POOR MAN'S TAPESTRY

By Oliver Onions

Oliver Onions

POOR MAN'S TAPESTRY

London

MICHAEL JOSEPH

First published in Great Britain by
MICHAEL JOSEPH LTD
52 Bedford Square
London WC1
1946

Reprinted once

This edition 1973

ISBN 0 7181 1146 X

Printed in Great Britain by
Hollen Street Press Ltd at Slough
and bound by James Burn at Esher, Surrey

To

(N. *or* M.)

OLIVER

*N*O green silk curtain protects it from the strong light, there is no glass lest the air should come at it or chemical to keep away the moth. Had it been an arras for a Rich Man's house it would have gleamed with the gold and silver thread of history and been carried away as conquerors' spoil. Yet Poor Man's hanging as it is history none the less went to its making. And history can take care of itself, but it is not an end in itself, so a word about it that we may be done with it.

The period of this story is the beginning of the Wars of the Roses, between the first clash in St. Alban's hilly streets and the skirmish at Blore Heath in Staffordshire, that is to say, between 1454 and 1458. The scene is the Yorkshire side of the Pennines and the Marches of mid-Wales. As Ann Thomas, however, was an old woman by that time her memory went farther back, and her Owain was none other than the fierce-browed Glyndwr, wronged and roused and aflame for vengeance. The "great battle" after he had seen his comet was Shrewsbury, fought on June the 21st, 1403, and his alliances with Hotspur, Mortimer, the Scots and the French, are no part of the present design.

Similarly, but fifty years and more later, "His Grace," my lord's overlord, was His Grace of York, sometime Protector of the Realm, himself to die at Wakefield in the year 1460, never himself king, but the father of an Edward and a Richard (the Third), both of whom presently became so. Calais, until the final expulsion from France, was England's other heart across the water, her bridgehead, home not only of the Staple but of prodigious merchandise besides.

But such things are not a Poor Man's business, and it is with him and his daily occupations that this story is concerned. And if the light in which he goes about his business and his love is not the light of to-day, what matter if that day was less unlike our own than we have got into the habit of supposing?

CONTENTS

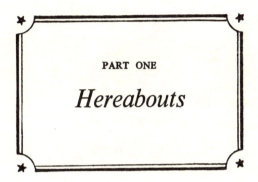

PART ONE

Hereabouts

1

ON A BYGONE MIDSUMMER MORNING, BUT HARDLY YET TIME OUT OF mind, a young woman stepped out of a stone porchway, all ready for the cutting of her teasel-thistles. About her middle she had passed an old hempen harden, dragged a man's frieze hood over her head, on her arm was a basket with a sickle and a tattered pair of gloves, and the wooden clogs on her feet made a short clattering on the sunny forecourt flags. But she had only come out of one door to disappear again into another, that of the adjoining mill, and here on the hard earth floor the clogs made no sound. At the shed's farther end stood a motionless waterwheel with a footbridge to cross the stream. Here, as she reappeared in the sunlight, the clogs knocked hollowly on wood, knock, knock, knock.

The teasels grew up the hillside, and at no time of the year was their blue quite like any other. In May, when it first appeared, it was a love-in-a-mist grey, yet already with a phosphor-glint of its own. Later this kindled, as if they were burning brimstone up there in the stone croft, and at night it did not sleep like other flowers, but continued its glimmering into the darkness. This morning it was cold witchfire blue, but as the young woman closed the gate behind her and threw off the man's hood the blue lost itself in that of the morning sky at the sudden blazing forth of her hair.

She had bunched it loosely together as housewives sometimes plait the last of their bread, but its outrageous red-gold might have been a stolen thing, herself condemned to wear it as a public penance. There were times when she hated herself because of it, and she had come out of the house to cut teasels, not to show that burning head a mile away down the valley. Setting her basket on the wall-top, she thrust her hands into the tattered gloves, seized the steel hook and sank to her knees. Her white nape lengthened by a couple of inches under its burden as she settled into her sacking and attacked the flowering burrs. In the parchment of an old will her name has come down as Hannah Thirlow.

But she had barely worked for five minutes before she sat suddenly back on her clogs, as still as a snuffing stag. Somebody out of sight down the hill was ascending, playing a merry tune on a whistle as he came.

It might have been the last sound in the world she wished to hear. Playing himself up to her father's house like a bridegroom bringing his own music with him! But she was no longer sitting on her heels. She was back at the gate, her hands fumbling hurriedly at her harden. Caught like a scullery-wench, and by him! Already her house-kirtle showed beneath it. Her back was twisted and a grey stocking showed as one wooden heel was turned up and she dragged the garment about her to pick off the burrs. Raking the cut thistles towards her with her foot, she reached for the scissors, and into the frieze hood snipped off half a dozen of the blue heads. Out of the basket she snatched an old carding-frame, and with a pricker began to prick the heads into its leather backing. Now let him come, whistle and all!

She heard no step on the footbridge, but the piping had stopped. Straggles of ivy and herb-robert and tufts of mosses had lodged themselves along the wall-top, and it was over these that there appeared first a leather cap turned back with badger fur, with points for tying under his chin. To right and left of this two arms in a sleeved leather jerkin spread themselves out, and over the clasped hands there jutted forward a short nose like a hawk's and a front-tooth gap you could have got a sixpence into, seen between lips that never quite met. So much at his ease did he seem that he might have been there only yesterday, and giving him a single glance only she went on pricking at the dead fibres of her frame.

"Rafe said I should find you here," he said, his eyes taking everything in in one look, her occupation, the sickle on the ground, the sacking, the hillside gorse beyond, mangy as a pelt with its last year's burnings. "So you've been left mistress here for a day or two?"

She began to pick at another hole. Let him not think himself any more welcome that her father had turned his back. And suddenly he removed his arms from the wall-top, lifted the latch and walked into the croft.

Now the rest of him could be seen. He was on the small side, but nimble and springy and restless-looking. Yet now that he had walked in unbidden it seemed to be for no particular reason, and the empty tackle of straps he wore on his shoulders jingled lightly as he placed himself on the lower wall with his back to the vale and began to drum with his heels. Then, as she still paid no heed he began to whistle softly against his twin teeth.

For what was all the parade of busyness about? Poking thistles into carding-frames was work that could be done in the house and at any time. He would have wagered that that sickle lying there was still warm from her hand. And suddenly he saw her toss her carding-frame back into the basket. It was not her best kirtle, and if it was no matter.

Somebody must work, never would it be he, and down on her knees she dropped again, the clog-soles once more turned up in their litter of blue.

But now he watched her with slowly altering eyes. Lord, what attitudes she took, that no other shape could ever have fitted itself into! Look at her now, by God, reaching so savagely forward with her hook that somewhere a seam parted with a tiny crack! Look at her again, that great red lump of a head among all that blue, and her smock working inch by inch out at her waist! But it was time she stopped showing him her back like a beast of the field, for in his belt he had a present for her, and suddenly ceasing to whistle he dropped his voice a couple of notes.

"Nan!"

She seemed not to hear, and more thistles were laid low.

"Nan!"

This time she heard and looked round.

"Where do you keep your scythe?"

"Ask Rafe. He knows."

"Come and show me where it is. I can have it down for you by dinner-time. Then you can give me a bite and I'll be getting on my way."

She rose to her feet. With the back of the glove she wiped the sweat from her brow and stood looking at him. But she yielded. The basket remained on the wall-top and the square of harden where it lay as they passed over the footbridge again and up the slope to the drying-ground behind.

The tenter-frames were set on the hill-side in tiers, one above another. They were ragged with bent nails, and resembled the posts and woodwork of a fair from which the canvas had been stripped or a market of stalls with nothing on the hooks to sell. At one time they had provided work for a whole establishment, fetching up the dripping slub from the trough, wringing and pulling and stretching it till the wind hummed on it like a drum, carding and kemping and teasing up the nap. Now they sagged as they stood, and the worst of them had been used to mend the others, and thistles and hawk-weed were once more breaking through the hard ground, and her lips parted of themselves for the first time.

"See, this is why my father's gone to Uthersfield," she said.

But he did not even give it a glance. He was looking east over the vale, for he had come that way, and now that he saw it from the height it seemed a long way to have come. Ellbeck township, with its thirty houses and twenty inns and a hump-backed bridge instead of a ford, was too close under the hill to be seen from there, and wherever else he turned his eyes he saw nothing but woods, and more woods, and woods to the very tops of all the highest hills. In and out among them swamps and marshes glinted and the rivers changed their courses as they went, and as trees and wandering rivers were no more than a platter of boiled kale to him already his fingers were at the pouch at his belt.

"Don't you want to see what I've brought you?" he asked her, and and as she did not answer brought it out. It was a small round locket, a token in a case, hinged so as to open, and with his nail he opened it. From it there looked forth her own likeness, daintily raised in the gold that might have been of the same red ingot as her hair and decapitated at the pit of the neck in a minute and graceful curve.

But she had suddenly turned as pale as parchment, shrinking back from the dangerous thing.

"Will!" she cried sharply, then in a tremulous voice, "Oh, have you no care what happens to you?"

But with his head on one side he was looking first at his work, then at her, then at his work again, comparingly back and forth.

"Hm. Perhaps it isn't all I thought it was now I see you again, but it's something of your neck with that great carrot on top of it. Turn your head a bit. . . ."

But she had struck sharply at it, so that it fell to the ground at their feet, and then she wrung her hands.

"Oh Mary Mother, what will he be doing next! Last time it was a pair of silver tweezers for my burling and my name on 'em too! Now he carries a thing like this about in his pocket and talks about *my* neck!" Then seizing him by the sleeve of his jerkin she shook it distractedly. "Out of sight with it before anybody else sees it! Where did you sleep last night?"

"Why, at the Shuttlecock, where I always do when I'm this way."

"And did you show them *that* at the Shuttlecock?" and he pushed back the furred cap to scratch his head.

"Now did I or didn't I?" but at the shaking she gave him this time the harness on his back jingled again.

"Carrying other folks webs in for them, you that never threw a shuttle in your life! Have you more such on you?" but he only stood looking at the glittering object of gold he had picked up from the ground again.

"No more than there are Nan Thirlows, and that's but the one."

"And where are you going when you leave here?" and he edged a little nearer to her along the rail against which he had placed himself.

"Where did I sleep last night and where shall I be to-morrow and nothing now I'm here! There's a welcome for man! If I'm coming this way why shouldn't I carry some honest weaver's piece in for him and save his legs a mile or two?"

"And get to know what money there is about, and borrow it for a couple of hours, and then——"

But she got no further, for his fingers had shot out quickly to her lips.

"Hearken, Nan. It's known what my calling is. It's not my trade to throw shuttles and slub weaver's stuff in troughs. Ah, I wish you could have seen a drinking-flagon I've chased for a gentleman since I've seen you, with huntsmen and hounds all round it so you could almost hear the music! And if I meet with him again I'm to do a sword-hilt for him, and if it wasn't for counting my chickens before they're hatched there's a certain nobleman's gold collar in the wind, too, a chain of SS-es with enamelling in between. . . ."

But she would have none of his sword-hilts or noblemen's collars in the wind. That locket he had made was too perilously like a coin, and the skill that can fashion one head can fashion another. It was in his hand and eye that the danger lay, and bluntly she asked him where he had got his gold from, at which he threw back his head and laughed.

"Her with a goldbeater's hammer of it on her head, asking a goldsmith where he gets his gold from!"

"Goldsmiths have their own gold. They have banks and lend it out. You're only an artificer."

"Where do I get my gold from! Not where do I get my eyes from, that can carry her picture in 'em since last spring! Who told you I wasn't paid for that gentleman's flagon in gold?"

"You said nothing last spring about noblemen and their gold collars. Who are these great folk you've taken up with all of a sudden?"

For her own father, though accounted a franklin, was still a fuller by trade, and neither he nor she had any part in such grandeur. Let Willie Middlemiss order his life differently and then, yes, he and she might hit it off. But again he was looking away over the rolling woods and bald hilltops. Where did his gold come from, where his new acquaintance? If the rivers wandered at will did not these great ones do the same? One domain picked to the bones they and their households and retinues assembled themselves, their furniture and belongings, their birdcages and barbs for hunting and their great destriers for war, and moved on to the next, and it was in the summer they migrated. She spoke in a low voice.

"Will, it isn't for me to tell you why my father's gone to Uthersfield. He's gone because there's no trade hereabouts. You can hardly pay for your yarn or buy a sack o' meal with the money that passes to-day. I can remember when we sat down four-and-twenty under this roof of

ours. Now we're six and three of them lads. My father's forbears dug
that dam and built this mill. They walked cloth the same as their
fathers did, and down in Ellbeck you'll not find an older fulling-name
on the registers. But look me in the face and tell me all's well to-day."

But he had drawn closer still on the rail and the coaxing note was
in his voice again.

"Here's an admiration to be in all over a bit of a locket! What is
it but a sort of token, such as any merchant can get licence to use?"

"Tokens don't carry images on them."

"Then is it because it's gold?"

"Gold or brass or pewter, it turns me cold to think of it."

"Then let's talk about something a bit warmer. Come, Nan. It's a
long time since last spring and it looks like being a longer to come.
Give me a kiss."

"First give me that that's in your pocket so I can sink it to the bottom
of the dam."

Their eyes met, his brown and bright and dancing, hers pale as a
pebbly stream, obstinately fighting it out. Then he gave a short laugh,
threw up his head, and began to fasten up the loosened buttons of
his jerkin.

"My neck for a rope and my handiwork for the bottom of the dam!
Nay then, when a man can do naught right it's time he was off, but
by God, you get handsomer every time I see you! Did you hear what
I was playing as I came up the hill?" and he whistled a snatch of
"Peggy Who Lost Her Garter." "If I'm to hang I'd liefer have had
my halter warm from your knee, but no matter. Maybe there'll be
ladies where I'm going won't think a pretty locket dear-bought at a
smile and a kiss. . . ."

But she had gone. She was already halfway down the hill, dipping
in and out among the tenter-frames, hurrying back to the house.

He had to follow her, for in asking for her at the house he had left
on the stone seat of the porchway the waist-pack that contained all he
had in the world. Past the herb-patch she sped, past the laithe where
the scythe was kept, without looking back. But as he, too, rounded the
house and set foot in its walled court-yard he stopped abruptly, for
she had not immediately sought the house and her chamber. Beyond
the pillars of the outer gate the trees had been cut away to make a
vista, and it was there that she was standing, her eyes strained and her
lips parted like his own. A procession of six or eight men was moving
slowly up the hill.

And Willie Middlemiss was also known as 'Somewhere-else-Willie,'
from a way he sometimes had of not being there just when he was
most wanted, and now could be seen the reason why. In one leap he

was at her side, then as swiftly back in the porch again, hastily buckling the wallet to his back. Another quick look first to see how many they were. . . .

But it was neither civil posse nor nobleman's outriding that toiled so slowly up the hill. Its single litter was a hurdle, and the men who bore it were unarmed, save for one who carried a halberd. They set down their load for a breathing-space, and uncovered their heads before taking it up again in a way that left no more to be said. John Thirlow, franklin and fuller, had been to Uthersfield for the last time, and it was his body that his neighbours were carrying home.

2

IT WAS ELLBECK'S BOAST THAT IT WAS A SETTLED COMMUNITY. IT HAD
its staple industry, its chartered market and fair, its thirty houses and
twenty inns, and a humpbacked bridge instead of a ford. Surely then
there had been no need to make a stronghold of John Thirlow's
house and mill?

Not so. As for the mill, well and good; it was a fuller's living; but
standing there with the mountains behind, it was an eye that looked
back east. York way and Ripon. No tree must obstruct its approaches.
Dressed, squared and mortared, its every stone must be thus and thus.
A crossbow was permitted for its defence, its inner staircase must be
so contrived that at need the inmates could withdraw themselves into
the house's upper part; and it was through its squat porchway and
into the ground-floor chamber that John Thirlow's bier was carried
and set down under the window at the chimney end. The heavy
shutters were swung to, but not quite closed, the scraping and
shuffling ceased to sound, and the spokesman delivered himself of his
tale.

He was a shepherd and it was quickly told. Out on the hills that
morning he had seen an unusual congregation of crows, and with some
thought of skin-wool in his mind, which is the wool taken from the
sheep after it is dead, had made for it. But he had first come upon an
empty shoulder-pack, then one by one the articles that had been
scattered from it, and these and the pack now lay on the window-sill
above the bier. They of the household who listened in silence were the
daughter of the house, the gaunt nun in her coffin-like draperies and
face-edging of white, Rafe who was in charge of the mill and his son
who looked after the sluices, for that morning the two fetch-and-carry
lads were elsewhere. Past the drawn shutters a single narrow shaft of
sunlight cut like a broadsword, and as the daughter bent to draw the
cloak aside from the dead face her head dipped through it like a
bloom of metal. The nun had dropped to her knees with a clicking of
jet beads, and the tale finished the bearers stood there shifting their
feet and fumbling with their headgear, then shuffled slowly away to
the end of the hall beyond the central stairs.

And now, though he knew every one of them as well as they knew
him, Willie Middlemiss felt himself a stranger among these men of

the region. There were a hundred neighbourly little things to do in which he could have no part. A coroner would have to sit, there would be a burial to see to, masses for John Thirlow's soul. But there were reasons why if needs be he must now outstay them all, and as he drew nearer to them, the constable with his halberd, the cloth-hall bailiff, the shepherd, the rest, he caught scraps of what they were saying.

Yet they were only the same things over and over again. It was but yesterday morning he had set out. It had happened within a few miles of their own doors. It was a way he had travelled hundreds of times without mishap; his staff hadn't been found yet. There were too many of these bedlamers about, with licence to beg, stout rogues lots of 'em and no madder than anybody else. But suddenly their heads all turned at once, for Willie had asked a question.

For a moment none of them spoke. Then it was the shepherd who answered him, civilly enough.

"Where did I come on him, Maister Middlemiss? Well, I could take you to the spot almost sooner than tell you where. It was a bit over the top, ay, a longish step over the top. There's a lot of new gorse just coming on there."

"Was it anywhere near where four birk-trees grow in a row?" But the shepherd became vaguer still.

"I know the birk-trees you mean. They grow in a row, as you say, but it was well-wide o' that. Constable Huddy, how would *you* tell Maister Middlemiss just where——"

But Willie had moved away again. Seating himself on the lowermost step of the stairs, he sat gazing at the stone floor, dangling his cap on the staff between his knees.

Tiptoeing on their heavy boots, the black-browed Rafe and his son Eggon was moving clumsily about, getting out the trestles for the long board. All was quiet over by the bier, where little could be seen but the dusty sword-blade of light. But Willie was frowning at his cap now. By God, but that was a queer sort of answer he had had from Dick Pope! The shepherd could have swum in the ale Willie had bought him one time and another, but now, when he was asked where he had found John Thirlow's body, he didn't know his own hillsides! Who too had been readier than the bailiff with his quip about the bit of off-and-on courting Willie Middlemiss was supposed to be doing up Thirlow way, or prompter than the constable himself when Willie had cocked an eye at the back door of the Shuttlecock when the front one was closed? Could it be that they were only fair-weather friends after all? But suddenly his name was whispered hoarsely in his ear. The space under the stairs was used as a pantry, and Rafe stood there with a large broken pasty on a platter in his hands, but when Willie asked him whether he was in the way sitting there he only shook his head.

"Bide where you are. I don't doubt but she'll be seeking her chamber in a bit, but 'tis the other wants a word with you before you go."

"The other?"

"The woman o' God. But maybe you might be best in the porch. They'll not sit down to their meat till they've carried him up."

"Do you mean Mother Ursula wants to see me?"

"Ay, the holy one," and Rafe moved cumbrously away again as Willie rose and sought the stone porch and the air.

The holy Sister! What could she want with him? But even as he asked it he was upright on his feet again, his fingers making a cross on his breast. Inside, four men were carrying the bier up the stairs. She followed, with the nun behind her, and for a moment he saw her face. It was as ashy as if that fire of her hair had burnt all the fuel out of it, and though four men had carried the bier up only two of them came down again, and again Willie's fingers made the cross. That was a thing he would have no stomach for. Short and sharp and finished with for him, and down again he sat, twiddling his cap of fur and leather on his stick and wondering what the bony nun could have to say to him.

Quietly the mill door along the yard was partly opened. Wedged in it he saw Eggon's face, making signs and mouthings. He had seen the nun go upstairs, but not come down again, and then he remembered that from the house to the mill there was an inner way. Eggon's face disappeared again as Willie Middlemiss stole softly to the mill-door.

It was in the shed that the long trough and wooden stocks were, but it was months now since the waterwheel had turned, and the only sound in it was that of the water that splashed in at one end of it and ran wastefully out again at the other. The iron cranks too were motionless, and the twilight of the shed was not a great deal more than that of the shuttered hall he had left, but what was this? No gaunt nun in cypress-black confronted him. She had taken off her clogs and got into her house-shoes, but that was all the changing she had done, and she was standing there as rigid as the crank arrested half-way in its descent behind her, one hand supporting her on the trough-edge, the other clenched on her hip. Her face was strained and bloodless, but showed no emotion, and still he could only stare at it, for why had she sent him her message as if it came from the other? Then, without any sort of preliminary, she addressed him by his proper name.

"Wilson Middlemiss," for he was not William as might have been supposed. His father had been the William, he was Will's son, wherefore his name was Wilson.

He could only stammer out a stupid-sounding, "Nan——"

"Nay, I'll not keep you, but come no nearer," for he was still standing just inside the door he had closed behind him. "Then you can be making for wherever it is you're going."

He found his voice with difficulty, for two hours had turned her into a person he didn't know.... "Leave all that till a fitter time, Nan," he muttered. "I'm not leaving you as long as there's any service I can do you. I can sleep in the laithe."

But a snake might have struck at her, the doubled fist flew back so.

"In my father's laithe, you!" but she swallowed it back. "Yesterday morning he went to Uthersfield. You heard that and it's why you came. Now see the way he comes back from Uthersfield . . ." and he tried to calm her.

"Nan—sweetheart—none saw you come in here. Get back and be getting on with your mourning. I'll stop and mourn with you, never fear," but she gave him a laugh that chilled him.

"And now he'll mourn with me! A mile away and a whistle in his pocket, and *he'll* mourn! But we're going to finish now, Wilson Middlemiss! You saw what was lying on the windowsill in yonder, picked up not ten yards from my father's body. It you didn't you can see it now!" and the fist that had been doubled on her hip shot out at him.

The object in it was of iron, much the size and shape of a thick thumb, and having thrust it at him she shrank back, lest the hand that took it should touch her own. He turned it over, and then his eyes went round the shed for the best light to examine it in.

For it required some milder light, the kind of light that engravers diffuse through their bowls of water. It was a hollow cylinder, and the portion of it he particularly wished to see lay at the bottom of its pit. A thin ray came from the closed door behind him, and to this he turned it, peering frowningly. Then he glanced up.

"Has Rafe a vice or a wrench anywhere about?"

Her hand was at her breast as she breathed a soft, "Ah, that's more easing!"

"But it has a look of being shrunk on—ay, they'd shrink it on . . ." and he turned it this way and that again. Then he made a sound of contempt, but now she was advancing towards him, her head thrust forward and her body crouching almost as if to spring.

"They haven't found my father's staff, but they found *that*, that never came out of *his* pack, Wilson Middlemiss, and when I want to know what a die for stamping a Henry noble is like I come to them that can tell me!"

"Nan!" he stammed. "What's all this strangeness?"

"Ay, what!" she glared.

"Of a truth, and from what I can see of it, it has something the look of a Henry. . . ."

" ' Of a truth'! "

"If you'd an end of beeswax or a candle I could take an impression with——"

Beeswax! A candle-end!

"—but a piece of bungling like that—the 'Rex' is a botch and a Henricus 'H' isn't fashioned that way. . . ."

"Praised be God you don't tell me you don't know what a Henricus 'H' is like!"

"But as for that being *my* work, if that's your meaning, may I never take a tool in my hands again . . ." but the laugh with which she mocked him cut through his words like a knife.

"Hear it then, my gentleman's gentleman, that thinks his fine neck's made for an axe instead of a rope! You wouldn't last time I said it, with love and tears, on my knees and my hands clasped on your breast, so hear it now! *You* carry in a weaver's cloth to save his legs! *You* that makes any your friend that can lend you a gold coin for an hour! These used to be honest cloth-lands, but the very sparrows know the trade that goes on hereabouts now! It's only because all their fingers are burnt with it that not one of 'em dares to fling a stone! And now my father goes to Uthersfield, to find an honest tradesman if he can, and there he lies upstairs, with the back of his head broke in!"

And he knew it, and she knew it, and the very sparrows knew it, but what was the use of their knowledge now? They could not shut their eyes to the slaying of a citizen, and for the cleaning of their township's name at whom would they fling their stone? Be sure at not one of themselves; now they would be simple tradesmen again, unwelcoming of strangers in their midst. Willie Middlemiss's dangerous trade—a coiner's die picked up not ten yards from a dead man's body—a scapegoat to hold for questioning—it would be for Willie Middlemiss that the hue and cry would be and the horns and the shoutings and the dogs and the staves, and he had better be giving it thought.

"I cannot but guess what's in your mind, Nan, but if you want me to go to a church and swear before an altar . . ." he was beginning when again that ironical sound in her throat cut him short.

"Nay, save your breath! Nobody's going to say it's Maister Middlemiss's dainty hand that does the striking! He's 'Somewhere-else-Willie' long before it comes to that! But craftsmen that can make dies don't grow on the whins, and only fools would use up blanks o' gold to put sweethearts' heads on them!" and suddenly snatching the piece

of iron from his hand, she stood before him like an accusing red
mænad, with only the desire for vengeance in her pale and shining eyes.

And by all the heavenly company, even then he wasn't sure her fury
didn't become her best of all, but he answered her reproachfully.

"There was no cause to snatch it from me like a wildcat, Nan. I'd
no thought of making off with it."

"As well not if you wanted to get out o' this house," she muttered,
her bosom beginning to rise and fall quickly, and suddenly he shot
her such a look as he had not given her yet. Now what the devil did
she mean by that? Was she thinking of the constable with his halberd
and the others eating her victuals in the hall? But if he was to be taken,
and she too was willing to hand him over, why had she not remained
upstairs in her chamber? Why, if not to give him an opportunity, had
she first sent him a message in the nun's name, and then herself stolen
down by the inner way? Suddenly, he began to improvise hurriedly.

"Still yourself a minute and hearken to me, Nan, for this too I'll
confess before a priest," he muttered. "There was a time when one, a
stranger, did come to me about some such matter, though it was
nowhere in these parts. He asked me if I could do this and that, and
I'd a notion what he meant when he fetched a Henricus from his
pocket, and I told him to put it away again. But even then I was wrong.
He didn't want any superscription, he said, only the head. He said it
was for livery-buttons."

Almost she could have found it in her heart to admire him. Livery-
buttons! With a likeness on them! But he was improving on his tale
now.

"I'll grant I didn't give it the thought I should. I can see now that
another might have put the superscription on afterwards, and it
might have been a Henricus or anything else for all the heed I paid
it. So seeing it was but a sort of punch, and for these livery-buttons—
that's a long way from murder, Nan. . . ."

The running water in the trough was now the only sound to be
heard in the shed. Even out of her hair the light seemed to die as the
sun, shining broadly in past the wheel, burned on the hens that had
assembled in the farther doorway. Yet how could she look at that
short nose and parted lips, the leather of his jerkin rubbed and frayed
like old velvet and his journeyman's tackle on his back, and not tremble
for him? Could nothing be done about it that he must be as he was,
she too so immovably herself? And yet, what sort of a life would it
have been with him? Lying awake by his side at night, and then the
low whistle under the window and him up and out of bed and off she
knew not where, with no certainty that he would ever return? Suddenly,
her voice shook piteously.

"Oh, go, go—for God knows how I rue it was this morning you had to come!"

"What, go, and leave you as you are?" he stammered.

Then she looked again at the iron object in her hand. She had seen it lying with the rest on the windowsill, but what was the use of stealing a thing so many eyes had already seen? She grew paler still. For murder they only hanged them, but this was treason and hanging was only the beginning of it. He had to strain his ears to catch her next words.

"As if half Ellbeck didn't know by this time! It must go back where I got it, for now it's missing it that would set them talking! Oh, how I dread the thought o' what you carry in that imp's head of yours! Begone if you want to be buried all in one piece!—and see you come here no more—yet stay—a minute if it's to be the last—wherever you go, Will—oh God!" and suddenly her voice failed her completely. "What's to do now?"

But he had heard it too, and it was not his eye but his ear that was at the door-crack now. Outside in the forecourt there was a confused sound of men's voices.

"The last I saw of him he was sitting in the porch. . . ."

"As impudent as they make 'em, with his cap on his stick. . . ."

"We were just sitting down to we'r meat. . . ."

Dangling from its short string was the wooden wedge that secured the bolt in its staple, and to this Willie's hand had stolen.

"The lad says he's somewhere wi' the Sister i' God. . . ."

Then the butt of the constable's halberd was heard on the flags. The door was tried from outside, but by this time the wedge was in its place.

"Then if he was here half an hour ago why isn't he to be found now?"

"It's their cunning, to be off while others are eating and drinking. . . ."

"Ay, crafty he always was. . . ."

Inside the shed Willie Middlemiss had swung swiftly round. It was she, not he, who must not be found there now, and he was pointing to the inner stairs, voicelessly waving her away. "Back with you!" his parted lips were shaping, with his thumb firmly on the wedge as again the door was shaken. "Quick, off upstairs!"

The stairs rose against the inner wall, with a rope instead of a rail to ascend by, but her hand had to fumble for the rope, for her head was turned back over her shoulder as she mechanically obeyed him, all of her that seemed to be under her own control. Further round still her eyes moved till she reached the door at the top, when the rest of her turned. She stood there for a space, with God knew what in her look whether it reached him or not. The door in the wall closed slowly behind her, and the next moment Willie Middlemiss had drawn out the wedge again.

The startled heads turned simultaneously as he appeared, but it was half a minute before a man spoke. Then the constable, his hands folded on his halberd, looked at Willie with his head on one side.

"Why, it's Maister Middlemiss! We were just beginning to think we'd lost sight of you!" he said in a jocular tone, and Willie answered him briskly.

"And what made you think that, Francis, my lad?"

"Nay, you were nowhere to be seen. . . ."

"Eggon could have told you. The holy sister wanted a private word with me, and came down by the house way, so I slipped the wedge in the door."

"Ah! That was how it was! And where, if we might ask, were you thinking of making for next?"

Willie's eyes moved from face to face, summing them rapidly up. Separately they would do nothing, but let one of them start something and they would all be of a mind, so as well do it for them. He gave himself a shake.

"Well, this is a sad morning's work, friends, but none of us needs telling that, so where am I for now? As some of you know, this morning I was for away and about my business. But I cannot go till I've seen Mistress Hannah, and this is no time to be troubling her. Where am I going now? I'm back for the Shuttlecock again, and as I take it that's your way too I'll be glad of your company."

So as for once 'Somewhere-else-Willie' was there and at their disposal there was no more to be said.

3

THE SHUTTLECOCK FACED THE STOCKS WHERE THE STRAGGLING STREET widened out at the bottom, and in its front window-seat there stood a slab-like table, sawn out of the thickness of a single great tree. It was at this table that Wilson Middlemiss sat towards midday the next day, wondering what had become of the customary company. The few who came in took their refreshment quickly and went out again, but if one didn't presently return another did, and so in odd ones and couples, in and out. Therefore, with the other side of the window better worth his eyesight than the one on which he sat, Willie watched the hogs that rooted and scavenged about the midden in front of the stocks and the wenches as they carried their buckets to the beck. He was thus killing time when there entered to him Gammer Alison with a full jug in her hand, though he had not called for anything. She filled his pewter and then gave a heavy sigh.

"They're opening the grave now," she said. "Eh, but I cannot sit still in one place for the thought of that poor lass up there, with none but that holy woman to see to her."

"What time's the inquest?" Willie cut her short.

"It'll be as soon as the body comes, and Dick Pope says she did nothing but stare like a madlin, without sound or cry."

"I don't take all that notice of folk when they're in their grief."

"Ah, you and me's different, Maister Middlemiss. We know when all folk wants is to be let alone. And I'm not one to open my house in Service-time like some. The clerk himself drinks in the Shuttle, and I've as good fish in Lent as comes out o' the streams. But when I think of that poor lass. . . ."

"Off with you and fetch a few customers in," Willie ordered her, and as she waddled away again turned once more to the window.

All Ellbeck seemed to be standing about or moving aimlessly up and down. There, with his nose well to windward of the pigs, went Stephen Akam in his square cap and knee-length gown, his cropped white beard and gold ring on his finger. He was the richest merchant in the place, and his ring was a seal that Willie himself had engraved, but Stephen was a Crown man, and the Crown stood opposite the Cloth-hall at the top of the street, not among the pigsties at the bottom. Now he had stopped to talk to John Roper, and John Roper was another of the better-house men, and if John Roper took a bill instead of money you could be sure somebody's house or livestock was behind it. So Willie's eyes wandered to the girls about the spout again. There was a slip of a wench now, the one with the yoke and two buckets; whose daughter would she be? Some of them seemed to shoot up into young women almost overnight, and by the Lord, who were these? Two customers, and two Willie knew! He nodded to them as they entered, and they nodded back, but evidently they had private matters to discuss, for they drank standing up in the doorway, and when next he turned to the window the girl with the yoke had gone.

But instead there strolled past the window and entered the inn a shambling, roughly-dressed man whose face Willie had an idea he had seen before, though he could not have said where or when. And instead of walking in and calling for his liquor this man must have gone straight into the kitchen for it, for pushing past the men in the doorway he came in with his pot in his hand. Then, just as Willie had caught sight of the girl with the yoke again, he heard himself suddenly addressed.

"I see you're looking at that table, Maister Middlemiss," the newcomer said. "It was my father felled that tree."

Willie looked quickly up. The slab of tree had been dressed with the bark on it, and along its edge the man was running a thick thumb-nail.

"You start counting 'em here, one for every year," he said. "Ninety's been counted, but you could add another fifteen to that. It's an elm," and as this was the sort of thing that now had to be stopped at once Willie wasted no time over it.

"And what," he asked, looking the man up and down, "might *your* name be?" and the thumb-nail paused for a moment.

"What, you can't have forgotten Sagar, Maister Middlemiss?"

"And your trade?"

"I'm a weaver when there's anything to weave."

"And your father felled that tree. And then what?"

But the fellow's hide must have been as tough as the elm-bark, for he took no notice of Willie's tone.

"Felled it *and* dressed it, for it wouldn't take a plane. It had to be fettled up wi' glass, broken bottles and such." Then, suddenly dropping his voice, "Are you stopping on after the funeral, Maister Middlemiss?" Then, in a voice lower still, "Because the money's what you like to ask, and one of us could meet you, but it might suit us all best if you came straight to the Pot o' One. . . ."

But Willie had heard enough, for the men in the doorway were straining their ears too. Down with a crack came his flagon on the tree-table.

"Stop grunting like one o' them hogs outside and speak up so folk can hear you! What is it you want with me?"

"Nay, Maister Middlemiss. . . ."

"Maister nothing to you! If ever I've seen your face before it was in the stocks, with a cowclap on it to mend it, so off where you came from before you're helped on the way!" and muttering to himself the ill-favoured fellow swallowed his ale and shambled past the men at the door and took himself off again.

Willie was angry that anything like a bad name should be thus thrust on him just when he stood in need of the best name he could get, and try as he would he could call nobody of the name of Sagar to mind. But looking out of the window he could still see him loafing by the stocks, and the rest was plain enough. Out on the hills some chawbacon had let the female half of a coiner's die slip through his fingers. Now they wanted another while they had a skilled man in the neighbourhood, and suddenly leaning forward Willie tapped sharply with his fingernail on the pane. There, passing the window, was the very lad he most wanted to see.

He was young Atty Cockin, the skinner's son, rising seventeen, as wick as they made 'em, and loyal to Willie though all the world had turned against him. Hearing the tapping he stopped. In a shake he was in the inn, his eyes on Willie's face.

"Atty, look out of the window. There's a flea-bitten fellow over by the stocks there says his name's Sagar and he's a weaver. Who does he company with?" for it was the practice of the more outlying men to band themselves together in twos and threes, those from the southern heights forming one company, those from the west another.

"He companies with none that I know of. He keeps the Pot o' One."

"And where just might that be?" and when Atty had told him Willie tapped his teeth thoughtfully. Out of demesne! If anything that made matters worse, for the law was that these waste and lonely places should harbour nothing in the way of an inn, but that these should be licensed only in the townships or under the walls of some stronghold. For some moments longer Willie tapped his teeth; then he edged an inch nearer to the lad's side.

"Atty," he said, "which think you's the best, to eat the devil or sup the broth he's boiled in?"

"I don't take your meaning, Willie."

"Tell me what the talk in Ellbeck's been since yesterday morning," and Atty's face fell.

"You ought to ha' got away while you had the chance."

"What do you mean, while I had the chance?"

"Weren't you up at Thirlow? From what I hear they laid hold of
you just when you were slipping away and brought you back here to
stand your examination," and Willie's jaw dropped.

Laid hold of him! Dot-and-carry bailey and that constable with
bones as rusty as his halberd! *Them* lay hold on him and bring him
back!

"Is that the tale they're putting about?"

"All but Dick Pope. *He* says he got you on one side and told you
where they'd set the guards."

"The guards!"

"Constable Huddy says he had 'em back and front of the house for
if you'd stirred foot or finger, and when you asked to see his warrant
he had to be round with you and show you the irons . . .," and Willie
drew a deep breath. Him all the time in the mill, and them running
here and there asking which way he had gone, and that liar Dick
Pope—but Dick Pope should hear about that, by God, and out Willie
broke.

"Guards! All they guarded was a firkin of ale and a mutton pasty!
Dick Pope! The best of his faces is the one he sits on! *Them* take me!"
and suddenly his hand went into his jerkin and came out again with
something in it. "Now don't move, Atty, but just go on looking out o'
that window and take no notice of what I'm putting into your hand,"
and under the elm-tree table he slipped the locket with the likeness
on it. "They're a pack of lying rogues, and I'm not back here because
of any of them, but the inquest will be in an hour or two, and it might
be as well if *this* wasn't found in my pocket. Can you feel what it is?"

"I can feel it's round."

"Round or oval, keep it for me for a bit. And now, can you keep
a great secret in your breast if I tell you something?"

The lad's eyes shone. . . . "That I can, Willie!"

"Even if I'm not here? If perhaps the next you hear of me I'm
Cheshire way, or the Duchy, or Denbigh, or some place in Wales?"

"Do you want me to cross myself, Willie?" and Willie whispered
into his ear:

"A certain lord, whose name I can't tell even you, Atty, he's heard
of me on account of his armourer being an old friend of mine, and all
being well I shall take service with him. That in your hand—(Body o'
God, you young jackanapes, don't go flashing it for all the town to
see!)—it was to show my skill, but I can make shift, for a gentleman
I'm in favour with can show 'em a flagon I chased for him instead,
and think of it, Atty! My lord there in his castle with his bodyguard
of knights, or taking the field it may be, with the horses all caparisoned
and prancing, and the banners and the trumpets . . ."

The stripling's face was all alight. . . . "Did you say you knew his armourer?"

"Do I know Humphrey Tull! Didn't we work on the same bench together, him a foreman while I was a prentice, and hammer on the same anvil and blow with the same bellows? Do I know him! But he hadn't my lightness of touch. Put a fine tool into his hands and his fingers were all thumbs, so he turned to steel and the heavy side. But when I join up with my lord I shall do the filigree and the damascus work, such as you see on coronets and panoplies of state. Huddy and his halberd! I've seen halberds, Atty, you'd think they were made of lace, with the gold and silver that's hammered into them! And I have word my lord's just got a new suit of body-armour, straight from Milan in Italy. . . ."

"And will you carry arms yourself, Willie?" the youth asked breathlessly, and Willie grimaced as Stephen Akam passed the window again with his hand on John Roper's shoulder.

"Wait till I'm shut of this lot, with their warps and wefts and moaning about bad trade!" but the lad's face had suddenly fallen.

"My father's only a skinner," he said, and Willie patted him on the shoulder.

"Isn't skinning leather, for bucklings and brigandines, and am I the one to forget my friends, Atty? It may be I shall be able to drop a word in his ear that I know the finest master-skinner this side of York— your father doesn't know the deal I've always thought of him. . . ."

"I'll tell him that, Willie."

"Ay, do. But now there's a little thing I want you to do for me. The body might be brought in any minute now and they're speedy to get 'em buried nowadays. The court'll sit the minute the inquest's finished, and there can only be one finding, so I want you to be there or thereabouts. Keep your eyes and ears open, and if you hear aught nip back here and tell me quick. If that man Sagar tries to get into any conversation with you——"

But he stopped, for he had seen what was happening outside. The pigs were being driven out of the way, the body was being brought in, every head was uncovered, but from the inn window little enough of the procession could be seen for the assembly in between. Even for the little there was Willie had no eyes, for he was speaking hurriedly to Atty again.

"They're splitting off for Akam's house till the finding's known. Away with you and do as I say. If I'm not down here, you'll find me upstairs," and he too hurried away for his cap.

And there were many in Ellbeck who said to their neighbours that afternoon what a seemly thing it was that young Middlemiss too should be standing outside the Crown with his cap in his hand, apart and speaking to none, for two hundred pounds was to have gone with Hannah Thirlow not so long back. But almost as many were not so sure, for they liked them Ellbeck-born, and if it was like that between them why wasn't he with her at Madam Akam's now, doing what he could to comfort her? But all agreed that the sooner the open grave under the south wall of St. Peter's was closed again the better, with quicklime too, for death entered in at the nostrils nowadays and the very crows that had congregated about John Thirlow's body might have stirred up a contagion in the air.

Then from the Crown a drawer came out, and round the whisper went. The finding was Misadventure. But still they waited, for in their hearts they knew it could not be let go like that, and when, nearly half an hour later, the true finding was made known and the word 'Murther' suddenly rose like a buzz of flies, there was no longer any Willie Middlemiss to look at. He was hurrying back to the Shuttlecock, there to wait for what news Atty Cockin had to bring.

But the buzz was there as soon as he was, and into the inn that had been half empty all day men were now pouring in a steady stream. And Willie forgot the crow he had to pick with Dick Pope, for there was no place for him at the table in the window-seat now, and the heat of their bodies stifled him, and after a single look he made for his own garret upstairs. It was immediately overhead, and its window was no more than a square hole cut through the wall. The seat before it was a wooden block, and his blanket and straw lay on the bare boards. There had been no movement yet towards the church, which was immediately behind the inn, so apparently the court was still in assembly, and he himself was unwatched and unfollowed for the first time that day.

Outside in the evening light the pigs were back at the midden again. Shadows were lengthening, and they seemed to creep over Willie too as each of the day's events joined itself on to the next; the avoidance of the better sort, his seeking out by Sagar, the eyes on him as he had waited outside the Crown. What with a name like his was he doing there, with his head in the lion's mouth? They were liars all in this town, and she alone, with the best reason of them all for turning against him, had stolen down into the mill to tell him to be off while he could. He could see her now, standing there at the top of the stairs with her face turned over her shoulder, and it was for that alone he had come back, for here she too was, up at Madam Akam's, also waiting for the next. Early in the morning he would steal out, go up to the merchant's house, contrive by some means to see her again if only for a few moments. Just to wish her well, to hear her say she

wished him well, and to have the weight off his heart. And as he sat
there he heard a push at his door as at last Atty appeared, with a
covered basket in his hand. He spoke breathlessly, for late as he was
he had been making haste.

"I got here as fast as I could," he panted. "Stuff this food into your
wallet, for I have to take the basket back, and then my father says
you're to leg it as fast as you can go. The court cannot agree, but
they've got a warrant all ready for signing and it doesn't take long to
sign a warrant."

Willie was on his feet. . . . "Your father says what?"

"Half of 'em's for holding you for question, but the other half says
nay, and they've been fratching about it this two hours. He says that
should be answer enough for you."

"How's that an answer?"

"He says if you were somewhere else it wouldn't take 'em five
minutes to make up their mind. Then they could make a show of being
on your heels. But you'd be miles away by then, and you're not to
forget that about the leather for the brigandines."

But now Willie stood suddenly irresolute. . . . "What else are they
saying?"

"There's all sorts of talk. Some want to know why Jim Sagar's here
slotting after you. Some says you've been warned before, and them
that won't take warning must abide that comes. My father's way's
the best."

But Willie was slowly loosening the straps from his shoulders. There
she had been, contriving for him even with her father lying dead,
getting the die privily into her possession and then saying the nun
wanted a word with him. . . .

"I cannot, Atty, I just cannot. Try as they will, they cannot fasten a
killing on me."

"But they're *giving* you law, Willie!" the boy urged distractedly.
"They'll sit for another two hours if you'll only be off!"

But Willie threw his wallet on the straw of his bed. . . . "Let 'em
sit. Cockcrow's going to find me at Akam's house, before any of them
are out o' their beds!"

But now it was the lad who seemed to be keeping something back,
something he seemed afraid to say. . . . "If you mean what I think you
mean, I wouldn't if I was you, Willie," he faltered, and Willie swung
abruptly round.

"You wouldn't what?"

"Try to see her," and he was seized roughly by the arm.

"What else have you heard? Sharp, out with it!"

"You said I was to keep my eyes and ears open—"

"Devil take you, out with it!"

"If I did wrong, Willie . . . I knew they were all at Madam Akam's because my mother was with 'em—there were eight or ten of 'em. . . ."

"You went there?"

"Yes. . . ."

"And you saw her?"

"I didn't at first—some were sitting and some were standing and coming in and out—she was crouched like a witch in the chimney-breast, all huddled up. . . ."

"Be quick!"

"Then she sees me, talking to my mother, and she crooks her finger at me like this, and when I got close to her, 'Are you from the Shuttle-cock?' she says. . . ."

"And you said?"

"Then she covers her face up for a minute, and when she uncovers it again, it was all a glare, and—I don't like to tell you, Willie. . . ."

"Tell me, Atty," said Willie, suddenly gentle.

" 'You can go back to the Shuttle,' she says, 'and you can tell him that's there he's naught to wait for, for it's all bye and over. I'm casting my garter for no man's whistle, you can tell him, and he's had more than two·years to make up his mind in, and he'll find his picking o' women in the world, and if one of 'em will but break his heart for him maybe he'll learn something he doesn't know yet,' she says, and with that she covers up her face again and I came away."

And warped as it was in the mouth of a jealous youngster who would have had no women in Willie's life, but only arms and accoutre-ments and horses, how often had she not said the same thing herself? For a minute Willie stood still. Atty, supposing himself to have done ill after all, seemed on the brink of tears. Then he started as Willie's hand was clapped in the old way on his shoulder.

"So! Now we can be about something! Have you got that locket on you?"

"Here it is," and the boy brought it out.

"Did you chance to look in down below as you came in? You don't suppose Constable Huddy has a cripple with crutches or a one-legged man at every corner of this house?"

"My father says they'll give you the bridge and the river too if only you'll get on the other side of 'em."

"Then by God!" cried Willie, cramming the contents of the basket into his wallet, "you can tell 'em to sign their warrant as soon as they like! My service to your father, and I'll not forget about the brigan-dines, and—Atty! There's a slip of a wench goes to the beck with a yoke and two buckets, fifteen years old, flanks like a greyhound and a blue kirtle. Find out who she is against I come again, and mind you practice your archery, for it's four marks a year and your livery for you, and now hand me my staff. We'll see which o' these Dick Popes downstairs stops me as I go through!"

But none of Ellbeck's cloth-men made so bold. He might have been transparent as the air as he marched through them and out by the door, with a thwack in the ribs for Dick Pope as he passed.

As for the court still sitting up at the Crown, it would continue to sit till Wilson Middlemiss, journeyman-engraver and worker in fine metals, was safely out of its jurisdiction.

4

THOSE OF THE MILL-PEEL KNEW LITTLE OF THE GAUNT NUN'S STORY
except that a long time ago she had been a lay-sister at Nostell Priory
and hoped to see Nostell again before she died. They never saw her
toes for the black muffles that lapped about them as she moved, and
her scalp in its close wimple was believed to have no more hair on it
than an egg. The furthest she commonly went from the house was to
her herb-patch at the back of it, where she gathered the medicines for
Thirlow's ailments. But now her herb was rue, which is the Herb of Grace.

Late on a sultry evening, with John Thirlow under his quicklime
three weeks and the shadow of the house across the forecourt flags,
the two women sat opposite to one another in the stone porch, taking
up the threads of life again where they had been broken off. Hannah,
back in her house-kirtle, had got out her basket with the shears and
odds-and-ends in it, but she sat idle, turning the funeral-ring on her
finger, for she knew without telling what was in the nun's mind. What
the place now wanted was a man at its head. Therefore, let her get
herself a husband, and suddenly the lay-sister's voice broke in on her
thoughts.

"If they've made a start on that will by Michaelmas it's more than
I look for, and Stephen Akam's willing to take those teasels off your
hands at a fair price," she said. "He did say something about helping
with Rafe's wages too," but Hannah did not look up.

"It's not sure Rafe will be here after Michaelmas. He's talking of
leaving," she answered, and into Sister Ursula's voice there came a
sudden snap.

"When did Rafe say that?"

"Yesterday morning. And if he goes Eggon will go with him," and
on the lay-sister's face the frown of an abbess gathered.

"This afternoon I heard Rafe with a graceless word in his mouth,"
for that was the other side of her holiness. Those who spoke lewdly
had best do so out of her hearing, but let one of the Ellbeck wenches
be brought to the straw and she would neither bite nor sup till she
had claimed the infant for the Church before the demons could clutch
at its young soul. "You can tell Rafe he's going when you give him
leave to go, and till then he's stopping where he is," she said, and
Hannah resumed her turning of her ring.

The numbness, that had been a boon while it had lasted, was passing now, and the way they looked at it any bachelor or widower would do. Down in the valley was a second fulling mill. It belonged to young Robert Safford, but in their eyes both mills belonged first and foremost to Ellbeck and its trade. To join mill to mill might even set the township itself on its feet again, and even the nun had returned to the dreaded subject, for at Nostell she had been a woman of affairs, and had learned to look at the other side too.

"They can make a deal of trouble for you if you fly in their faces," she was saying. "One fuller's sib to another, and it's true Robert's been sickly lately, a sort of sweating, but it may be there's cures he hasn't tried—nay, don't do that when these things have to be faced!" (For "Robert Safford!" Hannah had exclaimed faintly and closed her eyes.) "Or for that matter there's John Roper himself, for all his game leg and his grand-children, and he cannot live for ever. . . ."

But Hannah had shivered even more violently than before. John Roper, who had already seen three of them into their graves! A couple of dry courting kisses and a feather-bed with John Roper! But the woman of God went on.

"Now if his trade had but been cloth, instead of his father a skinner, there's young Cockin, coming a man and a skin as clean as a girl's. . . ."

But she could have pronounced no more luckless name. In Hannah's basket were still the same teasel-heads she had snipped off only three weeks ago, and back it all came, this time without the numbness. Young Cockin, the skinner's son! . . . There at Madam Akam's they had all been, those hard-eyed merchant's wives, who had paid the price before her. Her own valuation? A mill-trough with cranks and a wheel to turn them. Item, ten tenter-frames and a copyhold lease and no encumbrance but Hannah Thirlow and her alien red hair and tempers. Seeing it all in their eyes she had huddled herself up in the chimney-corner, and then looking up had seen the skinner's son. . . .

Now a dried thistle-head was enough. She heard it again, that merry piping under the hill. As fresh as ever it returned, the outspread arms on the wall-top, the short, self-sufficient nose, the strong white teeth with the gap between them, the eyes quick as a bird's. How should she remember, now, with what words she had charged the lad? She was casting her garter for no man (but again she heard his laugh as he had said that if he must hang he had liefer have had his halter warm from her knee). He had had two years to make up his mind in (and so he had, but sometimes they seemed like twenty). Off, off came the healing skin again, peeling the wound afresh. . . .

And now he was off again like a runaway dog with a kettle at its tail, all that this trembling township might whiten itself in its own eyes! North and east they were making their show of looking for him, but never west or south, lest they should light on some cousin whose house they dared not search or some other honest neighbour doing what they all did, and suddenly she thrust herself forward and spoke in a harsh voice.

"Who's this man they held for question for three days and then let go?"

But the nun had dropped her eyelids and her sunken lips were beginning to move.

"And what's become of that iron thing they picked up close to my father's body?"

But "*Adveniat regnum tuum*" the paternoster was clicking.

"All this blind-man's-buff over a man they aren't trying to catch!"

"*Fiat voluntas tua* . . ." and Hannah scoffed.

"There's absolution for you, that can wash a Henricus die away!" and the nun, opening her eyes again, spoke with severity.

"*Amen.* . . . Hannah, you're to be chidden for disturbing one that's withdrawn herself to her prayers. But for that ring on your finger I should put you to a penance. As it is, for those teasels Stephen Akam will pay you in such coin as there is, but he cannot pay Rafe but in kind, and that'll be cheese or something there's plenty of. Bear in mind they can make a deal of trouble for you," and rising, she moved stiffly away into the house.

Rafe the milner had got down the steel crossbow from the wall and with a rag and a pot of grease was seeing to its working parts. With his foot in the stirrup of the windlass he was easing the pawls of the twin wheels up and down as he oiled them with a feather. He took no notice of Hannah when she too entered, and when she asked him where Eggon was only growled that he was out with the other two, snaring rabbits. She then asked him, as she did nightly, whether there was any news that day, and he replaced the cords on the tackle's pulley before replying.

"Ay. There's a company stopping at the Crown, just in from Wrexham way. There's a dispensation about a burnt church, fifty days i' the year for them that builds it up again, and this 'un I spoke with his master carted the first load o' stones. It's a trade I've a mind to put Eggon to, stonework," and he turned to the other wheel.

Hannah watched his shaggy head bent over his machine. Again he was speaking as if he was his own master, and he had finished with the tackle now and was fitting on the steel bow. With the pawls clicking ever more slowly the powerful engine bent to the winding of the winch. Mary Mother, what things men made for themselves! He cast off the windlass and raising the formidable weapon levelled it at the farther wall, and though it carried neither bolt nor quarrell the twang of its cord brought her heart into her mouth as he loosed the pin. Jesu, have mercy on whoever received *that* in brow or breast! But Rafe only gave the cord a rub with his rag and slipped it off again.

"You could loose off six wi' a proper bow for one wi' that," he said as he replaced the weapon on the wall, and now Hannah was all raw and open again, yet unable to let the place alone. Twilight filled the hall, but it was not worth the lighting of a candle, and a bench stood before the trestle table. Suddenly pointing to it she told Rafe to sit down, and when he had done so, with almost space enough for a waterbutt between his great knees, placed herself at the plank's other end,

Yet her question was only the same one she had already asked the nun, who a man called Pot o' One Sagar was, but now Rafe, too, answered evasively. Who, he demanded in return, had been talking to her about that 'un? But her reply was sharp. A man couldn't be held for question for three days without folk hearing about it, she rapped back, but still Rafe only shook his head. Ay, that was true enough; they'd had him in the lock-up; but why come to Rafe, who had never set foot in his place? It was a place frequented by none but raggens and ragamuffins and such as had no regular trade, and out of her spite she was just about to retort that surely there could be no such place anywhere near righteous Ellbeck when she suddenly saw the mistake she was making. She would get nothing out of Rafe that way; therefore she must try another, and all at once she dropped her voice.

"So you've a fancy to make a mason of Eggon?" she said, and a growling came from Rafe's deep chest.

"Snaring rabbits isn't a trade," and she drew a little nearer to him on the bench.

"And with Eggon a mason what would you do yourself?" she asked, and again came the rumble.

"A man that can handle machines can take his pick these days."

"His pick of what?"

"Of twenty things. There's mangonels for casting stones, and setting booms i' rivers, and mining stuff out o' the earth, and when that dam up there gets clagged wi' weeds I've had a notion for scouring it out as clean as a pudding-basin, just by turning the stream," and Rafe might suddenly have become her idol of a man, such was the sudden admiration in her voice.

"I'll be bound you have, Rafe, and my father always said what a pest them weeds were. And just by turning the stream! Think of that! But what does Eggon know about mason's work?" and Rafe's voice dropped to a gruff softness.

"Let me but get him away from here. You cannot bring up a lad without a trade in such times as these. But set him in some border-country, where there's castles and works to set up and new ways of dealing wi' new weapons. . . ."

"But aren't they jealous of outlanders and such as come from strange places?"

"You cannot tell till you get there. He's all the son I have, and I wouldn't have his life go the way mine's gone. . . ."

And that was all that Hannah wanted to know. Suddenly she rose from the bench, straight-backed and imperious, the new mistress, and let those under her take notice of it.

"And a very fine plan for Michaelmas too, and only one thing amiss with it. What property have you, Rafe Bates, my father's man?"

Startled, Rafe had got up in his feet too. Whose voice was this?

"I misdoubt if I follow you, mistress. You asked me this and the other. . . ."

"They can wed *me* to a game leg or one that's little better than a leper, but *you'll* make a mason of your son and an engineer of yourself! Soon we shall be having more of your sort than we have beggars and bedlamers! Doing things to rivers and mangonels for flinging stones! *That's* what's to happen now my father's gone! But don't forget you're bond-born, Rafe Bates, and your son too, and if you're reckoning you've only a woman to deal with, we'll see what the manor has to say!"

But his astonishment over Rafe could be obstinate too. He had but to pay his fine, he told her sullenly, and neither she nor the manor could stop him, and now her raised voice might have been heard by the nun in her bed overhead.

"*You* pay, that'll soon be getting your wages in cheese! It's the strength o' that back of yours that's wanted here, not cheese! *You* step out of your bounden service at your pleasure! I'll tell you when *you'll* leave this house, Rafe Bates! You'll leave it when you can tell me how it comes about that when they have a rascal in their hands they shape their questions so they can let him go! You'll leave when you can tell me why they loose their bloodhounds over half a riding but daren't smell what's on their own doorsteps! Nailing a weasel-skin to a barn door and their own cellars running with rats! You'll stop here till they've made up their minds which way to look for them that murdered my father. . . ."

And the milner, struck dumb, could only fumble with his oil-rag in the gloom, but Hannah Thirlow turned quickly away, strangling back her sobs as she stumbled up the stairs.

The single great chamber overhead was furnished with poles for running curtains, and the cubicle nearest the mill was the lay-sister's dortoir, but no glimmer of candle beyond its grey hanging that night gave it the look of a chapel-ardent. Sister Ursula was asleep, and it was Hannah who, getting out of her clothes and drawing the coverings over her, lay awake, all raw and bleeding again but steeled by her triumph over the man downstairs. Why should she suffer alone when others could be made to suffer with her? Find out what lay closest to their hearts and then hold it over them that they had their victuals to earn! Set them to cleaning out the dam and get the rusty cranks turning again, setting the tenter-frames to rights and mending the treads of the sun-dried wheel! Only a woman in the mill-keep now? Soft exclamations broke from her as she vowed that from to-morrow Thirlow should be ruled with a rod of iron. She woke the nun, for from the other side of the curtain a fretful voice was raised. There was no need to make all that to-do about her prayers, it said, for they would be heard if they were truly in her heart.

But still Hannah lay awake, devising whips for Rafe and his son and the tenderest spots to apply them.

Commonly it was the nun who was the first downstairs in the morning, for some of her herbs had to be gathered with the sunrise, others with the waxing or waning moon. But Sister Ursula descended the next day to find Hannah already in the thick of it and the lower hall such a disorder as never was. Ah, the joy of showing these idlers how work should be done! The chest had been dragged from under the window, the trestles and boards carried out into the flagged courtyard. The chimney must be swept too, and two of the lads were up the hillside cutting a bush. That meant no fire on the hearth, their breakfasts must be what they could lay hands on, and Rafe, who slept alongside the pantry under the stairs, seeing Hannah in her harden with a cloth bound about her fury of a head, seized his newly-oiled crossbow from its hook and hid it away out of the dust. By eight o'clock the lads could be heard returning to the house, singing as merrily as if their chimney-bush had been a yule-log, and when they had finished their chimney sweeping they could be getting out the hooks and irons and giving Rafe a hand up at the dam. Get Hannah Thirlow properly into a rage and it was no good telling her that even work could be made a godly thing.

By the time she had begun to scrub the nun had fled to her herb-patch, and was flicking her beads aside as she cropped her camomile flowers.

So what fatality, on the day of all days and at half past eleven in the morning, must bring Stephen Akam all the way from Ellbeck to the house and mill on the height? Worse, why must he bring his wife with him, her short legs all swaddled up for riding and the garnets in her hair showing under the decent dark veil she had cast over her head because of Hannah and her mourning-ring? Rafe was already up at the dam. A monstrous hammering and clanking from the mill told where Eggon was at work on the cranks. Hannah, scrubber in hand, saw them from the window, tying up the hackney and palfrey for themselves. Then, with a word she had learned from Rafe, she sped out by the back way to fetch the lay-sister.

The merchant and his wife had advanced no further than the doorway, where they stood looking in. And to wake Sister Ursula from her first sleep, as Hannah had done, never boded well for the morrow, and as she came in by the back way with her camomiles in her hand her gaunt black figure was already charged with menace. Hannah was carrying in from the forecourt a bench for Madam Akam to sit down.

But Stephen Akam was renowned for his tact on all untoward occasions. It appeared that the purpose of his visit had been the inventory that must be made before the administration of John Thirlow's will could be proceeded with, and he carried a baize bag of papers that he had evidently intended to consult. But as he looked at the stripped walls and heaped-up utensils and the sooty chimney-bush still in the hearth he indulgently put all thoughts of business aside. Instead it was the lay-sister who was the first to speak.

"I don't doubt you were betimes with your mattins this morning, Madam Akam. You see the way you catch us. Had you but sent word you were coming . . ." but the hand with the gold seal-ring on it made sympathetic movements.

"Madam, no words are needed. We must come again at a more convenient season. Indeed 'twas little that a clerk couldn't do," and Madam Akam hastened to his support.

"'Twas a fine morning, such as we cannot expect many more of this time of the year. . . ."

But the nun still stood with her camomiles in her hand, and she too wanted a start made with that will, and for the trivial affairs of this world one time and place was as good as another. Also Madam Akam was still running on, about having to make an early start if you wished to be back in good time for your dinner, and suddenly Sister Ursula raised her voice.

"Hannah, bring the trestles in and lay the table. Madam Akam's famished. We can look at papers and break bread at the same time," and her eyes went to the poke in Stephen Akam's hand. "About it and do as I bid you," she ordered Hannah again, for both the callers were vigorously protesting. "When the law starts bestirring itself it isn't for us to hold back," and Hannah carried the trestles in again and turned to the cupboard under the stairs. "Nay, Maister Akam, there's no need for a clerk with all the years I spent in Nostell aumbry," and when Sister Ursula spoke in that tone there was only one answer. The merchant untied the strings of his bag and began to set out his papers on the space Hannah had cleared.

But even the way he began was not to Sister Ursula's liking, and as stiff as a rod she placed herself on the bench by his side. He was turning from one engrossed deed to another, then to other papers in between, his fingers playing with the point of his beard, reading and humming and humming and reading again, with skippings and etcetera-etceteras, and suddenly she snatched a parchment from him.

"Let's take it as it's written," she snapped. "We cannot have some things glossed over and all the weight laid on others like this. Nay, we can pass the '*Ego Johannes Thirlow*' and the '*Sanae mentis et memoriae.*' Start here," and the practised old fingers fluttered over the membranes as they had clicked off the paternosters. "*Uno messagio et uno molendino,*" but suddenly she gave an "Ah!" The doggerel Latin had been too much for Stephen Akam's scanty learning, and the interleavings were the English into which he had it put.

But in Latin or English it came to the same thing. "*The aforesaid mill with its dams and sluices and troughs and all fittings and appurtenance thereof whether of wood or iron, the same at all times to be maintained etcetera etcetera,*" and the woman of God first frowned, then broke impatiently out.

"Use your ears, Maister Akam! Hark to that racket out there!" for to judge from the sounds that reached them Eggon was taking down the cranks to their last bolt and washer. "Since six this morning that's been going on, and his father waist-deep in water up at the dam, and you're sitting there telling us repairs have to be done!"

The merchant's wife was seen to stiffen, but Stephen Akam only made placating movements with his ringed hand. . . . "Softly, softly, Mistress Ursula—we shall make better speed that way. . . ."

But to Hannah's astonishment the nun, who had never ceased to tell her what trouble they could make for her if she showed herself stubborn, seemed to be flying straight into trouble's face.

"The mill will be ready when you folk down there have found work for it to do, and I've had to do with wills before, and mills too! At Nostell we'd a couple of corn-mills, and rents and lands and revenues ten times what Ellbeck has to show! Ay, from a holy house, a thousand sheep were carried off by robbers in one year, and four hundred cows, half of 'em in calf! Is that will lodged for proving yet, with whatever claims there may be against it?"

"Gently, Mistress Ursula. . . ."

"You've no need to talk to me about inventories, for I've handled more of them than you have cloth, and no scrivener to put them into English for me either! Heaven forbid we shouldn't all live in peace together, but here's a young girl, come sudden and new to it all, and it's for them that knows the wiles to see she has her rights!"

Hannah had taken herself off to the window, but the barb about the Latin had gone home, and she heard the short nasal sound that broke from Madam Akam.

"Wiles, Ma'am?" but the lay-sister gave her her stare back again.

"I said wiles, Ma'am, and I grant you policy has its place, but it's the will of God it should be put back in it sometimes."

"We aren't all as privy to the will of God as some of you ladies from priories!" the clothier's wife flung back. "And you'd think something was due to them that's put themselves to the trouble we have this morning, with no thought but to help!"

"Your good man and I were talking executors' business, Ma'am," but back again flashed the answer.

"You spoke of wiles and young girls' rights and flung your Nostell at us! Nostell's no great way off, Madam, remember that! It's no further than just over Wakefield way!"

"I need no telling where Nostell is," and Stephen Akam, seeing the turn things had so unhappily taken, began to cram his papers back into his bag again. But now his wife was on her feet shaking out her petticoats and setting the veil about her shoulders, and again Hannah heard that short derisive sound.

"Policy and the will o' God! Here's a high horse to be riding! But when the holy set their own penances it isn't in nature they should make 'em too heavy!"

All were on their feet now, the nun too. . . . "Penances, Ma'am?" she said austerely, and hotly came the answer.

"Ay, or what you choose to call them, pilgrimages or sanctuary, or what you like! It's many a long year since *you* were at Nostell, Ma'am, but that doesn't stop others remembering! Wakefield and back!" but by this time her husband had her by the shoulders and was thrusting her towards the door.

The lay-sister's fingers had gone tremulously to her rosary. As if a white face could turn whiter, that dry oval framed in its narrow wimple seemed to blench of itself. "*Ave Mary*," she breathed shakily, but there was nothing but coarse contempt in Madam Akam's tone now.

"Nostell and its vows! Well may she be at a wench's bedside before the midwife's finished with her, for her pennyroyal's none the worse for having been blessed! Look at that one by the window, her with her dusting cloth on her head, and then ask Ann Thomas what colour *her* hair was before Nostell put its razor on it! For a pair o' foreign wild-cats—no more Ellbeck born than the Pope o' Rome. . . ."

There was a quick pattering as the string of a rosary suddenly snapped and aves and paternosters rattled in a flurry to the stone floor. The string of a shrivelled old heart must have cracked too, for the nun had given way at the knees and sagged down in a heap. Hannah had sprung forward, and Stephen Akam had clapped his ringed hand over his wife's mouth.

"Women! Get you mounted! Would you bring down the wrath of holy church on us?" but he was too late. The rest was flung back from the porch.

"Graveclothes as black as that chimney-bush, all whitened over with prayers! Sweep up your grandmother's beads for her, Hannah Thirlow, for it's time somebody told you, and as for her, when she comes round again, you can ask her. . . ."

But neither did she finish nor did Hannah hear, for she was on her knees. Dazed, she listened for a moment to the stir of hoofs and the sounds of mounting outside. Then, folding her arms about the corpse-like head, she made a cushion of her harden and gently eased it down among the pots and pans.

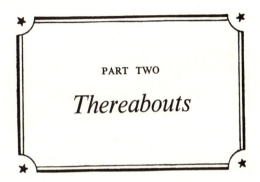

PART TWO

Thereabouts

1

WILLIE MIDDLEMISS LAY WIDE AWAKE AND LISTENING, BUT WITHOUT moving finger or eyelid. He was almost certain that what had awakened him had been a stone, but where up there should a stone have come from? As the valleys lay beneath the clouds, so here the clouds themselves lay half a thousand feet below. If a man would drink it must be water, if he would eat it must be what he carried with him or chanced upon, if he would weave or spin it must be the bogcotton or as the autumnal spiders span.

Yet Willie Middlemiss could have sworn that what had awakened him had been a falling stone.

Then again he heard the dull thud, but sometimes too stones were thrown blindly, to make some suspected presence show itself. As he lay, his furred cap and jerkin the same colour as the scrub, he was as indistinguishable as a hare at form as long as he kept still. Still therefore he kept, for another five minutes. Then, slowly, he raised his head an inch.

But still there was nothing to be seen but the daybreak evaporations, through the pallid whiteness of which the sun was just beginning to break like a burning-glass. Only heath, scrub, and the white tremendousness of the sky—still, it had been a stone, for there came another. It was time he was doing something.

Then came the third stone, as big as his fist, bounding over the bents not five yards from him, and raising his head he saw. Away to his right two men on nags moved, over on his left were two others, making four. Four, six—there were eight of them, closing slowly in a circle about him. As well to be taken standing as lying down, and he rose to his feet.

They were rough, tanned, small-built men, but breed-for-breed their nags were as small, so that their feet as they rode trailed only an inch or two from the ground. Three of them were naked to the waist, and those who had no stones in their hands carried pick-handles, and Willie did not understand the language they spoke, but all languages are one when, as next happened, a bow-legged fellow whose body from the waist up seemed to have been pickled in peat-water began to unwind a length of rope from his lean ribs and another, kicking his pony forward, challenged him in his own tongue.

"Who is with you and where are they hiding?"

With the pony's muzzle close to his face Willie answered that none was with him, neither had he been hiding.

"What are you doing on this mountain?"

"Being robbed by the look of it," said Willie, for already his staff had been wrenched from his hand and his wallet from his waist.

"Bring him in," and the ponies were headed about.

They had not far to go. A quarter of a mile away, where a rill of water winked up like a bright eye among the bents, were four tents of tarred canvas, with more long-tailed nags standing about. Stacked and strewn behind and about them were angle-frames and grids of iron, with rakes and pokers and picks and shovels and a couple of pairs of patched bellows. Over a fire-trench flour-cakes were baking on hot stones, and "Welshmen," Willie told himself as he was hustled and thrust towards a sloping bivouac the back of which was held down by yet more implements of iron.

Inside it a man was seated. The bedding on which he had lain had been thrust to the back of the tent, and on the folded blanket at his side he had set out a mixed assortment of stones. These however were not for throwing at Willie, but apparently ores and quartzes of various kinds, with a small hammer for cracking them and a mortar for crushing them to powder, and he was in fact crushing something at that moment and running the siftings through his fingers. Absorbed in his occupation he neither seemed to notice the sudden crowding of his tent nor to hear the half-dozen voices all telling of Willie's capture at once, but he looked up as Willie's wallet was passed to him, and opened it. By the side of his specimens he set out its contents, his cup and platter, his metal mirror and razor, his comb and spare shirt, his small stock of victuals, and wrapped up with separate care the tools of his trade. Meanwhile Willie too was observing him, his thick white hair like a thatch that had been snowed on, the rough sort of chieftaincy that seemed to inhere in his cheekbones and hollow jaw, and the intelligence of his furrowed brow. And suddenly, the man in the tent had had enough of their talk, and made a sign. Let those who were preparing breakfast get on with it. The entrance of the bivouac grew light again as they moved away, and not until then did he fix on Willie a pair of pale blue-black eyes, that is to say, the brows and the lashes were as black as coal for all his white hair, but the eyes that looked out from them might have been made of ice-blue water.

"What is your name?"

"Wilson Middlemiss."

"From where are you?"

"From back there in the cloth-lands."

"And where are you going?"

"To the Marches and Wales," and then came the same question Willie had been asked before.

"Who is with you?"

"Nobody is with me."

"Do you speak Welsh?"

"No," but now the eyes were as piercingly on him as if they gave him his last chance of saying 'Yes.'

"How long have you been on this mountain?"

"I got here last night."

"It was only a quarter of a mile away you were found. How came it you did not see our fire and join us?"

"It is in a hollow. There was a mist. I saw no fire," and the eyes flashed under their eaves of frosted hair.

"A night-fire only a quarter of a mile away and you didn't see it! You say you do not know Welsh, but do you know what Saes is?"

"Everybody knows that. It is Saxon, Englishman," and at that it seemed to Willie that the man began deliberately to work himself up into a passion.

"And you are going to the Marches of Wales, to tell them you know where there is a company of free men, ia, free men and the sons of free men, not butchers and cut-throats, to be seized and clapped into fighting-jackets and marched off and never heard of again! Was that your spy's business on this mountain?"

And somewhere before Willie had heard of these *cenedlau* or split-off fragments of clans, akin either by blood or by long custom and the habits of their trade, and now he could make a guess what that trade was. His close leather cap tied under his chin gave him the look of a hooded hawk as he leaned forward with his hand on the tent's framework.

"Are you miners?"

"And if we are? We are Cymri and we will not fight for the Saes in his quarrels," but the flash was dying down again, and he had removed the protecting cork from one of Willie's burins and was drawing its delicate point slowly across the ball of his thumb. "Ia. We are miners, as you or anybody can see."

"Then it may be our trades are not so different. What do you mine?"

"Ironstone," said the man absently, trying the tool again.

"Ironstone?" Willie exclaimed. "Then see how well-met we are after all! One man works in one metal and another in another, but if you get a seal-ring a year to do in those cloth-towns it's as much as . . . man, for God's sake have a care with that point!" for slipping through the miner's fingers the tool had clinked among his quartzes and pebbles. "What the devil, do you think a burin's a stone-chisel? Give it back into proper hands again!" and starting forward he snatched up the tool to see whether it had taken any hurt.

As it chanced he could have done nothing better. Burins were hard to come by, and his gesture had been swift and unconsidered, but that a leader, a *pen-cenedl*, should be addressed so by his prisoner was something new to this man in the tent, and he lifted his eyes to Willie afresh.

"What do you say your name is?"

"Middlemiss. Most call me Willie."

"I am Bartholomew Rhys, but I do not know what you mean by this metal-working. There is a blanket. Sit down."

The next minute Willie, seated on the blanket at the *pen-cenedl's* side, was showing him how an engraver used his burin.

"The handle, see, is rounded to fit your palm, and you never force it lest it should slip, but you turn the work round and round, like this," and he looked about him for something to demonstrate on.

The chief's breakfast had just been set before him. It was of freshly-killed meat and a flat cake still hot from the fire, and reaching out his hand to the cake Willie broke a portion of it off. Popping pieces of it into his mouth till he had got it to the size he wanted it he set the burin's point to the crust and worked for several minutes, the blue-black eyes as intent on what he was doing as his own. Then he passed it to Bartholomew Rhys.

It might have been some sleight of magic he had performed. First the head-man held it close, then at arm's length. An extempore scratching on the first thing to hand, half of it executed upside-down, and there it was, a resemblance of his own aquiline, hollow-cheeked face! He gave Willie an incredulous glance.

"You say this is your trade?"

"Not on crusts of bread. That point will bite into anything this side of a diamond," but still the chief gazed, as fascinated as a child.

"Ia ia, we live and learn," he said at last, but the next minute Willie's hopes were dashed again, for again that piercing, mistrustful look was fastened on him. "But this alters nothing. A wizard is as well able to betray as another, perhaps better. You were creeping about at night, counting us for all we know. It is that you haven't answered yet."

So—why not? Willie had no desire to be bound with ropes or to have animals breathing in his face. Bartholomew's bread and meat were a better breakfast than a stone, and snatching the piece of bread back again he made as if to crush it in his hand, but was checked by a vice-like grip.

"Leave that as it is."

"Not if you are going to call me a man-seller! And if I were to show you something else, how do I know *you* wouldn't betray me?"

"I am their *taid* and answerable to them all, of my own bed or not. They have told me where they found you. A fire in the night, not a quarter of a mile away . . . what is this?"

And now Willie could have eaten both breakfasts, for the *pen-cenedl* was staring incredulously at the locket that Willie had thrust into his hand.

"Dwu Mawr!" he breathed, as if the locket had fallen suddenly from the skies. "Take that cap off and let me see your face!"

Willie took off his cap. A face like any other face, yet behind it lay such wonders as these! But no, it was impossible, and the miner saw through the trick, for again he broke out harshly.

"Dwu Mawr did I say? Deowl more like, for it is pilfery! You stole it and it is some runaway you are!" and Willie made the despairing gesture of one who has done all he can and gives it up.

"You do it before their eyes and then they won't believe!"

"Will you swear it?"

"I will swear it," and Bartholomew raised his voice to a shout.

"Iorwerth! Pugh!"

"Nay," cried Willie in sudden alarm, "give me that back first! Before they as much as saw me they had a rope ready for me!" But Bartholomew only raised his voice the louder.

"Morgan, Gruffydd, *hwn a hwn!* More bread and meat! If there's honey bring it—and see if there's bilberries hereabouts! Then fetch fresh litter, for this young squire will share this tent! Peace, young sir. Not a finger shall be laid on anything that's yours. Iorwerth! Pugh!"

Yet though he gave the locket back into Willie's hand again, thrice before that midday he had begged for another sight of it.

That morning, seated with the head-man in his tent, Willie was given some idea of their rough and wandering lives. Ironstone was their trade, but before they could smelt it they must have fuel, for of what use was it to them that the broken cliffs of the shore laid bare the sea-coal if the ore was half a week's journey away, or that this cropped up at their very feet if there was not a tree to cut or charcoal to be had? It was where the two lay together that they sought, and for nearly a year they had been moving from place to place, as far away as Carlisle. Now they were headed south again, but whither was still uncertain, for the Forest of Dean was already too populous with just such forges as theirs, and always, by day and night, there was the danger that they might be overpowered and pressed and clapped into English haquetons and marched off and be heard of no more.

But it was the *pen* himself whose like Willie had never before seen, and he was not their leader for nothing. There was nothing in his rough attire to distinguish him from the rest of them, but he had his own crude and hard-won lore, and by means of it he sampled the land as they went, by experience and instinct marking its riches down. Unschooled save for that, a stranger to anything but sow-metal or a pig of iron from a sand mould, no wonder Willie and the revelation of his art should blind him like a peep into heaven itself. Nor was it now any concern of Willie's to shake him from this belief. Instead as he sat in his tent, eating his bread and cheese, he told him of the famous drinking-cup with the hunting-scene engraved round its bowl, and of half a dozen others that he invented with such facility that he began almost to believe in them himself. Whereupon the *pen* too began to remember his dignity and due. Raising his voice again he commanded that two ponies should be made ready forthwith. Then he thrust a short spade into Willie's hand.

"I shall take leave to call you Gwilym, young master," he said as he rose. "Come, Gwilym, and we will stretch ourselves a little."

It was no great distance from the camp that he took him, only a couple of miles or so back on the mountain, to a point where a peaty bed bordered on wide bog and marsh. There, dismounting, he bade Willie do the same, and pointed to a patch at his feet.

"Dig up a turf," he said, and when he had dug up the turf, Bartholomew took a crumple of touch-paper from his pocket. Kindling this he set it to the bared patch, and a thin spirituous blue flame flickered up from the ground.

"Try to put it out with water," and unstoppering his water-bottle Willie poured water on the teasel-blue licking. It floated and ran but still burned, so one miracle for another, and the icy eyes were turned to Willie as if some debt of honour was now as handsomely paid as needs be.

"No, nor all the pistylls in Wales will not put it out till it burns out of itself," he said. "Do you see that parched patch yonder where not a herb grows? Under it is fire, some pit or seam that no eye has ever seen. There are nights when I lie awake in my tent, unable to close my eyes for the thought of the things that lie under my head. If it is not the iron you smelt it is the glass-pebble you grind, or alum or salt or the firestone they call pyrites. Ia, ia, there are wondrous things down there among the worms too. To which part of Wales are you going?"

"I shall know better when I get a bit nearer to it," said Willie.

"If you go through the cannel-country, they waste no wicks for their lighting there. In the midst of the chamber they set up their hearth, and round it the family sits, and the women can sew by the coal-light and the men see to patch their shoes. Round Carlisle it is lead, but there is silver too—ia, ia, sixty pounds weight to the ton, in a horse and cart you could carry it away," and Willie laughed.

"There! Did I not tell you our trades were akin? The iron for you and the silver for me and we shall not quarrel!" but Bartholomew's eyes were gravely considering his fire-well.

"Sometimes I have dreams whether a man might not smelt with what sweats out of the earth like this, but no further do ever I get. Silver did you say? In Merioneth there is gold. They made Owain's crown of it when they crowned him king at Machynlleth. Dwu, but it is all very wonderful!" and leaving the fire-well to burn out of itself they turned for the encampment again.

Next in authority to Bartholomew seemed to be the Iorwerth who had ridden Willie down on his pony and the shirtless Pugh who had wanted to bind him with his cord. These two shared Bartholomew's tent, which was big enough for the three of them, but looked like being cramped quarters now that Willie made a fourth. But so far they had not been near it, and by the time Willie and Bartholomew reached it again the evening routine was in full swing. Besides the pack-animals the *cenedl* travelled with half a dozen lurchers and prick-eared corgies. These tracked down their food by day and kept watch at night, and now the men were turning them loose, and picketing the ponies and stacking up fuel for the night. In this Willie would have borne a hand, but Bartholomew would hear of no such thing. "Let them do it," he said, and out he went, leaving Willie in the lean-to, his hands the only idle pair in the camp.

So, with the night-noises of the mountain waking up, and that long-drawn sound in the distance either the belling of a stag or a wolf stalking its love or its prey, he turned his mind to his own affairs again. Very prettily indeed these had altered for the better. He had been brought in a captive, but within half an hour the chief had been shouting for meat and honey for him, and had set his band to scouring the bents for bilberries. But he had lost a day, the month was October, and it was no plan of his to spend the winter with a pack of Welsh colliers wherever their trade might lead them. And he was pondering his future when Bartholomew, returning from his round, entered the tent again. The fire in the trench had been made up, but he threw fresh wood on it, and then, lighting the candle of a lantern, began to busy himself among the litter at the back of the tent. Drawing a saddle-bag from underneath it he drew out a parchment or document and began to study it. It seemed to Willie to be some sort of a map, and Willie had no map, and many times had wished he had.

"How long are you camping here?" he asked, and Bartholomew lifted his frosted thatch of a head.

"It is what I am considering," he said. "By my reckoning there should be little in that direction. But even if there is nothing it will be knowledge for another."

"In what direction?" Willie asked, and again the *pen* looked up.

"It lies south of here, but a day should be enough, and then we can be packing up."

"What's that you have? A map?"

"Ia ia—see," and he passed it to Willie.

He called it a map, but a glance at it was enough to tell Willie that mapping was not among Bartholomew's gifts. Somewhere in his travels he must have come upon a map, and made a rude copy of it with his own unskilled hand, and that was as much as could be said for it. Towards its left edge it showed a clumsily-drawn coastline, with indentations for estuaries and ropy meanderings for rivers and knots for lakes, but it was on the signs and symbols that peppered it that Willie's eyes were fastened, and there could be little doubt what these were. They were the record of his observations as he went, and such-and-such a marking probably meant coal, another some other mineral, and so sprinkled thickly or thinly wherever the *cenedl* had wandered.

"And where's this place that's south you're talking of?" Willie asked, for of south or north the map bore no indication.

"Here," said Bartholomew, putting his finger on it, but that portion of the map was empty of markings. "And we may not pass this way again, and as I say it may be knowledge for another. Shall we ride out tomorrow and see, you and I?"

"As you please," said Willie, and Bartholomew put his map back into the saddlebag and buried it under his litter again.

Yet still the other two sharers of the lean-to did not return, and Willie lay awake, watching the fire at the tent's mouth and listening to the noises of the night. Apparently Bartholomew had the gift of sleeping at will, for he had rolled himself in his litter and was already dreaming of the hidden treasures of the earth; but the sound that startled Willie just as he too was dropping off came with no more announcement than the first heavy drop of a thunderstorm. There was something thunderous in its nature, too, that suddenly redoubled the loneliness even of the mountain. A single deep voice, as rough and salty as the food that nourished it, had been vibratingly raised. A second voice joined it, there was a pause as if the very night listened and then it lifted as a ship lifts to a wave. The miners had started a hymn.

But their God might have been of ironstone too for all the comfort they seemed to have of their singing, for at the door of heaven itself they seemed to knock in vain for the home they lacked on earth. That same hymn had mounted to the skies among the lead and silver of Carlisle, the Forest of Dean had heard it where the fuel and the ore lay together, for they carried it with them, the ark of the covenant of their toilsome lives. It was addressed to heaven, but something in it they shared with the belling stags and the wolves that slaked their hunger and their love, and Willie felt happier when it came to an end. It had awakened Bartholomew too, who was moving restlessly in his litter.

"I've heard many merrier noises than that," Willie grunted, and Bartholomew rolled over in his litter again.

"Ia ia. It's a month now since they sang a hymn. And always it is with a hymn that the worst of the world's troubles begin," he said, and the next moment he was once more asleep.

2

SOMETIME BEFORE DAYBREAK WILLIE AGAIN OPENED HIS EYES. THE FIRE in the trench had been replenished while he had slept, and from somewhere behind the tent came the sound of suppressed but contentious voices.

"I say it is ill-done to speak before him in a language he does not understand!"

"Are we not to speak our own language because a Saes is among us?"

"I have told you I am his *gwaesaf*."

"And we say he is a Saes and *aillt*."

"You tell me yourselves he offered no resistance. . . ."

"Eight to one! Does that make him less crafty? Pugh showed sense when he wanted to bind him! Ev-ery minute a pair of eyes should be on him!" and then came a third voice.

"I will not saddle ponies for a Saes, nor will Morgan here be set gathering bilberries. . . ."

"When I tell you I have made myself his *gwaesaf*. . . ."

"Every Saes is *aillt* and a spy. . . ."

But with words so incomprehensible running through it, it could only be a dream, and Willie rolled over and slept again.

He awoke to find Bartholomew already moving about the tent and their breakfast ready. The only cap Bartholomew ever wore was his thick eaves of hair, and this and the short sheepskin cape he had cast over his shoulders gave him the appearance of some rimed and top-heavy tree as he ate in silence, conning his map meanwhile. Whatever the mutiny of the night had been about the ponies were none the less ready, as was their packet of provisions, apparently for an excursion of some distance. This, as they mounted and set off, Bartholomew proceeded to make longer still, for hardly were they clear of the camp before he began to canter off in detours as this distant indication of the ground or that caught his eye. But Willie was setting a trap for him, and as he returned from one of these castings-off he suddenly sprang it.

"Bartholomew, what is good-morning in Welsh?" he said, and Bartholomew checked his pony just as he was starting off afresh.

"Good morning? It is *bore da*," he answered.

"And what is good night?"

"*Nos da*."

"And thank you?"

"*Diolch*."

"*Diolch*," said Willie. Bartholomew must have concluded that his ranging eyes had deceived him, for they rode on.

But at his next question, which was what *aillt* was in English, Bartholomew's eyes became all charcoal-and-ice again.

"*Aillt*?" Where have you heard of *aillt*?"

"And *gwaesaf*. I want to know what they mean."

"To whom here have you said good morning and not had your good morning again?"

"I didn't say to anybody. I asked you what *aillt* and *gwaesaf* meant," and the chief answered more slowly.

"*Aillt* is any not of their kin. Many Welsh too are *aillt* to them. A *gwaesaf* is a warranty or bail. Are there other words you wish to know?"

"Nay, these will do to be thinking over."

"Then you are not to suppose that I am abroad to-day for my pleasure, for I am their eyes, and unless I find it these will have no mining to do. Do you see that cairn, over on the skyline where I am pointing."

"Yes." It was faintly distinguishable on a crest, but a great way off.

"Then keep you straight for it, and I will join you there at midday," and off he circled again, leaving Willie to ride on alone.

About him was a desolation as dispiriting as even that mountain-range had to show. To left, to right, behind him, one stony barrenness succeeded another, sage-grey with scrub or brown with the velvet of rushes, and ending abruptly against the white blankness of the sky. And by this time it had begun to sink into Willie's mind that *gwaesaf* meant some sort of a protector, and *aillt* anybody but these stone-throwing hymn-singers themselves. But protection? Against what? There he was, with a stiff pony between his knees. Bartholomew was not to be seen. The whole wilderness of the range lay open before him. What more was he waiting for?

But just as the prospect opened out, three sufficient reasons closed it again. The *pen* had shown himself his friend. Instead of bringing his belongings with him he had left them behind among the litter of the tent. And the third reason appeared just as he turned to take another look about him. Three-quarters of a mile away behind him a mounted figure was just disappearing behind a hummock, while a second peeped round from an outcrop of rock.

The men of the band now trusted neither him nor their leader, and he was being followed.

Setting his face ahead again he rode on.

By midday, he had reached the cromlech, to find Bartholomew already there. He was busying himself with their frugal meal, but Willie only stood looking about him. A day's journey there and back for this! The very birds had forsaken that upraised mountain-peak. Not as much as a lizard's tail stirred among those heaped-up stones twice as high as himself, from which the rains had washed even the mosses away. The cleanness of the beginning and end of things had cursed it, and yet Willie, stooping, had picked up a shard of earthenware with its two inches of edge rounded in an unmistakable curve. It had been made in some ancient time by man, and hearing his exclamation Bartholomew turned.

"What have you found? A bone?"

"No. A bit of ware."

"Sit down and eat, for it is as I knew, there is nothing," and he handed Willie his bread and meat.

"Was there nothing where you went?" But Bartholomew had moved to the lee of the cairn, for their voices could hardly be heard for the rushing of the wind that was the lord of that place, and he shook his blown head.

"This is a dinas, an old battlefield, Gwilym," he said at last. "Dig here and you will find wasted iron without handles that once were swords. Those bits of green you can see once checked the mouth of a horse. Knuckles you'll find, and cob-bones from the backs of men, and that bit of ware was what they ate their porridge from or the cup they set to their lips."

"Diolch," said Willie, but Bartholomew went on as if he had been thinking of nothing else this past two hours.

"Gwilym bach," he said with a headshake, "those who journey through this world must take what they meet by the way. To say good morning or good night in Welsh would not make a Welshman of you. If you wanted to become a Welshman do you know how long it would take you?"

"If I what?" said Willie.

"If you, Gwilym, were to marry a Welshwoman, and your son after you married a Welshwoman also, and his son, and his son, and so for nine generations—six, seven, eight, nine generations—then another Gwilym might be admitted a member of this *cenedl*. But until then he is *aillt*."

"Then he must bear it as best he can," said Willie, but at something in his tone the frosted head was lifted as if a vanished crown settled on it again.

"Many of these are my kin, and in my veins runs the blood of Cyngen ap Cadell. In the north they have been, for a year, and there the fighting is against the Scot. But now they draw near their own land again the old things wake up in them."

"We aren't out of England yet," muttered Willie, but up went the handsome and authoritative head again.

"And what was England before it was what it is to-day? You call it Shrewsbury, but it is Amwythig to Cadell's blood. Ask them the way to the Dee and they will tell you where the Dwfwrdwy is. Tell that bit of shard the name of the lips that drank from it and where they are now! My men are asking what your business is in the Marches of Wales."

"This *cenedl* goes where its trade is. I do the same," said Willie doggedly.

"And as long as I am their chief I must see it their way," the *pen* answered him as implacably back.

And a few more words like those and Willie would be picking his luck all to pieces again. Was there not trouble enough to-day without stirring up the battles of the past? For all the shelter of the cairn he was shivering in this place of thin ghosts and nameless bones, and they had finished their meal, and all at once he was on his feet, trying to laugh himself warm again.

"Then you can tell them I care not where I go as long as it's a fine place with fine people in it, so up, man, and let's get out of this pot-shop! Who cares for dead lips if he can get near a pair of warm ones? Up, and let's be off from here!" and away he marched to unpicket the ponies, and for half the way home, to cheer Bartholomew up, talked about nothing but flagons with hunting-scenes on them and the lockets of women and their ear-rings twinkling in their ears like flowers of gold.

They heard the stir of preparation while they were still half a mile away from the camp. On the morrow they were moving on, but much of their packing could be done overnight, and all that evening their bivouac was noisy with the clanking of iron as the frames and fire-pans were carried to the loading-place and the implements bundled together for setting on the animals. And if they neither asked for nor wanted Willie's help then the devil take them and their Cadells and cromlechs and their wolfish hymns. Nay, you had only to scratch Bartholomew and he was of the same stuff as the rest of them, for on their way back, when Willie had finished with his goblets and lockets and ear-rings, Bartholomew too had resumed his solemn speculations on what went on in the darkness under their feet, whether in some sort metals did not breed from one another down there, else why were the silver and the lead so commonly found together? Just a rude philosopher in a sheep-skin!

And how long (God help us!) would it take Willie Middlemiss to become a Welshman! . . .

For all that he would gladly have been of their company later, for apparently it was their custom to break up their camp with singing, and it was not to hymns that Willie lay listening as they made themselves drunk on that ice-cold mountain-water and song. Their ditties were rousing and martial and wild, too wild for Bartholomew, for Willie heard him mutter, "Deowl, Iorwerth Rhys, but if you cannot smell Wales again but you must set fire to it it shall be Cornwall and the tin-mines for you!" But noisier still the singing grew, for it was only by the side of the Saes that these would not fight, and yet Willie had never as much as heard of that Cadwgan who had stalked through Wales whetting the edge of his axe away till there was no edge left and he had to get a new one, chanting his battle-call as he went. All he heard was Bartholomew's growling again. "Deowl! Is it so? . . ."

And after the battle the carouse, and after the carouse the sweeter sweets, for they were ravenous for women too on that mountain-top, and though Willie did not understand a word of it, it needed no understanding, and suddenly Bartholomew reached for his horn. On it he blew a peremptory blast. There was a pause, but the singing ceased, and again he muttered as he put his horn away.

"I am telling the world you are men of peace and you sing your song of Cadwgan! Ia ia, it always begins with a hymn, but any more of it and it shall be Cornwall and the tin, for all of you!"

Willie woke the next morning to find himself staring up at the sky. The tent had been taken down over his head, and the sudden flaring up of the fire showed where the trusses of bedding were being burned. Gathering his own up in his arms he rose and cast it also on the flames.

Already little of the encampment remained. It was a cold raw daybreak, with half-seen shapes that came and went in the whiteness, that became a denser vapour of breathing where the burdens were being adjusted to the animals backs. Tent-poles lay on the ground, and Willie folded the heavy canvas under which he had slept and then went to fill his water-bottle, but when he returned the tenting had gone and Bartholomew stood there between two great nets of fodder.

"Take these and wait over there by those four ponies," he said, and picking up the nets Willie did as he was told.

Half an hour later only the paler patches in the herbage and the still-creeping sparks of the fires showed where the encampment had been. Once more the *cenedl* was what it was—a score of ponies and as many men, with two travelling forges, wandering over the face of the land for where the fuel and the ironstone lay together.

Until the sun should get higher they did not split up, but kept in touch by sight, but now Willie saw that as well as Bartholomew Iorwerth and Pugh also carried horns. Pugh's charge was the right of their line, while Iorwerth took the left with Willie and the *pen* in the middle of it, and again they were headed south, but wide and west of the region they had crossed the day before. The whole business had taken little more than an hour, and clánking like an armoury off they set.

By nine o'clock the dazzle of the sun was beginning to splinter the whiteness. The mists were breaking, but still the long ridge to the left with the cromlech on it seemed to float on nothing, and the line of ponies were beginning to straggle out, till the farthest of them could hardly be seen at all. But Willie had got up out of the wrong side of the litter that morning, and was at odds with the *cenedl* from its chief downwards. The men let him sleep on like a sultan while they took down the tent over his head, and even Bartholomew had little time to spare for him, for he was here and there continually, trotting ahead, moving up and down the line, both comical and grotesque to look at with his shrub-like coat and mistletoe-tangle of a head and a great bundle of fodder propping him up on either side. Willie too rustled like a haystack with the fodder his pony carried, and this morning his breakfast had been forgotten—but no, suddenly he found it, a package half buried in the hay in front of him. But Bartholomew might at least have told him it was there, and opening the packet he munched sullenly as he rode.

The horns that Pugh and Iorwerth carried were the small horns of southern cattle, but Bartholomew's was that of some highland animal, twice as long and of a deeper note. Now, as it drew on to midday, all three of them sounded continually along the half-mile straggle of their line. The mists had steamed themselves away, Iorwerth's men were no more than dots among the hues of the hillside, and it was time for the burdened animals to be rested. Bartholomew blew a single blast. From left and right the thinner notes acknowledged it, and those of the centre closed in. The nets of fodder were opened, the animals munching with their loads on their backs, and again Bartholomew was off, this time on foot. The rest had flung themselves down to eat.

And now Willie was thinking what a barrier the Lord had erected when He had confounded the tongues of men. Pugh and Iorwerth, as he knew, spoke English, and possibly others, but these he guessed to be few, and there, not ten yards from him, were half a dozen of them, with the ponies standing by. And it was not in him to be ill-tempered for long when others were laughing, and his moroseness was passing, and he kept eyeing them. He could hardly offer to share his food with them, for each man had his own and it was their food he was eating, and when he held out a morsel to a corgie the animal took it when he let it go, but refused it from his hand. Repeatedly he glanced at the men, but each time he did so they seemed to have something to say to one another, and then, belatedly, he bethought him of a way. To be sure, his whistle! A whistle could speak any man's tongue, and he turned over on the grassy mound on which he had thrown himself down to get it out.

But he could not find it. Usually he carried it in his breast, but it was not there, and he turned to his wallet, half unpacking it on the grass, but it was not there either, and the chances were that it had slipped out of his jerkin while he slept and been thrown away with litter on which he had lain. Deowl, he muttered, for it was a new oath and as such to his liking. He had never lacked company as long as he had a whistle to set to his lips, and presently, with his hand inside his waist-band, he began to scratch himself. Still, it might have been his locket he had lost, and he could always whistle between his teeth, and suddenly he glanced over to see what the men by the ponies had been laughing at, and now he had taken off his leather cap and it was his head he was scratching. At that moment he saw Bartholomew returning, and picking up his cap again he found it infested with a million red ants. His waist too was a crawling of them, for unawares he had been lying on an anthill, and as the men tied up the nets and got ready the ponies again he heard their loud guffaw. Even Bartholomew's furrowed face was twitching at the sight of Willie, loosening his clothes, his face red with fury. The *pen's* horn had a metal band, and only yesterday he had been wondering what memento he should put on it before he left them, but now a plague of red ants on Bartholomew and his horn! To a double blast on it the cavalcade reformed its line, and once more the *cenedl* moved forward.

As the afternoon wore on the way became exceedingly rough. Because of its difficulty portions of the apparatus had to be lifted from the animals' backs and carried by the men themselves, the ridge-pole of a tent to two men, with the bundles of rakes and pickheads swinging beneath it. There was no riding for anybody now, for at every ascent the nags had to be helped by the headropes, and at each ravine the shifting loads had to be held back from slipping forward over their heads. Jangling and clattering and clanking, with outbursts of cursing every time a pony slipped and came down, the line huddled together when there was no other way, sprawling out again till only by the horns could it be told where half of them were, to this toilsome progress the sun began to decline. Soon it was half a sun only, a bowl rim-down that sank as you watched it. When that fire went out the mists would be on them again, already lanterns were being lighted, and they could go no further that day.

The valley-head they had reached was ill-suited for a camp, for each tent would have to be pitched wherever a footing could be found for it, but it had a brook tumbling down it and wood for their fire. A scattering of firs had straggled up with the stream, and at these the men were already busy with the axes. But Willie was down by the brook, without a stitch on him, hunting and picking and beating and shaking, knee-deep in the coldest water he had ever dipped toe into.

And now give Willie the wood and he would make do without the ironstone, for if the trees reached as high as that there would likely be more lower down, and hell and all its fires to these flaycrow Welshmen who didn't tell a man when he was lying among ants, and grinned to see a Saes tearing the skin off his body! He was planning his leave-taking now, shivering knee-deep in the pool.

They had pitched the *pen's* tent down by the stream, and the fire in front of it was just beginning to crackle when Willie reached it again. Higher up on a small plateau lanterns were making moving haloes, and twenty yards down the rocky stream more tenting had been irregularly stretched across the lower branches of the firs themselves. Willie was noting all these things as he got into his breeches again, and his shirt was over his head when Bartholomew returned to the tent.

"Be having your supper without me, for I have matters to attend to," he said, and Willie did not answer as he continued to clothe himself. "And streamside air is not wholesome, so light the lantern and drop the flap," and taking his map from his saddlebag out Bartholomew passed again.

No sooner had he gone than Willie became suddenly active. He did not know how long the *pen* would be, but first of all food. Coarse grasses and the podded stalks of spent flowers filled the newly-pitched tent's interior, and as he lighted the lantern and set it down among these he saw Bartholomew's stock of food as well as his own. Of this he took twice as much of the gammon as he could have eaten and a triple portion of bread, cramming them into his wallet and setting his freshly-washed shirt about the lantern to dry. There among the weeds the lantern resembled some miniature fantastic castle, all lighted up in the midst of a gigantic and scale-distorted forest. And he had done well to lose no time, for there after all was Bartholomew, back again with his map in his hand. Wearily he threw himself down, for these carriers of loads need not think that their chief had not his troubles too, but by this time Willie's thoughts were running far ahead.

It would not have to be down the stream, because of the ropes that might trip him in the dark. It would have to be by the way they had come, but avoiding the tents on the ledge above, and he had noticed exactly where Battholomew on entering the tent had placed the stone that closed its entrance. His food he had taken, his wallet and staff lay to his hand. If his shirt was still not dry he must make off with it wet. It was draped half over the lantern, and Willie was drawing it closer when suddenly Bartholomew spoke. Just a ray more of light he said, that he might study his map, and Willie twitched a portion of the shirt aside again.

Then, with everything as he had supposed ready, the one thing he had forgotten struck him like a thunderclap. All Creation! What had happened to his wits? As if first one veil was withdrawn, then another, it broke on him, his sudden, portentous and all-consuming idea. Bartholomew's map! Its ironstone and pyrites and lead? The silver round Carlisle? No, not even that. Then what?

What! Dazzling him so with its effulgence that even yet he did not see it! Why, the gold in Wales, man, *the gold in Wales!* It might not be on the map—it might be that even Bartholomew did not commit such secrets to maps—and suddenly he heard the snapping of the head of ragwort that hid him from Bartholomew. The *pen*, with his fingers in his thatch-like poll and his blue-black eyes shining with kindly mirth, had broken it off to see him better.

"The Welsh for ant, Gwilym, is *morgrygyn*," he said. "Can you remember that?"

Willie had an idea he answered, "*Diolch*," but could not be sure, and the chief went on.

"Indeed it is a long day that hasn't a laugh in it, and since morning I have had little time to give you. But I have not forgotten our talk yesterday."

"I'm thinking of my wet shirt," Willie grunted, and Bartholomew laughed.

"Prut, man, it will dry again, and Hwu Morgan meant no harm! Let me look at your locket again!"

Hoping his voice did not betray him, "Then let me have another sight of your map," Willie grunted again over his shoulder, and the exchange was made.

Yet now that he had it what was it? Breathless, as if he had been running, he had made a clearing for it about the light. It's *only* worth the symbols with which Bartholomew had sprinkled it? By all the martyrs who had ever burned, let Willie but find the symbol he wanted and that would be enough! Silver? That was 'Ag,' but what was the Welsh name for Carlisle? 'Aur' was gold, but did this pickaxe-wielder know that? Again he had to put his trust in his shaking voice.

"Bartholomew, what's the Welsh for gold?"

"*Aur*," Bartholomew replied, though he pronounced it in a somewhat different way, and Willie raised the steaming shirt to have another look at the map.

And almost suddenly he found it. Nay, his dancing eyes found it twice, once by a ragged estuary, and again by something that Bartholomew evidently intended for a lake, and he was persistently hunting for more recurrences when Bartholomew looked up from his locket again.

"Is this a likeness of somebody you know, Gwilym?"

"Ia," said Willie.

"Of what colour is she?"

"As red as a red ant," muttered Willie.

"And her skin, is it thick and white?"

"Clotted white like curds."

"Ia, ia, I have seen them. I have seen them in Wales, but they are not Cymri. You will find them in the north but they are not Scots. And faces too are different, as all things are different, yet in some ways it is very little they change. How if I were to tell you, Gwilym, that this was the head of a Pictish woman?"

"Her name's English," Willie grunted, but he was listening now, for it was necessary to keep the conversation as natural as possible.

"That was her father's name."

"Nor has she set foot out of England that I know of."

"I have not set foot in a palace, but Cyngen ap Cadell did. And forget this foolishness about the *morgrygyn*, Gwilym. If this *cariad* had not meant much to you, it would not show in her likeness so."

"I'm going to sleep."

"Then take your locket, and say good night in Welsh, and tell me in the morning what your dreams are. Sleep well, Gwilym bach, for indeed I shall soon be conceiving an affection for you, and begin to look on you as a son," and five minutes later the tent was still.

But the talk about the locket had been the last straw. Had this busybody of a chieftain no business of his own to mind that he must think that Willie's private affairs too were peats to be dug up and set touch-paper to till they burnt up with a teasel-blue flame? A son, forsooth! He would wake up to-morrow morning to find himself lacking one, and Willie was half in a mind to take that map with him too, but to that he could not quite bring himself. After all it was the sum of hard-won knowledge. He had helped himself to this man's food, had a use too for his lantern, and of what use were Willie's eyes to him if he couldn't fix a simple map in his memory? Fiercely they devoured it, but they found no more 'Aurs.' Just the one by the estuary,

C

the other by the lake, but by the time he had finished he knew where there were two gold-mines in Wales. Such a secret was worth some sort of a token, and folding the map up again, he raised his voice to a hoarse whisper.

"Bartholomew!"

There was no answer. Again the chief slept at a moment's notice, but he must make quite sure. Noiselessly raising himself he advanced his ear. Yes, he was well asleep, with his horn by his side, so let him have his map too, and Willie's hand stole to his belt. Out came his locket, and there was a tiny snap as he wrenched off its outer case. Gold for gold, and luck to boot. Bending over the sleeping man he slipped the quittance into his horn in such a way that when the horn was picked up again it would shake out with a tinkling sound. Then he blew out the candle, wrapped his steaming shirt round the hot lantern, and with shirt and lantern in his hand crept softly out by the tent-flap.

But Bartholomew never slept as deeply as that. Suddenly there came a voice from the tent's interior.

"Iorwerth! Is that you? Who's that?"

"It's only me, Gwilym," Willie called back.

"What are you doing there?"

"Making water," said Willie, and unstoppered his bottle.

For several minutes he waited, but no further sound came from the tent. He could fill his bottle again later. Noiselessly he moved away.

It was now the dogs he must most beware of, for corgies had not been given those funnel-like ears for nothing. But all was quiet on the ledge above, and the dank herbage through which he was creeping neither crackled nor snapped. Let him once get level with the ledge and he would be able to make better speed. But suddenly he stopped dead in his crawl, holding his breath. Not ten yards from him he heard Iorwerth's voice.

He was talking to Pugh, and again Willie cursed the alien tongue, for it was not English they were talking now. But he assembled his wits. These tatterdemalions had been threatened with Cornwall and the tin-mines. If it was the *cenedl's* destination that was in dispute he might presently hear a place-name that in English and Welsh was the same. Cowering behind another head of ragwort, he waited and sure enough, up out of the Welsh it suddenly popped. The place was Carlisle, and a few moments later it was followed by the Forest of Dean. Behind Bartholomew's back they were discussing it, and in all likelihood they were on their way to wrangle it out with him in his tent.

And heaven be thanked that when two Welshmen dispute their

corgies knowing their voices, rest their prick-ears for a while; but—Bartholomew's tent! The moment they entered it his absence would be discovered. The lantern too would be missed, up their suspicions would flame again, the horns would sound, the whole *cenedl* would wake. . . .

Suddenly the voices ceased. They passed Willie not six yards away, and no sooner were they past than Willie was on his feet, his knife bared for the first corgie to take him by the leg. So quickly now, 'Somewhere-else-Willie'—into the night-mists with all the speed you can. . . .

Sell them to the Saes for soldiers? Never for a moment had it been in your head. . . .

But by all their *Dwus* and *Deowls*, and if all goes well with you now, Wilson Middlemiss, never again will you, a gold-worker, have to tell anybody where you get your gold from!

3

LET NONE TALK OF NOSTELL NOW. LET THEM NOT TALK OF SISTER URSULA
either, but only of plain Ann Thomas, lying upstairs in her curtained
cell, as still as an image in wax. And let Stephen Akam cast up what
accounts he would. The time had come for Ann Thomas to cast up
the account of her life.

For many days she did not speak, but lay with the dried poppy of
her head raised so that she could see the priedieu at her feet. She still
wore the wimple close-drawn about her face, but her black garments
had been put away, and her food was thin gruel with a little sugar in
it, which had to be put into her mouth. And Hannah no longer turned
her cell into a chapel by drawing its grey curtains, for it was better
to have her in sight to the end.

But one day her hand was seen to make a feeble movement. The
light, the movement seemed to say, hurt her eyes, and as the days
passed this, next to the gruel, became Hannah's chief ministration, to
draw the curtain along its pole whenever the autumn sun came in and
then to open the cubicle again at nightfall. And she was doing this
one afternoon when she saw the eyes that went back and forth to
the priedieu, as if they mutely asked for something from it. It had a
niche in it for tapers and candles and other things appertaining to its
use, and Hannah was about to open it and to hold up the various
objects from it when again the lips moved.

"Not the priedieu? Then what? Another hot stone for your feet?"

"Not Nostell," she was just able to distinguish.

"Is your curtain as you want it?"

"Not Nostell," the whisper came again, and Hannah went downstairs to get her gruel.

Then, as she continued at least to get no worse, Hannah found a
small bell, which she tied to the toothpick of a wrist so that it tinkled
when she moved her left hand. Sometimes she heard it and sometimes
not, and often at night it was a false alarm, but it saved some of the
stair-work, and as day followed day the whisper began to gain a little
in strength. But even so Hannah could make little of what it said, for
so much seemed so long ago, so little to do with to-day. What, for
example, mattered this king or that—except to date something from,
as Hannah herself did, or else from some festival of the Church?

But now it was Hannah who was forgetting. This old woman had been lettered in her time, and had known the day of the month without kings and queens and festivals. They sometimes had these flickers before the end. She could only wait and see.

But why then did the poppy-head continue to shake, and the whisper to say, "Not Nostell," if she had finished with it all?

Then one day there came to the house, where Hannah now had all to do herself, a woman who from the belongings she had brought with her looked as if she had come to stay. Yet she was a stranger to Hannah. She was blowsy and full-figured, and before admitting her into the porch Hannah asked her who she was.

"I'm Joanna Cales," said the woman.

"And what do you want?" the young mistress asked, looking her and her bundle up and down.

"I've come to help in the house."

"And who sent you?"

"Madam Akam," and out shot Hannah's finger to the double-gates of the forecourt.

"Then my service to Madam Akam, and when I want help she shall be told of it," she flashed, and off the woman took herself again.

A pair of Akam eyes in *her* house and a tongue to prattle in Ellbeck of what they saw! *That* was what they wanted to be able to say, that now that her father had gone Hannah Thirlow had not been left to struggle on alone! Back into the house she strode, to find Rafe setting up a stack of firing.

"Rafe Bates, who's a woman who calls herself Joanna Cales?" she demanded, and Rafe gave his head a jerk in the direction of the floor above.

"There was a time when she could have told you," he said.

"When I ask you a question I want an answer to it."

"Joanna Cales is one 'o them she took her pennyroyal to, but she'd left it a bit late, so she put Joanna on a penance and christened the wean herself," Rafe replied.

So! Madam Akam not only stabbed, but poisoned the knife too! No money in the house, and only Rafe and Eggon now left, for by some sleight of executorship the two fetch-and-carry lads had one day vanished and were now in the service of Robert Safford, the fuller down in the valley! Hannah, furiously preparing the old woman's gruel, again spoke to Rafe over her shoulder.

"What's Stephen Akam paying you your wages in now?"

"I've seen no wages from Stephen Akam yet."

"Then what's he going to pay you in when he does pay you?"

"As you said, in cheese."

"When?"

"Come Christmas maybe. Or Eastertide. Or it might be Michaelmas next year," and Rafe rammed down his firing with his foot and lurched heavily out again.

And now upstairs was a grandmother from nowhere, lying as one newly-risen from the dead might be supposed to lie, Ann Thomas, gazing at the daisies on Sister Ursula's grave, and tremulously murmuring, "Not Nostell, not Nostell!"

"Then if not Nostell, where?" Hannah asked as she gave her her gruel that night, though she asked it only to humour her.

"Hierusalem. Campostella. Rome. Not Nostell."

"What, all of them?"

"Nostell is only by Wakefield. Further than that. A long way," and Hannah dried the face she had been washing, and tied the bell to her wrist, and went downstairs to see what was to do next.

And the cloth-folk had a name for it when the web, going sound and whole into the trough, came out again rent and ripped in a hundred places. 'A nail in the stocks,' they called it, and now it was plain enough that for all those years some such nail had been at work in Sister Ursula's heart, slowly draining it white. But what help was there for that now? Hannah saw none, rather the other way, for yet another little thing had happened. Thinking it would be something for the old fingers to occupy themselves with she had re-strung that fatal rosary and placed it one day on the bed. At the sight of it Ann Thomas had straightway fainted, and it had been two whole days before she had recovered the lost ground. Now again, she seemed to have no memory of the occurrence, but how shall we call those contemporaries whose hearts were crammed with old histories two generations before we were born? It might be that Hannah would never know more, and that might even be the best, for with this grandmother putting out these feeble feelers to life again, that shrank and hesitated like tendrils as they sought this support or that, to press her might well be to thrust her back into her grave again.

And now, if Ann Thomas was to creep back into the world of the living again, she would have to have something to wear.

It happened to be on a Christmas Eve that Hannah mounted the stairs and entered the upper chamber with the old black draperies over her arm. She cast the habits down on her own bed, and as tenderness was not now a thing to be played with, made a business-like clipping sound with the pair of scissors she carried in her hand.

"You'd better say which it's to be," she said. "Either you're going to wear them again or you're not, and we've no money to ware on new cloth."

The white pippin in its wimple moved, but the eyes did not see what lay on Hannah's bed. In changing her wimple Hannah had found the scanty crop of hair beneath it to be now as white as new-washed wool, but the colour of hair too was a thought she must set aside, and the old woman answered as if she continued some inner meditation aloud.

"Nor Campostella neither. 'Twould be too much for old bones, and I've never been on the sea."

"And which of us has, living in this inland place?" Hannah returned, and again those uncontemporary eyes seemed to be looking back, back, on so many things she had seen and Hannah had not, whereupon Hannah reached for the funereal draperies.

"How think you if I were to cut it plain up to your neck, with a button and an edging of white? There's enough to spare in these sleeves to make you a tippet almost."

"But that isn't to say I haven't seen the sea; ay, and more than once or twice . . ." said the voice.

"*I* think an edging of white and a button——"

"At one place it had a causey running out to it, but the tide was over it at that time and it was all white and terrible to look at——"

"And I might make a push to have it ready for you by the New Year, for you'll soon be wanting it the way you've taken the turn. Do you know it's Christmas to-morrow?" and some sort of a disturbance seemed to break in the old eyes.

"Christmas? That's a day for alms. And Rafe's wages."

"Never mind Rafe and his wages. Say close-fitting sleeves and a bit of a piping at the wrists too," and the momentary trouble in the eyes died down again.

"There's a Holy Island Anglesey way, and they say there's great ease to be had at Canterbury and Walsingham. But it will have to wait for the spring. Let's get April here first," and Hannah, leaving her to wander on as she pleased, set the scissors to the cloth.

She could not have named the day when Ann Thomas seemed to decide that she had lain among the dead long enough. Certainly Christmas had passed, and half January too, for later she remembered the roarer of a fire Rafe had ready for her the first time she was brought down into the lower hall. Hannah, with infinite care, managed to get her down alone, but to get her up again an hour and a half later was too much for her, three abreast on the stairs were too many, and Rafe, making no bones about it, ended by picking her up in his arms as easily as if she had weighed no more than a pod shelled of its peas. The cut of the new clothing was finally settled. The wimple remained, but by the time Hannah had finished with her she was just a thin, angular old woman, wasted almost to the bones over which the dry skin seemed to be stretched, in a plain black gown with close-fitting sleeves, a single button at the neck, and a narrow piping of white at the wrists too, at which she looked long and fixedly but without a word. January had gone too, for the snowdrops were out and Hannah had carried out her bedding to air in the February sun on the day when Rafe, making to pick her up and carry her up the stairs again, was pushed away with a shy and almost virginal refusal. She could now manage with Hannah's help alone, and one evening, just as Hannah had got her up again, out came the name of yet another island, for she had remembered the name of the one with the causey. It was Lindisfarne.

"Then there's St. Tudwals," she said. "It hasn't a causey, so they row out to it in boats. It's all coming back to me. There should be a pepper-castor church somewhere nearby, but I cannot call to mind its name."

"What's all this about islands and causeys?" Hannah asked as she carefully folded the new finery up again.

"They say Ireland's full of them too, very holy relics, and Mona as well," and Hannah, getting her into bed, tied the bell to her wrist and walked thoughtfully downstairs again.

For there could no longer be any doubt about it. In spite of everything, her fragility, her years, her miraculous resurrection, it was some sort of a pilgrimage she was turning over in her remote and wandering mind. This only became the plainer the nearer the spring approached, and first Hannah tried to turn the whimsey aside, then sought to reason with her, but now she had an answer to everything Hannah had to say. The standstill at Thirlow? Could not a strong man and a growing lad keep a few cranks oiled but two women must stand over them to see they did it? Then Hannah tried saying nothing at all, for to tell her the straits they were in would only be to stir other matters up, and at a word or a name all that had been so painfully won would be brought to nothing again. But one evening, out of sheer exasperation, she had to tell her the staring truth. This was that until something was done about that will of her father's they might consider themselves lucky to have a roof over their heads and food to put into their mouths. That, she thought, ought to put an end to it, and God send it gave her fancies some other turn.

But who who seeks, not Lindisfarne nor St. Tudwals, but that lost island of herself, forty, fifty, sixty years ago, is going to take that for an answer? She had had her gruel; it was time she was stilling herself for the night; but Hannah saw a beckoning, felt herself gently shaken by the sleeve. The tremulous old hand was pointing to the priedieu at the foot of the bed.

"And did you think I hadn't thought of that?" the cracked old voice triumphed. "Put your hand in there—behind the candles, right at the back . . ." and doing as she was bidden, Hannah drew out a small but heavy linen bag.

"Loose the strings. . . ."

This also Hannah did. Out over the bed there spilled the lay-sister's puttings-away, in all manner of coinages, nobles, marks, sols, florins, French moutons with the Lamb of God stamped on them. She could only gape at them, nor did Ann Thomas speak, but only held the poppy in its wimple almost as masterfully as when she had rebuked Rafe for his graceless words. There. Let her look at that. *Now* who was talking like a fool?

And so much for impossibilities, for once stared at boldly the rest went the same way. Hannah took yet two more days to think it over. Then, on the next night after that, with the sometime nun in her bed this three hours, Thirlow's grim hall saw a no less grim Rafe Bates, first choking, then dropping to his knees on the stone floor and kissing the hem of Hannah's house-kirtle, again and again. She had offered both him and his son their freedom, on the terms that they should guard Thirlow till its mistress's return. And rising again, his face wet with tears, Rafe got down his crossbow there and then, with bolts for it, as if before dawn he would have strewn the forecourt with dead.

And during the next days events followed one another with the like headlong speed. Eggon was despatched on one errand after another. Six months before, at the Crown in Ellbeck, a company from Wrexham had lodged on its way to York; now, at the end of March, another company was expected, travelling the other way. A litter must be bespoke for the convalescent, Hannah could ride on a galloway at her side. Let them not trouble themselves about any of these things; Rafe and Eggon would see to all; and now the stirring and exciting thing was to see Ann Thomas, with a close shawl about her wimple and a second shawl to hold down a great flat hat on the top of it, though she would only have to take them off again, sitting there in Thirlow's hall, pointing and directing and giving orders, as their light belongings were got together.

Then word was brought by Eggon one morning that the company from York had been reported a bare ten miles the other side of Ellbeck, and that same afternoon the litter and galloway stood outside the porchway. The peelhouse was left to take care of itself as Rafe and Eggon too accompanied them to the Crown, and at the Crown that night they lay. It was the beginning of April, and by seven o'clock the next morning all Ellbeck, saving only Stephen Akam and his wife, seemed to be assembled about the cloth-hall steps. From the back of a great grey Flemish stallion a red-bearded man of a loud and commanding presence was marshalling the travellers for departure. Place was made for the litter and the galloway in the middle of the cavalcade, and before eight all was in readiness. Down the straggling street they moved, past the Shuttlecock and the pigs at the bottom, bearing to the left by the stocks, making for the humpbacked bridge.

So, a little foolhardiness, a little blindness to the morrow, a little following of a glimmer that had not yet a name, and good-bye to Ellbeck and its trade. The western hills were a sunny tapestry of sere and evergreen and delicate springlike flush, only their bald tops uncovered to the morning sky. But the travellers were taking the valley way.

It was why such townships had almost as many inns as they had houses, for their company must have been nearly forty strong, merchants of this or that, overseers, bearers of letters, traders, with perhaps a factor or two or a clerk. So mixed an assembly must make its acquaintance as it goes along; but not from the start was there any doubt about who had taken upon himself its command. It was the red-bearded man on the stallion, and he was conspicuous not only by his stature, but also by his cap and doublet of gaudy purple camlet as he made his way backwards and forward along their line. He seemed to have great store of knowledge of such matters as fords and the state of the roads, inns and stabling and accommodation ahead, and this he imparted to all and sundry in a boisterous and overbearing voice. But Hannah, hoping that in that way their privacy might be preserved, had informed him at the outset that she and the occupant of the litter were pilgrims, and was already beginning to wish she had not done so, for now, whenever he found himself in the neighbourhood of the litter, he made exaggerated signs to those about him that the elder devotee slept or that her meditations must not be disturbed. Hannah, a mantle draped about her girt-up legs, bestrode the galloway at the litter's side, and thrice in the first hour she had found this great fellow bending over her, solicitously asking in his thunderous whisper how Ann Thomas fared. His name, he told her, was Hugon, and he came from Denbighshire, where he was a raglot or officer of a commote or hundred. Two pilgrims, he further told her, must have brought the company luck, for the roads were hard and dry, whereas he had known roads, and so off on his lore of roads and inns once more. But Hannah, unaccustomed to so long in the saddle, was already beginning to wish this first day was over, and had no desire to talk to the purple-capped raglot or to anybody else.

The hills among which they were beginning to wind were the furthest west she had ever travelled, and on her galloway she kept close to the litter, the curtains of which remained drawn. From time to time she peeped in to see whether Ann Thomas was asleep, but already the raglot had made of their privacy as it were a public matter, and at some time after midday, as Hannah judged, she saw the curtain of the litter shaken and heard the thin voice lifted behind it.

"Who is that you are talking to, Hannah?" and Hannah raised the curtain again.

"To this gentleman, a Maister Hugon," she told her, for again the great stallion was at the galloway's side.

"Then ask him how soon we shall come to our inn," but before Hannah could answer the raglot had answered for her, thrusting his red bush of a beard past her.

"We are now rounding a place they call Low Pike, ma'am. Stedham lies at the other side of it, and we should see it in an hour. I hope you are refreshed by your sleep, ma'am, and that the talk of these does not disturb you."

"Who is speaking?"

"It is Raglot Hugon, ma'am, of the lordship of Garwyn in Denbighshire," and making a sign to one of those about him to take the stallion's bridle he straightway dismounted, walked round to the litter's other side, and continued to accompany it on foot, holding back the curtain of the litter as he conversed.

The inn they reached at five o'clock that afternoon was a victualling-house too, and a couple of outriders had been sent ahead. Before its door the raglot raised his great voice for a footstool, pointed to where it was to be set, and himself handed Ann Thomas from her litter and conducted her with ceremony into the inn. With no less deference he inquired whether the pilgrims would sit down with the rest or dine in their own apartment, and when Hannah said they would sup apart he abased himself for the meanness of their accommodation. Their room was in fact little more than a store-closet or service-room of some kind, clay-washed and windowless, with a low bed-frame, a candle on a ledge and last year's rushes on the floor, but to make up for this, the raglot had busied himself to good purpose in other ways. Their supper, which was brought in half an hour later, proved to be the breasts of a boiled fowl with parsley sauce, a stew of apples and a small jug of spiced wine. This Ann ate in bed, with Hannah's mantle cast about her shoulders, and it revived her surprisingly, especially the wine, which Hannah gave her to sip from her own cup. She became as faintly animated as if those daisies of her resurrection tipped themselves with fresh pink.

"That is a very attentive and knowledgeable man and of a very good

conversation," she said when her head was at last on its pillow again,
and Hannah asked her what the litter-side conversation had been
about.

"It was only when he told me he was a raglot . . . to think I had
forgotten what a raglot was . . .!"

"Then you can tell me, for I never heard of one," said Hannah,
putting their supper things together.

"He keeps the rolls of the lordship, as I did when I was in the aumbry.
He pays the wages and receives the dues, just as I did too, and it is a
pleasure to talk to such a man. And that great horse of his has a
wind-gall. He should try horse-heal or a herb they call enula. It eases
the horse that he should get down and walk, and he has asked leave
of me to do so again to-morrow."

"To-morrow we're starting early. Shall I put the candle out and
come in with you?"

"Yes, do. It is a pleasure to talk to a man of such intelligent conversation," and Hannah put the supper things outside the door, blew
out the candle and crept in by her side.

So if this Raglot Hugon brought Ann Thomas the choicest portion
of the fowl and reviving wine to drink, and their conversation was of
a kind, he might weary Hannah with his inns and mileages and swollen
fords and ruinous landslides as much as he pleased. The next day,
mounted once more on her galloway while the raglot walked by the
litter, she even held the galled stallion's reins, for the valley way was
only a valley in a manner of speaking. Much was up or down-hill,
avoiding the bottom itself, as the invisible feet of countless populations
before them had learned to avoid it. There were long saddle-backs and
ledges, to be taken only at a walking pace, and places where but for
the cutting away of the trees there would hardly have been a road at
all, but it continued sunny and dry, with a fresh wind ruffling their
garments whenever they rode up into it, and then they might come
upon a breezy common or heath, with hardly a tree to be seen. So,
with the birds singing overhead and small life frisking behind every
bush and the raglot so attentive, why should Hannah herself alone turn
into a hedgehog? Shyly she began to return the greetings of those
immediately about her. If Ann Thomas wanted her curtain drawn
again, and one of these happened to be the raglot himself, was it not
something to be attended by the head-man of a household, with a
silk and long-wool doublet on his back and a purple cap nodding and
dancing in the wind? He became communicative to Hannah. He had
no daughters of his own, he said, but he was far too wise and merry
a man to make grief of that, since those who had daughters also had
the burden of them, whereas he was free to gaze on a pretty face for

nothing. Thus and much more, all as amiable as could be, he on his grey stallion and she on her shaggy galloway, to pass the time along.

Sometime that afternoon they passed over into the Palatinate, and thereafter as hour followed hour began to be aware of it. First another road joined their own, and with it other travellers, who rode with them for a space but presently were not seen again, for they had melted away by other tracks. From these other men appeared, on foot and driving cattle, but they too were soon overtaken and left behind, and all this time Ann Thomas slept. At a hamlet of half a dozen houses, however, where for some reason they stopped for a quarter of an hour, she woke again, and bade Hannah make enquiries for the herb called enula. But it was not to be had, and here others joined them, with panniers and baskets as if they were going to some market. And it was getting late, the marketeers were on foot, and the raglot would not have their progress impeded so. To such as wanted to be pressing about their business these stragglers were the curse of the roads, he grumbled into his red beard, and then some other detail caught his busy eye, and a moment later he was in a good humour again.

But at one of his sallies, which seemed to her suddenly over-bold, Hannah edged her galloway round to the other side of the litter again. The pilgrim whom she had not yet called grandmother was once more dozing, she herself ached with the unaccustomed jogging and jolting; and in her heart, she was beginning to be anxious about the whole adventure.

4

FOR IT WAS AN ESCAPADE THAT HAD BEEN THRUST UPON HER BY A stronger but, unhappily, no longer to be depended on mind, and this weighed ever more heavily on her as they approached their second night's resting-place. The first of its buildings to come into sight was its lazar-house. It stood behind palisades a space back from the highway, but she needed no telling what it was. Many men in rags peered through the palisades or squatted before them within throwing-distance of alms, but none approached them, and those of the cavalcade muffled their faces and kept their distance. A quarter of a mile further on the town began, but it bore little resemblance to familiar Ellbeck, settled about its market-hall and open straggling street. It had a ramshackle, temporary look, as if but for the castle that frowned down from its sudden cliff it would not have been there. Many men-at-arms mingled with the inhabitants of the place, and the crowds grew denser about its single stone inn, which was large and sprawling enough to have been mistaken for a barracks. Indeed at first it seemed unlikely that it would be able to receive them, but this turned out not to be so, for many of those who stood about were only there to hear the news of other parts, and such sudden inrushes of custom seemed to be no new thing to them. After much bawling and bad temper they were shown into a vast and steamy common chamber with a lofty beamed roof. It was deafening with noise and lighted only by smoky sconces on the walls and the great fireplace at its farther end, and at crowded boards many of all sorts were already eating. Burdened serving-men hurried to and fro, the clatter of vessels and the heavy odour of viands filled the place, and Hannah, fearing that the heat and clamour would be too much for her aged charge, shepherded her into a far corner, where she sat softly dabbing her face. Full as the hall was yet more boards were being carried in for the newcomers, and there were ill-tempered outbursts as those already seated were ordered to re-arrange themselves to make more room.

And here, for all his purple cap and doublets, even the masterful raglot raised his booming voice in vain for the creamed breasts of fowls and mulched fruits. Of heavy eating, venison and boar's flesh, they could have stuffed themselves full, but the best that could be offered Ann Thomas was a broth with toasts in it and a junket of goat's milk.

"And must we eat it here?" Hannah demanded of their burly protector, for her temper was getting short with this raglot who told other men's daughters he had no daughters of his own, and he bent over her to whisper in her ear.

"I spoke of the old one. She can have her broth when you get her into her bed. But what say you to a couple of spitted larks, with liver between, on the bench next to me?"

"Send that broth into her chamber, and a hot stone, and there should be no lack of wine here, so see she has that too," Hannah flashed back, and off the raglot took himself again, clapping his hands and bawling in his giant's voice for service.

But the populous place had its women's quarters too, separate and apart. These, as at Thirlow. were subdivided by curtains and rods, and one palliasse with a coverture on it seemed to be the bed of the mistress of the establishment itself, for better garments than most lay across it and from under it peeped a pair of wood-soled velvet shoes. But now Hannah spoke as sharply to the serving-wench as she had spoken to the raglot.

"Make haste before she gets past her food, and don't forget that wine," she ordered, and continued to fume after the wench had gone, all her fears back on her again.

Never would the old body stand the toil of it. At such an inn it could not be long before another company assembled, journeying back again. More and more it seemed to be the best to let the cavalcade go forward and then betake themselves home again.

But again the wine did its work. Propped up on her palliasse, with her feet on the hot stone, Ann Thomas began to pick up, and again Hannah, eating brawn, had to listen to her commendations of the raglot.

"He is a man of wide experience and travel," she said, "and it is surprising the things he brings back to my mind. He knows St. Tudwals too, and I was right about that peppercastor church. He knows it well, and its name is Llandegwning."

Hannah sighed. . . . "And what pray might a peppercastor church be?" and the old voice answered her promptly.

"Why, round like a peppercastor of course, and this one's plastered white, as I said. It had gone clean out of my mind what an *uchelwr* was too. It means one of pure descent, but that doesn't mean he hasn't his *amobr* to pay too."

"His what to pay?"

"His *amobr*. It is the tax they pay when any daughter of the lordship marries. He is a man of a very curious learning in these things, and in a place like this there ought to be enula for his horse," and on and on she ran, and as long as the greasy broth did not turn on her stomach things might have been worse, only if the time did come when they must turn back it would be better sooner than later, and if ever Hannah was able to get out of her an indication of where they were making for, she might be able to turn that into a reason. At the moment, it seemed to be St. Tudwals, wherever that was. At least it could not be Lindisfarne, for that was now the width of England away.

But suddenly, in the very middle of one of her sentences, the old woman stopped abruptly short, intent and listening. Such necessaries as they had brought with them had been packed into an old bag of hide, which Hannah carried before her as she rode, and this she had placed behind her on the palliasse to prop her up, with her mantle to ease its roughness. But from it she had started rigidly forward. The noisy chamber they had left was at the other side of the house, and by this time the men-at-arms must have finished their supper, for a distant unison of voices could be faintly heard, though Hannah would not have thought it enough to disturb anybody. Yet a startled "What's that?" had broken from the old lips. She was straining forward, holding her breath, and Hannah, thinking it might be the broth after all, quickly poured out a little more of the wine for her and held the cup to her lips.

"Drink this . . . nay, do not knock it out of my hand like that . . ." and at that moment the muffled sound rose long and sustained, and was followed by a roar. The men-at-arms were singing a soldiers' song.

"Listen . . ." and one old finger went shakily up.

"Oh God, her and her causeys and islands! Nay, let me cover you up—lay your head down . . ."

But Ann Thomas was half out of bed, feebly struggling with a Hannah who tried to put her back. The head in its wimple was beginning to nod grotesquely up and down, and the fingers that had counted the beads seemed to be moving to some instrument that was not there.

"Hark . . . after their supper they always sing . . . it's the soldiers. . . ."

"Stop—you'll do yourself an injury, struggling like that. . . ."

"Open the door . . . fling back the curtain . . . I want to hear them. . . ."

But at that moment the singing ceased. The fantastic movements of the fingers also stopped, but the old woman was trembling from head to foot. Hannah got her back into bed, but she let out a breath that seemed to sigh her soul away, and Hannah thrust aside the hide case that had propped her in a sitting posture and made her lie flat instead. Then, lest she should try to get out of bed again, she placed herself outside the coverlet, fully dressed in case of need.

But there was no need. In less than three minutes Ann Thomas was asleep, and only Hannah lay awake, asking herself what this new nightmare could be.

And now she saw plainly that she ought to have put her foot down at the beginning. If the singing of a few soldiers could set her off like that what other pitfalls might that uncontemporary mind not stumble into at any moment? Strange words in a strange tongue, peppercastor churches and trying to get out of bed because a barrack-room of soldiers unbent themselves after supper! Even sad Thirlow had been better, for it had not been without its happy moments if only all its troubles had not come at once. She must have slept, but it refreshed her little, and hearing the sounds of assembly the next morning, she went out into the courtyard to find that a dozen men-at-arms had now joined themselves to their company. This soldier-nightmare was to be a day-mare too, and hastily she sought the litter and busied herself with its curtains. It might be some small help if they were to open on one side of the litter only, and she was busily adjusting them when she was aware of Master Hugon standing over her. But even the raglot had no time for dalliance that morning. He asked her what she was doing, and she told him, and he then bade her leave everything to him, the curtains too, and an hour later, when she had got Ann Thomas into the litter three-parts asleep, he saw that a space was kept about it, on which even he himself did not intrude.

But now Hannah had mounted her galloway again to find that nothing went right. The footmen were heavily burdened with paraphernalia, they clung to stirrups to help themselves along. Hannah was not always able to keep her place, and she had no liking for strange hands fumbling at her leathers as she rode astride. And now in spite of the populousness of the region, there were few signs of industry, many of impoverishment. Sometimes it seemed as if an army had passed that way before them, so beggared was the land and so scanty the new sowings. Everywhere men seemed to be on the move, not in search of better but to escape from worse, and many of these too were burdened, not with military stores but with household possessions. She had muffled up her head in her mantle. Half of those who had joined the company at Ellbeck had now dropped off again, and their places had been taken by strangers. Not once were the litter curtains shaken from inside, and so, with the nightmare at her back, passed that weary day.

Its end brought them to a place where two roads met, of which the one by which they had come was no more than the tributary one. The other swept so broadly on through its clearings of trees that there must be other towns no great distance away, and at their junction stood a hostel so large and bustling that Hannah's heart sank again.

But Raglot Hugon, who had hardly troubled her all that day, now fell in by her side again and spoke to her in a heartening voice.

"There shall be no more of last night's jostling, young mistress, for it was a thing that even I could not help," he said. "I have sent ahead, and now all is bespoke. The great inn is the White Hart, and these will go on there, but you ladies will be better where I've put you. . . . Hey you!" and his voice rose again. "See that litter drawn in so the others can pass it!" and Hannah, peeping forth from her head-wrappings, saw small dwellings set back among their gardens and steadings, by the look of them the abodes of farriers and jobmasters and other purveyors who lived by the coming and going of others. This settlement had its own smaller inn, with its patch of orchard behind it and its poultry in front, and at its door the raglot bade them alight.

And now again Hannah thought less harshly of the man, for none can alter his nature. During that afternoon they had ridden through a shower, but now a fire awaited them, a welcome sight at the end of an early spring day, and the litter curtains could be taken down and dried before it too. He also promised that there should be no more greasy broth and goat's-milk cheese, and with that he left them, for now he must see the rest of the company settled in. At whose appointment he did all these things Hannah never knew. But it was helpful to have them done.

Their chamber lay at the end of a short passage, and it was a double one, in the sense that a wooden partition divided it, as if it had been arranged for some occupant who must have another person in nightly attendance. The partition, however, did not run from wall to wall, but stopped short, leaving it still one apartment, lighted by the same candle and warmed by the same fire. Before this Hannah set the litter-curtains, and when with no great delay their supper was brought in, lo! an infant's stomach could have digested those delicate sweetbreads and the neats-jelly that stood by their side. Except to put the tray out Hannah need not open their door again that night, and at the relief of it her whole being suddenly relaxed. Absurd that her eyes should be moist as she ate her sweetbread and sipped the spiced wine that smelt delicately of wall-flowers, and then, her supper finished and the old woman drowsily watching her from her pallet, she got out her comb. It was a good opportunity to take down that heavy blood-gold of her hair.

It was weeks since she had given it such a combing, and how it needed it! And as she tugged at its matted ends it was not a plaited loaf of sullen gold now, but spread out with the firelight shining through it it resembled a great red mane, through which the comb passed in sweeps a foot and a half long. In between she turned the drying curtains, and the old woman was cosseted and warm now, and the men-at-arms at the other inn might sing as much as they liked, for she had seen where the rest of the company had come to a stop, and it was nearly a quarter of a mile away.

"Your supper did you good," she said at last, peeping through the hair at the figure on the pallet, but the old eyes were looking now at Hannah's hair, now at the firelight on the plastered wall, then back at the hair again. Again she seemed to be searching the tired old memory for something, and suddenly she had it.

"Did you say there was another inn here?" And when Hannah had given a nod, "Then you must see if enula is to be had there for that good man's horse. Enula is sovereign for a gall," and Hannah yawned widely.

"I wish I'd remembered to bring the bell for your wrist. But it is only a partition, and I shall hear you if you call."

"Ay, get you into your own bed," and Hannah tied up the hair in a couple of places, so that it resembled the crinet of a battlehorse. She could finish dressing it in the morning, and she set her comb aside and began to prepare herself for the night.

There was no light in the outer passage as she carried out the tray, and closing the door again she gave a last glance into the inner-cabinet, then loosed her clothing and got into her own bed. For a time she lay, watching the shadow of the partition moving this way and that on the ceiling and the fire-light rising and falling on the wall, but her own eyes too were now heavy with sleep. The ceiling and the fire-light on the plaster became a soft sinking away, and the curtain of the darkness descended softly on her.

Sometime that night she awoke in dumb affright. The fire-light still flickered on the wall, but a hand was groping about her bed. It was a weighty hand, yet cautious withal, with a second hand in reserve, for she felt this stealing to the loopings of her hair. Her face was turning from side to side, avoiding a bushy beard, and her bed-frame creaked to the weight of a heavy form that was making a way for itself. It could only be the raglot, and as suddenly she saw it all her face was plunged not away from his beard but into it. Like an animal she bit, but bit only the beard, and she heard a choked but fiery muttering as a hand and arm were locked about her head like a vice.

"Softly my pretty . . . spiced wine for old blood but only enough to kittle up the young. . . . I rode ahead to see to all myself and none will come near us. . . ."

The two hands were also of an understanding, for what the one did not do the other did, and suddenly she wound herself up as Rafe wound up his cross-bow, as suddenly released herself. This time she heard his fierce oath as she bit on bone. From the hot suffocation of beard and breath she spat out the blood and prepared to bite again.

"So, my pretty pilgrim! Now we will see!"

From Hannah there broke a helpless, desperate cry. She called on a name she had never in her life called on before.

"*Grandam! Grannie!*"

And through what drugging of spices would not that reveille pierce? Hannah saw nothing, but the raglot had lifted his head. The last upleaping of the fire on the wall showed her grandmother standing there, in her wimple and smock, the old feet fresh from the bed-stone. Hannah heard the consigning of both their souls to eternal flame, but the weight that had stifled her was no longer there. There came yet another oath as the raglot struck himself heavily against the door, but only as she sank back did she hear that other voice, speaking out of another lifetime. Skeleton-thin arms were about her, and there was a mumbled murmuring in her ear:

"Little love! Did thy grannie hear thee call?"

5

ARE MIRACLES TO BE MEASURED AS GREATER OR LESS? IS IT NOT IN itself miraculous when an old woman who lately could hardly stand upright can get down on her knees before a dying fire, and grope for fresh fuel to put on it, and minister again as she ministered thirty, forty, fifty years ago?

But it is not enula for his horse that the raglot needs now. The ministration he needs is for his bitten chin as he lies raging in this traitorous little inn he has so craftily chosen, for under his beard is a redder and angrier wound to stain the kerchief he has bound about it. Yet it was a cowed lioness of a Hannah who made herself a lair in a corner of the floor, while her grandmother tottered about lighting the candle again, and fetched her bedclothes from the outer closet, and tucked them about her and then knelt again to blow on the ashes of the fire.

"Cease fretting." Hannah heard her voice as from a great distance. "They'll not tarry here now. Are your feet warm?"

"Yes."

"Then stop that rocking. Have done now and try to sleep."

"I daren't shut my eyes. He—he put something in your wine. . . ."

"Ay, ay, I've heard of such things. . . ."

"He rode on ahead to get all ready himself. . . ."

"Ay ay . . . you're telling me nothing I don't know . . ." but Hannah only went on rocking herself as if she hadn't heard.

And travellers in company cannot wait for pilgrims when a purple-capped man on a grey stallion curses out of his bandaged beard because there is neither surgeon nor apothecary in his train, but even in his departure he had left himself no choice but to do the two women a good turn. The night passed somehow, the day broke, and there came into their chamber the woman of the inn, a torrent of excuses, that the mistake had not been the raglot's but her own. Ay, they were on the road again, two hours ago and miles away by this—had she known the two pilgrims were to be left behind—had the brave gentleman but made it a bit plainer, but there, with so many to see too he had had too much to do—then she could have found them accommodation more suited to their condition and pious errand.

"And I was to tell you you'd find your horses at the Hart, for we've no stabling at the Rose, and it grieves him he couldn't take a proper leave of you, but in housing your litter he struck himself on a hook in the dark and went off in a plaister. So now we must see what can be done."

And at that a still heavy-eyed Hannah, shamed and humbled she knew not why, also took herself in hand again. It was she who carried their money, and from the linen bag she brought out a gold noble. Their first lodging had been on the ground-floor, but upstairs was a small and clean chamber that looked down on the orchard at the back, and to this their belongings were carried. But when she was asked how long they were likely to be staying Hannah could give no answer. It seemed to her that time hardly mattered now except for what it might bring forth, and even miracles have to be paid for, and in their new chamber Ann Thomas was put straight to bed, where she now refused food, and fasted in her spirit too, uttering no word.

So let her make a priedieu of the wall to which she had turned her face. Hannah also had plenty to occupy her. At their setting out Rafe and Eggon had seen to all arrangements for their journey, and since then the raglot himself had taken the cares of it off her hands. Now she must manage all for herself, the animals, whoever was in charge of them, what money would have to be paid and to whom. Also it was necessary that she should be at once informed if any new company assembled at the other inn, and all this was better than thinking. It was her grandmother who must do the thinking, for even the miracle would have gone for nothing if the seal of a closed chronicle was not broken now.

The old have been young, but the young have not yet been old, and the point at which they must meet is itself forever on the move. Outcries in the night too, that start the sleeping memories as birds rise in a flock from a tree, have no place in an orchard by day. Half-way up it was a small arbour from which the window of their new chamber could be seen, but Hannah was no longer watching it, sitting there alone, and trying to tell herself what was passing on the bed beyond its lattice. Up into the arbour she had carried a footstool and a couple of cushions, and Ann Thomas was sitting by her side. Somewhere in the inn she had found knitting to do, but it must have been a long time since she had last knitted, for her fingers fumbled with the needles and now and then reached out for wool that wasn't there. And at one time she must have worn a knitting-holder at her waist, for she knitted with her left elbow pressed to her side, a click of the needles, a movement of the elbow, another click and another pressure. She had just asked Hannah how old she supposed her to be, and Hannah answered without changing her position. It was odd and constraining, the way their eyes had not yet met.

"I haven't thought of it. I only know you're my grannie."

"Eighty you'd have said? Nay child. I was born in King Robert's time. I'm not eighty by ten years. Seventy's all I am, and that was the Second Robert, not the Third. What was that name you called me by?"

"Grannie," and the old eyes wandered from the knitting to the blossom on the boughs. The pear was out, the apple-buds beginning to burgeon, and it did not come in the dead of night now, plunging like a knife to the quick, but here in the orchard's peace. It was Hannah who gave the first little choke.

"Me . . . your own blood . . . and all these years you've never . . ." and the elbow ceased its motion for a moment.

"Never told you? Yet many's the night I've tossed there on my bed, with naught but a curtain between us, not knowing in the morning but I might have let it out in my sleep. Did you never hear anything?"

"Never."

"Nor from any other?"

"I only know how I used to dread you and your penances."

"Then bear with me now the penance is mine. What was it that woman said that morning? What colour my hair was? Was there ever a MacAlpin wasn't red? The very hair on their breasts and legs was red. Redshanks MacAlpin was my father, and of Scotland alone I've lived under five kings, and even then that hair of mine was their sport, making to warm their hands at it and light their torches at it and I can't tell you what. But mark you, child, any of 'em would as soon have braved Redshanks himself as lay a finger on me."

Hannah had closed her eyes. Now that it came what was it? It only made her feel suddenly alone in the world that this grandmother, whose hair under her wimple was now as white as wool, should once have had hair as flaming as her own. But once more the elbow was moving up and down.

"Ay. Redshanks MacAlpin. And earl or thane or King Robert himself, not one of them would he serve longer than he had a mind, and that might be a year but seldom was it longer than two," and Hannah opened her eyes again.

"Do you mean he was a soldier?"

"A soldier! He was captain of twenty of 'em, some with beards down to their waists, and pelts and skins on their shoulders and skenes and axes in their hands. Those we saw at the castlewick were princes to some of 'em."

The castlewick? Where was that? Then she remembered. It was where she had heard the singing at the other side of the house, and had tried to get out of bed, and had moved her elbow as she was moving it now. Slowly, the gap in time was narrowing and Hannah now helped it.

"And did you say all this was in Scotland?"

"Scotland or Northumberland or wherever it might be, for what's one place more than another to a bairn? . . . There! That comes of talking instead of keeping your mind on your business! Pick it up for me, child," and when Hannah had picked up the dropped stitch for her and put the knitting back into her hands she went on talking about what happened when folk tried to do two things at once. Yet she had only to think of the bagpipes she said, and knitting or no knitting that elbow of hers began to move, and when Hannah softly repeated, "The bagpipes?" she went on as if the bagpipes had been her burden all along.

"To be sure. I could play the bagpipes many a long year before I could knit. What knitting should there be the way I was brought up, that never slept but under my father's cloak till I was ten years old? I could play the bagpipes before I was six. Little Buchan taught me, and there I'd be marching at the head of 'em, skirling 'em on, and a feather in my bonnet and a little axe of my own and all those great hairy men fit to pittle themselves with laughing! When the moss was too deep for me they carried me on their shoulders, and when they'd finished their supper they'd have me dance on the board for them, clapping their hands and roaring their songs till the tears ran down their cheeks!"

"Grannie!"

"But it was little Buchan always made the most of me," she now ran garrulously on. "They never went on a fray but he'd bring me something back, a buckle or a comb for my hair, till I strutted about like a popinjay I was that pleased with myself!"

Hannah's eyes were on the plain black gown with its edging of white and the single button at its neck, but now she hardly saw them. What she saw instead was an unbroken colt of a child, bedizened with the spoil of half a dozen forays, her infant's axe at her waist and her baby lips joining the soldiers in their songs, and because a thing so old was a new thing to her it seemed inexpressibly shocking.

"But do you mean they were robbers?" she asked, and instantly wished she hadn't, for at last their eyes met. An even stranger grandmother was watching her from the puckered old lids, a watchful and jealous grandmother, whose battle-blood was the blood of Redshanks, though she had only knitting in her hand, not even a baby's axe.

"I said soldiers, Mistress Pert, and no more robbers than other folk, and a deal honester about it than some, so let it be a lesson to them that doesn't know how to look after what's their own!" she flashed back, and the one pair of eyes did not move from the other now as the message ran between them, that unless Hannah too sided with her own against the world, right or wrong, let her look for another grandmother somewhere else.

But it was the end of Ann Thomas's talking for that day. She, who had railed that Nostell had been robbed of a thousand sheep in one year, defending robbers now! Could it be that she refused to see the havoc it made of all her pious past? Trembling the fingers put the knitting aside. She rose uncertainly to her feet, and back upstairs Hannah had to help her, where she lay on her bed, moving her head from side to side, for her eyes would meet Hannah's no more that day.

As for Hannah, she could only muse on the strangeness of it, that not even this would have come about but for that shriek in the night, and those thin arms about her head, and that murmur in her ear: "Little love! Did thy grannie hear thee call?"

Not far from the other inn, standing back in a small field, was a diminutive church. Its interior was bare and white and its furniture of the rudest, but beyond its aisle-less nave was a painted wooden rood-screen, over which a single candle burned. And always heretofore, whenever Hannah had to confess herself, she had done so to the nearest ministrant to hand, who had been the bony Sister Ursula. But now she was gravely in doubt whether Sister Ursula was a proper person to confess to, and crossing to the White Hart the next day to see for herself that the animals were being properly cared for she learned that on the following Friday morning a small company was to set off for York. If, as she was once more pondering, they had best get back to Thirlow, this was their opportunity, and she hastened back to the Rose to report the matter. But at the mention of Thirlow her grandmother suddenly went into an extreme of agitation. Formerly, "Not Nostell," had been her cry, but now it was "Not Thirlow, not Thirlow!" and now the price that had to be paid for the miracle was beginning to show. Again the food had turned on her stomach, she seemed to be in haste to have something off her mind too. And this time she came down into the orchard of herself, and as she brought no knitting the elbow too was still. And when a tattered old chronicle begins to fall to pieces with the handling, and the memory that could have helped it out is dim, and whole pages are missing altogether, and to Hannah it all seemed a very great while ago, so let it be set down.

Incongruously into the story there suddenly thrust himself one Owain (it was all the name she called him by), threaped out of his lands by a certain Grey and bringing an action at law for the recovery of them; and this was neither in Northumberland nor Scotland, but apparently somewhere in Wales.

"So Redshanks," the failing old voice went on, "he sided with the Welshman, for it had to be one side or the other in those days. As for me, I was a great gowk of a lass by then, very sinful in the language I'd learned, but not past the gew-gaws that please bairns, and in one on these places there was a fair. Are you listening, child?"

"I'm listening."

"Six miles I'd walked to that fair, all by myself, and I'd money to spend, and I'd bought myself a trumpet, and a mannikin that jerked his arms and legs on a string, and a pot of honey. But I'd left my axe behind me, and I was licking the fingers I'd dipped into the honey when I was laid hold of by a couple of raging great men from behind . . . nay, peace, sweetheart! There's no cause to take on like that! They were two I knew, my father's men he'd sent after me, for he was stamping and raving up and down I'd given them the slip, for I hadn't learned the meaning of obedience at that time. And Ruthin I remember the name of the place was, in my lord Grey's domain, but 'twas a woeful thing, for of a sudden there was an uproar and a shrieking of women, and that fair was but built of canvas and wood, that a spark would set off, and before you could turn round all you could see of it was roaring red flames."

"But they got you away?" said Hannah, her eyes closed.

"Away from Owain and his Welshmen? Away where? Ruthin Fair was but the start of it, child. Come the King of England or Judgment Day itself, Owain had taken a vow he'd be revenged. Ay ay. When it comes to that there's no stopping it. And when both sides are spent there's always a third ready to step in and clean up what's left. . . ."

And now it was as if Hannah, drawing Thirlow's grey curtain aside along its rod, found an empty cell there, and only an impress on the bed, and the sleep-walking figure itself risen from it not on the hither side but on the farther one, where other phantom curtains seemed to open, and out through them the old figure was passing. She had left the priedieu behind her, taking only its candle in her frail hand, but as one sighing sentence succeeded another, to the sound of ghostly bagpipes, the twinkle of its taper was not to be seen for the smoke of burnings by day and the skies a glare of copper with them at night. But slowly these too died down, and it gave Hannah a queer little shock of stillness, for in the place of the fires there was suddenly sanctuary, and instead of the bloodshed protecting walls and peace.

"He'd seen to it, Redshanks had. He'd put me with a dean of St. Asaph's, to be out of the way of it all, and now he was at the other end of Wales, I didn't know where. Is there a church hereabouts, Hannah? Ay, a little one. Not a deanery, not a great palace of a place. Where was I? Ay. . . . There was fifteen of us women there, in a lean-to at the back o' the palace we all slept together, and the dean was a mild and gracious man, with gentle eyes and long silver hair, God keep him in His bosom. But then Owain must go and see a comet, and he won a great battle somewhere, but he might ha' done better to lose it, for after that it only burnt up again the worse. And this time the Church must join in. Him that was bishop at the time, first he'd been for the King, and then he'd been for Owain, but it was little his diocese ever saw of him, for if he wasn't in Gascony he was in Spain, not at Campostella or Our Lady of Lourdes, but at courts and councils, raising and furnishing men. Ay, it was holy banners now, with Keys and Crosses on 'em, and all this time I was in the deanery, but wait till I tell you. . . ."

For as with Ruthin Fair so at St. Asaph's palace, with the fifteen women asleep in their shed, and the sacristan stabbed at his vigil before he could give the alarm, and the shout of onset in the night, and the pillagers dancing-drunk, red demons in the flames, and no mountains thereabouts to take to and the bears and cats of the woods more merciful than man. . . .

"And I know not what became of the other fifteen, but there I stood in the yard, with a horse-blanket over my head. . . ."

"Stop, Grannie . . . you'll be in your bed again. . . ."

"And out o' the window at my feet the dean's body was flung, less its silver head. . . ."

"Nay, let's have no more," and now it was Hannah who had to take the old head to her young breast and rock it gently to and fro and make soft hushing noises like a dove.

So far all this had been in the orchard, with the pear-blossom already half on the ground and the apple-buds opening out almost as you watched them, but now the orchard would no longer do. The old feet must be moving, if only a little further along the road, past the garden walls with their glimpses of the doorways of cottages and peeps of what went on inside. Thus, it was in the orchard that Hannah pieced fragment to fragment; a lanky overgrown girl, armed against cat and bear only with her infant's axe, avoiding one burnt-out homestead after another as she tracked down this cateran father of hers half the length of Wales away. It was in the orchard that she learned how she had found him, and remained with him, and how little Buchan had died apparently twice, first in Westmorland and then again as he was setting a ladder against a castle wall in Flint. It was still in the orchard that one Hughie Thomas, as doughty a man with a bill as ever hooked a horseman out of his saddle, had wanted to marry her. But Hughie was never to be trusted when the spoil was wine, and he had been found one morning after his carouse, drowned face downwards in a shallow pool of water.

Then again the old discipline of Nostell would have her in its grip, and the little church was only a few hundred yards away, and they could take half the day to get there if they wished, and the indomitable old feet would not rest. Mattins and evensong were performed in that tiny church, but other services went by default, and the sanctity of the place helped a little to set things in proportion again. The image in the trefoiled niche over the rood-screen had been newly painted, the Mary in blue and the John in red, and the ever-renewed candle burned like a crocus between them, so what were lesser agonies to that Agony? And long years spent in an aumbry relax observances somewhat. The words were only whispered, but what she could not have told in the orchard she could tell more easily here, the fluttering eyelids lifted to the apostle in red and the Mother in her new coat of blue and the Figure in between.

And it was all that Hannah for very pity now wanted to hear, yet when it came what was it? For it had neither place nor date, and Hannah too knew its meaning now. She seemed to have known it ever since that "Little love, did thy grannie hear thee call?" Only another rape in the darkness, by an unknown man, but this time a consummated one.

And when her babe was born it must be given a name, and Hughie Thomas had always wanted to marry her, so now she might as well call herself by his name as another. With Hughie dead in his drink what odds did it any longer make to anybody?

"Bronwen means White Breast, and never was maid's breast whiter. But my little chuck wasn't going to play the bagpipes like her mother or to swear vainly by holy things. By the time she was sixteen I couldn't call myself a young woman any more, and it was time to have done with camps and pillage. I'd seek some other part of the country, and if some steady sober man with a trade offered, why God be thanked for a husband for her."

"But Redshanks?" Hannah managed to get out.

"What say you, love?"

"What of your father?"

"Did I not tell you he died at Montgomery siege? There was only my White Breast and me now, till your father wed her and you were born. Then she died of her second, that was stillborn, and there was only you and me."

Only Hannah, growing up year by year in Thirlow's peel-house, wondering until she had ceased to wonder, and asking her father until one day he had bidden her ask him no more, who the bony lay-sister was who presided like an abbess at their board.

Only a grim old woman, whom even Nostell had failed to tame, who had seen the Ellbeck wenches through their troubles and, a freebooter's daughter, would fight tooth and claw sooner than see her own robbed.

Two days later a Hannah, heavily muffled and alone, heard faint strains of music from the little church in the field. She had not been to the White Hart that day, and entering the church she saw nobody, but the music seemed to be coming from a small recess that lay beyond the rood-post below John's side of the candle. Treading softly she advanced. At a table a man sat before a small regal or portable organ, of seven double pipes. The fingers of his right hand depressed the keys of the instrument while his left worked a pair of bellows, but looking up and seeing Hannah he brought the flat of his hand down on all the keys at once and the music expired in discord.

"There's passing-notes for you!" he scowled as if he was glad to hear the last of them. "And where did you spring from, Mistress?"

"Play again," said Hannah.

"What, start again after the amen? Then get you where you can't see me for I'll not be stolen on and watched," and Hannah retired into the church again and placed herself under one of its three high-up windows with her head against the white wall.

But now the music was not the same as before. Heard from the fields it had had a sweet and consoling sound, solemn and fluty, but now something graceless seemed to have crept into it, as if the man deliberately set himself to play the fool both with his instrument and her. Nor was there much of it, for after no more than a minute or two down came his hand as before and she heard him coming towards her. He was tall and middle-aged and saturnine-looking, dressed in a church-like habit of sober grey, yet almost certainly not a churchman, for his scowling face was as mobile as that of a mime, and the long fingers that had depressed the keys were as restless as the fingers of a pickpocket.

"What, aren't you in tears?" he asked with a grimace.

Hannah shook her head, which still rested against the wall.

"What, not at the nightingale-warble, with the little drop of water slid into the pipe, that sets tipsy lords leaning to their lemans and the dish-wenches dreaming they're in heaven?" and Hannah got up quickly.

"I'll leave you, sir."

But the thin man stood at the pew's end, and as Hannah would have had to push past him to get out of it she stood still, but suddenly it was he who moved lightly and noiselessly aside.

"Your pardon, mistress. Are you not one of the two pilgrims who stayed behind?"

"Yes."

"Then if you pray as you go spare a prayer for Gandelyn, that once in a while crawls into a church to make his peace alone. That was plain-chant you caught him at, but swan-songs count for more than plain-chant in this world. Your pardon, and tell the other one Gandelyn asked her prayer."

But now it was Hannah who sank to her knees in the pew and spoke from the mantle about her head. . . . "She's prayed her last," she said, and down her head sank on her breast.

For Ann Thomas had finished with the vinegar and the hyssop. With no more struggle and no more pain, her pilgrimage had ended in her sleep the night before, and Hannah was now far from home and alone.

6

NO DOGS HAD BARKED, NO HORNS HAS SOUNDED BEHIND WILSON
Middlemiss as he had sought the darkness and security of the wood.
To let his feet follow the fall of the land was to have brought him to
the valley and the houses of men. Now let them talk of the fall of the
the land who had a tent over their heads and a map to guide them.
In a darkness hardly less dense than night itself, he was now seeking
a way back whence he had come.

But already there was no way back. He had entered the wood
where birch and sapling oak made a coppice about it, and these had
been his cover and his bed, but now his eyes were open to the snare
into which he had fallen. The saplings themselves had been thrust out
by the wood as an unnatural mother casts her babe upon a doorstep.
Let young trees find light and air for themselves. The parent-wood
had its dying to get on with.

Even on the gloomiest mountain-top he had always known day from
night, but here the difference was disturbingly simpler. It was the
difference between life and death, yet that was not simple either, for
even in its dying the wood was re-procreating itself in a myriad new
forms of life. The dead are silent, but all about Willie were soft seethings
and almost human sighings, and never had he conceived of trees so
ancient and monstrous. Their very identity had gone, for as tree
leaned against tree because there was no room for it to fall they put
forth stools and suckers, growing incestuously back into one another
again. Hoary and grey and moss-rimed branches interlocked overhead
as the antlers of contending stags interlock, when dying they have to
be decapitated, still locked together. They wreathed themselves into
fantastic aisles and tunnels, but with no passage through, for as a
ruin is blocked with its own masonry, so holly and thorn and giant
bramble closed the way again, with a thousand ivies to knit all together.
Cat or bear here? A chimera perhaps, or the squint of a unicorn or
some gliding thing that suddenly hissed. Sun-ray pierce that sickliness
of eld and beetle-gloss of green? Its only light was the phosphorescence
of its own rottenness and decay.

And twice in the last hour Willie Middlemiss has sunk to mid-thigh
in a morass with stagnant water beneath, that had broken into gaseous
necklets of bubbles, to a shimmering of insects' wings.

He had breakfasted only sparingly, for he did not know the size of the wood; how if it were a forest, such as might stretch with scarce a break from Humber to Solway-side or from Lincoln almost to the gates of York? Now he was reclining against a weeping face of rock, rank with pennywort and orange with agaric, wishing he had helped himself to a second candle. A light would have been company, and less than half of that of the night before now remained. Now he dreaded lest the food in his wallet should be tainted by the quag. But he still had his staff. Before him the roots of a water-rotted and dislodged tree upreared themselves into the twilight higher than himself, and better all the red ants in the forest than to lie long on that spongy ground. Rising again, trying the ground step by step with his staff before he trusted his foot to it, he groped his way round the rock face.

By this time he was telling himself there was nothing in his situation to be afraid of. It was true people had stumbled into woods before and never been heard of again, but they had always seemed to him a different sort of people, set apart for such things to happen to. For himself, the bright and beckoning things of the world had always been reserved, and it was on these that he must fix his mind. No dogs had followed him, no horns sounded behind him. The *cenedl* was away and about his business by this, and if he could only find his way to the daylight again Willie would take good care not to be seized a second time. Besides, the wood was too busy preying on itself to have time to spare for a harmless journeyman, strayed it might be a little out of his proper path but sure to find his way in the end. Therefore pick out all the best from the past, the reassuring and hopeful things, and suddenly, just as the snapping of a dead branch in his hand had almost caused him to lose his balance, he was scraping together such fragments as he could now remember of his meeting with Humphrey Tull.

Getting on for a year before, with a score of other prentices all merry and noisy together and bragging of the things they would do when they too were turned loose on the world, he had sat one evening drinking ale in a tavern in York. In the midst of the noise of the room had opened and framed in it there had appeared Humphrey's knotty four-square figure, and than Humphrey Tull Milan itself could boast no more renowned a master-armourer. And but for the eyes of his fellow-rabble on him Willie would as soon have marched up to the King of England as address so great a man unspoken to, but only a minute before he had been out-bragging the noisiest of them, to show the white feather in his tail now? Suddenly up on his feet he had been, his leather cap in his hand, louting low with civilities, while the less bold ones held their breath at his daring. If the famous armourer would but honour such small fry as they by drinking a cup of wine in their company. . . .

And good-humouredly the armourer had accepted the cup, and drinking to them had told them to be good and diligent lads, and (with a glance round the tavern) to stick to their money when they had got it, and so had departed again; and that was the only time in his life when Willie had been within a bowshot of Humphrey Tull.

But now, in the presence of the trees, it gave him a solemn and religious sort of feeling to realize how different had been the tale he had told to young Atty Cockin. And not only that. What you tell often enough to others you end by telling yourself, and now he had the further little matter of the drinking-flagon on his conscience. He had indeed chased a drinking-flagon for a knight, adding the bit about the sword-hilt to round the tale more neatly off, but he had executed it to the order of a master-worker he had fallen in with by the way, and was now willing to admit that he did not even know the knight's name.

As for my lord this or my lord that, never a living lord had Willie Middlemiss set eyes on in the course of his life.

But to tell Atty these things had made them easier for Atty to understand, and now that he was shirven in the presence of the trees peace and justification stole over him again.

Now he was groping his way blindly by the fall of the land and trying to picture woods as he had hitherto seen them, rolling wide and free in the sunshine, dropped like a mantle over the earth that thrust up a bare shoulder where the hills rose highest. But already he had lost count of the time. Wastefully he had lighted his candle, for without it he could hardly see his way from one tree to the next, and the wood had made him drowsy and the stump in the lantern had lighted him to a hollow beech. In spite of the sumph out of which it grew its cavity was stuffy with dry-rot, and he thrust the candle into it first to see whether it was already tenanted. But no glint of eyes met his, nothing speckled lay coiled up inside. Creeping in he curled himself up like a bear in its lair, and calling on the past again he slept to a vision of himself, seated in some shadowy but very great lord's hall, with my lord himself at the high table, drinking from one of Willie's own goblets, his dogs nosing at his hand for food as he bade some squire regale the minstrels with a cup of wine.

Yet he was nearer deliverance than he had known, for the worst oι that dismal wood was in fact over. When next he opened his eyes it was not to pitchy darkness, for into his burrow there crept a wan half-light. Fox-like in his leather he crawled out and looked up. The antlers overhead were still locked in death, but now, almost level with

D

his eyes, they were patterned in places against a morning-flushed sky. His end of candle had burnt itself out, and the lantern he left in the tree would never be seen by mortal eye again. Where another generation of shivering saplings had been cast out the wood ended at a steep declivity. A southerly wind blew in his face, there was clean grass under his feet, and the first thing he did was to roll himself over and over again on this, as cattle cleanse the mire from their sides. Then, getting on his feet again, he looked about him.

With a far-off undulation of hills beyond it an autumnal valley lay spread before him, through which a river wound. Sometimes this river enlarged in shining expanses, three or four of them visible at once, then again it contracted itself to a single channel, fringed with willows. And now Willie's eyes danced, for trees in lines spoke of husbandry again. Hardly more than a mile away roofs were set about the spire of a church, roofs under which men lived their lives and a spire where they came together for worship. Blithely he made his way down, and in ten minutes the dark rampart of that cannibal wood was one with the other memories behind him.

But as he descended he began to walk more slowly for all the easing of the steep track, for first he came upon a dead sheep. It belonged to somebody, for it had a marking, but it seemed to lie unusually flat to the ground, and he turned it over with his staff. At the sight of the silvery crawl beneath it he turned it back again, just as the yellow eyes of a cat gleamed at him for a moment behind a bush and then were gone again. A little lower down somebody had been cutting brushwood, for by a sodden piece of sacking he came upon brown chippings, and wheel-tracks ahead now showed him the way. He had finished with mountain-tops and nomads, and just below him were the buildings of a small steading.

Yet not an animal was to be seen, and between its rye-patch and bean-strip the ditch was yellow and level with weeds. Trodden mud had set hard about its gate, but as he pushed at this and called no voice of dog or man answered him. Entering and crossing its yard he stood before a stout timber house with a newly-mended roofing of rushes, and as its door stood open he looked in. The ashes of its last fire were still grey in the hearth but not a stick or utensil did the place contain, and crossing to the byre, he found it a mortuary of stiffened rats.

The neighbouring houses were the same. Five or six of them with their sheds and outbuildings were scattered irregularly about the church, but there were no people, and in the churchyard he found the reason. The graves were recent and not even limed, and let no man who valued his life pluck a blackberry from those tainted hedges or eat a mushroom from those autumn fields. After the stricken wood, this!

As Willie Middlemiss took to his heels it was early morning by the sun. He would have held his breath till midday if he could, and say now that he carried it with him in his clothing or his remaining provisions? He tore open his wallet in a panic as he ran, casting the food from him. Then, taking a stocking, he bound it close about his nose and mouth.

Food in the hedges, water in the brooks, meat for the lifting of a stick, but not a morsel he dared to put into his mouth. From one danger only he felt himself free. The hardiest robber in the land would not knowingly have ventured into that region of pestilence, so deceitful to look upon in the pale October sun.

Yet with the very bees perished in the hives how came it that the rabbits throve so? Mid-morning found him on a common, amid such a warren of them as he had never beheld. The earth itself seemed to move with the flickering brown and the white dots of their scuts, and now he would have welcomed even a bedlamer's voice to tell him whether the peril was past, for to-morrow would be the beginning of the fourth day since he had spoken to a fellow-creature. But there was no praying to a pestilence, and he must make quite sure, and all that day he walked, till the mists began to drift in patches over the unbanked river and for very weariness he must find somewhere to lay his head. As the rabbits seemed to be immune let it be among them. The ground he chose for his bed was above the level of the mists, rising to a coppice on a hillock. The moon was not yet up, but by the last of the day he had seen the falling away of the land and had felt a colder nip in the air. At least it was better than leprous woods and infected sheepskins and rats lying in heaps in the byres, and presently, as the mists crept up and sleep crept down, he lay there like a log.

At any other time he would have known instantly what the smell was that woke him, for who does not know the smell of burning when it fills the air at night, the spark a flame and the flame a conflagration before the sleeper is aware? But the smell grew stronger, and sluggishly he raised himself. Fire might be a cleansing and a purification, and God knew the place stood in need of it, and where fire was man was; but men, here? Then, suddenly wide awake, he was on his feet. He would see better from higher up, and to the coppice on the hillock he made his way. The moon was half-way down its arch, and across its face heavy acrid smoke was drifting. The mists in the hollow below had a central core of rusty light, and slowly the moon went out as the smoke began to thicken in volume and to spiral. Muffled cracklings had broken out, and all at once these were followed by a soft rushing roar, as if some unseen roof or floor had fallen in.

A few seconds later and the very air was red about him. High into the heavens shot the sudden streamers of flame. The half-stripped coppice behind him became a dull tapestry of gold, the light shone on his leather cap and parted lips. And in the glare and fluctuation of it he saw stumbling up the slope towards him a hopping, hobbled-looking figure that fell to the ground, and lay motionless there for a space, and then laboured on again on its knees, with a clinking sound of irons.

A "Name of God!" broke from Willie as he started forward, but already his hands were under the man's armpits and he was dragging him up the slope and into the shelter of the coppice. He got him a little way within it, out of the light of the fire, and there he lay heaving with his back against a birch, gasping for water.

"What's to do down there? Who are they? Who are you?"

"Water!" and Willie saw that the man's feet were iron-ringed and that the rings were linked together by six inches of iron chain. "They landed from the sea . . . water . . ."

"I have none. I'll try to find some. Who landed from the sea? Is somebody after you?"

"The gaoler loosed my wrists," the man panted, "but when he heard the petard burst he fled. . . ."

"Who do you say landed from the sea? What place is this?" and now Willie could see that the man's wrists must lately have been manacled too, for they were swollen and purple and puffed, but his features could not be seen for smoke and grime and mud.

"Water. . . ."

But Willie did not know how long it might take to find water, and already he had turned to the man's fettered ankles. The bands about them would have to wait till he could come by a picklock or a file, but to cut through a single link would at least give him two legs again. Christ! He had frog-hopped it for half a mile with those torturing things cutting into him at every heave!

"Pirates . . . they landed in six ships this morning . . . *ai!*" and the blackened face bared its teeth as Willie twisted the chain into position. "Nay, go on . . . I'll suffer it . . . they put me in the *siambr ddu.* . . ."

"Patience . . . my burins were not rightly meant for this work . . ." and the man's breast heaved and his lips writhed as he began to ply his tool.

"The bonds of the captives . . . nay, a moment's ease . . . there's a string somewhere round my neck with knots in it . . . put it in my hands. . . ."

"Are you a priest?"

"With water I could bear it. . . ."

"All day yesterday I feared either to eat or drink. Courage . . . the tool is doing its work," and the man made not another sound till the link was cut through and forced apart. But no sooner was this done than he flung himself flat on his back, with his stiffened but liberated legs thrust out, and lay there, whether asleep or awake Willie could not tell, for his lips continued to move incoherently though his eyes were closed.

But in setting him free Willie had snapped one of his precious burins, and for the rest of that night hardly slept for cursing the tool, the man and himself.

So good-morrow to you, Willie Middlemiss, waking to a gnawing belly and a crippled stranger by your side whose face you·cannot see for its besmirching. But—pirates from the sea? By his reckoning he should not have been anywhere near the sea. Tightening his belt he rose, and making his way to the crest of the hillock rubbed his eyes. Below him a broad estuary lost itself gossamer light. Dark on its silver breast lay the six ships, clustered round with barges from which cattle were being lifted in slings and the rest of the spoil hoisted with tackles. The Mersey? The Dee? But from where he stood he could see no more than the smoke of whatever had burned below. Far inland it drifted, sullying the morning air, but the next moment he did not even see the smoke, for what was this? A hazel-bush, by God! and bunched with nuts, whether tainted or not he no longer cared. Ah the joy as he stripped them and cracked them between his strong teeth! Then off came his leather cap. By the time he had filled it not a nut remained on the bush, and now for water. After a little casting about this too he found, and before the sun was well up a sleeping man woke with a loud cry as cold water splashed on his face.

"Up and wash yourself, for I want to see what you look like! Then you can eat."

The cleansing however was something of a surprise. The man might have been a year or two older than Willie, but so eager had he been to show himself of man's estate that the tender brown beard he had allowed to sprout actually made him look as much younger, and the lips beneath it were at once timorous and over-ready. His hair was long and tangled and unclean, and after another glance at his swollen wrists Willie no longer wondered that his young cheeks were wasted and his eyes still haunted with fear. By the time he had washed and drunk the bottle was empty again, and though it was only bit by bit that his story came out, as much of it as matters can be set down in a piece.

His name was Matthias, and his was an itinerant scholar from the University of Cambridge. There he had studied and been fed by the charity of his college, and with the ranks of the lower clergy thinned out by successive sicknesses he had himself aspired to a living. But he was a teacher who should have been still a scholar, he was not ordained and his degree was doubtful, and when his benefactor had obtained preferment his troubles had begun. Setting out with letters from his chancellor he had hoped to minister to others and improve himself as he went along, but he had found his half-knowledge more dangerous than no knowledge at all, and being of a perfervid and obstinate nature he had made as many enemies as friends. When finally a pretext had been found for having him up and questioning him his answers had been judged too overweening for his station, and at that point Willie put a word in.

"What was the pretext?"

"They took me at the communion-table itself, asking by what authority I celebrated. I showed them the chancellor's letter, but they said I had forged it, and after many delays they brought me before de Saule."

"Who is de Saule?" and the fear-ridden eyes were lifted to the smoke that thinned away overhead.

"You do not know these parts?"

"No."

"That . . . yesterday . . . was his house. It was the court and the prison too, but at first they did not put me in irons. Then one day there came one who swore I had some skill in penmanship, as indeed I have, but still de Saule said nothing about the forgery, but charged me with making a riot in the church and fined me three hundred marks. Of this I had one sixpence, so I cast it into the poor-box, which angered them."

Up went Willie's brows. Angered them! He himself was careful not to anger people till he was safely out of their power, but he only said, "And then what happened?"

"They cast me into the *siambr ddu*, for by this time they were devising other things against me. A month, five weeks, I have been there."

"In those irons?"

"The moat filled when the tide came in. But for its being half empty the weight of the irons must have drowned me," and Willie clicked his teeth.

"What is the name of this place?"

"The river is the Mersey. Yonder at the mouth of it lies Liverpool."

"And what lies across the water?"

"A region thay call Wirral."

"And how does one cross over?"

"A mile from here, by a beacon, there is a ferry. It was that way they brought me to de Saule."

"And these ships? How came they to get past Liverpool?"

"The river is boomed and chained but they must keep a way open for the traffic. It may be that they have closed it again," and Willie, who had neither time nor tears to waste on burnt-out court-houses and had not spent a month in the *siambr ddu*, leapt to his feet.

"Can you walk if I help you?"

"I must try."

"Then up. Sixpences into poor-boxes and you with those on your legs! Was that the best you could think of? But we can talk as we go. Gently now on those feet and let's see how you can frame yourself. Sixpence in the poor-box! What other saucy answers did you make 'em?"

Bartholomew's map could not be as wrong as all that, and Willie had his bearings now. If Wirral lay just over the water then a day's walk would bring him to Deeside, and out on the estuary the ships were getting up their anchor-stones from the mud. The barges were being roped up for towing, and a multitude of seagulls whitened the water as food and dunnage were flung overboard. The sun too, piercing the gossamer, shot the estuary across with opal light, but half a morning had gone and the crippled man had to rest a dozen times before, keeping as far from the burning ruins as they could, they at last reached the bank. Heavy piles had been sunk deep into the mud, with a great tub on a platform and a ladder to climb up to it. But the beacon set in it had not been lighted, and seeing the ships and the flames the ferryman had fled.

In his hut, however, they found salted fish and a green cheese standing over its bowl of whey, and Matthias closed his eyes in a Benedicete as on a shelf Willie discovered half a rye loaf, still fresh. The oars of the ferryboat stood behind the door and the boat itself was tied up to one of the beacon piles; it lay on its side, for the tide had ebbed, and now a broad waste of shining mud separated them from the stream. There was nothing for it but to wait for three hours, and the ferryman's bed was a bin of old nets on the floor. On these Willie made Matthias stretch himself out and then took off his gabardine. Already he had kindled a fire. While waiting for the tide he might as well be cleaning some of the mud from his new companion's clothes.

7

WILLIE'S FIRST OATH WAS NO MORE THAN A PANTING, "MY GOD!" BUT Matthias, lying in the bottom of the boat, heard it and turned up his eyes in a beseeching look. It was the look of one ready to flout those who could cast him into the *siambr ddu* but less ready to offend this saviour who scraped the mud from his clothing and cut through the links of his fetters, yet out it came.

"Let your conversation be Yea and Nay, friend," he pleaded, and Willie's next "My God!" was under his breath.

Yet he had need enough of an oath or so, straining and tugging there at the oars, with Matthias lying there in the bottom of the boat. The mark for which they were headed was a tall pole with a sort of iron basket on the top of it, but it seemèd to be running away towards Liverpool as if on wheels and soon was no more than a small receding dot. All about the boat was a thick yellow marbling of tossing water, that whitened and seethed as it broke on shoal after shoal. Colonies of birds rested on it, rising in flocks from time to time to quarrel overhead, and now Willie was redder still, flushed by the reproof he had received. Did the fellow want the tide to turn on them again, leaving them stranded among the birds in mid-stream? But now Matthias for his part also avoided his eyes.

Nor did that restless estuary seem to have more than a moment or two of slack water. No sooner had the flood made than it seemed to Willie to be setting outwards again, and again the seagulls settled in white congregations as one shoal after another uncovered itself. What sort of a giant could that ferryman be who could contend with stream and tide like this? What too if a wind should arise?

And if he did manage to get them over this tide, what was he going to do with one whose ankles were ringed with iron to tell the world of the prison he had escaped from? Curse him and his *siambr ddu*!

As it was they grounded just in time, for already the flood was in full set the other way, and the gulls screaming and rioting and settling again as ever fresh flats emerged. Under a bank that seemed to be passing them at a swift walking-pace a current had cut out a cove as cleanly as if out of a piece of cheese. Willie seized an overhanging branch. Hoping that boat might rot before ever its owner found it again he noné the less made it fast. He helped Matthias to drag himself up the bank, and then flung himself down too to get his breath again.

But the rebuke about the oath continued to rankle, and there was no great warmth in the tone in which he asked Matthias, some little time later and looking straight up at the sky, what place he had thought of making for next. If he couldn't stomach a My God once in a while let him make shift to find it.

"Valle Crucis," was the reply.

"What's that?"

"It is an abbey, but travellers may rest there," and now it seemed that in a holy cause Matthias could sulk for a long time too, for again it was Willie who broke the silence.

"Would you be among friends there, or getting into fresh trouble?"

"I do not know, but there is an infirmary, and except for the Office there is no preaching at Valle Crucis. They are Cistercians and vowed to silence."

"The devil. . . . I should say are they indeed! And would they take you in?"

"The master of my college in Cambridge was in charge of the muniments. Sometimes there would come in a rubric it might be, or a missal or a psalter or a book of hours, with an initial or a border they wished to have copied. So in return for my meat and my tuition I put myself to school to this."

At that Willie pricked up his ears. . . . "What, to limning?" and the scholar inclined his head.

"To copying and illumination. I had my pots of ochres and lapis lazuli, and brushes and pencils and a burnisher and a small pipkin of gold, and they do such things at Valle Crucis too," and already Willie was beginning to forget about the oath, for this was talk he could understand. Soon the winter would be here. Except that by some lucky wind he hoped to get tidings of Humphrey Tull's whereabouts, he himself had no more immediate plans than the gulls racketting there over the banks and shoals. Therefore he answered thoughtfully.

"Then was that how they learned about your penmanship and then charged you with forgery?" he asked.

"I was falsely accused, and to copy an initial is not forgery, and you have not told me yet what your trade is," Matthias replied, and as Willie had been in a sense charged with forgery too, away to the winds the last of his resentment went.

"A lucky one for you, Matthias, or you'd have been still frog-humping it and crying out for a mouthful of water the other side of the Mersey!" he laughed. "Which way does this abbey lie?"

"This is Wirral, and over it, missing Deemouth, is Flint. Hold south and you come to Wrexham, and Valle Crucis is hard by Llangollen."

"I don't know what else you preach, but there's little amiss with your geography!" Willie admired. "You've walked better in your time than you're walking now!"

"I have preached my way from Cambridge across England, and I shall spend the winter in retreat and meditation and then preach again."

"Then let's hear a bit more about this Valle Crucis, and then when you're rested we'll be moving on."

For now Willie had another idea. When all was said Humphrey Tull was an armourer, not a goldsmith. It might indeed happen that damascening came into his trade or that to a basnet a gold circlet had to be fixed, but such things were hardly in the regular day's work, whereas it was notorious that in monasteries and great churches employment was found for the finest goldsmiths in the land. From masters themselves Willie had heard of the patinas and chalices and other vessels that on high days of Celebration made their altars glow with their treasury of silver and gold, and if this Valle Crucis could find a use for Matthias and his limning, why not for Willie and his craft too? It was to be considered . . . indeed it was well worth considering. . . .

That afternoon, and within a mile or two of Mersey's swirls and shoals, there were signs that cultivation was beginning again. Drains began to cross the land, for it seemed to be a region of meres and ponds staked for fish, and once, creeping slowly along the far-off skyline, a plough drawn by eight oxen passed. So many to a plough meant that a commote or township was not far away. But Matthias's progress was slow and painful, and in one important respect was not progress at all, for only the chains had been cut through, and as long as he had those gyves round his ankles there could be no seeking the company of men. Therefore Willie must bestir himself. By mid-afternoon they had reached an old marl-pit, where for want of a better chamber they could also make their beds that night. Suddenly bidding Matthias wait there till his return he strode away.

The township was half an hour's walk away, but there, outside a wheelwright's door, Willie saw a grindstone. Asking its owner's leave, he got out his broken burin and busied himself for a time in bringing its stump to a point again. He then asked whether there was an apothecary in the place, and on being directed to the barber's brought out this fettled-up tool and his best and friendliest smile. In so thriving a place they doubtless had harness to mend, he said, and for piercing holes in stiff leather he could show them such a sprig-bit as never was, warranted of the finest steel, forged in Spain. . . .

"Nay, I'm not asking money for it," he hastened to say. "All I want is a ha'porth of salve for a poor pedlar that's come down on a flint and cut his knee to the bone," and the exchange made he sped back to Matthias again before the light should fail. He had been careful to keep the broken-off portion of the tool, and now never had he peered into mould-bottom or die-punch more intently than he squinted into the lock-hole of the first fetter, seeking for the point to attack it. Then he inserted the cutter. Matthias winced and groaned, but after half an hour's picking and scratching something was heard to click and yield. A sharp tap with a stone, at which Matthias cried aloud, and one ankle was freed.

But it was dusk before the other was released, and then Willie straightened himself again in triumph.

"*That's* more than your limning-pencils could do!" he exulted, and in the marl-pit they lay that night.

So now the choice rested with Willie. Matthias, his only sixpence thrown into the poor-box, had no money. Only stumblingly could he get about on his feet, for a glance at his ankles the next morning told him how cruelly he had suffered. He would be to provide for, for nobody picks a man out of the ditch to throw him into the quagmire. The best use he could make of a chancellor's letters was to get himself cast into the *siambr ddu*, and (Willie was already beginning to notice) because he had lived in a college he was inclined to look down his nose at Willie, as his betters looked askance at himself.

On the other hand, Matthias had no need of money. Apparently his knotted string and gabardine were his title to beg, and he had but to show his empty scrip and there was his meat, at no more cost than a blessing with two fingers. When God had found him in food there was Willie to provide him with salve for his hurt, and as for the *siambr ddu*, even there there had been a gaoler to take pity on his plight. What with the gaoler, Willie and God, Matthias was not without friends after all.

There were also other things. In his progress across England, besides geography, Matthias had acquired certain pickings of knowledge that Willie now greatly desired. He must therefore bear with it that he imparted these just a little from on high, explaining them at length when they needed no explanation, but falling back on nods and headshakes whenever (as Willie shrewdly judged) he was in doubt about them himself. Now too, with the width of the Mersey in between, he was beginning to have prickings of conscience, whether after all it had not been his duty to remain by that smouldering court-house, to see what had befallen the humane gaoler or even to succour de Saule himself. Willie would have thought it somewhat late in the day to be troubling about that now.

Next there popped up two other small matters. Matthias was a limner, Willie an artist too, and there at least was a bond between them. It further appeared that on his mother's side Matthias was Welsh, in which language he could also preach, and the first time Willie slipped into a "Diolch" he started and asked Willie where he had learned that word. Whereupon Willie began to plan subtle sentences into which he could drag his three and a half other words of Welsh also, and this seemed suddenly to raise him again in Matthias's estimation.

Lastly, and to settle it all, Matthias had a fine of three hundred marks against him, and Mersey or no Mersey there was still the chance that he might be seized again. He could keep his wrists tucked into the sleeves of his gabardine, but his limp would still betray him, and it would be days yet before he could mingle freely with other men.

Wherefore let it be so. Matthias should do the begging for the pair of them. Willie for his part would snare the fish, for the flat land they were slowly making their way across was still everywhere broken by meres and ponds. But the bad weather would soon be upon them, and the shelter and warmth and occupation of Valle Crucis became ever more attractive.

It was on their fourth day together, resting on a dry bank and watching the wind-bent grasses and the poplars ruffling their white against the sky, that Matthias suddenly asked Willie where he had picked up his few words of Welsh. Willie considered it for a moment, then saw no harm in it, and out came the story of Bartholomew and his *cenedl*, including the silver that lay about Carlisle, though of the gold in Wales he said not one word. Matthias listened attentively, for he was as willing to be edified as he was to edify, and when Willie had finished he delivered himself with some sententiousness.

"It may be as you say, that to know such things is itself a sort of riches, Wilson," he observed, for he called him Wilson, as if the Willie had been some sort of levity. "But even if you knew all this for certain which you do not, what would your knowledge profit you?" and Willie, laughed.

"Profit me, by—by Yea and Nay! But my lord would quickly see it profited him."

"What lord?"

"What lord? Whisper such things in any lord's ear and think you his eyes wouldn't start out of his head?"

"And then?" the catechism went on.

"And then? Why, wouldn't my fortune be made? Would he not make me his treasurer, and set me above all at his board, and pledge me every night in a cup of gold bigger than my head?" he crowed, and Matthias stroked the virgin beard.

"Have you known many lords, Wilson?"

"That's not to say I never shall," Willie retorted.

"Have you known many de Saules even, and he was not a lord?"

"Then tell me about the lords you've known, Matthias," said Willie, impatiently humbling himself again.

"Indeed no, for I must not boast of the little knowledge that is mine. But say this lord of yours listened to you, and smiled on you, and drew you on, but then went away to take counsel with others, of which you knew nothing?"

"What, better counsel than what I could tell him?"

"And say that one supper-time your seat at the table was empty, and when they asked what kept Sir Wilson the Treasurer so late from his supper one or two exchanged a look and then told the minstrels to play louder?" and at that Willie laughed till his sides ached.

"Your failing, Matthias, is measuring other men's pecks out of your own bushel. It isn't everybody's way of doing things, to flout 'em with a sixpence in their faces and then expect anything but the *siambr ddu*. If the fire's out o' those ankles yet shall we try another mile?"

Yet none the less he continued to question Matthias as he adjusted his own pace to his limp, for Matthias might know no more lords than himself but he had kept company with those who did, and such things loomed ever the larger the nearer they approached the lands to which their faces were set.

Indeed, by the fifth afternoon of their journeying together, the whole look of the country had again changed. To the west and south-west wooded hills were beginning to draw in, and the distant patches of cultivation were becoming fewer and straggled only a little way up the rougher slopes. And where the hills closed in to a valley there perforce the road must be, and the sun was declining as they got there, and Matthias had stripped his ankles to rub in more salve, and Willie was examining them with critical eyes.

"They might be better and they might be worse, but another mile or two and we shall have no choice," he said. "Where do you make out we ought to be now?"

"Can you see anything of a stream, that soon gets bigger, first on one side of the road and then on the other? If we're there we're well on the way to Wrexham."

"You get on with your salving and I'll go and see what I can see," said Willie, and he strode away.

It was from a small eminence of crags, that dropped in mossy rock-shelves to the valley below, that he suddenly saw the road, and brought to a standstill on it the most gigantic structure he had ever seen on wheels.

It had eight of them, four a side, squat and stocky and getting on for a foot thick, and they carried an edifice four stories high, of beams scarfed and bolted together and draped round with raw hides. Both before it and behind many oxen were yoked, and it was accompanied by a horde of men with steel sallets on their heads and armed with glaives and iron-shod staves. But the road at that point was ridged and rocky, and there the great tower had lodged, immovable either backwards or forwards, and men swarming up it had fixed ropes to it, while others unyoked the rear oxen and sought stones and branches with which to fill in the ruts. Angry peasants were protesting at the breaking of their hedges and the inroads on their land, and Willie, having observed all this from above, made his way back to Matthias again.

But now this did not seem to be the information Matthias wanted, for he looked up from his salving of his second ankle.

"Didn't you find out who they were?"

"I only went half-way down."

"Could you pick out no livery or device?"

"It's all but dark down in the road."

"Which way are they headed?" and when Willie had pointed out the direction, "So. They'll be for Wrexham, and it's true there's another way, over the mountains, but get you back and first try to find out who they are. Look out specially for Silver Swans, or indeed any device," and obediently Willie trotted off again.

For if, as they drew near to roads and men again, Matthias remembered the *siambr ddu*, and kept his pangs of conscience for when it was too late to do anything about it, Willie thought none the worse of his prudence in keeping away from anything that savoured of de Saule. This time too, he sought a watching-place somewhat lower down. The men in the road had begun to lighten the sow of some of its top-weight. Thrusting the hide curtains aside they were passing out ladders and grapples and man-high shields, and the engine, eased of its load, was rocking cumbrously to and fro to the heaving on the ropes and the thrusting of the levers. Somewhere ahead whips cracked, and men shouted continually as forty oxen strained at their yoking, and they had lighted torches, and the glare shone ruddily on the turned-back hides, roan and brindled and black all laced together, with here and there the ragged eye-holes of a skinned head gazing mournfully out. And now Willie looked on spellbound, for there was something world-old and primal about it all, that reminded him of the dinas and the handleless swords and those scattered bones that had done this self-same thing unnumbered ages before. There was the obstacle, settled in and not to be moved; there were the men, swearing in their sweat that it should be moved; and there was Willie, watching those flayings of whole beasts, and remembering a skinner's son and his own windy vaunt about brigandine-leather for my lord's meinie. Those squat foot-thick wheels put him in mind of an inn-table he had seen somewhere, sawn out of a single tree and finished off with glass because it would not take the plane. For a quarter of an hour he watched and then returned to Matthias, who had got his stockings on again and looked up with a sharp "Well?"

"They're in such a stew I was in two minds whether to join in and give 'em a hand," said Willie.

"Did you see any Silver Swans? What did you see?"

"You know a bit about fetters. What's a fetterlock with a falcon on it?" and Matthias's face cleared, so Silver Swans were very evidently what he had most feared.

"Are you sure?"

"I might have been wrong about an odd one. I wasn't wrong about half a dozen of 'em," but just as suddenly Matthias seemed irresolute again.

"There is the other way, over the mountains, and I'm used to journeying alone," he muttered. "Which was to have been your way, Wilson?"

"It's not a place I seek. It's a man."

"There is the mountain way," the student muttered again, and seeing him unable to make up his mind Willie made it up for him.

"Mountains did you say? Have they woods on 'em?" he demanded.

"They are wooded enough."

"Old woods?"

"Older than memory," and Willie looked round to see where he had put his staff.

"Then hark you, Matthias. I'll be your *gwaesaf*, (is that right?) there's no Silver Swans down yonder. And a slow-moving thing like that will scarce make two miles an hour, so tuck your wrists in, and hold on to me. Now—on your feet."

Twenty minutes later he had him down by the roadside, resting again under a hedge. Now to find out who was in charge of the sow.

He found him, a stiff fellow with a soiled falcon-and-fetterlock stitched to his quilted jacket, holding a blazing torch above his head. They were loading up the stores again, and the stiffened integuments had been flung back so that the light of the torch shone into the sow's yawning belly. It was full of slackened cables, and the great beam with its ramshead of iron lay along its floor, and Willie addressed the man in charge in a masterful voice.

"Have you any orders concerning a manor on Merseyside that was sacked four nights back?" he demanded.

"No," said the man, and turned to shout an order behind him, whereupon Willie became still shorter with him.

"When I speak to you give me your attention. You are for Wrexham?"

"Where else in a needle's-eye like this?" the man growled.

"Then if you want a shirt of mail on your back instead of that bag of puddings heed what I say. I am seeking Humphrey Tull the armourer. The learned gentleman who is with me has hot tidings of Merseyside for your master, and he too has suffered from these accursed Silver Swans and can scarce stand on his feet. Make him a place inside the sow."

The man was looking Willie up and down. . . . "Did you say Humphrey Tull the armourer?"

"I am his journeyman-graver, making haste from Yorkshire to join him. How soon will this machine of yours be on the road again?"

"Sooner than you'll catch up with Maister Tull, for the last we heard of him he was in Ludlow, and that wasn't yesterday."

"Come, make a place for this learned gentleman. Sir Matthias!" he called. "All is set for you. Bid two of these help you forward."

"Then see he has neither flint nor steel on him," said the other and turned away.

There was a re-doubling of the whipping and shouting ahead and a running back and forth. All at once the sow came up with a lurch, and before it could slip back again skids of rock were thrust under its wheels. Men paused to wipe their streaming faces, and Willie helped Matthias up the ramp. The remaining stores were bundled in and the swinging hides laced down again. Four guards thrust themselves through the passing-in flap, and stretched among bales of tallow and buckets of resin, kegs of gunpowder for petards and slow-match for their combustion, Matthias lay fingering his downy beard.

But Willie Middlemiss, seated on the iron head of the ram, was now face to face with the wrecking of all his plans. Humphrey Tull in Ludlow! The stores about him rocked and shifted continually as the great engine lurched this way and that, the four guards cursed as they as continually set them back again. The skins bellied and flapped and the light of the torches outside flickered through cracks into the gloomy interior, but—Humphrey Tull away in Ludlow! Never had his dream seemed brighter than now it lay in ruins. Himself installed in Humphrey Tull's atelier or drawing-shop . . . my lord chancing one fine day to enter and ask who the new journeyman was, and then to be shown some cunning design that Willie had artfully prepared to catch his eye . . . the gold in Wales and the word softly whispered into Humphrey's ear, and Humphrey as secretly bidding him wait till he had

had a word with my lord about it . . . all, all now vanished. With the next break in the skies the winter would be upon them. Nay, unless he was mistaken he could feel it already, for new regions bring new weather, and Wirral with its meres and ponds lay behind them and they were approaching the mountains, down which the gusts swept without warning, bringing the rains and making a torrent of the stream that brawled white, now on one side of the rough road and now on the other.

And it was even as he feared, for the tardy day came greyly, with sullen sag-bellied clouds too cold for rain. Men cursed the icy wind that now blew straight at their backs, and now that they had got it going again the sow did not stop, and Willie, clambering out of its flap while it was still on the move, knew the signs of snow when he saw them. It began in fact to fall that very morning. Slowly treetop and hillside greyed, whitened, and the oxen were given no rest, for siege-towers on the road were trouble enough without snow. The white flakes settled on shoulders and crusted on the iron sallets, and now even their destination had to be changed. It was to have been Berwyn, hard by Valle Crucis. Now it was good-bye Berwyn, for they would be lucky if they made Wrexham that night.

Yet not even of Wrexham had Willie more than a glimpse. The coming of the snow had spurred other travellers to haste too, and coming out of the town with the snow still falling steadily and without a break, was a company that could not have far to go, for otherwise it would not have been so foolhardy as to set out. They were in fact going no further than Valle Crucis, now a bare dozen miles away, and what was a hindrance to them was a boon to Matthias, who now that he was rested again could keep up with their slowed-down pace with ease.

Valle Crucis stood by its stream, its great eastern face mitred with white, its five towering windows ledged and cornered with snow. Its vast courtyard, at other times as busy as a fair with merchants, hucksters, pilgrims, men-at-arms and those of every make and sort from the outside world, was a white and deserted square. The porter asked their business, not as refusing them but as ascertaining their station, and those in charge of horses were shown to the stables at the north of the forecourt, their masters to the row of buildings to the south of it. Before them rose the great west door of the church, with the cloister-porter's lodge in the shadow of it, and to all his dreaming Willie now finally said good-bye, for everything had settled itself over his head. He and Matthias were conducted to the pilgrim's lodging, until the prior should have given further directions. So, stamping the snow from their feet, they reached their winter quarters.

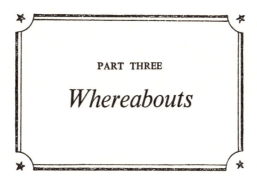

PART THREE

Whereabouts

1

THE GREAT SALT WAS UNQUESTIONABLY OF FRENCH WORKMANSHIP. OF
wrought gold and the best part of a yard high, its belly swelled out
midway to the shape of a plump fruit, where its cover joined it. It
then took an inner curve, tapering upwards till it ended in a spindle
or spire, with a decorated finial for its weathercock. But instead of
gleaming, its gold had a dulled finish, as if the fruit of its belly was
rinded like a nut, and this was the tracery of diagonal diaperwork
that enmeshed it, with a jewel or gem or glint of enamelling at each
knot. The whole grew out of a six-toed circular base, and the bud
that pointed to the hammer-beamed roof clasped a single turquoise
in its filigree calyx.

The butler himself had set it midway down the long board, and
now, with a group of stripling squires about him and the older of the
younger lads, was instructing them in the decorum of their table-
setting.

Spring sunshine slanted in at the great window that looked out on
the inner courtyard, and in the hall itself all was stir and bustle. The
head-panter had placed the wine-hanap on the table raised on the dais,
and from secondary sideboards the lesser servants were handing out
the platters, the napkins, the bread. The wine-hanap, like the Great
Salt, was French, and the two of them together were probably worth
more than the ship that had carried them over.

Now their owner, the most illustrious John, lord of the baronies of
Wharram and Wickware and Tollington and Wyke in England,
deputy-warden of the Middle Marches and also seised in his wife's
right of the castles of Briniau and Coed Isaf and Coed Uchaf and
Quellyn and Gwlad in Wales, was on his way home.

From one end of the castle of Gwlad to the other it was the same.
The gatehouse stood open, since morning the messengers had been
arriving almost hourly, the barrack-quarters were all cleared for the
incoming men-at-arms. The great octagonal kitchen was a swelter of
seething and boiling and roasting, and still more quarters of beeves
and split hogs were being carried in from the store-house tubs. In the
bakery fresh sacks of meal were being opened, barrels trundled out
from the brewhouse. The dogs had been kennelled, the high roof-
lantern over the butchering-table was dimmed with steam, and the

cooks cooled themselves at the openings of the walls or quenched their thirst in the open air.

The sentries who paced the wall-tops had to circle the south-east turret, and as they made the turn they could see for a few moments into the window of the great solar, the projecting oriel of which stood open over the backwater of the moat. Here the stir was of another kind, for it was into the solar that the women had withdrawn themselves to open the wardrobes and get out their clothes. They too could see the sentries as they passed, but that morning their minds were on the garments that strewed the solar floor. The pages had been sent about their business, the half dozen younger children did not matter, and they were in their cottes and smocks and deshabille, choosing among this and that.

The Lady Margaret was no longer of a figure to be peeped at by sentries passing along the wall. She was short and meal-coloured and as jowled as the great talbot that lay stretched out in front of the fire-dogs. But well worth any young man's glance was Mistress Joslin Covil, nearer to the open oriel than there was any need for her to be as she stood with her stripped arms above her head, trying on a steepled structure taller than the Great Salt itself, from which floated a cloud-like wafting of stiffened gauze. She was twenty, lush as a blackheart cherry and ticklish as a balsam-pod, and she had been married just a year. But her husband, who was the least robust of the younger lads being taught their table-setting by the butler in the great hall below, had been dismissed the solar for the undressing, and suddenly the Lady Margaret raised first a heavy eyelid and then her voice.

"Joslin, do you shut that window at once and come away from it. No, not that one," for Mistress Joslin's hand was at the oriel's other bay, "the one towards the turret. Then place yourself further within."

"Yes, Madam. I was but looking to see if they'd raised my lord's banner yet."

"You'll hear the trumpets when we all hear them, and take that hennin off, that is far too set-up for your years. I was half again your age before I wore a hennin."

"Yes, Madam," and Mistress Joslin threw the hennin on the solar floor without folding it and turned to her perfume-box instead.

But she kept the lids lowered over her walnut-dark eyes. Hennins forsooth! As if any but these exiles in their stone castle had worn a hennin this last twenty years! But wait. It was money that talked, as my lord knew if my lady didn't, and she was not a wealthy London mercer's daughter for nothing. Straight into my lord's pocket the best part of her dowry had gone, for her boy-husband had been one of my lord's wards, and now, as soon as my lord saw fit to dub her young

Ferdinand a knight, she would not be Joslin but Lady Joslin, and she had lived in this heart-breaking castle for a year, and she had only tried the hennin on to have a peep at her own round shoulders against it. The Lady Margaret coveted that enamel and silver gilt perfume-box for herself too, so let her mouth go on watering for it till my lord made her Ferdinand a knight and herself a Lady.

The messengers now stretching themselves in the gate-house had ridden in in stages, a stage the fewer with each that my lord left behind him, and as half of them had not seen my lord they had little of news to relate. What the stay-at-homes had to tell was even slighter, for it was no news that the arrears of wages had not yet been paid, and they had seen for themselves that nothing had yet been settled about the waste and the common-rights, for the fences my lord had set up before his departure had been once more laid flat and again sheep and cattle strayed in and out.

With the drawbridge dropped and wide open the waste could be seen from the gatehouse, beyond the barbican and a furlong away across the moat. That row of dilapidations to the left of the whipping-post had once been dwellings. Now its broken roofs and walls hardly served for cowsheds, and the dispute about the cattle and sheep had joined itself to a still older feud, the chickens that must be provided for the feeding of my lord's falcons. Hens clucked and scratched about the old sheds, and it was on this that the corporal of the guard was loudly holding forth.

"What's a hamper of pullets once in a while, laying or not?" he stormed. "Think o' what they get out of my lord! A pack of pilferers and poachers, and I warrant you from to-day on boilers and roasters and half-cheeses will be going out o' this castle by the sackfull! Whipping's too good for 'em. . . ."

"But let 'em see dust in the south, and strange pennons rising from it, and they're swarming outside there, on their knees to be let in . . ." another supported him.

"If they know a better castle let them go seek it . . ." and they continued to wrangle, while the cattle continued to graze and the hens to scratch and the riffraff on the waste to assemble.

The castle of Gwlad stood at the head of the south valley, with the gate into the western hills behind it. It had a circuitous and winding way between its double walls, and with its garrison at full strength it housed five hundred souls. That was why its great octagonal kitchen hissed and spat and steamed so that day, for it had to victual the great hall at one end and the garrison at the other, and the meats the panters passed out by the hatch were received by the waiting camp-cooks and orderlies who carried them to the barrack hall. And, hurrying panters and sweating cooks and indeed everybody in the castle of Gwlad heard, at five o'clock that spring afternoon, the faint and faraway thrilling borne on the light wind from the south.

It was heard first by the four sentries high on the barbican wall, who stood still for a moment to listen. After a few moments it came again, and suddenly one of the four raised a trumpet to his lips. Thereupon the whole castle of Gwlad leapt to life. The seneschal, hearing it from the great hall, clapped his hands, and squires and pages raced to their stations. The banners on the walls were broken out, and at the same moment the solar window became a nosegay of faces. On the waste by the broken fences there was a running of the township's nondescripts to the long timbered approach, nay, even the prisoners in their vault beneath the postern of the back-court raised their sullen heads at the sound. The massive chains rumbled and rattled in the drawbridge walls. Ponderously and spilling its chippings and straw and dust the gateway came up, only to be lowered again at my lord's recognition and command. Nearer in its dust the cavalcade drew, two hundred and fifty strong, and this time the trumpet spoke in a challenging "Who goes there?" An outrider galloped forward. There were calls and counter-calls between him and the captain of the guard. Down clattered the bridge again, and the next flourish told all the region of Gwlad that its deputy-warden was once more in residence among them.

By six o'clock that evening knights had bathed in their chambers and got into their camlets and says, their ladies were resplendent in their velvets and silks and furs. The great hall was a leaping and barking of the released dogs, the first rush of greetings was over. But most were travel weary, for the nonce ceremony was relaxed, and the dignity and precedence of the guests my lord had brought with him could be determined to-morrow. To-night they might arrange themselves as they pleased. The chaplain said 'Grace,' and down they sat.

Humphrey Tull the armourer sat in the highest seat below the Great Salt, next to the marshal-at-arms who occupied the lowest place above it. And Humphrey Tull's anvil-days were long since passed, and there was nothing to choose between his fingers and the marshal's as they helped themselves from the same dish, which none the less was set first before the marshal, who courteously signed for the master-armourer to help himself first, who as courteously motioned the dish back again. They were waited on not by the squires, but by the younger pages, and as the marshal's word was law when the lists over by the quarry were dressed they were in a sense two of a trade, with their joint affairs to talk about.

"A suit came in just after Christmas," the marshal was telling

Humphrey as the two pages who had brought the ewer and bowl retired again, "I'd like you to cast your eye over. It was the seneschal brought it to me, and I say a suit, but it's scarce that, for it's little more than nursery-size, made for some sprig of a dauphin as like as not."

"What make?" the armourer asked.

"There's no mark on it, but Spanish at a guess. But the casque's had a knock and doesn't seat right in to the mentonnière, and I though best not to send it to your smiths, for it's a pretty piece of work for a boy."

"I'll have a look at it in the morning."

"I'd be obliged. I gather it would please my lord well if it could be furbished up for young Ferdinand. It was seeing him brought it to my mind."

"I'll see it, but it's a waste of good steel making suits for children."

"And so say I, but my lord knows what he's about, and you and I know our business best when we leave my lord to his," and the master-armourer nodded, and they went on to speak of other matters.

At the table raised on its dais my lord sat in his high-backed chair, with the Lady Margaret on his right and on his left a French lady of such rank that nowhere else might she sit than at his side. She was indeed a protégée of His Grace himself, who in person had seen her horsed at Ludlow, standing gazing after her long after the stirrup-cup had been drained. But the others sat in alternation, a knight and then a lady, a knight and another lady, so many now of them that they overflowed the ends of the high table and sat with their backs to the hall below. Before my lord stood the wine-hanap, and he made a sign. The chief butler wore a slender gold chain about his neck from which depended a portion of a unicorn's horn, and my lord, who had been talking to the Lady Estelle in French, now spoke to him in English.

"From which bin is this wine?"

"My lord, from your own bin," and the butler proceeded gravely with his office. There was little likelihood that my lord would be poisoned at his own table on the day of his return, but into the great silver-gilt vessel the butler dipped his cup of assay. No seething or clouding agitated the talisman at the end of his chain. He was ordered to fill, and my lord raised his cup, to right, to left, to his wife on returning to her bosom again, to the guest whose charge he had been honoured with.

Mistress Joslin, who had stood in her cotte too close to the solar window, was one of those who sat at the dais's end with their backs to the hall below. She sat elbow to elbow with the knight who was known as the French prisoner, though he was no prisoner of my lord's

taking. How he had come to be left out of the general amnesty perhaps
only my lord could have told, for he had acquired him by purchase
until such day as his ransom should be completed, and for all he was
called a prisoner he was free as the birds, inside the castle or out, for
his parole was still to his original captor. He was a lithe and dark-
skinned young man, with a poetical little pointed beard trimmed to
fit the shape of his lips, and as it had cost three men their lives before
he had been overcome it went to Mistress Joslin's heart that he should
thus be languishing his prime away.

"So now," she was pouting, "with one of your own countrywomen
come to Gwlad, you sigh for your France again?" and he answered
without raising his eyes.

"I have not yet been told that the Lady Estelle is here to visit
prisoners."

"But in France you are a sieur. Do not tell me there is no lady in
France who does not sigh her heart away to have you back!"

"English knights have their pick of the French ladies, since English
kings make them their queens," and his downcast eyes were on the
tapering fingers she dipped into the bowl.

"Then the French sieurs should recompense themselves on the
English ladies," and the prisoner glanced up. Over his shoulder he
had seen the busy pages down below.

"To find them already married?"

"He is a Covil, and he too will be a sieur."

"Vous parlez Français?"

"Oui."

"Quel age a-t'il?"

"Quatorze ans."

"Est-il . . . terrible?" and his look was both cool and bold, but at
that moment the Lady Margaret's voice was heard, and others were
looking towards Mistress Joslin too. "Tais-toi. It is my compatriote
and they have been speaking to us. See, my lord is raising his cup to
you," and as for a lady-in-waiting this was a signal honour Mistress
Joslin lowered her black cherry of a head and dipped her knee dutifully
under the table.

In his place next below the Great Salt, Humphrey Tull the armourer,
content now with meat and drink, had summoned this same young
husband forward from the service-table again. He seemed but a
weakling for his years, yet spoiled withal, and the last months had
done little to fill him out; yet he was a Covil and to be reckoned
with.

"And how goes the world with young Master Ferdinand?" Humphrey asked. "I hear from the birds you're on the way to being made

a squire and a knight, and then you will forget us blacksmiths. Is your lady well in health?"

"She is always in health, sir."

"And you are exercising yourself as you should? How goes the riding?"

"I now have as good a knee-grip as the best, sir."   .

"What is this I hear about a new armour? At your leisure I shall have to take your measurements again. Not to-morrow, for I must see how my work has fallen behind, but how say you to the day after?"

"I am at your call, Master Tull."

"Then after to-morrow I will run my tape over you," and as the lad fell back again the marshal turned once more to his neighbour.

"What was that I heard young Ferdinand saying about his riding?"

"That he had tightened up his knee-grip and now had as good a one as any," and the marshal's eyes stole to the upper end of the hall, where Mistress Joslin sat.

"Barring one," he said out of the corner of his mouth, and the armourer gave him a quick look, but no more was said.

Far different was the scene half the length of the inner court away, where the men-at-arms sat noisily at their meat. No silver-gilt stood on the sideboards here, and instead of two a dozen dipped their hands into the same dish. As for all the sayes and camlets they had, such as wore breast-armour had doffed it, and they sat in their rust-stained leather and studded jerkins, and there were many bald and greying and scarred heads among them, for most of the younger men were elsewhere. And as some had left their sons behind at Ludlow with His Grace it was of these that they spoke.

"Think you your two will be for Chester, Diggon?" a battered footman asked his neighbour on the bench. "There's talk of my lord of Salisbury making ready in the north."

"Who told you that?"

"Richard, the second-cook, and he had it from the head-cook, who had it from the seneschal himself."

"What Richard the cook knows about it he could put in his eye and see no worse. Half Cheshire's a swannery by this and they'll keep the young 'uns back i' case o' need."

"Ay, the same as the Calais men;" but at the name of Calais another voice was raised.

"Calais! Calais 's stunk too long of riches, and them Calais-men's half French with their marrying and mixing and whoring! Calais!" and he spat on the floor, as another fellow called across the board.

"Hey! What talk's this? When were you in Kent?"

"In '50, if you must know. . . ."

"Ay, keeping an ale-house. . . ."

"Richard the cook, that's never stirred out of his kitchen!"

"It's often them that hears the most . . ." and out the quarrel broke.

For these had known what to do with French prisoners when they took them, and those had been the days to live in. With a sack on his back and a French street to loot a man had been able to pay his own wages, and any lad of spirit could raise a Free Company of his own. These knew Westerham and Avranches, Saint Lô and Caen and Rouen, better than they knew their own country, not to speak of Gascony and Guienne. Now it was Hereford and Shropshire and what was happening south of Ludlow. Silver Swans or a Falcon-on-a-fetterlock, a Boar, a Sun behind a Cloud, a bird, a bear, a red rose or a white one—they were not eating now, but drinking, and drinking again, and fighting their old battles anew as they thought of their sons whose battles were still to come.

Those who dwelt outside the walls were well known to the guard at the gatehouse, and back and forth over the waste they moved, the graziers of half a dozen sheep, the pedlars of anything that offered, the pickers-up, the blind with their dogs, the beggars with their pokes. They were forbidden the central court, but they had leave to wander between the walls, and there were women among them, for where there are soldiers there are always women. Old Mother Jule, who squatted in her cowshed-cottage none knew by what alms or permission, had put on her battered black steeple-hat and her scanty shawl, smelling trade. She told fortunes, which all remembered when they came true, and it was the sport to bar the way to her as she swung between her two crutches with one clubbed foot off the ground. As she now approached the portcullis a footman thrust a pike across her path.

"The watchword, you with the beard," he demanded, while the guard on the benches looked on, and the crone wrinkled her nose and beckoned.

"Come nearer while I whisper it then," she wheedled.

"Who is it you seek?"

"My truelove, boy bach, that I gave three hairs off my chin to charm the arrows away. . . ."

"How do we know that isn't the devil you have in your poke?"

"Nay, the whole world's scarce big enough for him, but it's big enough for a crust of bread and maybe a jellied pigsfoot and a fish-head for my cat. . . ."

"Then tell us a fortune for your passage," but even as he spoke he shifted the pike in his hand, for a shadow had fallen across the draw-bridge planks. A figure they didn't know was advancing, with a leather cap on his head and a package under his arm, and a stranger was a stranger, and a couple of the other guards were on their feet too. But the old woman had thrust forward her bearded chin.

"Soldiers ought to know their fortunes by this, but here's one whose luck I'll tell!" she cackled, her eyes on the newcomer. "Save you, my pretty young man! Do you seek your truelove too?"

But though no order was given, the man with the pike was already asking the intruder his name and business, and at that up went the leather-capped head, and from behind two large white teeth there came a noisy laugh.

"Speech in my ears again, by God, and sinners with tongues in their heads! Nay, more clamour! What do you say, friend? Shout it at me, as long as it isn't the midnight bell and the shuffle of frostbitten feet and a look like doom if a man as much as whistles! It's like coming up into the world again! And a woman too! Greetings to you, mother...."

"We do not know your face. The watchword?"

"Is Master Humphrey Tull back with my lord?"

"They are at their supper. Come, your errand," and the stranger glanced at the pikes and the furniture hanging on the gate-house walls and then gave a friendly salute.

"My business is I'm the journeyman from York, and the watchword is Humphrey Tull the armourer. Middlemiss the metal-worker, tell him, that drank with him in the Ainsty Arms in York city. Where shall I find him?"

"Enough, Stephen," the corporal's voice was raised. "Let him pass. If it isn't as he says he's got to get out again," so at last, through the outer gate of Gwlad, Willie Middlemiss passed.

Beyond the inner arch the stables and storehouses stretched to right and left, with more defence-works to flank them and the frowning walls overtopping a sunless canal. Their close-mortared masonry seemed the jaws of a trap, and Willie was wondering whether to turn to the right or to the left when he heard the tapping of crutches behind him and waited for the witch to come up.

"Nay, that takes you to the smithies and the back-court," she said. "They're having their dinner, and you'll find Maister Tull in the great hall."

"So I shall, mother, and thank you," but still she detained him.

"Let me look at you, for I see luck in your face," and her battered steeple-hat wagged to one side as she peered up at him. "And to think of your coming the same day as my lord! There's fortune to be starting off with, pretty boy!" and Willie laughed.

"And if your own eyes aren't the brightest I've seen these six months!"

"Eyes, says he, with that merry pair of his own!" and the steeple-hat was cocked the other way. "What have you in your pocket, boy-bach?"

"My winter's wages, mother."

"And a coin for Mother Jule?"

"To be sure," and the wrinkled hand into which he pressed it held his own as she put her nose into it and peered and mumbled.

"Keep it still a minute, for I cannot believe it . . . for a fortune I never saw the like! Chimney-smoke! I can almost smell it, and they say the best of all luck's that that comes out of the muck! Why, 'tis a king's hand! Are you wed, pretty boy?"

"Not yet, mother."

"No, nor this year's leaves aren't fallen yet, but Mother Jules sees her on her way! Yet stay, for I see a check. Nay, it's gone and all's well. Did you say you had your winter's wages?"

Lightly a second coin passed. Valle Crucis and its bell, the shuffling feet, the grave-like silence and the whispering half-hour on Sunday with the abbot sitting there like an iceberg in his white, all were over and Humphrey Tull was found. Just ahead a low gateway broke the inner wall and from it there came a deep surge of voices. They were the voices of the men-at-arms, still drinking in the crowded barrack-hall.

2

"I CANNOT CALL ANY SUCH OCCASION TO MIND, YOUNG MAN."

It was Humphrey Tull speaking, at eight o'clock the next morning, and Willie, trimmed up as if for a wedding, stood before him with his leather cap in his hands. The armourer's office was a ground-floor room at the foot of a turret, with the smithies clinking busily across a wide yard and a row of horses standing outside waiting to be shod. But it might have been anybody's office, for nothing in the way of armour was to be seen, only many papers on the table, bills and nominal rolls and memoranda of one sort and another.

"Where do you say all this was?"

"In York, Master Tull, in the little tavern where the prentices used to go," and the armourer raised his grizzled brows.

"Prentices in taverns?"

"It was but an occasion, sir, and if I don't make too bold you told us you'd been a prentice yourself."

"Meaning that if I shut my eyes once I'm a blind man from then on. Well, as I cannot deny it it may be as you say. Why did you leave York?"

"My time was up, sir."

"And where have you been since?"

"All the winter I've been at Valle Crucis."

"That's a monastery. How came you to fetch up in a monastery?"

"I went with a priest, sir, who is also a limner. I left him there copying a book of hours."

"And what work were you engaged on there?"

"Work enough, for there was always something to be replaced or made good or something, chalices or vessels or the image of a saint. For a month I was at a great book as big as a bakestone, all bound in solid silver."

"Have you brought any of your work with you?" and already Willie's fingers were at his package, from which he promptly brought out a quantity of working drawings, fine pencillings of details, a patina or the ornamentation of a pastoral staff, at which the armourer hardly glanced.

"I have no time for these. What about metal?"

"Yes, sir, I have that too."

But now Willie found that Humphrey Tull was no Bartholomew

Rhys, to stare his eyes out at a broken locket with a girl's head on it and to beg to be shown it over and over again. . . . "Is this all you have?" he asked as he looked at it for a moment and passed it back again, and Willie's heart sank. "What did you say your name was?"

"Middlemiss."

"Any would say it was a middle you missed, upsetting monks with your wenches' heads and bringing this pastrycook's work to an armourer. Don't you hear 'em in that smithy? It's welding and riveting for us, not whimwhams."

"I thought, sir, there might be graving or chasing or some finer work. . . . I've seen basnets and swords-of-ceremony. . . ."

But he stopped, for the armourer too seemed suddenly to have bethought himself of something. He glanced round his stone office as if in search of it, then remembered. Stooping he brought out from under a bench behind him two pieces of harness, a sharp-peaked mentonnière and the casque that should have fitted snugly into it. As he set the casque on a pile of papers Willie saw that it was delicately chased all over with an intricate pattern of vine-leaves, into which silver had been hammered. The armourer was looking first at the head-piece, then up at Willic.

"Was this that you had in your mind?" he asked, and Willie's heart rose again.

"Ah, sir, but that's pretty work! But it's no more than an infant's size."

"He'll grow in greatness if he doesn't in inches, and it would look ill if I had to tell my lord such a thing was beyond us. My men can hammer out the dint but they cannot restore the pattern, so how if I let you try your hand at it?"

"It's done, sir!" Willie cried eagerly, the headpiece in his hands. "Give me half an ounce of silver and a bench to work at. . . ."

"Yonder's the smithy. Ask for Sizar," and the interview was over, for Humphrey Tull had turned to his nominal rolls and lists of requirements again.

Hugging the headpiece to his breast Willie walked on air across the court to where the anvils clinked and the horses waited. All this bustle and blowing and the smell of singeing hoofs was suddenly life to him again after the frozen silence of the brothers and the chilblains on his hands as he had tooled and shivered over his cold silver binding. But the hammering out of that dent in the casque was no work for the first blacksmith's striker who offered, and standing at the smithy door, inhaling the smell of hot iron-flake and listening to the puffing of the bellows and his eyes dancing like the glow that rose and fell on the hearths, he called loudly for the head-smith.

"Is your name Sizar?"

"Ay, I'm Sizar."

"Can you take a rubbing of a pattern?"

"It mightn't be past me."

"Then we can make a start."

And a start was made there and then. The rubbing of the vine-leaves must first be taken, then the casque must be swaddled and packed, with only the damaged part left exposed. Soap and pitch must be got, nor was the head-smith to let the thing out of his own hands, but at that he only nodded, for he had seen the casque before, also one trades-man can quickly tell when another knows his trade. An hour later he had the casque between his aproned knees, and he and Willie were pitching and packing it up, till it resembled a swollen head muffled up against the toothache, with only the bald patch of its tonsure showing.

And by noon that day, at a wink from the smith and without anybody's permission, Willie had installed himself in a small chamber immediately over Humphrey Tull's, with winding stairs leading to it, and was sitting on a stone seat with an oilstone on his knee, getting his burins and gravers ready for action.

His heart was bounding with exultation. That to be sure was the way, begin as you mean to go on. Never take no for an answer, and if anybody asked him who had told him he might instal himself in that turret in which he sat, tell them it would do well enough till something better was got ready for him! And he was preening himself thus when there walked into his new quarters a knock-kneed wreckling of a lad of fourteen, dressed in brown velvet, who addressed him much as he himself had addressed the foreman-smith.

"I'm told you have my headpiece," this youngster said, and Willie looked up from his sharpening.

"It's across at the smithy," he said.

"How soon will it be ready?"

"Two weeks maybe. Maybe three."

"I want it sooner than that. I want it by the end of this week," and at that, Willie went on with his sharpening.

"Did you hear what I said?" the boy demanded, and Willie looked up.

"Is it for you?"

"Yes, and I've got to get my horse used to the weight, and he shies at the noise too," and Willie wiped his tools and stone on a rag, put them aside and rose.

"It is a princely suit, young sir, the two bits of it I've seen, and you can be getting your horse used to the weight of the rest of it. Such of it as is in my hands is going to be princely used, and by the time it's

E

finished you'll not know where that dent's been. But you cannot have
it in less time than I say."

"Curse of Christ!" the boy muttered pettishly, and Willie watched
the knocking of his knees as he turned to the stone stairs again.

And now, with nothing for the moment to do, Willie judged it time
to be making himself better acquainted with this castle of Gwlad,
and this he proceeded to do forthwith. The sooner his face was known
the better, and first by way of the moat backwater he strolled as far
as the gatehouse. Here the corporal, remembering him from the day
before, asked him whether he had fetched up with Humphrey Tull
yet, and Willie nodded, and after some little talk asked whether a low
heavy door by the chain-slot led up to the battlements. Told that it
did he passed without hindrance up dark twisting stairs and out on
the ramparts, with his vine-leaf rubbing in his hand in case he had to
answer questions, and there stood looking about him. First he looked
at the ragged township and beyond it down the wide southern valley,
then proceeding further stood standing opposite the gate into the
western hills. Further round he wandered still, nodding to the sentries
as he passed and noting this and that, until he had completed half of
the castle's circuit. Then the clinking of anvils told him he was nearing
the backcourt again, but before reaching it he saw that a floor below
him a sort of flying-bridge, window-pierced for light throughout its
short length, spanned the way between the outer precincts and the
castle's inner apartments. It was the only communication of the sort
he had seen, so it was evidently a private way, and he turned to the
other side to see what else there might be. But there was little else.
Some yards further along the wall-walk took a turn round a tower,
and as he rounded the turn an oriel window came into sight on the
level below and allowed a glimpse into its interior. But except for a
number of children's toys strewed on the floor and a long-eared talbot
stretched lazily before a hearth it was empty, and as he must now be
somewhere near his starting-point he tried a low wooden door that
looked as if it might lead down to the armourer's office again. But
there was no entry by it, and the sight of the roof-lantern of the octagonal kitchen at the next turn and the smell that rose from it suddenly
reminded him he was hungry.

But where to eat? All Gwlad had bestirred itself for my lord's
homecoming, but no special provision had been made for a dusty
young journeyman who chanced to have strayed into the castle on
the same day. The night before he had slept in a forage-shed in the
shadow of the gatehouse. The turret-chamber he had made free with
would serve for the present, but its furniture was little more than a
bench and the niche in its wall, neither had Humphrey Tull opened his

arms very wide to receive him. Sizar the smith was the man he must seek, but the smiths, he learned on asking one of the cooks, had their food sent across the yard to them, as it would be a waste of time to make themselves clean when in an hour they would be as grimed again as ever.

Next he wandered in by the lower door of the great hall, where he found much movement and preparation but no dinner, for under its high hammer-beamed roof a dozen pages and squires were still setting the tables. The torch-brackets on the smoky walls had been trimmed with springtime greenery and the high table decked with early flowers. A dozen dogs nosed about among the floor-rushes, and Willie was patting the head of one of these when his eyes fell on the Great Salt, reigning like a monarch in the middle of the board. In a moment he had sprung towards it, almost overturning a page with a tray of cups on his way. Great Jupiter, but there was a piece! French, for all the money in the world, and what workmanship, what cunning, what art! It was almost common with its cuspings and its gemmings, so that a man's eyes had to come back anew to its beauty! God, but he must see that a hundred times, hold it in his hands, murmur soft praises to it! In the meantime he saw that under the great window some seven or eight men were already eating. They seemed to be the upper menials of the household, who must take their meals at different times because of their duties—the bakers, the saddlers, the tailors, the what-nots. Their trestle table too could be whisked away when they had finished, and there they sat, with a great crock of stew in front of them, the baker with a dusting of flour on his sleeve, the saddler eating with his leather-knife. So the Great Salt might be such a piece as a man might not see thrice in a lifetime, but he must eat every day, and in a moment there was Willie at the board too, dipping his fingers into the crock with the rest.

"Didn't I see you talking to Sizar the smith this morning?" he suddenly heard in his ear. The man he had placed himself next to had addressed him.

"Yes," said Willie, his mouth full of stew.

"Yours is a new face here?"

"Since yesterday," said Willie.

"What's your service?"

"The armoury," said Willie. "What's yours?"

"Head ostler I am. What are you doing about your wages?"

"I'm scarce settled in yet. Who's that down the hall there, the lad in brown velvet carrying the wine-jug?" for it was the same youth who had been at Willie about the headpiece that morning, and the ostler looked up.

"Young Covil. He's no need to worry about *his* wages. His wife's seen to that."

"A wife, that bantling?"

"Whisht if you only came yesterday. There's a deal more goes on in this castle than meets the eye. . . . Dick! Tom! Harry!" and he leaned forward and called along the trestle to his companions. "Here's a new man of Humphrey Tull's. I didn't catch your name, young man. . . ."

But Willie, his belt tight again, had now thought twice about his company. With his cap on his head again he was at the door, and the next moment outside it, with his face towards his own turret.

As well too, for that afternoon, as he sat moodily looking at his Valle Crucis odds and ends, one of the smiths entered. The master-armourer wished to see him, and descending to the stone office he found Humphrey Tull with thunder on his brow. For some minutes the armourer went on checking his lists; then he looked up.

"So," he said. "You've had enough of Gwlad already, have you?"

"Sir?" said Willie.

"Not having been here a day you're for back to your monks again?"

"I'd no such thought, Master Tull. . . ."

"No, but that's not to say I hadn't. News doesn't take long to get round in Gwlad. Where did you have your dinner to-day?"

"I snatched a bite where I could, sir. . . . I have my way about to find and no orders have been given me yet. . . ."

"So you sat down with the storekeepers and victuallers and grooms?"

"If I did wrong, sir . . . it was yesterday I last put anything into my mouth, and I shouldn't have had a bed but for the horses' fodder. . . ."

"I care not where you sleep, for none sees you, but I'll have no man o' mine hobnobbing with bakers and chandlers. You seem to have started with a tavern, and if you cannot respect yourself there's your calling to respect," and Willie hung his head, for when such storms blow up the less said the better. On for some minutes longer Humphrey Tull rumbled, and then his wrath began to abate. Where had he put himself now? Humphrey Tull wanted to know. With the mongrels in the kennels?

So, the storm over, to set things on a more regular footing. Willie had best keep for the present to his chamber overhead, for then he would be within call, and for the rest, Humphrey would have a word with the seneschal. Bedding should be taken up and such other necessities as he must have, but after that Humphrey Tull made no promises. It might be that when the treasurer heard they had among them a craftsman who had passed the test of Valle Crucis he would find him something, but that had nothing to do with Humphrey Tull.

"Where's that headpiece now?" he asked.

"Over at the smithy, sir. That knock it got has to be hammered out first."

"And what comes next in your gimcrack trade?"

"Then I can make a start with the pattern."

"Throwing good steel away on such puppetry!" growled the man who might never have seen a Milan breastplate or a Spanish blade in his life, and with that Willie had leave to go.

He and Sizar did the hammering between them, and it took them the best part of a couple of days. Even when the packing was removed there was still work enough for Willie, for between the planished-out patch and the surrounding pattern was a cicatrice where the two came together, that must be tapped out the merest pinpoint at a time. The broken ends of the silver veining had also to be picked away and put frugally aside for use again, and so to work he set. The foreman-smith's assistant, who spent half his time running back and forth for Humphrey Tull, saw to the furnishing of his turret. Running deep into his chamber-wall was a V-shaped embrasure, narrowing at its outer end to a tall arrow-slit. Across this he stretched an awning of muslin to make diaphanous the light. He set up a small bench in it, and was supplied with such other tools and appliances as he did not possess, a vice, a shaving-hook, tweezers and files. Buffing and polishing he could get from the pantlers. So, tracer or burin in hand, tapping and picking-out, peering and feeling the surface with his fingers, Willie began to spend day after day. Only once did Humphrey Tull come near him, and then the only remark he made was a grudging grunt of approval of the way in which Willie carefully set every scrap and shred of the old silver aside. To waste nothing was the way to wealth, he said.

But neither Humphrey nor anybody else said anything about the new silver that would be required for the hammering in.

Then came a day when, his incision of vine-leaves complete all but its filling, Willie sat looking at it, softly tapping his teeth with his burin knob. Looking at it with him was young Ferdinand in his brown velvet, for some reason or other nearer to tears than became one so soon to be raised in his degree. He was in a petulant temper, which Willie did his best to placate.

"Don't wreak it on me," he said. "I can cut the pattern, as you see. But I cannot make silver."

"Where's the silver that was there before?"

"Some I have. Some had to be lost."

"Then get some more from Tull."

"Patience, young sir. I told you it wouldn't be ready in a day."

"Get some from the treasurer. Tell him I want it. Here's the marshal out of humour with me, and all the other casques are too big for me, and now my lady's mocking me, and I'll not be mocked. . . . I tell you, I'll not be mocked. . . ."

"Did you mean my lord's lady?"

"No, *my* lady, you dolt! And the French sieur's showing me how to dress my lance, but my lady only makes a face and says 'Eat and drink and make yourself a man!' and I do eat, I eat till I'm stuffed, and I am a man. . . ."

And Willie thought of young Atty Cockin the skinner's son, who ran like a deer and never as much as glanced at the girls who filled their buckets at the stream. But it brought him no nearer to the silver he must have if his work was to be finished, and when he spoke to Humphrey Tull about it the armourer all but went into an apoplexy. But coming round again he asked how much silver would be required.

"The weight of a penny piece or more. Say two silver pennies, melted down and drawn into wire."

"What! For a brat's casque! Young man, there's melting enough in this castle, gold by the ounce and silver by the pound, but never ask 'em for a coin! Silver-gilt to eat off, but the Great Salt and the hanap together wouldn't begin to pay the wages that's owed! Tell the young table-bird flesh and fortune go together. He'll know what you mean," but when Willie reported this young Ferdinand gulped outright.

"She locks everything up the minute she comes into our chamber and I don't know where she hides the key," and again Willie tried to soothe him.

"You haven't got my meaning. I'm not putting it into your head to steal. If she's all that finery surely she has a silver twopence! Then it's but rendering it down and drawing the wire and the hammering wouldn't take two days," and the boy lifted pathetic eyes.

"The French knight killed three men before he was taken."

"Is he the tree-cat looking one in the dark clothes and the little pointed beard?"

"Yes. . . . Gaston his name is, and the marshal will set us up a barrier in the quarry. . . ."

"And I'll come and see the sport. You get me that silver," and the boy went disconsolately out.

Once more with nothing to do, Willie sat looking round his new quarters. The bowmen's slit was his atelier, a second bench had been joined to the first to make his bed, and for eating he had now been allotted a place in the hall, though it was a long, long way below the Great Salt. It was in fact at the very foot of the lower board, and the Salt was almost as far as he had yet dared to raise his eyes, lest they should meet other eyes. From fifty to eighty sat down daily, a throwing together of men of all ages, their velvets edged with fur and linen at their wrists, yet all it seemed to Willie with the same high look of captaincy and authority. Their dogs waited behind them or gnawed their bones among the rushes, and he wondered what their jests might be, for the mingled hubbub of their voices would sometimes change suddenly to a peal of laughter; but seeing the faces of the pages at the sideboards immovable Willie schooled his own face too. As for the high dais itself, even if he had looked it was almost too far away to see, except when the Lady Margaret in her hennin rose and she and her ladies passed out over a horizontal bending of backs, the French Sieur's in its blue-black velvet the lowest of all. . . . But suddenly he yawned and stretched himself. Covering up the headpiece and putting his tools away he got up on his feet. He passed through the low door-way, but instead of descending the stairs he took the upward winding. If that closed door he had seen opened from the inside it was the nearest way out to the battlements, and after his breath-holding work he wanted air.

Only a heavy bar secured the upper door, and closing it he had perforce to leave it unbarred behind him. It was a breezy, ruffling sort of day, with white clouds rolling overhead, but again he was pursing his lips over his lack of silver. Silver by the cartload round Carlisle, but here not enough for the re-veining of a small round patch of vine-leaves! Why, even Bartholomew Rhys had known better than that! Bartholomew knew where such things were, not in pennyworths at a time, not the frugal melting down of old things, but to be had by the cartload and new! Ia, ia, in a horse and cart you could carry it away! And he was idling moodily along, nodding to the sentries as they passed, when all at once he found himself at an inner embrasure, looking down at the flying-bridge he had noticed before.

It was no more than a light structure, most of it of wood, but the windows that pierced it were designed as if for stone, narrow and pointed. There were six of them on the side nearest to him, with as many on the other, so that the light came through, and along the bridgeway a figure was moving. It was the figure of a young woman, and her business had been somewhere in the outer precincts, for she was passing the first of the windows on her return, but the interval between the windows hid her again, and Willie next saw her at the second glazed piercing. If she was some serving-wench she was an extraordinarily pretty one, and a mantle hung down her back, which a servant would hardly have worn, and she was just passing out of sight again when she chanced to look up, and at the third window stopped dead.

Yet if she was more than a servant she was not dressed for the hall, but rather as if she had relaxed herself for the afternoon and put on only her second or it might be her third-best. Her twin-bunched hair was richly dark, and the meshing of green silk that contained it hardly seemed enough to hold it from tumbling down over her shoulders. At the pit of her neck a peep of under-cotte showed, and she was now at the third window. She gave a quick glance behind her and another at the window on the farther side. But there were still three more windows to pass.

It was at the fourth of them that she looked covertly up at Willie. The eyes that did so were dark and slumbrous, and about her pouting lips there hovered the faintest of smiles. And a No can sometimes be only half a No, and may even not be a No at all, but who says No before they are asked? Yet it seemed to him that she gave the minutest shake of her head, as if something could not be, alas it could not be! so the look must be a farewell too. After that, she did not turn again, but sped quickly past the remaining windows with her mantle floating behind her and was gone. He heard the approach of a sentry. No sentry must find him standing at a battlement embrasure, gazing at that glazed gallery down below.

But as he turned about again it seemed to him that the only thing he did not know of this lady, so shyly yet boldly forthcoming with her secret thoughts, was her name.

He had not long to wait before he had that also. With time on his hands, and willing to make a show of zeal before Humphrey Tull, on the following morning he sought Thomasson the second smith and asked him if there was any way in which he could give him a helping hand in the armoury. This was the turret's main lower room, only to be reached through Humphrey Tull's office, and it was something of a disillusion to Willie. Indeed the whole castle was beginning to surprise him in a number of ways. It was to have been merry with music from morning till night, but so far not a sound of minstrelsy had he heard in the palace. Now its armoury, instead of showing a pageantry of crests and inlaid burgonets, was little more than an ironmonger's shop. A few pieces of plate-armour indeed there were and a sort of rag-bag heap of discarded gusset-mail, but for the rest the irregularly-shaped chamber was timbered round with heavy shelving, binned and compartmented for humdrum pins and rivets, hooks, buckles, and the iron heads of bolts. Squares of brigandine leather were stacked on the floor, and the rest was as miscellaneous as the stores among which he had ridden in the sow. All however were tabbed and docketted and labelled, with a book lying open on a ledge to check their receipts and issues.

"Body-armour?" said Thomasson in reply to Willie's question.

"Them that wears it keeps it close to hand these days. Arrows, they're the fletcher's charge, but here's the heads for them and the blades for the bills, and in checking them in and out see you get them right unless you want Humphrey jumping down your throat," and he was thus putting Willie into the way of things when there burst in on them young Ferdinand, his face alight and two silver pennies in his hand.

"See!" he cried, "I've found the way! The Sieur Gaston was there, and he laughed and clapped me on the back, and *he* said that was the way!"

"The way to do what?" Willie asked, looking at the two silver pennies.

"To bring women to their senses! At first she said no, but I took a high hand with her, and asked her if she wanted a whipping, and you should have seen the Sieur Gaston laugh!"

"Do you mean your lady?" Willie asked, while a queer little turmoil went on in his head. It was about that scrap of a headshake and that mouth-shaped No. "*No silver*," was what it had meant, but the boy was crowing jubilantly on.

"And the marshal's got a lance shortened for me, and I'm to tilt at a dummy-man first, and now where's that headpiece? Do you have to melt the silver first? You said you were only waiting for the silver, and it's here, and why are they always setting us to make poetry for them when all they want's a bit of bullying? Where is it?"

"It's up in my chamber."

"Then come and get it," and with the silver pennies in one hand he shook Willie with the other as if he would have given him a beating too.

But up in Willie's chamber was something besides the casque. The boy had evidently sought him there first before descending to the armoury, for he had left it on Willie's bench, a silver-gilt sweetmeat-box, on six small toed feet, lined inside with some fine wood; but its lid lay detached at its side. Willie picked it up to examine it.

"Who left this?"

"You're to do it when you've finished the headpiece. It's what she keeps her essences in, but she's broke the hinge and wants it mended. What do you do with the silver when you've melted it?"

"Draw it . . . or a bit of cold hammering might do," Willie told him.

"Then be setting about it, and I want to see you do it, for there's too many in this castle only work when somebody's eyes are on them. . . ."

But instead of stirring himself Willie picked up the box and smelt its fine wood lining. It smelt fragrantly, and then he turned to its lid. It had two minute hinges, and the slender pin of one of them was missing. But the pin of the other was in its place, and the lid had very much the look of having been wrenched off, as he himself had once wrenched off the outer cover of a golden locket. Then he looked at the boy.

"Tell me something, young sir. When jewels and suchlike come out of their setting, or any little job like that, what do they do about it in this castle?"

"They send them along to the treasurer."

"And what does he do?"

"I don't know. I'm sick of women and their flimflams."

"But by and by they come back mended?"

"For all I know they do. Get you moving. You said you were only waiting for the silver and here it is."

But now Willie Middlemiss's thoughts were miles and leagues away. That No? It plainly did *not* mean the silver, for there the silver was. Again he saw that figure, pausing in its walk along the glazed gallery to look up. A carelessly clapped-on hairnet to hold that prune-dark hair in its place, a peep of cotte at her neck and the headshake that said No but the drowsy eyes that said Yes—and at that his thoughts ranged more widely still. One day during his winter's purgatory at Valle Crucis, Matthias had come to him as he had hammered at something in an outhouse far beyond the cloisters, for when hammering had to be done it was done as distantly as possible. Matthias wanted him to come to the scriptorium, for he had something to show him, and to the scriptorium they had gone. It was an illuminated border, of branches and birds and stiff little figures, at a first glance exactly like fifty other such borders. But Matthias would not have fetched him merely for that, and he looked at it again, and it was the second look that did it. With their bills parted the tiny birds were singing their little hearts out, the small animals were intent on their private affairs. Shyly peeping among their branches the decorous little people smiled and smirked and lifted their mischievous eyes, but their lips said "Hush," for it was a secret and nobody was supposed to know they were all the time gently breathing and as full of life and wicksomeness as they could be. Just little people at play in their vermilion and lapis lazuli against their sheen of burnished gold, but even Matthias had seen the joke and fetched Willie all the way from the outhouse that he might see it too.

And Willie, picking up the vine-leaf casque and the silver pennies in one hand, picked up the perfume-box with the other, and snuffed in its fragrance again, and his teeth too peeped mischievously out as he smiled.

3

ALWAYS THERE IS SOME LITTLE THING WE FORGET. TWO DAYS LATER Willie Middlemiss heard Humphrey Tull's foot on his stone stairs, and there on the bench before him the comfit-box from the hinge of which he had been tapping the pin stood in full view. Luckily the casque stood by its side, and hurriedly Willie covered up the box with Ferdinand's headpiece. At the same moment he contrived to interpose his body too, and there before him Humphrey stood. It was the casque he had come to see, and to the end of his days Willie could not have told by what sleight he managed to drop his leather cap over the box as he picked up the headpiece.

"So," the armourer said, turning it this way and that in his hands. "How did you come by the silver?"

"I cannot tell you where it came from, Master Tull. The young master brought it to me."

"Then the rest's a blind-man's guess. Is it what you call finished now?"

"All but. Another rub over and a bit of buffing and I think it will pass," and setting the casque down again the armourer stood looking at Willie with an old-fashioned sort of look.

"Young man, you didn't by any chance have your fortune told before you came to Gwlad, did you?" and Willie laughed.

"Not before I came, Master Tull, but I'd scarce smelt the place when there was an old body at my elbow, swinging her club-foot and trying to sell me the skies for a groat."

"Then never say she hasn't been a good mother to you, for there must be something in this trade of yours after all. It seems you're to see the treasurer."

Willie's step back almost swept both cap and comfit-box from the table. . . . "I'm to see . . .! Which is he, sir?"

"Sir William? To be sure, you wouldn't know, as it's little we see of him in the hall these days. He's plagued with a rheumatism and can't get about on his feet the way he used to. But see you walk your shoes straight when he's anywhere about. Maybe he can't see through walls, but for anything in this castle that's on his charge, I warrant he knows where it is any moment of the day or night."

Willie had recovered his breath again. . . . "When am I to see him and where's he to be found, sir?"

"The message is he'll see you this afternoon, and you needn't go ten times round the castle asking for him. You go through the armoury and up the stairs, and along a gallery you'll find, and then it's to the right, and then to the left and down a floor again, but over the gallery you'd better ask somebody," and the armourer turned his broad back and, by the grace of God, left without a suspicion of what the leather cap hid on the bench.

No sooner had he gone than Willie had the casket in his hands again and was hiding it behind his bed. It was eleven o'clock in the morning and Humphrey had added over his shoulder that he was to see the treasurer at two. That gave him three hours for his toilet, and first of all to get his hair cut. The treasurer himself, by God! What a world in little this castle was, and how with one's wits about one it was possible to climb in it! From the scullion's trestle to the foot of the board and on the way to the Great Salt itself . . . snatched from Humphrey Tull's service the very moment the rumour of his gifts got about . . . vine-leaved helms and filigree boxes on which to show the world what he could do . . . in those three hours his fancies had taken three thousand shapes. In the great hall he could hardly eat his meat that day. Sir William did not sit at the board, but Sir William had the ear of my lord himself, lord of a dozen castles, lord of the broad southern valley, lord of the mountain gates and the lands beyond, lord of the kites and eagles above them and the treasures in their bowels beneath. . . .

A quarter to two found Willie Middlemiss passing through the armoury. At its farther end was a second door, inside which narrow stairs rose, which he mounted. A door at the top opened into some kind of a small warehouse or store, down the middle of which ran an unusually large and long table. Snippets of cloth strewed its floor and it smelt of stuffs and fabrics, for it seemed to be some sort of a tailoring-shop, many flat packages wrapped in linen stacked its tiers of shelves, and on the long table lay a large pair of shears. But Willie, hurrying through, stopped abruptly as he opened its farther door. He stood in the glazed gallery itself, with the pointed windows to right and left of him and the well between the walls below. Instinctively his eyes turned to the right. There, a storey nearer the sky now, was the embrasure at which he had lingered, and he tried to picture himself there, looking down at the lady who had stood where he stood now. But he remembered the time. At the end of the bridge the door stood open, and he was to turn to the right, then to the left, and then ask.

But there was nobody to ask. The corridor ran only a little way, then there came a branching off, where the thick masonry of the walls showed, and he was leaving the light behind him and had the feeling that at any moment he might be touched by some unseen person on the shoulder and asked who he was and what was his business there. But he had been told to descend, and before him was a narrow and doorless stairhead, down which he began to feel his way. He was standing there at the bottom, in complete darkness, and on the point of turning back again, when the very thing he had been thinking of suddenly happened. Out of the gloom a voice said, "This way, sir." The darkness broke as before him an opening appeared and closed again behind him, and he stood in a room full of a dim multi-mingling of coloured light. It came from a painted window, mildly effulgent with crimsons and blues and ambers, and under the window stood a couch. Except for the great hall and the barrack-room such of the castle's apartments as he had yet seen were smallish in size, nor was this apartment very much bigger. Its walls were hung with arras, against which stood a couple of inlaid chairs on curule legs, a strong coffer, a trophy of arms and little else. A sharp shuffling turn was heard as a sentry turned in his pacing outside, and on the couch under the window a man reclined.

He was wrapped in a long gown of cloth-of-gold, and against a low table to his hand leaned an ebony stick. He was of a fleshy build, with puffy cheeks that sagged like a pelican's pouch, and the armourer had told Willie that this invalid knew where every piece in the castle was at any moment of the day or night, and he was intimidated already, the more so when from his small mouth came the most mellifluous trickle of a voice Willie had ever heard.

"You are from the armourer?" said the man in the cloth-of-gold, and Willie bowed low, wondering whether his low "Yes, sir," should have been some address more august.

"Stand where I can see you," and Willie moved in obedience to a plump white hand. "Your name?"

"Middlemiss, sir."

"You are a fine metalsmith?"

"Yes, sir," and thereupon the inquisition began.

But it was a putting to the question such as never in his life had Willie had to stand up to before. Humphrey Tull had received him gruffly. Humphrey's voice was abrupt and rasping, and though he had asked him the questions that masters usually ask those who offer themselves for work, Willie had been prepared for just such questions and the armourer had not been difficult to satisfy. But neither Humphrey Tull nor anybody else had told Willie that he was now to stand before the man who in his time has been Master of his London Guild, and thereafter had been appointed to watch the ports for foreign counterfeit, and that among English gibbets he neither picked nor chose, but before all other French ones he preferred Montfaucon, where they could dangle thirty at a time. The soft voice issuing from the expressionless mouth seemed to creep under his very skin as he realized that this flabby man in the cloth-of-gold knew more about his craft than Willie himself.

"Who was your master in York?"

"Master Habbord, sir, close by Monk Bar."

"What is his mark?"

"Two Henricus H's turned back to back, sir."

"That is a maker's mark. How comes it that those in York, though they have a touch-mark of their own, make no use of it, but accept the London assay?" and at a question so deep Willie began to fidget.

"I am but a craftsman, sir. Such matters do not concern me," he stammered.

"Do you know anything of the practice of Newcastle or Lincoln or Durham?"

"It is all out of my depth, sir."

"Then I will ask you something simpler. Are you able to silver a copper spoon?" but that instead of being simpler was more searching still, and Willie, seeing the trap, answered virtuously:

"No, sir. The law is express against it."

"Do you work both in gold and silver?" but again Willie was aware of the snare, for if artificers must not gild or silver any inferior metal, neither of gold or silver might they work in both.

"Prentices aren't trusted with either of them till they've learned the use of their tools, sir, and this is but my journey-year," he answered, and the fleshy man nodded.

"It is not an answer, but we will pass it. Then you know nothing of assay or the purity of gold, but receive it with its London mark, and work in it as it is warranted to you?"

"Nay, sir, not quite that, for we prentices must obey our masters, but there are tricks in every trade, things we must know even if we do not practise them," and again the treasurer nodded.

"Tell me how you would set about to check the purity of a sample of gold."

"To eight grains of it, sir, you add thrice its weight in silver and lap it up in its due proportion of lead. Then you heat it to a red-heat in a cupel . . ." and he described the process.

"And what do you do with the little button that's left at the bottom?"

"It is called the comet, sir, and you take your acids and heat them, and dissolve the silver out, and then you weigh it, and after that . . ."

"Enough. You evidently know or have heard of it, and a little curiosity not strictly within our business is sometimes commendable. When were you last in those northern parts?"

"Last summer, sir."

"And what brought you to Gwlad as an armourer?"

"I knew none but Master Tull, sir, and I hoped he might have employment for me."

"You presented yourself and he found you in work?"

"A chance job, that is now finished, sir, but I cannot think that in a great household like this, with tinkers to mend the kettles and cobblers the shoes, never a jewel comes out of its clawing or the stem of a cup is not sometimes to straighten," and at that the gentle dribble of a voice was silent for so long that again Willie heard the step of the sentry outside the coloured window, pacing his thirty yards and turning and pacing again. Then he heard the treasurer's heavy sigh.

"Those were the happy days. It is not so now. It is not making but melting, beating down and rendering, and it goes to my heart to see the cunning and skill that has to be thrown into the crucibles like bones into a pot. I will not say that once in a while there are not such odd things as you spoke of to do, for there are always those whims must be humoured, but the crucible and the bellows and the hearth . . . they eat all . . . they eat all. . . ."

And hearing this dismal account of things, Willie's heart sank. That dim coloured chamber was the apartment of a man of knowledge and taste. His curule chair was inlaid with ivory, his stick was of ebony, he dressed in cloth-of-gold, and gold too was the locket that burned a hole in Willie's belt. Delicately he had furbished it up that very morning, considering what light he should display it in, yet now he was not even asked for it and unasked dared not produce it. His casque was finished, now for further employment he had no more than a hinge to fit with a pin, and if he wished to remain in Gwlad he had best go to the marshal and enrol himself with the men-at-arms. And he was about to cast himself on the treasurer's mercy, to tell him he would hammer or melt or aught else he liked so it but kept him in touch with his trade, when again he felt himself touched on the shoulder from behind. The door in the wall had opened again and the treasurer had turned his face away as if to compose himself for sleep. Dejectedly he bowed low, and did not even see the servant who touched him. The wall closed behind him, he stood in the darkness of the passage once more, and his feet were being directed to the lowermost of the ascending stairs.

So back empty-handed again where he had come from. Issuing at the top of the stairs again he saw nobody in the upper corridor. Its daylight seemed suddenly bleak after the multi-hued twilight he had left, and he reached the turn to the flying bridge. Slowly, he made his way past its double row of windows to the drapery-closet.

But pushing at its door he stopped abruptly. Standing at the large table that filled the middle of the room, with her back turned towards him, was a young woman. Above her twin hair-nets a soft roll of plum-coloured velvet cushioned her brow, and her mantle was thrown back so that her arms, closely sleeved in velvet of the same colour, might be free for her occupation. This was the patting and smoothing out of various irregularly-shaped breadths of cloth, apparently some garment she had picked to pieces, and these she was spacing out over the new material beneath, contriving and fitting. She did not hear Willie, but as she reached far forward over the cutting-table the plum-coloured robe was raised by the leg she extended behind her for balance, and then recovering her former position again she stood considering her work. She was the lady of the gallery. The lady who stopped in her walk between the windows, and raised her eyes, and shook her head in a minute No before she was asked.

"*Oh!*"

A piece of chalk she had been holding in her hand dropped from it. With a shake the mantle was back on her shoulders again, and a pair of startled prune-dark eyes, dark as the netted hair above, was fixed on Willie's as she caught her breath.

"Who . . . what are you doing here?"

Willie had not advanced beyond the doorway.

"Passing through, madam, if I may."

"This is the women's closet."

"I was directed this way, madam."

"It is the solar way. Where have you come from?"

"I am on my way back from seeing the treasurer, madam," and suddenly the dark eyes seemed to fill with enlightenment.

"Ah! Are you he who wanted silver for my husband's helm?"

"Yes, madam."

"Will it soon be ready? Is my life to be made a plague much longer because of this toy of a helm?"

"It is ready for the fetching, madam," and the lady looked at him again and seemed sorry she had shown irritation.

"And then perhaps you will have a moment to cast away on my poor patient little box?" and to that Willie, still standing in the doorway, did not reply in words.

For if he was the judge he considered himself to be of such things words counted for least of all. Hair dark as the blots on a pansy, eyes like night in the afternoon, that small round neck with the pulse in it, and her whole body one warm stream of life as she had balanced herself over the table—these and not words were her portion in life. Her voice too had a sort of pigeon-note, and her puny husband had threatened to beat her, and the French Knight had laughed, and what more would you? Now she had picked up the piece of chalk again. She was dimpling it into her cheek, and the linen-wrapped packets on the shelves were a soft willowy-grey for her to set herself off against, and she had neither sent him away nor given him leave to pass through, but was shifting the unpicked sleeve to another position on the cutting-table and then moving it back again, almost (but not quite) as if he had not been there.

"It's well this wasn't in the morning," she said softly at last.

"What wasn't in the morning, madam?"

"Why, you being here. In the mornings they all come, besides the pages in and out all the time."

"Don't they in the afternoons?" and again he heard the pigeon-laugh.

"Ask my lady what they do in the afternoons, for you can hear her snoring half the passage away! It is the siesta. They put a guard before the solar fire and turn the children in there, and the rest do as they please."

"And so you busy yourself here, madam?"

"Sometimes," and again he found himself at a loss for something to say. For that 'sometimes' seemed to mean that other times might be more tiresome. Her husband might come to her and tell her he would beat her unless she provided him with two silver pennies. Sometimes too the boy-husband came away in tears, weeping that his lady had mocked him, and storming that he would not be mocked now that he was grown-up and a man. Then perhaps the afternoons would become heavy with sighs for her too, and angers and sighs again, and the door still stood open behind Willie, but suddenly he closed it and took a step into the closet.

"Have I your leave to go through?"

"Where does the other door lead to?"

"Downstairs to the armoury and the back-court, madam," and it seemed to him that the dark eyes were lifted a little less boldly now.

"And what of my casket?"

"If you are in a push for it, it will not take long."

"It will be to send back by the same hands, and I have a silver girdle-chain too that has lost three links and I cannot be troubling Sir William with every little thing. But now you must go, for they will be waking, and if the French gentleman gets to hear of this there will be more of those smiles of his that are like tickling your back," and her nape showed as her panniered hair dipped over her pattern.

And what was there amiss with Willie himself for a brisk and serviceable young man? He had barbered himself for his visit to the treasurer as he had never been barbered before, his hands he had specially tended, for he had been ready to show his golden locket and in taking the locket the treasurer might have had a glance for the hands too. They were not the hands of a man-at-arms; this No-lady who paused at windows had Sir William's ear; and the treasurer himself had said that though all was melting nowadays there were still those in this castle who had to be humoured in their whims and caprices. Respectfully he drew a little nearer to the table.

"Your coffer, madam, shall I press on with it?"

"Oh, they will be waking! Yes . . . no . . . to-morrow will do or the next day. Have it ready for him when next he comes."

"You said something about a girdle-chain, madam."

"I stuffed it away in a coffer and it will be to seek. Can you come to this closet whenever you like?"

"Nobody would stop me, madam, but it might be remarked on," and she stood irresolute, looking round the closet, and then suddenly pointed.

"Do you see that package at the end of the top shelf? I could leave the chain there for you and you could put it back in the same place. Listen . . . no, 'tis nothing, but go now. To-morrow I will bring it."

"Madam . . ."

"Oh, one of them might come in at any moment . . . you should not have shut the door. . . ."

"First, my knee. . . ."

The hand she put out, looking bashfully the other way, had the same perfume as the wood-lined box. Dropping to his knee he kissed it, rose again and backed bowing away. But by the time she had raised the night-dark eyes again the door that led to the armoury was closing behind him.

4

GWLAD CASTLE WAS OF NO GREAT AGE, ONLY FROM A LITTLE BEFORE Owain's time, but its stones had not been to fetch from a distance. They had been quarried on the spot, and there the quarry was, the cliff of its excavation already romantically grown over and weathered, mossed and ivied, with wallflower in its crannies and gorse to crest its skyline like a battered crown. Immediately beneath it the lists were dressed, and at other times the levelled space served as an exercise-ground for the youths and a parade for the men-at-arms.

Now, at various hours of the day there was to be seen wandering about it a certain Wilson Middlemiss, who had come to Gwlad at his own invitation, and was finding it a totally different place from the castle of his dreams. There each man had fitted hand-and-glove into his place; here all was misfit and mis-appointment. As renowned an armourer as England had to show spent his days counting rivets and checking lists of men. A treasurer, instead of amassing riches for his master, ransacked the place for stuff to melt down. A subtle workman like himself was given a bit of patching and matching to do, then the hinge of a box to tinker, after which he might enlist for a man-at-arms and whistle for his wages with the rest.

Yet, dig into those hills and there were riches waiting for them ten thousand times more precious than building-stone. Why scrape and melt and pawn and redeem and pawn again when Augsburgs and Nurembergs of gold lay not a day's journey away, gold for wages, gold for goldsmiths to work in, gold for my lord, gold for my lady, gold for what you would? Now the thoughts dogged him wherever he went, and with it another thought, though one almost too temerarious to entertain. Did he stray to the stagnant moat-end, as near to the solar window as he dared venture? It was speckled with the rising duckweed, and its green put him in mind of a green hair-net, that seemed too filigree to bind its baskets of ripeness together. Moored to a ring was a waterlogged boat that the ditchers used when the moat had to be cleaned. That meant that later there would be lilies, and lily-white her nape had been as she had reached out over the cutting-table with her outstretched leg to balance her. Did he idle to the gatehouse or smithy, just to drag himself away from these thoughts and have somebody to talk to? Smiths and sentries were no more his proper company than the ostlers and victuallers had been. His daily neighbour at table was now a man called Potts, one of the seneschal's factotums, and from Potts he was beginning to learn a good deal of what went on above the Salt. He knew many of their names and faces, these Sir Richards and Sir Etiennes and Sir Hughs and Sir Guys, where they had fought, what castles in France had surrendered to them and what places they had governed. The French knight, the one always in the same suit of dark-blue velvet, who moved like a cat and wore the little sportive beard, had been in Italy and called the glazed gallery the Bridge of Sighs. By that he meant love-sighs, and to sigh in the right poetical way made just the difference between the knee-bending of the courtly and the grubbling courtship of the boor. As far as Willie could make out it was the fashion to be stretched on a rack of love one minute and to forget all about it the next. But it was an aptitude that had to be learned early or not at all, and Willie was little likely to acquire it now.

About the ladies however he had not dared to question Potts. The little he knew of her was that her name was Joslin, that actually her origin was no more distinguished than his own, but what of that when she had that bursting purse of her father's behind her? She might have the whims and fancies, but it was the mercer who would pay for them, and so (Potts more than hinted) the French knight saw his way to his ransom. But Willie was beginning to flush and mutter whenever he thought of the French knight. She herself had told him that sometimes his gallantries were like somebody tickling her back, and now that struck Willie as his foreign impudence and an affront. It might be her husband's back to whip, but it was not his to tickle, and who but a Frenchman would suppose she was married and a vestal too?

And when was she going to leave that broken girdle-chain behind the package on the shelf of the clothing-closet, so that again he might be touching something that was hers?

It was May, the days long, the nights short. Willie, lying awake in his turret and fretting that he was the only one in that castle who had no settled place in it, might be awakened as early as four or five o'clock by the lively noises outside, the smiths beginning their day or the trumpet for the men-at-arms to parade. And one morning, hearing the bustle he rose and went down to wash himself at the smiths' pump. But that morning the sounds he had heard were those of the youths assembling for the daily exercises, and making his way towards the quarry he could see them under the cliff, lightly clad, chafing their bare limbs, with doublets and towels cast loosely about their shoulders scuffling and leap-frogging about. Already a posse of the taller lads were half the length of the castle away, loosening themselves up in a run, and thirty yards beyond the quarry opening was their apparatus too, the staves and bucklers on the ground and the great ballista by its pile of stones. This was for the exercising of the younger lads, for they too must learn to heave on the windlass and set the stone in the socket of the great flinging-arm, and as Willie came up he heard young Ferdinand's querulous voice. He didn't want to heave on a windlass. He wanted to be in his vine-leaf headpiece calling, "A Covil, a Covil!" but it was the marshal's orders that he must first put muscle on his bones, and nobody paid any attention to him.

The senior squire in charge of the engine was a blonde ox of a lad of sixteen, a giant in the making, who nevertheless was himself under the instruction of two brawny engineers, with no shirts under their jerkins and their arms bared and knotty and brown. The engine's arm was wound back at its tautest and lacked only its missile of stone, and the blond youth was on the point of taking charge when his instructor stayed him with his hand.

"Nay, Master Hal, a thought less haste. You are about to fling a heavy stone. At what are you hurling it?"

"Straight past the quarry face," said the young bullock, but the engineer pointed. Thirty yards away, as if the path of the missile mattered nothing as long as they kept well removed from the engine itself, two watching figures stood. Like grey sweet-peas on one stem they looked with their fluttering lawns passed over their head-rolls and tied in an apex under their chins, and again the instructor's voice was heard.

"Friend or foe, always see first to your field of fire. A pretty breach you would make laying two ladies flat before they have had their breakfasts!" and the youth called Hal was opening his mouth to shout when Willie saved him the trouble.

"I'm returning that way. Where would you have them?"

"Fifteen yards back, nearer the quarry."

"Then stay your engine a minute," and Willie was off, motioning the two watchers back yards before he came up with them.

And what more natural than that Joslin Covil should have risen from her bed betimes to see her husband's prowess on the exercise-field? But the younger sweet-pea was one Willie had not seen before, and she was round-faced and moist-mouthed and pink and timorous, and scarce had they taken up their new stations when there hurtled through the air a hundredweight of rock, that struck the ground with a dusty thud and rolled past. A faint "Mercy on us!" broke from the younger of the two and she began to gather her mantle about her for flight.

"The children will be waking. . . ."

"Tush, my lady will sleep for another hour yet. . . ."

"She daren't use you as she uses me. . . ."

"But don't you want to see your Hal at his engine?"

"They will be waking, and she will call for me and I shan't be there . . . you have a husband here and I haven't. . . ."

"You have your Hal . . . Bessie! Nay, stop . . . wait . . . Bessie!"

But already the other was off and away, like a rabbit at the clapping of a pair of hands.

And thrice in two days Willie Middlemiss had been up to the drapery-closet to look for a chain girdle that had lost three of its links, but he had found nothing, and with Humphrey Tull to pass each time he must be wary about such visits, and already he had done far more thinking than he was accustomed to, and to what had it brought him? Out to the exercise-ground at six o'clock in the morning, where he had as a good a right to be as another, but not in the company of a lady whose place at the board was the high dais itself. And he had only come to warn her she was standing in danger, and now the danger was past. At the morning exercises too you had to be constantly changing your place, for there were more squads than one, running their distances and shifting their ground, so that a spot that was empty one minute might be the busiest of all the next. But Mistress Joslin seemed to know all this too, and he was looking at the fluttering triangle of her head as she moved towards the quarry gap. At its entrance was a great bush of broom with arrowy young bracken standing up knee-deep about it, and the rock-face beyond was tufted with yellow wallflowers that scented the air like wine. Half-way up a cliff a couple of sheep stood motionless on a ledge, apparently unable to get either up or down, and at the catapult a dozen of the taller youths had picked up helves and bucklers and were running in a body towards them. Best out of the way. He too had slipped round by the broom-bush, and it might be that they must now remain where they were till the exercises were over.

She was wearing the same plum-coloured gown she had worn in the gallery, and she had gathered it about her against the heavy dew that drenched the bracken. But the bright little showers spilled again from its folds leaving them as dry as a nasturtium leaf, and where the slope stopped at the rock-face was a narrow ledge, just wide enough to rest against. She had reached this before she turned her face again, and then he saw that it was in a pet of vexation.

"Letting me arrange everything for her and then running away like that!" she pouted, and Willie, standing before her in his leather, could think of nothing to say except that he hadn't seen the other one before.

"She looks after the children, and everything she does she's frightened of it the minute she's done it, and now it's that glove, and oh, how sick I am of this everlasting castle!"

"What glove, and who is she?" Willie asked.

"She's Bessie Wickes, Sir Walter the cupbearer's her father, and she gave him the glove, and now he says he's going to wear it at the tilting, and if she didn't want it to be seen why did she give it to him?" and she snapped off the delicate brown caterpillar of a fern-tip and began to tease it to bits between her fingers, not looking at him, so that suddenly he was wondering what in such an emergency the French Sieur would have said. Something sprightly no doubt, but not so Willie, who might have no manners of his own to boast of but was not going to ape those of any French Sieur.

"You never left the chain where you said you would," and at that she snapped at him too.

"I know I didn't, and now he's got his silver for the vine-leaves he's forgotten all about the box and I suppose I shall get it sometime."

"Shall I put it back in the closet, behind the bale?" but she only went on picking at the fern.

"And what about my lady? This castle's dull enough without being locked in my chamber and being put on bread-and-water for a week!"

"But . . . but . . ." He had understood that the ladies at least were free of the drapery-closet whenever they wished to go there, but she threw the frond-tip angrily away.

"I know, but it isn't just that . . . it's everything, and when I do try to amuse myself in my own way it's sure to be wrong, and I wish I was back with my father in Cheap and my little room all to myself, and the barge on the river on Sundays and the other girls to talk to and I'd never seen any of them or their mouldy castles!" and to Willie's dismay she fumbled under her mantle and brought out a little handkerchief, and first blew her nose loudly and then dabbed her eyes.

So here was a pretty way to be starting the day. First this unhoped-for encounter, and now sniffs and sobs and tears! When Mistress Joslin sobbed moreover she made no pretence of keeping it back because people saw her, but let it go, and the words too came in a flood as she blew and dabbed and gulped.

"And Bessie's always saying they don't use me as they use her, but they use me a hundred times worse! All of them! Gaston knows better than to say those things to the Lady Estelle! If *she* says something about the King he doesn't say to *her*, 'Do you mean the Prince of Wales's father?' as he does to me, and I'm going to tell him so! Nothing's too good for *her*, because she comes from His Grace, and I can't be expected to talk French the way she does, because I'm not French and don't want to be, and the others are just a lot of English cats for all their 'dear Joslins.' My lord doesn't know half that goes on behind his back, and my lady'll go down on her knees before she gets my sweetmeat-box, and I wish I was back in London again. . . ."

And seeing them like that Willie had always judged it best to let them get it over and then slip in a soothing word about something else. The thwacking and cudgelling beyond the cliff had shifted away, but now the ballista was at it again, and he could hear the muffled clack-clack of the windlass, the commands of young Hal in charge, the thud of the arm as it fetched up against the great pad of its cushion, the crash and rolling past of the stone. Evidently young Hal had his troubles too. A girl had given him a glove and said he was not to wear it, but Hal just told her bluntly he was going to wear it, and by the time they had turned their handkerchiefs into unsightly little crumples they usually stopped. She was better already, and had put the handker-chief away again, and it was time he spoke, but she was the first to do so.

"I'm . . . I'm sorry," she said contritely. "I don't know what brought it all up just then. Perhaps it was because I didn't sleep very well."

"How came that about?" and as she re-set her disarranged head-cage straight again he saw a little twitching at the corner of her mouth.

"You'd never guess. I . . . I had a flea in my bed."

And just when their little tempests are blowing over is not the time to be thinking of *morgrygyn*, and perhaps she didn't mean that kind of a flea at all, but he left these things for Frenchmen to say, and he was on the point of asking her what about that girdle-chain when her very next question struck him suddenly open-mouthed.

"There, I'm sorry, and now let's talk about something else. You haven't told me yet what Sir William said."

He drew in his breath. Sir William! True she had asked him what he was doing there in the drapery-closet, and he had said something about having been to see the treasurer, but for what Sir William had said . . .

"Sir William! Who the devil . . . I mean, who told you about Sir William?"

"Didn't he send for you again? He said he would," and he stared.

"Who did he say that to?"

"To me of course."

"When?" he rapped out, and now there was no guile whatever in the large eyes she lifted.

"Why, that day he came into the solar, saying he wanted more gold, and he couldn't pay us for it just then but he'd keep a faithful account of it, and I asked him if that was why he'd stopped mending our trinkets, because he wanted the gold himself. And my lady checked me for being forward, but I didn't care, and I said what was the good of having a goldsmith in the castle if he wasn't given something to do...."

And suddenly Willie could have fallen on his knees before her, and covered that velvet gown with kisses that would have rolled off it again like the dewdrops, but he was far too stupefied to do anything of the kind.

"And then he said he would see me?" he gasped at last.

"Yes, and I knew you went, because you were seen in our corridor coming away, and you haven't told me yet what happened," and at that Willie's face clouded over.

"No. There's nothing to tell, because nothing happened."

"But you didn't go and just look at one another and neither of you say anything!"

"I mean it ended in nothing. He asked me a lot of questions, but he hadn't any work for me, and he didn't even ask to be shown what I could do."

"I did the best I could, and all I got for it was a scolding from my lady," Mistress Joslin sighed, and there was a silence.

So a word in your ear, young Willie-my-lad, for never in that castle will you have such an opportunity again. Whether you have noticed it or not, you are not calling her 'Madam' any longer, and she cannot say the first motion was not hers. She is not repulsive, perched on her bit of a shelf, with the wedge of her head-covering like a lavender butterfly against the rock and the scented wallflower ten feet above her, and only the two of you there, for the two sheep so stationary on their cliff disappeared long ago. It is there in your belt, the locket that the treasurer didn't ask to see, and she may hate this castle, but none the less she seems to be a somebody in it, or the French knight would not be dangling at her skirts nor Sir William himself wheedling her for scraps of gold. Strike then while the iron is hot. If nothing comes of it you are no worse off, but if all goes well . . . please yourself, young Willie-my-lad, but don't say afterwards that you never had your chance. . . .

And as suddenly as if it had spirited itself there, it was out of his belt-pouch and in his hand. The next moment it had passed to hers, and he could not see her eyes, for they were veiled by her lashes as she sat there looking at it, and she did not look up but just went on gazing.

"Who is it?" she asked at last.

"It's just a head," he mumbled. "I show it when they ask me what I can do. But he didn't even ask."

"Is it somebody you know?"

"I'm telling you. It's just a head on a bit of gold."

"How did it get broken?"

"A man told me a sort of trade-secret one day, so I gave him the other bit," and she looked sideways up at him.

"I knew," she said softly, "I knew in a moment that afternoon in the closet, and I said to myself, 'He has a lady of his own!' and I'm never wrong about those things! Oh, do tell me who she is, your pretty mistress! Has she sent you away on some service, like Hal wearing Bessie's glove?"

"No," said Willie, suddenly short, and she looked at the locket again and sighed.

"If my father hadn't been rich I should have been washing dishes in Gwlad, and if I'd only *one* friend of my own I could tell everything to, and what's the good of being married when sometimes you cry half the night for loneliness? Will she be coming here?" and he answered doggedly:

"I tell you it's but a sample I show. I showed it at Valle Crucis, and it kept me through the winter."

"But what do you want me to do with it? Take it to Sir William for you?"

Heavens, if only she would, was his first thought, but fool that he was, here she was, unasked and actually offering it! Suddenly he felt himself abashed to think how he had misjudged her. The handkerchief-dropping sort as he had at first supposed? When she could get away from them all she used her poor wisp of a handkerchief to blubber and cry into. She had only to think of other and happier girls and her very voice altered, and the exercises must be over, for no more sounds of thwacking reached them, and it was a hazardous thing that she should be seen with him on the exercise-ground at all. And if she was spied on every time she crossed the windowed Bridge of Sighs there was no saying when he would see her again, and she was still waiting to hear what she was to do about his locket.

"Madam . . ." he began so humbly that he hardly knew himself, but she shook her head.

"Talk as you were talking, and Ferdinand only calls you the armourer's man, so tell me your name."

"It is Willie, and if only in your goodness you would see the treasurer again . . ."

"And show him this? But how if he asks me how *I* came by it?" and he hadn't thought of that, and stood tapping his teeth.

"I only know that I should be your servant for ever. . . ."

"Besides, if he does send for you . . . stay, I must think," and she sat there considering it. "It's the women who make me the talk of the castle, but when they go hunting sometimes we ride a little of the way with them."

"I have no horse."

"They follow the hare on foot."

"I am not even a squire. They would ask who I was."

"But there must be ways. Hal finds ways. He has to, because he mightn't be seeing his Bessie much longer."

"But what has Hal . . .?" he was beginning, when suddenly he broke off. She had jumped from her ledge, for she too had noticed that no more sounds came from the exercise-ground, and already she was in trepidation again.

"Jesu, how quiet it is! Have they gone? If they have they will all be having their breakfasts, and there will be such a coil as never was. . . ."

"Wait, I will see," and he dashed down the slope. It was true, and he returned, and they stood looking at one another. Then she spoke hurriedly, but the locket was still in her hand.

"Lord, the trouble now! And what's to be done about this?"

He too looked at it. He had crammed the same bit of gold into Atty Cockin's hand and within an hour he had had it back again. He had shown it to Bartholomew Rhys, who had gaped at it like a fish, and to Humphrey Tull, who had called it a whimwham. But when he had shown it to Matthias, he in his turn had shown it to them at Valle Crucis, and without speaking he looked at her face's oval in its bird-trap of a veil. "Let me get away first and don't follow me for five minutes," she was saying quickly, and down on both knees he dropped, burying his face in her velvet and kissing its folds again and again. And suddenly the velvet was not there. She was speeding down the slope, the butterfly of her head disappearing round the quarry gap.

And she had asked for five minutes in which to get back to the castle first.

5

POTTS, THE SENESCHAL'S FACTOTUM AND HIS COMPANION AT TABLE, had more likely than not incurred somebody's displeasure, for otherwise he would hardly have been set down so many places at the board that only Willie himself sat lower, and more than once Willie had wondered whether his offence had been talking too much. Now he was on his best behaviour, and when Willie asked him a question that day he glanced first up the board to where Robert Burnage the grizzled seneschal sat, and then answered, hardly moving his mouth.

"Hal Sibbald? There he is, waiting on Sir Mordaunt . . . nay, I'm telling you wrong," for that had been precisely Willie's question, how it was that the blond youth who had been in charge of the ballista was not at his usual station that day. "He'll be seeing to Sir Mordaunt's mastiffs belike. They're hunting to-morrow."

"Where?" Willie asked, his eyes too searching the table, for he saw nothing of Mistress Joslin either.

"They meet at Dame Kate's, at seven o'clock."

"Dame Kate's? Where's that? Do you mean that tumbledown place with the ivy?" Willie hadn't known it by that name, the five-square fallen-in ruin a bowshot beyond the gatehouse, out on the waste where the hens scratched and the cattle strayed.

"It's tumbledown now, but it hasn't always been. Before the new wing and the solar were built all that used to be a separate estate, and those old cowsheds were its stables and granary. It was a dower-house, but they took half its stones away and then made it into a kennels."

"Are the ladies hunting too to-morrow?"

"No, that is to say, we've no orders about horses for them, but it's likely they'll be there to see them off."

"Before I came to Gwlad I thought castles were all hunting and junketting of one sort and another."

"It might have been so once upon a time, but we have to work for our livings now. I remember this hall . . ." and the fallen servant glanced furtively round and dropped his voice, and now all Willie had to do was to listen.

But instead of listening he was wondering why Mistress Joslin was not in her place that day, and whether she had been chidden for being late for breakfast and shut up in her room and put on bread-and-water for a punishment. Poor, bruised, soft-hearted . . . nay, what was he saying? . . . poor lady, as out of her proper place in this castle as he was himself, and only wanting a friend, any girl of her own age, to squander her loneliness of heart upon! But what was her lot instead? A few half-mocking courtesies she might think herself lucky to get, and then whispering behind their hands about how rich her father was! They looked down their noses at her, but coveted her comfit-boxes and her cast-off clothes, and what could the mercer himself be thinking of but the feather it was in his cap to have a daughter a lady and as good as the best of them? But *she* must endure those humiliating, empty afternoons with her little-finger of a husband, who came away whimpering that he was a man, a man!

Yet she had only to see such a man as Willie was and she felt her broken wings stirring again. It was not 'No' that the glance in the gallery had said, but 'Alas, alas, that it must be so!' And insecure and with his way to make, what a friend to have at his side! Her casket was waiting for her in the cloth-closet, and whether she had fetched it or not he did not know. Now she had his locket, to show to Sir William or whom she pleased, and that afternoon, to ease his heart of its anxiety, he went for a walk. Out past the gatehouse he strolled, along the moat-side and across to the waste. To-morrow there was to be a meet at Dame Kate's, and there Dame Kate's was, its crest of ivy spilling down one of its angles and half its roof open to the sky. Advancing to it he looked in. It had been used as a kennels, Potts said, and its door had been burnt by the waste-prowlers for firewood, but a portion of its interior was still roughly furnished, with bins and a bedshelf and a bench for the kennel-man and an inner door, that was closed and for some reason had been let alone. Bits of lead-set glass still remained among the fragments of carved masonry, and Willie was coming out of it again when he saw, balanced between her crutches, a figure in a steeple-hat with a wicker pottle slung round her neck. It was Mother Jule, hobbling towards her outhouse dwelling, and seeing him she stopped and beckoned.

"If it isn't my truelove come to see me again!" she cackled as he came up. "And how speeds the fortune, my pretty young man?"

"In need of hastening, Mother," he answered moodily.

"Then come you in," and suddenly there was a hot mothy smell in Willie's nostrils as she pushed at her door. The ceiling of her hovel had been patched and mended with sacking, and its single small window was also closely stuffed up. The walls were beehived and bird's-nested with countless ricketty compartments of old wood and sticks and wattle, and strewn with worm-eaten leaves. On these rested

hundreds of greyish egg-shaped objects, and the crone, unshipping
her basket, proceeded to distribute its contents, which were the young
mulberry leaves she had been out to gather.

"Eat, Dewdrop, eat!" she crooned in a cracked voice. "Eat, Plump-
kin, eat and spin! They're fresh, for your grannie gathered 'em this
morning, so spin hose for a lady's fine legs and a shimmy for her
pretty breasts! Leave nibbling them veins, my Tinklet, for here's fresh!
Mulberry-leaves, fine fresh mulberry leaves!" and seeing her hobble
from post to post Willie could not help but laugh.

"What, have you names for your silkworms, mother?"

"Names for 'em, bless 'em! Come, Comfit, wake up, lazies! Here's
a gentleman from the castle to see you!" and from one to another of
them she went till she had distributed her last leaf. Then again she
ogled Willie and asked him how his fortune sped.

"I fear that's what you'll have to tell me, mother," he sighed.

"Then set you down, set you down here on my bed. . . ."

So with his life at a standstill, why not? We do not believe, we do
not disbelieve, for that is what we have come for, to lull belief and
doubt alike to rest. Nay, lest even a witch fail us we are ready to tell
her a little to set her in the way of it, for soothsayers' lives are made
of ears and whisperings. Not a word can fall from our lips but it tells
them if not one thing then another, and home to us it all comes again,
so that we do not see the dribbling lips nor feel the scratching of the
finger-nail on the palm. We do not believe. We do not disbelieve.
We are only waiting to be told . . . only paying for being told. . . .

"What do you see, mother?" he asked, and the hag held her breath,
not to break the spell.

"Eih, 'tis not to be believed!"

"Tell me what you see."

"If these old eyes aren't dropping out of my head with the sight
of it!"

"Tell your true love, Mother Jule."

"On a white horse and hunting! You'd never believe me! It would
go to your head!"

"Leave the believing to me, mother."

"I cannot see clearly what it is you're hunting, but see it has gone
to earth . . . they're digging it out . . ."

To be sure, to be sure . . . to earth, where blue flames slept in the
ground and the silver married in the darkness with the gold.

"But I misdoubt you've been talking about it, and suchlike often
gets dim again once you start talking about it. . . ."

"Not to a soul in this place have I said a word, mother. . . ."

"And I can see you have journeyed . . . a long journey. . . ."

"Come to the fortune," he urged her, but here her voice began to shake as it dropped lower.

"And you have friends in this castle, as would to God I had, for there's things I scarce dare name even to my pretties because of ears. . . ."

"What things are those, Mother Jule?"

"'Twas no more than a trumpery matter for my lord to fly into such a spleen about, one of 'em selling a loaf or so of bread of his own baking and the other a few manure-scrapings last cattle-fair. . . ."

"This is not telling me my fortune. . . . Come, you promised me a pretty mistress."

But instead of peering into his hand, now she was drawing it to herself, and plucking at it and trying to get her lips and hairy chin to it.

"Oh, sir . . . you have friends in the castle, and for two years they've seen none but the gaoler . . . there's a fear they may have been forgotten all about, and they're my own two sons, and it might be that if you could speak a word to somebody for them . . ." but at that up Willie had jumped from the edge of the wretched bed, shaking her off.

"Think you I'm paying money for a heel-tap of a fortune like that? Not I . . . let be . . ."

"Nay, let me speer again . . ." she besought him, but the spell was broken, and as he cast her off she fumbled for her crutches and hoisted herself up between them and from her toothless mouth revilings began to pour.

"Then if you willn't say a word for my own two bonnie lads, may the devil's double curse . . ."

But he was no longer there to hear her. He was out in the air again, with his face set for the castle once more and the waste and its cattle and its fowls and its silkworms and fortune-telling at his back.

He walked moodily, his eyes on the ground. Prisoners, too! Well, it took all sorts to make a castle. For that matter the French Sieur was a prisoner, a prisoner in torment too with his vilanelles and his Bridge of Sighs, but he had only to look into the next lady's eyes and he was healed again. Well might the ostler have told him on that first day that there were more things in this castle of Gwlad then met the eye! He had also gathered that some were absent, and when they returned Willie would have to ask Potts who they were, but they for their part would look at Willie and ask who this stranger was they had never set eyes on before. He had crossed the moat again, passed the gate-house and was following the windings of the walls. They too had a grim and menacing look, with only the arrow-slits to break their blankness and an occasional trap or jutting overhead, and suddenly where the wall turned ahead of him he heard a voice calling, "Hollo, Tinker, down I say Nell!" The next instant he was face to face with the great lad who had been in charge of the ballista and who, for all Willie was the older, could have eaten bread-and-butter over his head. He held two great mastiffs on a double chain, and the dogs were sniffing at Willie's legs, and their master too stopped on seeing Willie.

"Quiet, Nell! Have no fear, I can hold 'em. Have done, Tinker!" and then he looked at Willie again. "Fear nothing. I'll see they don't harm you. Are you he that silvered young Covil's helm?"

"Yes," said Willie.

"Then I'm the bearer of a message to you," and he proceeded to unburden himself of it.

And even when he had it the message was no news to Willie, for it was only that the meet was to be at seven o'clock on the waste, but he looked up at this blonde young Hercules with the sullen short nose and the neck like a tree and the powerful shoulders that heaved on the two heavy brutes. The verses young Hal Sibbald wrote to his Bessie might be few and lame, but he would bang and buffet and hack for her, and now there were other things about that message Willie wanted to know.

"Who sent this word?"

"She did."

"When, young sir?"

"An hour back and I went to your turret, but only Tull was there, so I got some grease from him and came out to look for you."

"Then she isn't punished?" and he could tell by Hal's eyes that no further explanation was needed.

"She would have been, but she kept close to the Lady Estelle, and you cannot check ladies-in-waiting before guests, and it blew over."

"What are you doing with the dogs?"

"Exercising them and keeping them out of the kitchens."

"Could one that isn't a squire offer to come with you?" and Hal, putting ceremony where it belonged, saw nothing amiss with that, rather the other way.

"Ay, you can take Tinker, if he won't run away with you," and separating the chains he handed the mastiff over.

For Hal was one of Sir Mordaunt's squires, and should Sir Mordaunt's place at the board be seen to be suddenly empty there would be no Hal either, for Hal would have taken the field with him. And where Hal went Mistress Bessie's glove would go too, but not Bessie herself, wherefore Hal must make the most of the remaining time. That was what she had meant by that "Hal's the one to find out a way," and Hal for his part, wholly relieved that no further introduction or explanation was needed, plunged as headlong into matters as a bull at a gate. They had hardly passed the stables on their way round to the exercise-ground before both their heads and wits were joined together over it.

"But I thought the ladies might not go beyond the gates," said Willie as they passed the sheeted ballista by its pile of stones.

"A hunt's different, and even if it wasn't a quart of wine goes a long way with the guard," Hal answered.

"What do you mean . . .?" Willie left to himself could hardly have pictured raspberry-mouthed, white-mouse of a Bessie, who had fled like a rabbit lest the children should wake, slipping past the gatehouse like a bat in the dusk while her Hal inside bribed the guards with a quart of wine.

"I mean you can but try it, and the children will be asleep by then, and she'll have me with her," rumbled Hal, and the dogs nosing the kitchens, continued to drag them along.

"Do you know when you'll be off?" Willie asked at last.

"No, and if it wasn't for this I shouldn't care how soon, for squires cannot ride against knights, and as for Gilbert, he's the one next to me, I could throw him over my shoulder, saddle and lance and armour and all."

"You seem in a great hurry to get your neck broken."

"It'll be to break first," muttered the youth, "but I sometimes wish I had the brains of some, for the Sieur Gaston says I'm nothing but a great stirk, and if ever I'm to be a knight I shall have to cudgel my way to it."

"I was past Dame Kate's an hour ago," Willie murmured.

"Did you go in?"

"I didn't see aught to go in for but broken stones and an old bench or so."

"I'll show you to-morrow. I'm not hunting because I've told Sir Mordaunt I wanted to run over his harness and soften the bucklings up with grease. But I shall be there at seven, and if for any reason it cannot be there there's the herb-garden, and I know a way into 'em both. Peace, you two! You're not going into the kitchen!"

Late that evening, meeting Potts as he took the air where the moat ran under the solar window, Willie asked him whether the castle had a prison and if so where it was, and for the first time it seemed to Willie that Potts thought twice before he spoke.

"The prison? It's back there under the postern," he said.

"Who's in it?"

"None that doesn't deserve to be," but Willie persisted. "What's

F

this about two men having been there a year and more, something to do with bread and the droppings after a cattle-fair?"

"Baking-rights are my lord's, and so's manure, and if he didn't stop these things at the start he'd soon have little left. Who's been telling you that?"

"An old crippled body I met on the waste."

"Ah, Mother Jule and those two of hers! Ask her the next time you see her if she wants a whipping too. One of them shot a falcon with a bolt, and it's well known who was the ringleader about that fencing trouble. You cannot expect my lord to thole affronts like that. You be thankful it isn't you!" said the man whose tongue had brought him down to the foot of the table, and walked away.

But who can be thinking of dungeons on a hunting-morning? The castle's central court, besides by the large window of the hall, was overlooked on one side by the upper windows of the private apartments. It was grassed and daisied, with two intersecting paths and a sundial where they crossed, and already by half-past six the ladies were were beginning to assemble there. The horses would be taken direct to Dame Kate's, but the dogs were kept back, and with a sweet early smell in the air and the birds singing their hearts out never was there such a yelping and gambolling as they made. Cooks stood in the doorways to watch the kennel-lads struggling with the great lymers, and now and then a horn snapped out its tuning-note, and the gay group about the sundial grew in numbers, and even Sir William the treasurer had ease of his rheumatism, for there he was too, in a furred robe and his ebony stick in one stiffened hand. But Willie Middlemiss kept to the side farthest from the private apartments. He would follow when the group about the sundial had moved away, and they were still waiting for my lady and the Lady Estelle. And she—no need to say which she—must have been out of her bed a couple of hours or more, for hardly in less time could she have adorned herself so. Her hair was not bundled into its net of green now. She had put on her pearls, with a fillet across her brow to join her right temple to her left like the beam of a balance, and her girdled gown, for she wore no mantle, was of a soft strawberry crimson. Her eyes roved as she whispered to Bessie, but all at once there was a hush and the whole group dipped in a low curtsey. Across the grass my lady and the Lady Estelle were advancing, with my lord himself between them, and as they came forward Willie moved away.

Out on the waste the scene was all animation. About Dame Kate's the knights and their attendants and the grooms with the horses were gathered, with the townfolk some thirty yards back. The grudge about the pullets was forgotten at the sight of the beaters with their sticks and the huntsmen with their short spears. Across the moat the leaping and straining pack was advancing, with the ladies following behind, but again Willie backed away, for he had seen Hal and his Bessie, not in attendance on any lady, but only the young girl who looked after the children. They were standing where the ivy draggled over the broken angle of the dower-house, and the other was too beginning to edge that way, and the French Sieur was riding with the rest, but Hal was not riding, and hearing the horns and the sudden cries of "To horse, to horse!" he was now close on the place of assignation. The riders were mounting, moving off, thirty and more of them, the sweating huntsmen dragged on by the dogs willy-nilly. Out by the broken fence they streamed, about again outside it, and there a coppice of trees hid them for a space, but beyond it they could soon be seen again, dropping to a walk as they breasted the westward slope, headed for the gateway of the hills. There was a castlewards stirring among those who remained behind, but she had seen him now from where she too stood by the ivy, and the No in her eyes was a sparkling Yes. Even as Willie looked at them they vanished from his sight. In another moment he himself would not have been where he stood either, but suddenly he heard a soft voice in his ear.

"Well met, young man. I need not now put myself to the trouble of sending for you."

Turning he saw the treasurer's flat and fleshy face, his furred robe and the ebony stick on which he leaned.

6

THE COLOURED LIGHT OF HIS GROUND-FLOOR CHAMBER HAD BEEN kinder to him than this merry wide-open morning. With the sun behind it his face was of an earthy yellow, but his eyes showed recollection and interest as they rested on Willie.

"Well met, very well met," he said again, looking about him at the townsfolk on the waste and those already on their way back to the castle. "Ah, what sweet weather! It makes me young again! Not for two summers have I walked so far and yet I am not tired! Yet somewhat gently, for a pleasure such as this must be lingered over. You have not suffered from rheumatism?"

Willie managed to get out a "No, sir."

"Ah to be young! But shorten your pace yet a little, for the way back is never so short as the way there," and Willie did as he was ordered, for they had nearly a furlong to go. But to Dame Kate's he had only had a few steps to take.

There could, however, be little doubt what had happened, and as the invalid tapped his way across the waste, and then his stick sounded on the wooden bridge, and at the gatehouse the guards suddenly raised themselves as stiff as pokers to their feet, it seemed to Willie that two hovering familiars preceded them, as strife about him. One of them could only be the angel of his locket, and now Sir William had seen it and was all-athirst for more. But the other? And suddenly, Sir William stopped and fumbled inside his robe, and the next moment there was an iron key in his hand. He had stopped at a point between the walls where through the bars of an iron grille a glimpse of narrow garden showed, with an espaliered apple-tree growing against an inner-wall, and it was not a furlong after all, for evidently there was a shorter way. But the treasurer's cramped and twisted hands had trouble with the key, and he seemed pleased when Willie deferentially offered to open the grille for him, and locked it again when they had passed through. The garden inside was only a few yards wide but of unexpected length. It seemed to be the back way to the dwellings of the principal officers of the household, and suddenly he remembered that Hal had said something about a herb-garden. No window pierced the high inner wall that supported the outspread apple, but growing in the plots and strips were medicinal herbs, camomile and hellebore and aconite and the herb of St. Martin for the bowels and eyes. And to lock the outer grille was apparently enough, for the narrow green door under the apple stood half open, and it led to a short stone passage, at the end of which the green of the central grasscourt suddenly appeared again. But a second passage led off to the left, with two doors that the treasurer passed, but at a third stopped. This he was able to open for himself with a smaller key, and he motioned Willie towards it.

"Perhaps I am a little more tired than I thought, but for that there is a remedy," he said. "It is a cup of wine, if you will be so good as to pour it out for me. Pray enter," and thereupon Willie found himself in the room he had been in before, the room with the coloured window and the couch and the pacing sentry outside, but by a different way. By the couch stood a small table with cakes and wine on it, and this time the treasurer did not cast himself down on the couch, but sat on the edge of it, with his hands on his stick and his stick between his knees. This time too Willie was told he might sit, and the treasurer had hardly said ten words before Willie was caught up from the earth in an ecstasy of pleasure and hope.

"Why, when I sent for you before, did you not show me what I have now seen?" he asked with a fixed and reproachful look.

Willie, enheavened, could only stammer that he had not been asked to do so, but Sir William's lids fluttered, and Willie glowed again at the soft indulgence in his voice.

"I did not? True. Too seldom, alas! has such a question to be asked. But tell me, young man, have you never found this modesty of yours stand sorely in your way?"

Willie's modesty stand in his way! Never until that moment had the thought entered his head. Nor did he know what the wine was that he had poured out and was now himself sipping at the treasurer's bidding, except that it was sweet and strong and that he was drinking it in the company of Sir William Stone himself, and he scarcely heard the next question, which was an inquiry what work he was engaged upon now, but he recollected himself.

"On none, sir. Finding none to do I was on the point of enlisting myself among the men-at-arms," and this Sir William found so preposterous that he dismissed it as one dismisses an absurdity that is past.

"A pretty thing that would have been, my young friend! But ah, how you have wasted my time, as the young will who know that others die but are so sure they themselves are to live for ever! But enough. When I sent for you before I questioned you about foolish things, makers' marks and assay and I cannot remember what. That was because I

did not know. Tell me," he said suddenly, thrusting forward to Willie
the round knob of his ebony stick, "what do you think of this for a
trifling but not wholly unpleasing bit of work?"

The knob was of gold, orientally patterned in delicate arabesque
and exquisitely wrought, and to be asked his opinion of it went to
Willie's head more than the wine, but even that was as nothing to
what came almost before he had finished praising the knob, for the
treasurer gave a deep and troubled sigh.

"Ah, this art, this art! Tell me what it is, you fortunate young man
who know! Which is the master and which is the slave? When you say,
'I will do it thus,' does it answer, 'No, you shall do it thus?' Does it
come shivering to your door like an outcast and then when you have
warmed it drive you away from your own fire? For every moment of
joy has it a thousand despairs, yet were deliverance to offer itself, you
would be back at your torment again? Tell me these things, you who
know, you who alone among us know!"

And Willie, understanding not a word of it, could only sit there in
confusion, but the flattering voice dropped still more tragically.

"Yet you are happier than we, who admire and envy but cannot
move a finger towards it! Sometimes we would ease ourselves by
taking even your moment of joy from you again, yet even that we
cannot do, for you have known something we have not! Oh that I
could set you to a task worthy of your gifts! But the world is as it is,
and I cannot!" and his lids began to blink rapidly. "So on such terms
would you enter my service?"

Bewildered, looking down at his feet, Willie nevertheless stammered
out a "Yes."

"When you would perhaps be happier among the soldiery, anywhere
else? I have told you how little I have to offer."

"I wish it, sir," and the invalid rose.

"Then finish your wine and I will show you," and with his stick he
tapped upon the wall. Again the door by which Willie had formerly
entered was opened from the outside, and a man with a lighted lantern
stood there. But a few yards along the outer passage the lantern
showed, not stairs that ascended to the floor above, but others that
dropped by an opposite way to the regions below. Until the day before
Willie had not given a thought to the cellarage of that castle, but now,
as he followed the lantern with its bearer in front of him and the
treasurer behind, he saw at the end of the crypt a pale light ahead.
An arras was flung aside. He stood in a chamber that seemed to be a
sort of workshop, half open to the day again, that smelt of coke-fumes
and acids. But its outlet showed a blank wall, hardly more than a
couple of strides away, and down this there slanted the latticed shadow

of a heavy grating overhead. At one end of the room was a raised hearth with bellows, and its walls were hardly to be seen for racks and ledges of retorts and phials, tongs, swages, hammers, crucibles, and a vice. At a sign from Sir William the man with the lantern had retired again, and the treasurer was speaking.

"I told you, now I am showing you, that is all. It is here that all your making is sweated to its elements again. Here the Great Salt itself may have to come if I can find no other way. Would you see the wretch who does it?" and clapping his hands he raised his voice in a language Willie did not understand.

"Do not expect much speech from Pietro, for he is not talkative," and in a corner an old rag of hanging parted, and from behind it there emerged a small elderly man in dusty black, whose natural growth seemed to have been arrested many years ago. The obeisance this fire-dried and broken figure made to Willie was only a little less profound than the cringing with which he bent before the treasurer himself.

"But he hears as you do," said the man in the furred robe, for Valle Crucis had nothing in the way of silence to teach the other, and how often he had longed for the shorter shrift of Montfaucon and its gibbet was between himself and the God who had forgotten him. "Come, wake up your fire, Pietro," the gentle voice commanded, and the man passed a leather apron about his black suiting and from a ledge took a pair of darkened iron goggles. He crossed to the hearth and the coughing of the bellows filled the cellar. "Set a cupel in it," and this too was done and the grey ash woke to a glow. "We are now about to assay the purity of a specimen of gold," the treasurer murmured as if to himself, and his hand went to the pouch of his girdle. In cold dismay Willie saw what he produced from it. It was his locket, and the fire under the cupel was now ready.

So what of the bone-ash pipkin and the comet of silver and lead and the little button at the bottom now? His own locket! Willie, wringing his hands, had cried aloud before he knew.

"Sir, sir, you cannot! It is all I have to show! The very gold was saved out of my wages! Sir, for pity, you would not rob a poor journeyman in search of his bread!"

Not only for one moment did his cry seem to be ecstatic music in Sir William's ears, but for the endless moments he lingered it out, blinking rapidly at Willie as he did not remove his eyes from his agonized face. Then Willie heard his voice again, sinking to softness once more.

"Who said your gold was to be stolen, young man? If I returned you the gold could you not easily make another?"

"On my knees, sir . . ." and to his knees he would have dropped, but as suddenly the blinking ceased, and the treasurer's twisted hands were uplifting him, and in his ears was an easy, natural laugh.

"What, before Pietro? Whose master I had a mind to make you? Timorous, fearful boy! I, who have had them flogged for a fingermark on a chaffer-dish, mar such art as *you* are the thrice-happy master of! Before I trust a man with things that are not to be spoken about shall I not first see what he is made of? Fie, young goldsmith! Set your heart at rest! Pietro! Quench your fire. And you, young master, give me your arm, these cellars are death to me, and I did but jest, for did Isaac slay his own son? But I see you are shaken. Come, and we will take another cup of wine to restore you. Then you shall see where I propose to bestow you. Come, let us up into the air," and clinging affectionately to Willie's arm he drew aside the arras and turned again to the crypt way and the stairs.

Utter abhorrence of the man now surged through Willie's breast. It was not yet nine o'clock, and he had been roused that morning by the clamour of dogs and the twanging of horns. He had been within a few yards of an ivy-grown doorway, his heart throbbing with trepidation and hope. The sun had shone merrily on the cavalcade bound for the hills, but it was no longer the same sun, for what had it shown him since? Sir William's coloured window with the sentry pacing outside. A cellar, deeper as he guessed by many feet than the moat and its back-water, with the shadow of iron bars slanting down a wall. Now he was back in the apartment with the red and amber and blue window again, but in what company? In that of a man who talked incomprehensible things about Willie and his art, affected to be moved that beauty should be brought to naught, but oh that lascivious blinking of his eyes and the unction in his voice as he had offered to destroy Willie's work before his very eyes! And it had been Willie who had poured out the wine before, but now he was pouring it out for Willie, softly jesting and rallying him that he should even for a moment have believed him. And as he said something about bestowing Willie in new quarters, he was asking him where he was lodged at the moment, steadying one cramped hand with the other as he poured him out his third glass of wine.

But it was a heady, confusing sort of wine, and for more than a cup or so Willie would have preferred ale; but still the third was better than the second, and the last time Willie had drunk in exalted company it had been with Humphrey Tull in York. But now the thought began to beat in his head that he was drinking cup-for-cup with Sir William Stone himself, at Sir William's express invitation. They were talking familiarly together, at least Sir William did not cease to talk, and again he invited Willie to admire the arabesqued golden knob of his stick.

But whether it was Willie, or the treasurer, or the wine, the stick was not passed over very skilfully, for as Willie took it the knob came suddenly away in his hand. It showed an eight-inch blade of slenderest steel that ended in a needle-point, which Willie was about to touch, but at that the soft voice was raised in a warning cry.

"For God's sake have a care! Did you touch it?"

"No, sir."

And again as he replaced the delicate blade, "Touch only your burins, young artist, for indeed you have brought me into a sweat at the thought of it!" And Willie fancied he heard the faint click of a spring.

"Never touch such points!" But the little incident was the end of the interview. Sir William rapped once more with the stick on the wall. Again the servant apeared, this time without his lantern, and he seemed to have his orders, for Sir William was committing Willie to his care.

"Punshon will show you where you have been placed," he was saying. "To-day is a holiday and there is nothing to do, but for to-morrow, Punshon will tell you if I am not there. And a word about Pietro. Use no gentleness with him. At the first sign do this," and with a bent finger Sir William drew a square in the air, but Willie had not yet learned that Montfaucon the gibbet was a square one. "And Punshon, before you go, help me off with this robe and get me my cloth-of-gold," and this done, while Willie waited, he stretched himself on his couch again, for he too had had a full morning. "Ah, this sweet weather!" he murmured as he settled himself. "I shall now sleep a little. But I am not far away, and Punshon is always here. . . ."

Some hours later Willie, raising his head from the arms to which it had dropped, looked about him wondering where he was. He woke at a table before a window, and its open casement showed other windows at the same level, but they seemed a long way off, and he too must be somewhere upstairs. He pushed back the chair in which he had fallen asleep. He was looking towards the inward part of the castle. Below him he could see the grass-court with the sundial where its two paths intersected, and suddenly from below rose the voice of a girl. Leaning forward over the table he looked down.

"Then three of you go to the sideboard, with your eyes modestly on the ground, and one takes the basin, and the other pours the water and the third has the napkin ready. Jacqueline, you are not attending. Come you here and take the ewer, and you Philippa hold the basin. . . ."

Willie did not know how long he had slept, for it was the governess, Bessie, back long ago from her assignation at Dame Kate's and diligently at her duties again. With their gowns like thistle-stars about them the children were sitting on the grass in a ring, and Bessie was in their midst, holding out the invisible basin and ewer as they went through their mimic ceremony. And looking across at the other windows again Willie now knew where he was. There, a little to his right, was the seneschal's house, with the marshal's next to it, and somewhere below him that of the treasurer himself. To his left lay the priest's, then my lord's own retiring rooms, with the solar beyond them facing the other way. Withdrawing his head again he next looked round his own quarters. He saw no bed, but in a niche in the wall saw his own wallet with his tools in it, and if he had been a little intoxicated it was passing off, and there being no bed might mean that there was a second room. And so he found it. He had to go out to a cramped angle of stairhead to get to it, but it adjoined the first room and he had no need of a third. Suddenly he sat down heavily on the bed, at first thinking of nothing. Then, hardly believing it yet, he sat there, trying to set it all in order. His first bed had been among the horses' fodder. On the second night he had had none, for no provision had been made for him in Humphrey's turret opposite the smithy. On the third night it had been two benches joined together, which had been his couch ever since. And now this. His lips parted, his heart rose. By God, but those were the stars to follow! His heart began to thump as he counted other things too—the clothing-closet, the quarry, that morning's broken assignation at Dame Kate's . . . and had not Hal said something about a herb-garden? Now he even knew where that herb-garden was. It was within a stone's-throw of him, the long-walled strip behind the grille for which Sir William had a key, and if H al hadn't a key for it he knew some other way of getting in. The room in which he was sitting had a window like the first, but no table stood before it, so that he was able to rest his elbows on its sill. Again he looked about him. By the Universe and its Maker, he was here . . . here! He, who had fawned on clothiers for a seal-ring to do, he who had shivered on a barren mountain with a lousy Welsh *cenedl*, and walled himself up alive among a lot of monks who never spoke, was here! God's blessing on Mother Jule and the pearl of a mistress she had found him! What need had she of those twin baskets of them who was the mother-of-pearl herself? And now what could he do for her in return? It must be something that all the money in the world could not buy, and if he could toss a locket-cover to a collier who carried himself like a king what should he not do for such a queen among women as this? Of her and her fillet and her pearl-panniers he would make such a locket . . . such a locket . . .

And suddenly dropping his eyes he saw her below, but could hardly believe them, his breathing was suspended so. She was walking slowly along the farther side of the court, and with whom? With none other than my lord himself—just the two of them, walking together, with no other in attendance. . . .

But what? How? My lord? It could not be that the hunt was back yet, and had he not, with his own eyes, seen my lord set off for the mountains, four, five, he did not know how many hours ago?

But no, he had not, for now he recalled the scene. My lord had indeed been at the meet, but Willie had *not* seen him on a horse. Sir Mordaunt and Sir Francis and Sir Etienne and the French Sieur, *they* had mounted, but not my lord. Some business had kept him behind and there the two were, pacing the farther side of the court and turning to walk back again, in earnest conversation. About what? Her boy-husband and the knighthood? Money again? Not rondeaus and vilanelles, for when my lord paid his court to ladies be sure it was something more substantial. His face was grooved and lined with cares. In London alone he must have business of state enough to break the backs of twenty men, and these idle haughty ladies might make the mercer's daughter their by-play, but these grim and elderly ones knew better. Suddenly the walkers changed their direction. They were crossing the daisied grass, and though Willie had not seen them go he knew that at my lord's appearance the governess had whisked her charges hurriedly away. They were passing the sundial, advancing towards him, and raising her eyes she saw him at the window. The dark, wistful eyes were looking up as *knowing* he would be there, for she herself had brought it all about, as she was perhaps even now busily bringing other things about. Quicker than the flicker of a snake's tongue the upward glance was, but added to what Hal had told him it was enough. If not Dame Kate's that morning, then the herb-garden later in the day. They passed and were gone, and Willie roused himself from his stupor.

No higher place at table had been allotted to him yet, but his way to the hall now lay directly across the court. Slowly he sought his wallet and unpacked it. Ten minutes later he had made his toilet, thrown his leather cap on his bed, and was descending bareheaded. As he passed the sundial he paused for a moment to read its motto. "*Labuntur et imputantur*" it ran, but he knew no Latin, and to the hall he passed on.

But except for the underlings he found it almost empty. The dais had not even been dressed, the Great Salt was shrouded in napkins, the meats were cold and a few curs only moved about the benches. In crossing the herb-garden with the treasurer he had noticed that a little way down it, past the espaliered apple, there was a small summerhouse. He did not know what he ate, the horn of ale he tasted seemed to unsettle the treasurer's wine, and getting through his meal hastily he left the rest of it undrunk. Back across the court again he made his way, into the short stone tunnel under the low arch, past the seneschal's and marshal's closed doors to the left and out into the herb-garden by the green door under the apple tree. There at the end of it was the summerhouse, with a briar to make a hanging-basket of its opening, and down on its rustic bench he sat with his hands clasped between the leather of his knees. No saye or samlet, but still the leather between his knees. No higher place at table yet, though he all but shared a house with the treasurer himself—but patience. He sat there, thinking of nothing.

Then a little at a time it began to come to him, his waylaying by the treasurer that morning, the harangue about his art, Punshon and his lantern, the workshop in the cellar. He smelt its fumes of coke and acids again, its damp for all the sleeping fire on its hearth, saw its imprisoning wall with the shadows of the grating above slanting down their oblique pattern. At the soft raising of a honeyed voice an old rag of arras had parted and a small wasted figure had crept out, a grey and early-aged figure in dusty black, who answered with his fingers because no speech remained in his mutilated tongue. And at that Willie tried to stop, for he had no wish to recall the rest, the cough of the bellows, the reddening of the fire, his own breakdown as the crippled hand had brought out his own locket and prepared to cast it into the bóne-ash pot. But they would not be shut out, that satanic quivering of eyelids, the ineffable lip-licking, his own torment turned to delectable music—oh, beyond words inhuman and abominable! It seemed to Willie, brooding there under the briar and blinking at the fallen petals at the apples' foot as if a bride undressed herself blush by blush, an impossible thing that the God who had made that spring-time freshness should have made a man who turned such things to his sport. It was more coldly cruel to think of now than it had seemed in the cellar itself.

Yet stay. The mimic torture over had anything happened? Nothing, nothing at all. Had not Sir William, the real Sir William, the other only the one he gave himself out to be, explained all? *Was* it to be supposed that he would commit the deepest secrets of his breast to Willie before he knew who he was trusting? Was it so that Willie himself had trusted Atty Cockin? No, no. He had no sooner satisfied himself than he had been all care and solicitude for Willie. He had had him back into his chamber, had comforted him with wine, praised him again, made much of him, and when the little accident about the stick had happened he had cried aloud in terror lest he should have been hurt. It was his office and its responsibilities that made him what he was, as Willie might have known even by the way his chamber was guarded. Any jack of a sentry might pace the upper walls, but Sir William and his business must be given closer protection than that. None might approach within thirty yards even of the outside of his coloured window, so Willie would have to make up his mind. He might stay outside if he wished, but once admitted he must put up with what he found. And suddenly and strangely quiet a hunting-day seemed to make the castle, but in this garden between the walls it was doubly quiet. As if something from the herbs stole over him, and even though he had slept already, a heaviness began to overtake him. Camomile and poppy, aconite and hemp and myrrh mingled their astringent balms, and another spell of sleep ought to make a new man of him. For some moments longer he saw the apple, sturdily ruddy against the grey and windowless wall. He supposed that was the way Hal saw his Bessie. Then he closed his eyes.

The small green door under the apple opened and his eyes again with it. She had come, and was closing the door again behind her.

7

THERE HAS BEEN NO SIESTA FOR JOSLIN COVIL THAT DAY. SHE WAS still in the girdled crimson and hair-diaper of pearls, and there was no need for her to place her finger on her lips as she closed the door again behind her, for complicity and connivance seemed to load the very air of that secluded garden within its wall. The cloisters of Valle Crucis had not been quieter, and what was all this about bread-and-water and punishment? She walked on the grass with my lord instead, and he was on his feet, for she had seen him under the briar and was advancing towards him. And no knee-bending or stooping over her hand for his duty and service now, for she was weary and sick of such scrapings, and there was one service he alone among them could offer her, and his eyes were already at it—not a profile like a shadow on a wall this time, but the oval and the pearled baskets together, full and flush as a kiss on the mouth. But the next moment they had dipped under the briar and she was sitting at his side.

"How long have you been here?"

"I . . . I don't know." The sun over the outer wall had begun to catch the espaliered apple, which it had not done before. "I think I fell asleep."

"But you knew I meant here."

"Yes. Hal told me."

"Hal got some oil from the armourer and oiled the lock of the grille so that it wouldn't grate. Now I only have to slip out and unlock it for him and a push will open it, but it still looks locked and nobody else knows."

He was wide awake now. So that was another of Hal's ways. . . .

"What happened this morning?" he asked.

"I waited at Dame Kate's for twenty minutes, but you didn't come, so I came away again."

"Have they come back yet?"

"Have no fear you won't hear them when they come back. So then I went up to our room, very cross and vexed, and then Ferdinand began to be tiresome, so I left him in his new armour, but he was fighting battles one minute and crying the next," and with one hand she began to crumple up the velvet of her lap, pushing out a pointed crimson toe under its hem, and for a moment she seemed to think twice about something, but then went on. "And I've given her the perfume-box."

"My lady?"

"Yes, and it pleased my lord, so that he sent for me, and now I'm to write a letter to my father, but he'll tell me what to put in it, and he'll see Ferdinand's advancement is pushed on, and he was graciousness itself to me."

And now Willie sat wondering how to tell her what he for his part had to say.

"It seems the advancement of others is pushed on too," he said at at last. "Didn't you see me coming away with the treasurer?"

"No."

"I was with him over an hour, and you gave him the locket. Did he ask you how you came by it?"

"Yes, and I said my husband saw you with it in your hand, and then a long story, but I don't think he was listening, because he was looking at it and turning it this way and that, and then he shook his head, and said that at any other time he might have done something, so I reminded him."

"How, you reminded him?"

"How stupid it was having a goldsmith in the castle and not giving him anything to do. So he said he would have a word with my lord about it, and I don't know any more, and the rest is for you to tell me."

So how much of that was Willie going to tell her now? The things he didn't want to think of himself, that he didn't like a man who played with people's nerves and could not forbear to linger out the torment a few moments longer even as he stayed his hand? Shame on him for the thought. It was indeed only too likely that he would be set to do his share of the breaking-down and melting for a time, but Willie was young, and the bad days pass, and in time to come there in Gwlad or some other castle Willie would be, with a history of faithfulness and willingness behind him, and Sir William by that time an old man and none but Willie to hand things over to. Now he wanted to see that full face again of which she showed him only the pretty nose and the pouting mouth, still tremulous from the pestering of that afternoon and her husband who whimpered in his vine-leaf armour as he postured before the glass with his shortened lance.

"That window you saw me at," he said slowly, his hands again between his leather knees. "It is where I am put now."

"I guessed that," she answered.

"I had only one room before. Now I have two," and she sighed.

"Then you have one more than I have, for if it isn't your own chamber it's the solar or the hall."

"One of them has a table to work at, not the things Sir William says it must be, but the things *I* want to do."

"What are they?" and straight out now he told her. He wanted to make a locket of herself, he said, pouts and pearls and all, and it should be such a locket as when my lady saw it she would not rest till she had one too, for comfit-boxes were only comfit-boxes, but into the likeness everything went; and hearing him she began to crumple the crimson folds again.

"If it is anything like the one you made of your dainty mistress. . . ."

"Turn your head. Nay, straight to me. So. But there will be a drawing to make first. This garden, have I now the freedom of it?"

"Surely, if they have put you where they have."

"Who uses it?"

"Do you mean Hal and Bessie?"

"I mean can *you* come here when you like?" and she smoothed out the crumple she had made.

"I might."

"Then, barring Sir William wants me, to-morrow?"

"I will see. Shall I wear my green?"

"No. And nothing on your head but what you have now. Then when I get my locket back . . ." but he stopped. He had been about to say that then he would have the gold too, but the questioning dark eyes were raised to his for a long moment before she dropped her head, showing him the cheek and the pearled temple as before.

"If Sir William talks to you as he talks to us all you'll see of that locket again will be a quittance on a piece of paper," she said, and he sat stiffly up.

"But . . . but . . . he said he would give it me back!"

"Did he say when?"

"He . . . he . . . no, he didn't say when."

"Don't look like that," she went quickly on. "If I can find a silver twopence for my husband I can find a scrap of gold for my own locket, and this old velvet is but a dowd of a gown, only fit to go out on the waste in, but my new green my father sent me is like a spring meadow, with a hundred little white buttons like daisies from my neck down to my toes," and the point of the crimson toe peeped out again.

But now it was he who was not listening. Not have his gold back, but only a bill for it! They had been the treasurer's own words when Willie had wrung his hands and cried aloud, that none would rob a poor journeyman of his hard-earned gold. Was that a word he could take back, even though she did find him the gold blank as she had found the silver for the headpiece?

And now another thought was drawing each moment nearer, growing, looming, overshadowing. It was no new thought, for at Valle Crucis he had brooded over it for the whole of the winter, turning it over, waking from dreams of it to the sound of the midnight bell, rising to it in the chill dawn, almost glad of the silence of the refectory bench and that no brother asked him what was in his mind. They were of the gold in Wales, gold for the taking, the gold it might be over which the hunt had ridden that very morning. Augsbergs and Nurembergs of gold, and here they were scraping lockets and trinkets together, all for lack of a word from Willie! How if, without betraying anything, he were to sound her a little? Nay, he had already hinted at it that morning in the quarry, when he had said that in exchange for a sort of trade-secret he had given half his locket away. The sun-flush was still on the apple on the seneschal's wall. The crimson toes were rising and falling again. Was she thinking of her boy-husband, his puny horns still in the velvet, a brocket fretting and rubbing himself against a tree? The devil take her boy-husband, and give him a baby's pitchfork to play with! Suddenly she turned her face to him unasked. Ah, that was as he wanted her, unconscious, herself as she was, just the oval and the ripe lips and the nets about her temples and the eyelids downcast again. Upstairs in his new chamber was paper, Valle Crucis paper with crosses and foliations on the other side of it. Lacking paper, a crust of bread would have served, and suddenly he was talking to her about Bartholomew Rhys.

"Where was this?" she asked presently.

"Many days back, on the English mountain."

"Were you then from England? What adventures men have!"

"And that morning in the quarry, when you told me you had had a flea in your bed, it reminded me of some red ants one day, *morgrygyn* they call them . . ." and he told her that too. "That was the man I gave my locket case to."

"Do you say he was a collier?"

"Such a collier as maybe Sir William or my lord himself might give something to have an hour's talk with!"

"Then why don't they send for him?"

"He might come if I sent for him, but not at my lord's bidding. And now I shall be put to hammering things down in a cellar and melting them down over a hearth and trying them with acids. . . ."

But again he checked himself, for it seemed he hadn't finished with the things of that morning yet. Why should the treasurer have told him that if Pietro began to give trouble all he had to do was to draw a square in the air with his finger? It put out of his mind the things he had been going to say about Bartholomew Rhys, and suddenly he knew that none of this was in the least what he had come into that herb-garden for. It was what she had been set on earth for, what she pined for too but for frustration, and when it comes, what matter

how it comes about? He had seen them sitting so before, moving their
toes and fiddling with their clothing with their eyes cast down. He
knew too that some kissed with their eyes open, some closed, but closed
or open it saved many words. And no wasting time with hands either,
though it lay on her lap for his taking. The oval, the pearls, the eyes
again. . . . "Look up," he suddenly ordered her. She did so showing
no profile now, but face turned to face in a pause of suspense. Her
thirsting lips parted, and the "Yes" was never spoken. The next
moment her breast was on his and his sleeve was passed about the
crimson. The kiss was not interrupted, only renewed in surrender.

"Joslin! Jo!"

Still she did not seek to free herself. The sun would have gone from
the apple, night fallen over Gwlad castle, before she had begun to make
up for all her flushing youth had lost. But even so it could not last for
ever, and at last she made to release herself.

"In the afternoon!" she said, shamed and abashed.

"All day. . . ."

"Oh, how unhappy I have been!" she sighed.

"Are you unhappy now?"

"You have made me so that I cannot think. . . ."

"Then don't think. . . ."

"No, no . . . *bien, la main, mais ne recommencez-pas* . . ."

"Talk any language you like with those lips. . . ."

"Then gently with me, for I must not stay much longer. . . ."

"What, more afraid than Bessie?" he softly taunted her.

"There . . . sit so, a little away, or I will not come here again."

"When shall I see you again?"

Now the bosom had to calm down and the upstart colour to settle
again in her cheeks, and what is a hand after a pair of lips? Yes, he
might do as he liked with that, and it was a long time before she spoke
again tremulously.

"Heaven send that when next I sigh it is the right name that slips
out! And I am weary of your coalheaver. Tell me more of what passed
between you and Sir William."

But of that Willie would now never tell her more than he saw fit,
and he was glad he had said nothing about the gold in the mountains,
for with all else shaping so goldenly worlds of things were now best
left out of it. A quarter of an hour longer she stayed, and then shook
herself and got up. They were of a height as they walked slowly to the
green door under the still-sunny espalier. As in the quarry, she must
have a few minutes the start of him, but—*pas de recommencement.*
Tenderly this time lips met lips and severed again. Then he returned
to the summer-house alone.

If Willie now thought that to use the same archway and private passage as Sir William was to be in the bosom of the treasurer himself, he was quickly made aware of his error. Punshon, to whom he had been turned over, was a thin, bald, servile man, with Sir William's badge on the breast of his suit of civil black and hardly more words than the tongueless Italian down below, and his footfall was quiet, and of door Willie's new chamber had none. If therefore its arras happened to be flung back Willie was likely to hear Punshon's voice behind him before he heard his step, and this happened on the very next morning, so that again Willie had to cover up the occupation that engaged him.

"Pietro will have all ready in an hour, sir," he said, but even the 'sir' did not quite set one doubt at rest, whether Punshon was his servant, or in some sort he was to take his orders from him. "Do you know which is my room?"

"No," said Willie.

"Because when Sir William is not to be disturbed he leaves all in my hands. It's just round the corner from his, but I'll leave the door open so you can see, and you'd best have your working clothes on," and as he retired as noiselessly as he had come Willie first drew the arras behind him so that next time he would hear the running of its rings. Then he uncovered that which he had so hurriedly covered up. It was his pencilled full-face. She had not sat for it, for it still floated before his eyes like an aura, that harmony of oval and fillets and scaled pearls as he had played pat-a-cake with her hand, and now he looked long and measuringly at it. He would lose it, but like the kiss, it had been, and like the kiss would be again when the time came. Till then he had committed it to the Valle Crucis paper, with a drawing of a ceremonial cross on the other side. Again, he looked at it before setting it aside. No more dreaming for the present, but to be about the work in hand.

Punshon's room round the corner from the treasurer's was in a sort Humphrey Tull's armoury-office over again, yet at the difference Willie frowned. His eyes had missed nothing from dresser or side-board, for the hall would be the last to be despoiled. The Great Salt still reared itself in its beauty, before my lord's seat the hanap still stood for the butler to dip his talisman into. But when a castle is combed for its gold a multitude of lesser things come to light, and there they were heaped together on Punshon's table, the turning-out of closets and chests, old trinkets and ornaments, rings and broken garnishings and odd things of pairs, the pommels and clasps of the knights and the collectings of the women, the gold and silver-gilt to be broken down. They were carefully sorted and separated and ticketed as Humphrey ticketed his glaive-heads and rivets, and Punshon was writing down his inventory in a book. He continued to write for some minutes, while Willie waited behind him, and then closing his book reached for a great voider such as they used to sweep the broken bread from the table into. To this he transferred his treasures, lighted his lantern, and handed it to Willie. Then, carrying the voider and its condemnings before him, and except for a couple of doublings by the same way as before, he clinked and jangled his way down the narrow stairs and into the crypt. Willie held aside the rag of arras and set down the lantern. The cellar already glowed hot with the smothered fire on its hearth. The Italian was waiting in his apron and smoky goggles, and to a bench he had fixed his vice and on it set hammers and crushers and crucibles and tongs. Punshon was the only one of them to speak.

"There's your acids, sir. You'll keep them all in the same lots as you find them, and each is to ticket as it is assayed. Then you'll be so good as to deliver them back to me. Your food will be brought down to you, and you'll not finish to-day nor to-morrow, but you'll know by the wall when it's a fair time to knock off. If you want me you know where to find me," and with those words he was off, and Willie saw him no more that day.

So to it, Willie Middlemiss, artist in silver and gold, and forget what you were told about putting on your oldest clothes, for this cellar is no place for samlets and sayes. The clothes you work in are the same clothes as you make love in, and you will soon get used to this gulping, stifling heat, for see, the hearth with the bellows has a funnel and a pipe to the grated air-space outside, and the shadow on the wall will tell you when it is time to knock off. And do not ask yourself how long this humiliation is going to last, for it cannot be long, and be glad that there are two of you and that Pietro knows his business. For all he cannot speak his hands are nimble and intelligent, always ready with whatever you are in need of, wrench or nipper or hammer to crush with or tongs with which to twist, and it may be that he was once an artist too, and a lover like yourself. And remember that even Sir William mourns that he must set you to this. When your prison-clock tells you it is time to put on your doublet again you have a fair chamber upstairs in which you can breathe, and look out over the daisied grass-court, and the summer evenings are long, and what after all is a voider full of leavings and trash? Into the crucible with it, and then to the testing and the assay. If you find that some of the gew-gaws are no more than common latten gilded over it is too late to do anything now, and that precious little button that is left at the bottom is gold—gold, gold, pure gold!

But with one thought do not play. Do not, as your food like the smiths' is sent down to you, and you burn your fingers to bronze with the strong acids, toy with that other perilous musing, that up there in the mountains is gold, and of gold coins are made, and the hand and eye that can make one image can make another. Remember that before Sir William became the treasurer of Gwlad he watched the ports for counterfeit, and all this moiling and melting is that the men-at-arms may be paid their arrears of wages, and still there are more things in this castle than meet the eye. Therefore be advised, and leave treasurers to find their gold in their own way.

How balmy-sweet now was the end of the day when, cleansed and brushed again, cool save for the fumes in his eyes, he could see hope beginning to shine again like a star in the skies! For by the third day the voider was three-parts empty. When the last of the trash had gone there would be a respite, for though the scouring of the castle still continued the spate would be over till some lesser quantity had accumulated again. But now he looked at his hands, and reddened with humiliation and shame. Those an artist's hands! For all his scouring, the powerful acids had burnt his fingers to umber, and now he envied Hal, for if Hal went away he would return again with scars of honour to show, not the ignominy of a tradesman. He knew that no fingers in that castle were cleaner, but they must dip into the same dish with other fingers when he sat at table again, and already he saw the eyes, glancing to see whether anything came off them. Nothing but time would remove those stains, and bitterly he wished he had been a baker or a cook instead of carrying his occupation about with him like a dyer. And oh for money, for the fingers of those with money remained as spotless as the French Sieur's! For three nights together now he had wandered into the herb-garden, where the apple on the seneschal's wall had almost ceased to blush, for its blushings lay like shredded lacework on the ground. She had been unable to come, or for some other reason had not come, and he had waited there, sullenly scouring his hands with dry sand and rubbing them with thyme to make them sweet again. But on the fourth evening the green door opened, slowly at first and only a little way, as children play at 'I spy,' so that he wondered whether she was being watched again, or perhaps he was, or perhaps both of them. But the next moment he had forgotten even his hands and was nothing but eyes. She had put on the green she had told him about. No pearls went with it, for her nets too were green again, but instead of pearls there the hundred little white buttons twinkled all the way down her, from her neck to her hem. They rippled like a daisy-chain as she advanced towards him, but even as she came slowly on and placed herself at his side she did not speak, but crumpled the green on her knees as she had crumpled the crimson before it. Again something had happened, and she did not look as if she wanted to be kissed or her husband to be made a knight or anything else. And it is a fine thing to know all about them when they are like that, but not when you cannot play pat-a-cake with their hands because of your own unsightly fingers, and Willie too was tongue-tied as she still sat there and crumpled but did not speak. But suddenly she did speak.

"I wish I was dead!" she broke petulantly out.

He was on the point of telling her she wished no such thing, but changed his mind. . . . "Three nights I've been here," he mumbled. "Where were you?"

"She's taken it into her head now that Sir Mordaunt must have a new banner to go away with, and we all have to sit round in the solar sewing it, and that's where I've been."

"Oh," he said.

"And you can guess what that means. If she happens to want some scarlet or some blue, it's 'Oh, Huguette, that kirtle you never wear, or 'Oh, Joslin, if I could only match the blue of that old mantle of yours!' . . . First Sir William wanting to know what we've got, and now her wanting the clothes off our backs. . . ."

"Oh," he said again.

"And she's in and out of the stuff-closet, and the tailor has to cut into new cloth, and there in a ring we all have to sit, saying, 'Yes madam,' and 'No, madam' . . ."

"And then will Hal be going?" he asked, but instead of answering she looked suddenly at his knees. For all his working apron the acid splash had splashed one of them, and in colour the spot was a red as a *morgrygyn* or one of the agarics of the infected wood, and he flushed again, but worse followed.

"And your hands! What have you been doing to your fingers?"

"Don't look at them," he muttered. "It will have worn off in a day or two."

"But what is it?"

"Only what Sir William put me to do," but it was a great deal more than that, and it would be longer than a few days before his fingers were fit to be seen again. Now she was looking at the rest of him, at his shoes, clean and newly-mended, but the same shoes in which he had wallowed in the sloughs of the wood. She was looking at his only doublet and at his acid-splashed breeches, at least if she wasn't he thought she was, and until now she had only looked at the jaunty set of his head and the handsome teeth over which the lips never quite closed. A knight might bear a scar or lack an eye, but they didn't find that unsightly, and did they think their lockets dropped from the

skies, with never a tool slipping or a blackened finger-nail? He wanted
to tell her that somebody had to handle Mother Jule's sticky cocoons
before she could put those clothes of hers on her back, but thought
better of it, and instead asked her whether Sir Mordaunt knew about
his new banner, or whether it was supposed to be a surprise for him,
and she answered crossly:

"If he doesn't know he's the only one in Gwlad who hasn't heard
of it, and I've been thinking of that you say you're going to make of
me. Who'd want a locket made of another woman's gold?"

Ah! Now Willie began to feel himself on firm ground again. That
other whom she had at first wanted for a friend had become a rival
now, so let her look at his fingers as much as she liked, for here was
something he could handle. But her little flash was followed by another.

"And whatever else they collect they aren't going to have my pearls,
and that blue mantle she called an old one was new for me to come
to Gwlad in!" and he softened his voice the way he knew how.

"To be sure, Jo, but this melting will soon be over and then I shall
have time to myself again. And lockets aren't made the easy way you
think. Sir William's always prying and asking how it's done, not
knowing how they come from the heart (for I don't think he has one.)
And I shall want you to put those green nets on again, and here in
this garden would be a good place, and I warrant you by the time I've
had two or three sittings . . ." and mounted on the only horse he had
Willie began to put it thoroughly through its paces.

And he did so with success, for after he had talked for a few minutes
she lifted her eyes again.

"All that! Do you know what I thought, that afternoon when I was
coming back from the closet and looked up and saw you on the wall?"

"What did you think, Jo?"

"I was fit to weep with it all, and I thought, 'Here's a face, not a
shut face like the faces in Gwlad, but an open one, such as we long to
make friends with, and . . . and . . .'"

"And what, Jo?"

"I wondered what you might be thinking of me. . . ."

"I can soon show you what I think of you now. . . ."

"No, no. . . . I mean, just let's sit and talk. . . ."

And when Hal kissed his Bessie it was a stirk's kiss, just kissing
and nothing else, but set Willie showing Willie off in the best light
and he could go on by the hour together. She was pampered and
spoiled yet slighted withal, and he was not troubling about his stained
hands any longer, but clasping them between his leather knees, his
eyes on the herbs in their shady beds. The pot-herbs grew in the kitchen
gardens over by the quarry, but these herbs were physics, and at some

of their brews the butler's talisman would have sickened and changed its colours. Run down and silent again he looked at them, the foxglove rods breaking into their purple below, the rhubarb for purging, the monkshood, the coltsfoot, the lectuaries, the gums, the banes. But the summerhouse briar she was crushing between her fingers bruised with a fragrant smell, and the most those fingers knew of work was once in a while a needle prick, and he sank back into moodiness again.

"When you feel things are your due, and nobody gives them to you, then I suppose you can go on wanting them," he grumbled.

"What things, Willie?" she asked.

"What not? Almost averything. Look at what they give an artist like me to do! A stray job Tull happened to have, and now Sir William can find nothing but melting for me! What do I ever see of that fine new chamber of mine till the sun's down? Even my dinner's sent in to me, and look at these . . . look at them!" and he spread his hands out before her eyes.

"In the hall I daren't look round at you all. Where do you sit at table?"

"At the bottom of it, and I didn't come to Gwlad to sit at the bottom of tables, and I'm in two minds whether to pack up again and be off," and she threw away the briar-leaf and started on the buttons again.

"I've felt like that a long time, but you can go and I can't," and at that he grew heated.

"If it hadn't been for you I should have been off a month ago, but first it was that headpiece, then it was your box, and an odd trinket or two isn't worth staying for, and curse Gwlad and its castle if that's all!" and she gave a little gulp.

"I did what you asked me, Willie."

"I know you did, but if I'm stopping I want a hundred things I haven't got. I know I'm neither knight nor squire, but all the kings in Christendom couldn't make one of my lockets, and I want clothes, and a horse to ride, and to walk where I can be seen, not clothes-closets and quarries and you creeping in here as if it was a scullion you'd come to meet."

"I did my best," she sniffed, not the pearled lady now, but as unhappy as himself, and ready—who knew, when again and again such things have happened?—to cram a handful of her pearls and pussings into a casket one dark night, and in a dark cloak slip over the bridge while Willie kept the eyes of the guard on himself, as modest Bessie flitted out while Hal drank to them in their quart of wine.

And that would have been a tale indeed, Somewhere-else-Willie not alone this time, but Somebody-else with him, and the mastiffs and lymers of the castle with their noses to the ground, and the western mountains a clamour of pursuit, and young Ferdinand weeping in his vine-leaves for his stolen plaything, and in his frustration Willie broke out.

"And all for what? What's lying under their noses if they but knew! All this stew for every gramme and quarter-grain of gold! By God, but I was a fool not to seize his map while I had it in my fingers! Hadn't I given him gold for it too? When I'd found what I wanted couldn't I have got it back again to him somehow? Scrapings of silver-gilt when there's barrowloads of it for him that knows! Nay, I must have taken leave of my wits!"

But as suddenly he stopped, for of what prudence was he not taking his leave now? Letting such things slip him in his petulance, and to a woman! Or was it something about that herb-garden itself that engendered rashness, lulling the clear mind like a soporific? Though that apple espaliered against the seneschal's wall bloomed like a bride it never came to fruition. Of what grew about it, potions could be made that would poison the wine in my lord's hanap and made deadly the point of the treasurer's stiletto. Nightshade weeds! . . . But in the lady herself there was never any harm. Only a little later, when her frail spouse ran a foot-tilt against a smaller lad than himself and his casque was lifted from its lacings so that his blanched and terrified little face was left looking over the throat-piece like one of Mother Jule's caddices out of its broken cocoon, she tucked him into their bed and comforted his sobbing till he slept like a babe at the breast. No harm in her, nothing irredeemably wicked in himself. Perhaps it was only that he was he and she she, and what might have been right for any other two was wrong for them. He stammered and muttered.

"Take no notice. Forget I said that. Sometimes we don't hold our tongues the way we should," but now she was tapping her foot and musing.

"I know that, and then am I not told about it! But what is it you gave somebody gold for? Do you mean that collier your were telling me about?"

"Nay, I'm saying no more, except that with a horse and a few days to myself I might come back with something in my pocket that would set even Sir William looking five ways at once!"

"If you were to tell me perhaps I could help, Willie," she said timidly.

"Ay, in one way but not in another. They'd want to know what I wanted a horse for, and that 'ld be as good as telling."

"Then they'd be better guessers than I am, for I cannot guess."

But besides a horse he might want another man or two to help, and perhaps other things, and while she might be able to do little he could do nothing at all without her, and she had reconciled herself to the state of his hands, for she touched one of them lightly.

"If you don't tell me how *can* I help?"

It might too be better that she should know a little than be guessing at large and dangerously, and he hesitated, looking almost mistrustfully at her.

"Even if this time it's something you're *not* to tell Sir William or any other living soul?"

"I swear I won't," she answered earnestly.

"That is till I give you the word you may?"

"I promise."

"Then draw a bit nearer, for these aren't things a man wants to shout," and though there was no fondling now, and he could have told her it all in three minutes, it took him ten, and even then he could see he had *not* told her, for its momentousness passed entirely over her head.

"Of course I won't breathe a word, but is that all of it?" she asked, All of it! A goldmine 'all'!

"But if you have it all in your mind, as you say you have, why do you want the map?"

"To bear me out, that it *is* knowledge and I'm not just guessing."

"So there's no need for all this turning the castle upside down after all?"

"It may be only ironstone he works, but he's spent his life among these things," he answered doggedly "Why my lord himself couldn't get him here is that he moves about with his own kin, and they'd as soon fight with the devil at their sides as the English. They tried to stone me because they thought I was spying on them to sell them, so you can guess what respect they'd pay to my lord."

"Willie! When you come to think of it, it takes your breath away!"

"Ay, see it does," he answered grimly, "and now forget all about it, and promise me again."

"Oh, I vow and promise!" she breathed.

So if Willie, pottering about a lakeside in the mountains, could but light on some trace of those old workings that only a few score years before had furnished the gold for Owain's crown . . . if the treasurer of Gwlad could be brought to see that under Willie's guidance the men-at-arms could be paid, and the pawnings redeemed, and Gwlad set on its feet again, and all his troubles but his rheumatism be at an end . . . if only a number of other things would stand still as, acid or no acid, the pat-a-cake of hands began again, and again she whispered how wonderful, how wonderful it all was—then everything would be well. But events, like poisons, take time to brew, and the herbs, grey rather than green between those castle walls, had made no promise.

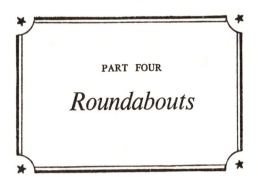

PART FOUR

Roundabouts

1

THE CATAMOUNTS AND THE BOARS HAD THE FORESTS TO THEMSELVES, the *cenedlau* kept to the mountain crests, but here below all sorts mingled. High summer was here again, those whose business took them far afield lost no time, and the towns themselves, thronged as no man remembered them, spilled out their overflow into the surrounding meadows. At the White Hart they were sleeping and camping in the open fields. Beggars swarmed abroad and such as lived by pickings, and only the hardiest now travelled alone.

But at the little inn with the orchard behind it Hannah Thirlow now had to look her situation in the face. She had never known whither her pilgrimage was to take her. The chance-met man whom she had heard playing the regal in the church had taken the care of her litter and horses off her hands, but when he asked her where she was bound for now she could only sigh, and say she supposed back where she had come from. But at that his restless face began its twitching again.

"With the roads like this you'd never get there. They're setting from the north this way too. Who was she, her you've put away?"

"My grandmother." And back came the thought of Stephen Akam again, and Robert Safford and the rest.

"Have you any money?"

"Yes," and at that his restlessness seemed to centre in his eyes.

"Who knows that besides yourself?"

"I gave him that made the coffin an écu, and her at the inn a noble."

"Where do you keep the rest?"

"In my bosom."

"Then please yourself, but it would be safer with me, and there's no knowing when I shall finger a regal again. When there's no going back we all have to go forward."

And Hannah did not answer there and then, but as well be robbed by this man who had tided her over a funeral as raped by a raglot, or both by those who now infested the roads. But no sooner had she shown what was in her linen bag than the man did an extraordinary thing, which was to begin making quick and nimble passes with his hands. "Look," he said, holding one of her own coins up before her eyes, but when she looked it was no longer between his lively fingers. "See," he said, "a spider on your arm," but when he picked the spider off, lo! it was her gold piece again. "And if here isn't another!" he exclaimed, and this time produced a Henricus from under Hannah's chin. "Now did you see what I'd done with the rest of it?"

And she stared in dismay, for suddenly both bag and money had vanished. Then she started as a strange rough voice spoke behind her, but started even more at seeing nobody there, and the next moment he was speaking in his own voice again.

"That's my trade, not singing plainchant," he said in a bitter voice. "A Joseph's coat's what I wear, and a bladder in my hand, and I mop and mow at them and they laugh, and that laugh's my wages. Here's your money again. Count it if you doubt me, and if you gave her at the inn a noble for your reckoning there should be money due back to you. I'll see you on your galloway for wherever you want to go, and you're right to trust none, me least of all. So if that's what's in your mind, God be with you."

And passing-notes died away, and candles before Maries in blue and Johns in red burn down and are renewed, and there was a company waiting at the White Hart to which he was joining himself on the morrow. Already she had had to cover that head of hers from the men who washed and ate their breakfasts in the open field and called to her across the ditch. He spoke of a Joseph's coat, but still wore his monkish habit of sober grey, and though he had mocked her with the nightingale-warble of his regal and talked about tipsy lords and their lemans, as soon as he had learned she was a pilgrim it was as if a false face had dropped from him, and he had said his name was Gandelyn, and if any needed a prayer Gandelyn did. So let it be so. Ann Thomas had prayed her last, Hannah had none but herself to pray for. He did not ask her how many sweethearts she had, nor tell her he had no daughters of his own. Instead he asked her what she could do, and she answered that her father had been a fuller and that except for cloth she knew nothing. All this was as they paced slowly back and forth past the plots and gardens between the White Hart and the Rose, turning and turning again. Then, once more outside the Hart, he asked her whether she could dance.

"No."

"But you can sew?"

"Yes."

"Then wait you here a minute," and striding into the inn he presently returned with a bundle under his arm. "Are you going to trust yourself to me?"

"I trust in God, sir."

"Amen, but God had best shut His eyes sometimes. Can you be ready to start in the morning, till I can find some place to bestow you?"

"I see naught to stay here for."

"Then I'll see you to your door and do you be running over these for me," and at the door of the Rose he thrust his bundle at her, and she spent the last of the light over a fantastically-petalled harlotry of yellow and red, with a combed crest like a cock's. He had her money, and now all else she left to him too. In whose litter Ann Thomas had ridden she had never asked, but neither litter nor its horses did she ever see again. But he kept her galloway, to which he now added burdens of his own.

The soldiery in the fields, watching from their crowded camp the next morning, saw them pass, the small company to which he had joined himself, some seven or nine strollers, apparently of his own trade, two of them women, and one of them with child. Their costume and apparatus travelled with them in a basket-tilted cart, from which painted poles stuck out. But Hannah bestrode her galloway again, with Gandelyn walking at her side, his restless face for once composed and still.

The coming together of the two roads had already told of some large town ahead, and that same afternoon its broken roof-line came into sight, but they were aware of it a good mile before that. Save for a windmill on a small hill the land thereabouts was flat, and out to a wide common the whole population of the town seemed to have poured. What fair or festival it was Hannah did not know, but she heard the tumult of it even before the tilt-cart came to a stop. A throbbing of drums and piping was borne towards them on the air, and the pious might be on their way to church, but it was for no church-going that those whose company they had joined were now making ready. About the tilt they had gathered, from it their fripperies were flung out to them. Out on the open road they set the feathers on their heads and the clowning garments on their bodies. Down too was flung their paraphernalia, their masks and beards and coloured balls and spring-rattles to announce their arrival. They painted faces on one another, and Hannah fell back as out of a savage pelt of dyed flax-combings a rough bear's head was flung back, showing a man's face beneath. But Gandelyn got into no motley, and they moved forward again, the tilt-waggon now a triumphal chariot of painted ribaldry and mirth. A tomfool with half a peacock's tail on his head had mounted its single horse, and the bear, his staff in his arms, was tipsily leading the music. Hannah closed her eyes for a moment as the woman with the child inside her got out a great greasy bagpipe and the others their horns and rattles, while the hubbub of the fair swelled about them. But Gandelyn was again the Gandelyn who had slipped the drop of water into the regal-pipe and then asked Hannah why she was not in tears.

"Me know such as these!" he said with deep contempt. "I did but see them in the inn, and show them a bit of fingerwork, and they opened their arms to me as one pickpocket hugs another. We can sink low enough in the world without supping the dregs too! But what's taken you? Have you never seen a fair before?"

She was looking about her with an intimidated look, for indeed she had never before seen such a fair as this was. It seemed to wake something up in her, some other fair she had heard of, that a long time ago had suddenly blazed, and a gowk of a girl with a pot of honey in her hand had been seized roughly from behind, and much more better let lie. But the bateleur at the galloway's head had made an abrupt sign to an oafish lad who stood by and bidden him come hither, and from his ear had suddenly plucked an egg.

"What's this?" he demanded harshly of the youth, his brows working up and down again, while the yokel gaped, for by some legerdemain the egg was suddenly two eggs. "Here's witchcraft!" he bawled. "Where's the constable?"

"Here, sir," said a gruff voice, but turning the lad saw nobody, and as suddenly the eggs too had vanished. "Nay, we're having no spells cast on us here! What's your name?"

"Cozens . . ."

"Then cease your cozening and take this bridle and hold it, and if you stir a foot from this place you'll find the Bashaw of Gallimaufry on your heels with his crickcrack! Are you there, Bashaw?"

"Yes, lord and master!" said the deep phantom-voice.

"Then sic him if he moves a finger, and call Devil Dusty if he moves two," and with another grimace he flung the bridle to the lad, pushed Hannah forward, and they mingled with the fair.

Banners flapped about them and horns sounded stridently in their ears. Brawny men lifted great weights, and some rode skirted hobby-horses, but the two legs beneath them were their own, and in one place they were dancing in a great ring and at another archers shot at a butt. But now Hannah was half afraid of this prestidigitateur she had fallen in with and whose yellow wattles she had sewn. His stripped and expressionless face was like a vellum blank or a still pool for any wind to ruffle. His eyes did not cease to dart and rove as through the fair they passed, with the windmill on its hill decked with flags too, that as they turned seemed to be fluttering signals to the roofs of the town beyond. And the mummers with whom they had travelled had set up their poles, and the bear was a rope-walker now, balancing himself up in the air with his staff, but for some reason there was an uproar about it, and men in authority from the town suddenly appeared, for their business was to keep the peace, and by this time Hannah was wondering why this man should be travelling with these scrapings he affected to despise so. But the acrobats were taking their poles down again, and where the fair thinned out was a booth where he bought hot tripes, playing however no tricks with his money this time, but buying the tripe as soberly as anybody else. The tricks were for when he came to the galloway again. The lad was still standing as stiff as if the Bashaw of Gallimaufry stood with his crickcrack behind him, and putting his hand into his pouch Gandelyn brought out a gold quarter-noble, but when the lad's fingers closed greedily upon it it was no more than a common tester, and with a kick on the backside he was bidden begone.

"Are we not waiting for the others?" Hannah asked as he helped her to her saddle again.

"No. I've a bit of business in Wroxeter. We shall be picking 'em up on the road again, and there's no fear such company won't stick to you. Are you set?" and he took the bridle and they were off once more.

Though Hannah now had the name of the place she was little wiser than before, for she had never heard of Wroxeter, and as her conductor avoided the town beyond the windmill she supposed that was because on such a day there was nobody left in it. But on the common that skirted it they met not a living soul, and presently she asked him where Wroxeter was.

"Hard by Shrewsbury," he told her. "South and east of it."

"And what's this business you left the fair for?"

"Marking swans," he answered.

"Marking swans! Pray what for?"

"Arrow-feathers," he said, but as it was no more than a put-off she drew into herself again.

"In the parts I come from they quill them with goose," she said, looking straight ahead of her, and he grunted and nodded.

"Ay. Goose will do. But geese hiss, like this," and the pony itself started as a goose hissed at its head. "Swans only sing when they die. Didn't I tell you my trade was swan-upping?"

"You said you were a droll, and I mended your motley for you."

"So. But I hook swans too, with a hook they don't see, and nick 'em and mark 'em down in a book, and you don't put on your velvets for that," and she was in a huff now, for it is ill-manners talking riddles to those who don't know the answers, and the rest of the common was crossed in silence.

Yet after Wroxeter, where, and for what, and for how long could she put up with such fantastic company? He had said something about bestowing her somewhere, but he seemed to travel by byways, which

G

began to look like bestowing her only after a fashion. The afternoon had become evening, and the common had changed now to light meadow-land, that yellowed with buttercups as the daisies shut their eyes for the night, and she knew what raglots in their purple caps had in mind when they chose secluded lodgings and bade young girls sleep quietly for none would come near. The mean house under a wood-edge he finally led her to had but two rooms, one of them occupied by the old woman who kept it, yet one could hardly guess what she lived on, for if she had had sheep there was no sign of them, and if she had had cattle they too had been driven away. But her fears, that had increased on her hour by hour, vanished like a coin between his conjuring fingers. It seemed that his swans had to be attended to by night too, for presenting himself in her doorway he bade her sleep well, and he would be back in the morning, and left her, and so in fact it was. At their outset he had taught her a whistle, of four short notes. In the morning she heard it, and there he was, calling outside that breakfast was ready. Again they set out.

Yet more mystifications were to come. Sometime that morning, as they passed what was left of a broken barn, no more than a stub of wall and an unhinged door, he asked her whether she had ever seen a knife thrown. "Because if you haven't, get down and I'll show you," he said, and from she knew not where produced a short thick-bladed knife and pointed to the door. "Make a mark there. Nay, make it within a hairsbreadth," he said, and as she set her finger on a thread of graining he stepped back. The knife glittered in the air. Quivering it came to rest on the very spot she had touched. "Again," he said, and thrice he repeated the feat. Then he put the knife away and helped her to the galloway once more.

"You could spread your fingers out against that door, and as long as I could trust you not to flinch I could put knives between all of them," he said. "Can't you feel 'em in that bundle?"

"I can feel something," she answered, for though the bundle had no swan-book she knew it had other things besides his yellow and red.

"There's twenty of them there, that I polish up like silver to make them glitter, but it isn't all you'd think. Have you never seen a knife-board?"

"Ay, for cleaning them with emery," and he nodded.

"You'll see it when we come to Wroxeter, where I left it, and I saw you were in fear last night. You were in fear of me and of what I might be after with you. Set it to rest. I have too much on my mind for such trifles. Pilgrimages don't end when an old woman dies, may their souls have rest. Think of me as just Gandelyn, that played the music in the church and hopes for rest too. Have you understood?"

"Yes," but it was spoken so low it was hardly to be heard.

"Once for all and no matter what?"

"No matter what," she answered out of her relief and thankfulness that at least he was no raglot.

"Then it need not be spoken of again."

Nor was it, and she could give her thoughts more freedom now, for already she was beginning to puzzle her head about another thing. He put spells on yokels with his talk of Bashaws of Gallimaufry; with his pranks of goose-hissing he sought to mystify herself; but if his trade in the world was to make folk gape and laugh, why then had he saddled himself with such a burden as Hannah at all? But he seemed to have a reason even for this, for on their second afternoon together he suddenly broke a silence that had lasted an hour.

"Did you tell me your trade was cloth?"

"Yes, that is to say, not weaving it, only burling and fulling."

"And you can sew, and a needlewoman's always worth her keep and I know more than one place where there's things to do in sewing closets and wardrobes and what-not. But that great flare of a head of yours . . . and it's all a trick and there's nothing to flinch from . . . but leave it for the moment. It can wait till Wroxeter," and on he strode again, never leaving the galloway's head, working his skipjack of a face, so that she wondered what twist or grimace would come next.

Never was there such a midsummer for weather. If he was able to find her a roof to sleep under at night, well and good, but if he couldn't, half the world seemed to be sleeping out of doors as well as themselves. And now that that first fear of him was over, if she wished to bathe her feet in a brook she took off her stockings and did so, and if she wanted more than that he too had his bag-of-tricks to overhaul, or something else to do. Only at her hair did he continue to look as if it had been an eruption in the sun. Often she dismounted to walk with him, and once in a while he might borrow the galloway at night, and that would be the last she would see of him till the morning. They were journeying south and west, and she was beginning to take to the life and movement as if it had been something in her blood. So they drew near to Shrewsbury town.

But she was glad they did not linger there, for she felt herself hardly able to breathe in the place. She had swilled forecourt flags, with her feet thrust into wooden clogs, but never before had she seen a whole high-street paved with stones, never such dark and frowning houses or such a loafing of soldiery as sprawled outside its taverns. They wore feathers for badges and roses-in-soleil and fetterlocks and harts, but Gandelyn made her keep herself covered up, and stalked through them as if he wished neither to know nor be known, and only when the river was crossed and the town lay behind them did he tell her that Wroxeter was only six miles away and that they were to lie there that night.

"And now for what's on my mind," he said. "We have to make our way as we go, you and me. You say you've never seen a knife-board?"

"No."

"There's taking their money too, for they think double of that they have to pay for. Bladder and bells and a trick to fool their eyes—they gape at me when out of the air something's suddenly in my hand—but a great flaming lass with her hair all gummed out and in peril of her life, and her face whitened, Jesu how they'd catch their breaths! Think you you could bring yourself to try it?"

"I know not what you mean, but if you say so," and even as she spoke, Wroxeter came into sight.

It was in an empty barn behind an inn where he seemed to be known that she steeled herself for her ordeal, with only the galloway standing by to see. First from his bundle he got out his twenty knives, but of board for polishing them she saw none, till mounting a short ladder he thrust forward from the rack where it had lain a great flat package swathed in sacking, which he lowered to the floor. It took him five minutes to loosen the knots that bound it, and even then it was not one board but two, each as tall as himself and almost as wide. These he clamped together from behind, by what mechanism she did not see, set the board up at the barn's end, bade her stand back, and the knife-play began.

It was brilliant and terrifying. Beginning at the edge of the board knife after knife flashed through the air and stuck quivering in the wood, the blades not an inch apart. He did not look at her, but when his knives were expended advanced, plucked them out and began again, but this time the hemming of knives was creeping closer to the centre of the board. Thrice he did this, and then looked at her with eyes that glittered like the knives themselves.

"You have seen I throw straight. Now I wish you to hold up your hand."

Without a word she advanced to the board.

"You're not to look at the knives, but keep your eyes on mine, and only if you flinch may there be a mishap."

With eyes glassy with apprehension but rigidly on his, she set her hand against the board. A knife flashed, a second, a third, each one nearer. "Enough!" she wanted to cry, but she must be held to it now, and not until the last knife had left his hand did he advance to the board. What he did there she did not see, but suddenly, each with its little twang, knife after knife began to appear on the board from nowhere. They took the shape of a human figure, outlined with knives, but still her martyrdom was not over, for "Now again" he ordered. "No, not your hand—place yourself against the board. . . ."

But the first time over such things are not to do again. There was nothing in the barn for her to sit on by the time he had finished, so he placed her against the pony for support. "You may close your eyes now," he said, and when she opened them again knives were popping up from the apparatus as if the board itself was bewitched.

"Are you faint?"

"My heart's pumping. . . ."

"Will you do it again—not now, but to-morrow?"

She did not answer, and his voice was now as gentle as if instead of flinging knives at her he had been making love.

"See how little there is to fear," he said. "No knife I fling comes within a foot of you. Those that do you work yourself," and as he pressed the back of his own hand against the board a knife started up at his fingertips. "You stand flat against the board, so, and your eyes must never leave mine. If you see 'em on your right hand, press back with it. If it's your left the same, and if it's your head, force it back on that side, and if it's your buttocks you thrust with 'em. It's the knives in the air they gape at, not them that's bedded in the board, the same as they look round when I speak as if there was somebody behind 'em. I shall have to change things round a bit, but when I've got the springs eased and all to fit you'll have as pretty a mantle of knives as if a tailor had measured you for it. Fairs and foolery don't stop no matter how the great wrangle over our heads. Think you you can face it?"

And there were no long-bearded caterans in Wroxeter for her to skirl to with a bagpipe, no Redshanks to spread his cloak for her on the moss at night, but the answer in her blood woke of itself. At Wroxeter too there appeared the next day the ragamuffin troupe they had joined themselves to. They had a waggon into which the knife-board could be stowed, and for the whole of that day and the next he busied himself, borrowing tools, altering the knives and springs and filling in the places where they had been. If any now cared to say that a homeless mountebank and his red-haired mort had passed that way, why let them. There can be no two minds when between eyes and eyes messages flash swifter than the knives through the air, and two whole days of it that barn at Wroxeter saw, three crucifixions a day, that she might learn crucifixion as her trade. At the end of them she could bristle herself round with knives till she was a hedgehog of their glittering blades. From Wroxeter under the Long Mynd was the way to Church Stretton and Ludlow, but now back for Shrewsbury they made, with Hannah on the galloway again and the knife-board in the tilt.

But from the rest of the troupe he held himself coldly aloof. Evidently he esteemed himself a cut above them, they carried his board for him, and often he wandered off at night alone, and when this happened Hannah must walk the next day, that the animal too might have its rest. Yet for all they had started off back for Shrewsbury he avoided its pavements as he had avoided the town by the windmill, letting the tilt go on. West of Shrewsbury was a place called Ford, where they were to meet again, but Hannah now doubted whether the woman with child would get there before her time came. She was the one who played the bagpipes, and Hannah waved to her as they parted, but still she saw no reason why they should not all have journeyed together, for again Gandelyn seemed to be idling away the time. But that same afternoon, near a place called Meole Brace, they came to a small mere, where he bade her await his return, and took himself off again. Now she had a shift to wash, and here was her washing-place, with none to see but a pair of swans and their two squab-brown cygnets, striping the mere with long feathery arrows that rippled away to the sedges of the marge. Crossing to the galloway she got the shift out and began to take off her stockings. The water was glassy enough where the swans were, but muddy at the edge, and into the mud her feet sank as with her skirts held up about her she waded a little way out. Happily she rubbed and washed, for it was joy and happiness to be alone for once, but again she must stir up the mud as she came out again, so that now her feet had to be seen to. Spreading the wet shift over a thistle she set to work on them. Running water would have been better, but one cannot always have everything as one would like it, and she was putting on her stockings again when she heard him returning, and glanced up as he appeared.

"You've been missing trade," she said, for she could talk with ease to him now. "Look, there's something for you to nick."

For a moment he stood looking down on her, the smock on the thistle and her shoes by her side. Then he placed himself by her.

"Trade?" he said. "We mustn't let trade slip through our fingers. I'm beginning to have hopes of you. Have you ever been in Cheshire?"

"No, and I want to see how you set about this upping of yours," but at something in his tone she already wished she had said nothing about the swans.

"You should see Cheshire. That's the place for swans. I've nicked eight thousand of them in Cheshire, one way and another. But you've been in Shrawardine, that was where the fair was. Did you see no swans there?"

"What, swans at a fair?"

"Ay. I marked down half a dozen of 'em, when the constables bade

Hob get down off his rope. Prudent men they were too, for trouble's always best stopped before it starts," and as she had her other stocking on now she asked him where they were making for next. But he had turned himself flat on his back, and did not answer for a long time, and when at last he did so it was to the sky over his head.

"We're not moving from here till two people, that's you and me, have come to an understanding about certain matters," he said. "Haven't you wondered what all this soldiery's on the move for?"

"Nay, I belong to other parts. For all I know it's a way they have hereabouts," she said, but there was no jocularity of any kind about the abrupt way he raised himself on his elbow.

"Remember, I could put two knives into those eyes of yours and it would but be said my hand had slipped."

She was suddenly silent.

"The last that stood before that board," he went on, "he was a man; but man or woman, they both have to be schooled. When he saw a fool in dyed flax capering on a rope with a bear's muzzle on and a staff in his hand he saw what he saw and didn't talk about it. And the same with a hart or a fetterlock, or a rose-in-soleil, or any other cognizance. I taught him to count 'em too, the same as I do, and note how they were equipped, and how many joined 'em, and how the rest stood affected, and hold his tongue about it. But I've never had to teach it to a woman before, and I found you on a pilgrimage, and a prayer's fitter than a jape about swans on a pilgrim's lips. *Hai!*" and his cry flashed as suddenly out as lightning in the night. "Ready with those eyes! To the board with you, and remember a slip with a knife's but a slip, you with that tongue on wheels! Think you I carry my swan-book where I carry my bauble and bells? Eyes at the ready! Be praying the first knife's the last!"

And had it been in his hand, and the board there by the lakeside, she could not have been whiter than she was now before the implacability of his face. All the voices of which he was the master seemed to be united in one.

"I lost one that was near to me, and many swans will have their necks stretched longer before a quittance is cried to that! *Hai!*" and terrified she saw it all, in store and to come, his secret betrayed, the slip of the hand, the flash, the shock, the blood, the dead Hannah that would be herself. "A Warwick, a York! Sell this head o' mine with what's in it and which think you'd be the first to die, you or me?"

Yet there was no need for it, for she carried that board and its discipline in her heart now, and submission had made its home in her eyes.

"You saw me through my trouble, Gandelyn . . . my worse since my father . . ."

"Your worst since . . .?" he glared.

Sitting there on the marge of the mere, reaching back into the faraway past till it unfolded itself again before her eyes, she unburdened herself of that too.

"Where was all this?" he demanded.

"A long way off, in Yorkshire. . . ."

"In Yorkshire . . .! Where in Yorkshire?"

"A place called Ellbeck, that's Uthersfield way."

"Not east Yorkshire, or north?"

"No."

"And you're alone, and you've no other?"

"None."

"And you've seen my way of living, and what a word would do?"

"I've seen."

"Then," he said, and they were almost the same words as before, "it will not be to speak of again."

Nor, as before, was it spoken of again. An hour later, on their way once more, with her shift spread out over the pony's quarters to dry as they went, he was talking about what was to be done with her hair.

2

BUT WHEN HE SPOKE OF GUMMING IT SHE NO LONGER LOOKED AT HIM as a victim. Where had *he* got his knowledge of women and their hair?

"And am I to spend my days in washing it?" she answered him back. "Do you know how long this burning-bush of mine takes to dry? Tell me what it is you want."

"I want a blaze, a house afire, a sun-in-splendour, a petard, a keg o' gunpowder going up, and your face powdered white as a sheet beneath it, stricken white with terror," and at that her mouth twitched almost like his own.

"Marry, I should be pitying myself instead of watching you! Gum my hair! But leave it till we come up with Meg again. Women know more of their own hair than men do," and on they trudged, mountebank, woman and the galloway with its packs.

Meg was the wife or fancy of Hob the Bear, and they came up with the tilt again just outside Ford. But there was no sign of Hob now. Meg was groaning like a bagpipe herself, which the other woman was urging her to do, saying it all helped, but the men had taken themselves off to an inn together, and it was falling evening, with rooks darkening the air overhead, cawing and calling as if they too told one another that a child was to be born into this world below the trees. One or two of the women of the place had also appeared to help, and a kettle was boiling on a fire on the ground, and instead of the mumming-clothes cloths and towels were set in readiness about it. There was nothing for Hannah to do but to stop her ears against Meg's ever-renewed passing-notes, but the other woman saw her face at the opening of the tilt and bade her fetch a priest quick, and seek the worthless Hob, for Meg's groans were indeed as if her spirit was taking flight. So off Hannah sped to the town, for all this was on a patch of ground outside, where gipsies such as they lighted their fires and countless rats grew fat on Ford's refuse. She was unable to find Hob, but coming out of the church she chanced to see a tender-bearded young man in a gabardine who talked to himself as he walked with his gaze on the ground. She asked him if he could help her to a priest, and he lifted a pair of irresolute brown eyes.

"For what office?" he asked.

"A woman in labour."

"*Emitte lucem tuam. I will come. In montem sanctum tuam . . .* show me the way," and he placed himself at Hannah's side.

It seemed to her good fortune that she should ask a stranger to direct her to a priest and then discover that the man was a priest himself. His name, he said, was Matthias, and when he was told that the woman who needed his ministration was one of the strollers it seemed to give him an austere sort of pleasure. It was those of the highways and hedges who needed the succour, he said, not the great in their high seats, and so fervently did he just hold forth on this text, stopping in his walk to enforce his point just when Hannah wanted him to make haste, that by the time they reached the tilt again there was nothing for him to do but to wait outside, for the groaning and droning had brought it on, and the curtains were closed. But twenty yards away she saw Gandelyn, attending to the galloway, and he was displeased, and wanted to know where she had been, and gladly she turned the earnest young priest over to him.

But an hour and a half later, with the last rook home and the western sky a fireless grate, there was no need for Matthias and his prayers. The birth was over, and Meg now wanted nothing but to be let sleep. So the young man blessed them all first in Latin and then in English, and took himself off again. But Gandelyn had been closeted with him an hour, and what had passed between them Hannah did not know, but now it was she who had the talking-to.

"There goes one who will talk himself into more trouble than he'll ever see his way out of," he said. "Where did you find him?"

"She sent me for a priest and I found him coming out of the church."

"Then have a care how you pick up with those who have lucklessness written all over them. More have heard of Master Matthias than Master Matthias knows. Valle Crucis was the safest place for him, not trying to shame prelates into what he supposes their duty to be, so let there be no more gadding. And I begin to see my way about that red head of yours. Maybe not gum, but it's got to be flared out some way, with points at the tips or maybe a pin or two set in the board to spread it about. . . ."

For half that night Hannah thought of nothing but Meg and her babe, and she got out of her blanket the next morning to find Gandelyn appointing yet another meeting-place with Hob; but now she must see the babe, and taking him too by the sleeve she drew him to the tilt, where they stood looking in over the tailboard. Under its wicker hooping, with her head on the bagpipes that had been her pillow, Meg was munching cold bacon. The mite seemed to Hannah sooty-polled and crinkled and angrily-red, but there Meg was,

with her teeth in the cold bacon, and it was Gandelyn who first
scowled, and then turned up his eyes as if he was listening to some
unseen regal, and then scowled again. "East Yorkshire," he
muttered to himself as he turned his back. The pony was ready. He
gave Hob a last order, who nodded, and leaving Meg to her bacon
and her babe they made their way past the still-closed doors of
Ford.

But now instead of keeping to the tracks of the bottoms Gandelyn
seemed to be on the look-out for hills to mount. The streams were
summer-low, at times they could walk for a mile and more over water-
less stone and pebbles, but let a hill appear and he would walk
the mile back again in search of a ford to cross it. Yet to breast one
hill was only to come to another valley, and the region was neither
chase nor forest, but a maze of broken woods, and he still wore his
hodden-grey. Indeed he would have passed for a schoolmaster conning
his lesson as they left this or that bright hillside for shade, and in
the shade sought the green again because of the tangles and the
insects and the white and purple wastes of summer weeds that
grew higher than themselves. And on the fringe of a glade, but
whether in England or Wales she did not know, he suddenly asked
her whether she ever gave a thought to that money of hers he carried
for her.

She had forgotten all about her money, for if he had been going
to make off with it he could have done so long ago, but he produced
it for her reassurance, and as Ann Thomas's savings were in écus and
French moutons and other foreign coinages a glance told her that
they were still as she had handed them to him. But now the money
seemed to be on his mind, as if it was little safer in his keeping than
in her own.

"The mischief with money," he said, "is that if you could but call
it when you were in need of it, like this handkerchief you didn't know
was in your ear . . ." and out of her ear the handkerchief magically
came as he fluttered it before her eyes, "that would be all anybody
wanted of money. Something must be thought of," and they set their
breasts to the next rise.

It was from the crest of it, on the following daybreak, that they woke
to find what he had apparently been seeking, spread out before their
eyes. On a flat mead below them was a regalia of pitched pavilions,
set in the midst of a camp. Light palisades fenced them about, and the
rays of the early sun caught their painted tops, gilding their silken
castellations and the flags that flapped lazily over their pride of crests
and cognizances and shields and devices. The camp was awake, inside
the palisades young squires could be seen adjusting the tent-ropes and

setting in order the pleated folds, and Gandelyn too had seen, for she heard him on the other side of a brake, apparently moving the galloway to a fresh place. Hurriedly stirring herself she called to him from where she had been lying.

"Have you seen? Who are they?" and his voice came grimly back,

"A few more Earls of Fitz-Somewhat. They shall be attended to. Are you to be approached?"

"Ay, there's little to hurt your eyes," and he appeared. He had her bag of money in his hand, and he had not put on his grey habit, but was no more than half-dressed, in shirt and loosened laces.

"Now hearken, Madonna, but first withdraw yourself further out of sight, and heed me well. Do you see yon farther hill, with the wood on the top that breaks in two?" and he pointed away to the skyline beyond the camp.

"Yes."

"Then I might be back before noon, ay it's certain I shall be back before afternoon, but if I'm not you're to make for that hill, keeping well this side of it and missing a bog you'll see on your right, till you come to a place called Corndon. That's where you ll find the waggon again. It might be mid-afternoon, but if it's later than that you'd best not wait here. Now say all that after me."

"I'm to make for a place called Corndon, missing a bog, where I shall find Meg and Hob, and if you're not back by mid-afternoon I'm to be off."

"Mid-afternoon will be when the sun gets just round that red gewgaw you see on that second tent. And now keep your own side o' the bush while I get into my robes of state," and again she heard him, moving about in the bushes, but when next he appeared her eyes nearly dropped out of her head with astonishment. He had got into the red-and-yellow she had mended for him, and he had a red-and-yellow toy of a zany in his hand, and he was grimacing and talking to it, and the marotte was answering in another voice.

"Shall we make 'em laugh, Titus? Ay, we'll make 'em laugh, and then we'll see who laughs last, and praise the Lord for the day He made fools! Who but a fool would laugh at a puppet on a stick? A smack o' lewdness, so, while Madonna isn't looking?" and he performed an antic. "And count 'em, queens of birds and their eggs and all! That's the jig! . . . And now for that money of yours. See, this is where I'm putting it," and he tried several moss-grown stones till one of them came up at his lift. Digging under it with the stick of his marotte he deposited the linen bag there. "Or take it with you if you like, but its best where it is, and if aught happens see you get a strong-backed wittol to look after you the rest o' your way. But I'll be back.

Bid her be of good heart, Titus," and Titus squeaked out a "God be with you, Madonna." Then, a stalking-horse with his tinkle of bells and twirling his zany as he went, like a tawdry fire in the daylight he danced away down the hillside, dropping to the camp and pavilions below.

And false fire as it was, no sooner had it gone than something seemed to die out in her breast too. Thrice he had said he would be back. It had shocked her that he who had played so sweetly on the regal in the church should bedizen himself after that ungodly fashion, perform a lewd antic, and that would be the last she would ever see of him. For there was no shutting her eyes to what he was about now. Into their own camp he had adventured, and suddenly she wished to God he had taken her with him, for without him in what a predicament would she be now?

Yet what for that matter was life with him? From night to night she never knew which roof or hedge or bush she would be sleeping under next. He terrified her with his "Hai, a Warwick, a York!" He flashed her about with a thicket of knives, in surrendering her eyes to him she seemed to have surrendered all else too, and already she saw it coming, the something else that was only a matter of familiarity and time. She was young, unprotected, in hourly need of protection, and the protection would have to be paid for with all she had to give. Of herself, she would creep to the other side of the bush one night and place herself by his side and not even whisper his name, but just lie there, still and waiting, and if nothing came of it, then it was nothing, but if it did she would at least know who her child's father was. Ann Thomas had had a Hughie who had wanted to marry her but had died in his drink instead. Raglots and the ribaldry of the fairs and soldiers everywhere, but if Hannah Thirlow was seized brutally from behind and bore a nameless brat she would wish she was with her grandmother in her grave.

But at least there was a new and heart-lifting liberty in it all, and now he had stirred up the memories of her father and the past too. What freedom had those days had to show? Twenty houses and thirty inns and a humpbacked bridge instead of a ford, and the furthest from their tether-post such as she ever got to take their buckets to the beck, and whisper over penny fortunes, and giggle about which weaver's or skinner's son they would be lying in bed with next year! What Ellbeck woman would have placed herself before the flying knives, not knowing, should some black mistrust enter his riddling head, which of them the next moment would find its home between her eyes? It was torturing, garish, fantastic, in some way all wrong, but who could say that after each breathless moment there was not the air to draw in in great new gulps and deep waters into which to plunge? Her money under the stone? Nay, it wounded her he should be thinking of the money! A few écus and florins, safe for a few moments, was that all? As for love, she could have spat at the word. A sackful of such loves and still a woman would not know the hungering that ailed her. Her grandmother the nun, dancing on the table for the caterans—a canon's silver head flung out of the window of a blazing palace—a Gandelyn away down there with his marotte, aping obscenities and nicking his swans as he went. . . .

But the morning wore on, and the sun stood at high noon, and still no folly-in-flames was to be seen making his way back up the hill. And if he did not come? With his conjuring fingers he had pointed out the way to Corndon. At Corndon she would find Meg and Hob, and there lay the bag of money under the stone. Now she could have hated him for making her suffer thus. Oh, if only a body could sleep at will, sleep the time away, get it over! She was keeping out of sight as he had bidden her, and for company she sought the galloway. Peering round the trees she could see the red cognisance of the rose on the second pavilion, and when the sun came round it it would be mid-afternoon, and she saw that into one of the galloway's packs he had stuffed his scholastic clothes. What now ought she to do about those? She supposed she was to take the animal with her, but lacking his clothes would he dance his way over the hill into Corndon dressed as he had danced himself down to the camp?

Then she made ready for the worst, for the red rose on the tent was beginning to be edged with ruby now. It was time she was off. But the next moment she had almost screamed aloud with fright, for she had heard neither whistle nor tinkle. To steal upon her he had tucked in the points of the coloured triangles, and the first she saw of him was his marotte flung down at her feet. He was grinning from ear to ear again, and on the palm of one hand he carried a great golden tansy-cake, which the next moment he was spinning like a top on the point of his finger.

"Ay, it's made of honest eggs and butter and no foolery," he warranted it as he handed it to her. "Have you eaten?"

"No," she gulped.

"Then be cramming a lump of that into you," but he was watching her strained face as a cat watches a mouse. "Have you been at my budget of tricks while I've been away?"

"No. . . ."

"Titus 'll tell me if you have. . . ."

"No . . . it's only that I'm so thankful. . . ."

"Nor my bleeding thumb, that I sometimes cut off like this?" and with a knife from nowhere he cut a deep gash in his thumb, and passed his motley over it and it was straightway healed again, but she only closed her tired eyes.

"No more pranks to-day, Gandelyn . . . just let me get breathing again. . . ."

"Then breathe yourself away from my chamber while I get out o' this trumpery, and don't make yourself sick with that cake," and taking her by the shoulders he thrust her away.

How his errand had sped she did not even ask him. He dug up her money again, and the swallows were almost out of sight overhead and golden gnat-clusters spun in the air and the pavilion were sunny on the farther side when again he took the pony's head, leading it out of the wood by another way. But his swanning seemed to be drawing to an end, for now he only talked of what lay ahead.

"Do you think you could manage a bit more walking than you have been doing?" he asked her as the notched wood on the skyline closed its gap again.

"I might be none the worse for it. Why, Gandelyn?"

"Because at Corndon we shall be seeing the last of that muck-button crew and their tilt, and the galloway'll have the knife-board to carry too," he told her.

"All's one to me, Gandelyn," she sighed, still tremulous.

"And you'll have their groats to take too, you and your white face, shaking your begging-bowl like a palmer with his shell."

"As you say, Gandelyn."

"And after that it'll be time to be thinking of that needlework I spoke of. But castles and such'll be no news to Madonnas like you."

"Nay, I know more of fulling-mills than I know about castles. Castles haven't come my way."

"What, you haven't seen a castle wi' roofs of beaten gold, and pavements slabbed with silver, and diamonds for windows and rubies and chrysoprases and beryl growing in the garden beds?"

"I've seen no more in gardens than just common flowers. Where is this wonderful castle?" and this time it was he who heaved a deep sigh.

"In Spain, for if the castle of Gwlad's become like that it's strangely changed since I saw it last," he answered, and they set themselves to the farther rise.

3

USE A MAN HANDSOMELY ENOUGH AND HE HAS VERY SOON PERSUADED himself that he has deserved it all and more. Who has been a better friend to Willie Middlemiss than Willie Middlemiss himself? Always he had been at the call of the right people, picking up with the other sort only when he had to. Now his journey-year was over. As a nobody he had come to Gwlad's castle, it was now his home, and if he wished to admire the Great Salt he now sat as one of the household, only a few seats below it, *vis-à-vis* with the marshal and Humphrey Tull. He, he was the young goldsmith-artificer, who had been fetched all the way from York because of his special gifts. If he had to be called to account it must be by the treasurer or my lord himself, and to crown all, he could rest secure in the interest of the easy-hearted lady whose favour he was now requiting with a miniature image of her own kind face.

But that image was not for all eyes, and it flustered Willie when, hearing a tapping behind him as he worked at it one morning, he turned to find the treasurer himself behind him, his shrunken hands on his ebony stick as he stood there in his cloth-of-gold. Impossible to cover up what he was doing. There was too much of it, too many objects spread out before him, the drawing on the Valle Crucis paper, three or four pieces of green wax, and a plaster mould. Already Sir William had one of the waxen objects in his hand.

"What is this?" he asked, peering curiously at it, as well he might, and Willie had turned as red as fire.

"But a notion that caught my fancy, sir, and having begun it I went on with it," he mumbled, on his feet in the treasurer's presence; but a smile had stolen over Sir William's flat and mottled face.

"No more than a notion, young artist, when 'tis somebody's very coiffing, and the fall-away of her cheek, and the exact turn of her pretty nose? But at what keyholes have you been listening? Now it seems another secret is abroad!"

"A secret, sir?" Willie stammered.

"That young Ferdinand is to be made a knight. It was known to no more than three or four. Are you something of a courtier too, to spy out those due for advancement and ingratiate yourself with pictures of their ladies, as we say *pour les beaux yeux?*"

"Nay, sir, I know of no such secret," Willie returned, redder than ever. Yet for all that he was not ill-pleased, for if Sir William thought that his miniature was destined for young Ferdinand then he was keeping Willie's secret too; but the treasurer had picked up a second green object, and a third, and was attentively comparing the impressions. Then he shook his head sadly.

"Ah, how it all takes me back! Three trials, each as the work proceeds, and then another hour at the matrix and then another impression . . . ah, make the most of your youth, young man, for little did I think either that I should end up with these crippled hands! And what are you casting it in?"

"In a bit of silver I have left over from a headpiece, sir," and again Sir William shook his head in a melancholy way.

"Ah, would I could spare you the gold . . . but stay. Have I not in my possession a bit of gold that's rightly yours? Sir Ferdinand in his bed, sweated away to a dewdrop with all this exercising, nay, he cannot be offered his lady's picture in anything but the best! Ay, it's herself, all but the voice, and we must see what can be done. Bid Punshon remind me," and putting the impressions down on the table again he helped himself with his stick across the floor and the arras fell behind him again.

Willie gave the treasurer time to get down the stairs again, but no more. He never knew when the quiet-footed Punshon entered his chamber in his absence, but as far as he knew this was the first time the treasurer himself had mounted his stairs, and now he wanted his piece of gold back, and he was downstairs in Punshon's chamber almost before Sir William could have reached his own apartment. The clerk's head was bent over his books, and whereas a short time ago Willie had sat many places at the board below Punshon, he now sat as many above him. Yet on hearing his entry the clerk did not rise immediately, being busy with figures.

"Be so good as to let me finish the casting of this column, sir," he said, and when he had cast it pushed his ledger aside and got up, and placed a second stool for Willie, and showed him other deferences.

"A cup of wine, sir, such as you won't get in the hall. I can commend it to you, for it's his own," and a sideways jerk of his head told whose the wine was.

But Willie would have none of the treasurer's wine. After drinking it a man nodded off in his chair and woke wondering where he was, and to wonder where he was was no longer Willie's business, which was to set himself higher still. But by Willie's leave Punshon filled a small measure for himself, and when Willie told him what he had come for said, 'Ay, he knew the bit of gold Willie meant. It had a

wench's head on it, and it should be seen to that very afternoon.'
But Willie sat on, and presently was asking Punshon about the last
assay and how it had worked out.

"But thinly, sir. Those knops were hardly worth the firing, no more
than five grains the lot, and ah me, the quantities of this licked-over
latten you find when you come to look! You'd wonder they went on
making laws, the shameless way they're broken!" and so shocked did
he seem by such illegal practices that Willie had to laugh.

"Come, Punshon, that last lot was but the heeltaps! You and I know
there's been enough stuff melted these last weeks to pay the wages of
three castles and their soldiery!" but first Punshon shook his head,
but then seemed to think twice, for when one man is going up in the
world and another wants to be taken up with him this last must show
himself off to the best advantage he can.

"Ay sir, as you say, melting enough; but soldiers are housed and
fed and ha' no clothes to buy, so there's a-many comes before them,"
and as the clerk's eyes rested on the books on the table it came over
Willie again that Punshon's was one of the sort of faces he didn't
quite trust, for deferential as his eyes were there were times when
something shot out of them that bit like the acids in the cellar below.
But the clerk took another sip of the wine, and it seemed to embolden
him to go on with what he had begun.

"It's all in those books, sir, where the money goes. And you're one
of us, if I may make so free, but for all that keep your voice down,
for you never know when any stone in these walls isn't an ear. It's all
in those books, and they aren't for all eyes to see. Have I your leave
to speak, sir?"

"Talk on, man," and drawing one of the ledgers to him the clerk
began to turn over its engrossed pages.

"See this lot," he said, his finger resting on a detailed inventory
with its precious yield to balance it opposite. "That was sent to Salop,
wherever it gets after that. This other went to Hereford, and these,"
and he turned over the page, "all these were for Gloster and South
Wales. And so with the rest. Men lie, sir, but not figures, and when I
go to bed at night the box I keep these books in is chained to my body."

"But why does it go to all these places?" Willie asked, and at that
Punshon became the underling, suddenly brought forward into the
light and magnifying himself and his office.

"What used to be salt-cellars and flagons, Maister Middlemiss, is
what you can call new money now, and they keep the new money for
that they have to buy on the hoof, as we say," he said.

"What do you mean, 'on the hoof'?"

"Such as are not caught and listed yet. Where there's new men to raise, that's where the new money goes, for you cannot catch the recruit with a pinch of salt on his tail. He wants to see the money, and look you, sir, it isn't as if all England was swimming in it. There's starvation little of it, and what even the new 'uns get isn't going to choke them either, for first there's the agent, and then his men, and their men, and the more hands it goes through it gets no bigger. What's wanted isn't old stuff made new. The man that could make himself king of them all, he'd be the one who . . ." but suddenly the wine seemed to have been too much for him, for he gave a hiccough.

"Yes? He'd be . . .?" said Willie, but the clerk's face was swollen with coughing and his mouth protruded and he seemed about to choke.

"He'd be—but you were right, sir—I wish I'd denied myself that wine. . . ."

"Go on with what you were saying. . . ."

"So early in the day—it's led me on to say more than I set out to say. . . ."

"Come, the king of them all would be the man who—what?"

"That could make newer money still—*ugh ugh*—nay, with your good leave I'll seek the next chamber a minute . . ." and rising from his stool he moved unsteadily across the floor.

Now had Willie but glanced into the cup from which Punshon had been drinking, and sipped of it himself, he would have found that the wine in it was no whit stronger than that that was served daily in the hall; but as he came away every other thought flew out of his head at the sight of what he found waiting for him when he entered his own chamber again.

For weeks now he had been looking forward to it. The acid-stains had gone from his fingers, he sat within arms-length of the Great Salt, but still he had been wearing his weather-stained old jerkin and the leathers in which he had first arrived at Gwlad. When his livery was ready it would be black, like Punshon's, but what use had stirk Hal for sayes and velvets now? Hal was for the field. Working-steel for Hal, Sir Mordaunt's device over his chain-shirt and Bessie's glove in his cap, these were all Hal needed to buffet his way to a pair of spurs, and Hal had clothes to fling away. The suit on which Willie had set his heart was a velvet of murrey with fine branchings stamped all over it. Its mulberry-hue was sober and seemly, but the branchings gave it a richness as it caught the light, and Hal had royally refused to accept anything for it. Now here it was, back from its altering by the tailor, waiting for Willie to try it on.

The transformation took half an hour. He had entered his chamber an artisan; he came out of it again a courtier, a personage, bearing himself assuredly, a figure to step aside for, a Willie come into his own

at last. Now for the glass in the stuff-closet, and hastening to it he
looked long at himself and then made himself a bow. A fig for the
French knight in his blue-black and his poetical beard! And even as
he looked he had now a further use for Hal.

For Hal, squire of Sir Mordaunt's horses too, sometimes rode with
the grooms up into the mountains to exercise them, and those heights
to the west now overshadowed the whole of Willie's life. Say that Willie
himself rode there with Hal one day, and while the grooms watered
the horses at the lake he and Hal strayed off together, as leaving the
cenedl he had moved off with Bartholomew Rhys? Hal, no doubt,
would be bellowing out some battle-cry, but Willie? Willie would have
his eyes about him. Workings only fifty years old did not disappear as
quickly as that, and say he found no workings, but only a random
stone or two to put into his pocket, for crushing when he got back?
'*Aur*' for gold? Deowl, but Willie was not a fool! He did not expect
to cry "Ha!" and pick up a lump of gold with every step he took! But
the next time Sir William looked over his shoulder he would have a
new occupation to be discussed. He would have opened a way to a
momentous subject, a subject only to be discussed with Sir William
himself, a subject it would be his plain duty to bring to the treasurer's
notice. Now his talk with Punshon had set him all on fire again. It
needed no Punshon to tell Willie how starvation little of gold there was
in the world. Hal would not be in the castle much longer, it was time
things were set in motion. First warn Punshon against that wine of the
treasurer's taken too early in the morning, then find out what else he
knew, the treasurer's moods, when he was to be approached and when
not, anything else. For all this Punshon was the man, and Willie made
his way slowly back along the glazed gallery again, counsellor-like in
his new mulberry, and like a counsellor his head bowed down with
its weight of thought.

For already he was beginning to see other differences that Hal's
departure would make. Four with a secret are close company even if
two of them do meet in a herb-garden and two at Dame Kate's, or
it might be the other way round, and now other changes in the castle's
life daily drew the bond closer. The morning exercises were being
hastened on. There were fresh comings and goings, as if for the con-
tinuation of Gwlad and its tapestried life fresh warps were being set
up, to work an altered pattern upon. Yet in what did one secret differ
from another that Jo had not told him that Ferdinand was so soon
to be made a knight? Somehow that was little like herself, and instead
of returning to his quarters that afternoon he had sought the air and
was pacing moodily by the dead-end of the moat. Lily-pads patched
its scummed surface, their flowers like broken egg-shells on their green

platters, gently rocking whenever the waterfowl dived. Above him the solar casement stood open, behind him lay the grating of Pietro's cellar, but it was the hour of the siesta, and the quietness of the backwater put him in mind of the day when they had all ridden out hunting but my lord had remained behind, and from his window he had seen them down in the grasscourt together, walking slowly, deep in talk. They had paused by the sundial with '*Labuntur et Imputantur*' on it, and Willie knew what that meant now, for he had asked Hal. It meant that the hours and days crept on but what you did with them was set down in your account, and it might have been that mulberry was not his lucky colour, for now he could not shake off that picture of her in her crimson and pearls, pausing by the sundial when Willie had supposed my lord to be miles away up in the mountains. Could it be that she had known about Ferdinand even then and had been keeping it back from him ever since?

And now that it had begun it went on. On that same day, in the evening, they had met in the herb-garden for the first time. It was there that she had told him she had given his locket to Sir William, and he had told her of a Welsh collier he had once met on an English mountain, but presently had come their first kiss, a kiss so long and deep that for a time it had had to be pat-a-cake with hands, to give reason time to steady itself again.

But now he was beginning once more to wonder whether kiss by kiss he had not kissed his reason completely away. For after that, either in her grass-green with the daisy-buttons or the crimson again, or the night-blue mantle she cast about herself to slip past the guards to Dame Kate's, or whichever of her clothes it might be, there had been nothing he had not told her. In the end he had even told her of a map that would have set Sir William looking five ways at once . . . yes, he remembered the very words, and the puzzled look she had given him in return. Now a bauble for her baby-husband outweighed even that, and she had kept his trumped-up knighthood back from him, and suddenly Willie felt that that needed some sort of explanation. He would have it that very evening, unless (as had already twice happened) she sent him some last-minute excuse; and their meeting-place for that evening was neither the herb-garden nor Dame Kate's, but in a new one of her own choosing. It seemed that Bessie's duties with the children did not end with the day. Two of them were in her charge at night too, and Bessie could not be folded in Hal's bear's-hug and within earshot of Jacqueline and Philippa too, so that night Jo had promised to take her place. Hal, who had been her messenger, had been clear enough in his directions; but Hal had also been in a stew of a hurry, and his last words had been over his shoulder from the saddle.

"It's but five feet, and there's a notch for your toe. . . ."

"*Bien*," growled Willie in his mulberry, but it sounded more like "Deowl," and Hal had been off, and Willie had turned in under the treasurer's arch, and finding his old clothes where he had thrown them on his bed had begun to fold them and put them away.

He thought it a foolhardy venture from the start. Already he knew the way by which he had descended into Sir William's apartment with the coloured window; now instead of descending it it seemed he was to mount. When the new solar wing had been built a portion of the old turret had been left for buttress and support, and where old and new met Bessie and her charges had been wedged away. The lower half of an old loophole had been walled in again but the upper half left open for light, and this it was that "was only five feet high," with a notch for his toe too. At eight o'clock that evening Willie stood looking at it, then at his new clothes. Hoisting himself carefully over, he brushed the dust away again with his hand and then stood looking about him. The angle of the passage had only one recess, and into it he cautiously peered. Inside it a door had been left partly open.

But the white cells of Valle Crucis itself were not more sparsely furnished than the narrow cubicle in which he found himself. It had a pallet with a wooden crucifix over it, a scrap of matting to kneel on, a chest, a linen-covered ledge with a few objects neatly laid out on it, and from every appearance it was none other than the chamber in which governess Bessie nightly cried herself to sleep. And by this time Willie had worked himself up into a masterful mood. He would give Jo her due for planning, but this was too foolhardy altogether. A greensick virgin's bedroom, and she not even there herself to tell him he had made a mistake and must take himself off as he valued his life! But he had not long to wait. In the doorway by which he had entered she stood, and for a moment he almost thought he had mistaken his way after all, for as swiftly she fell back again.

"*Oh*! Who . . ."

But he had made no mistake, and the next moment all was plain. What her eyes had rested on had been a stranger, in soberly-rich clothes, dark against Bessie's white walls and bed, and with clothes to pick and choose among herself she had not recognized him now that he too had a second suit to his back. And though she had quickly recovered herself she spoke in a low and hurried voice.

"I thought . . . coming in so suddenly . . . but listen. It mustn't be for more than a quarter of an hour. . . ."

Indeed no, and now he had noticed that that virginal cell had an inner door, behind which the children probably slept, but for all that she was at no pains to drop her voice, and now he spoke.

"Why had it to be here?" he demanded.

"Because of the children. They're playing games in the solar, but I shall hear them coming and keep them till you're away, and it had to be here or not at all. . . ."

"And will it be the same to-morrow night?" and as he had not moved she advanced and placed both her hands pleadingly on his breast.

"Not so harshly, Willie, for indeed it's getting beyond my wits sometimes. I've seen her when it would go to your heart the hard way she takes it, and I'm in my lady's favour now, and you'll be here when Hal's not. . . ."

"Then is this to be every night till he goes?"

"Of course not, for he's in a sweal of things too, and he cannot meet her every night," and now she was gazing at him in his velvet with the branched stampings, nor had he seen her before dressed as she was dressed now. To play with the children she too had turned herself into a governess, and something had happened to her hair-nets, and she had torn them off, and now it was just her ebon hair, not made to be groomed by any tirewoman, but by other fingers, that would lift it from her head like a truss of riches already half their own. She was admiring him, holding him back to see him better.

"Willie! Have you been to the closet and looked at yourself in the glass?"

"You'd say it became me?" he asked, turning himself.

"Nay, the dignity! It puts their finery to the blush! Let me feel it," and she ran her small hand over its pile, but then she gave a light sigh. "And yet . . ."

"Yet what?"

"Yet it was in the other I saw you first, when you didn't look the same as them all. But let's not waste the few minutes we have, and indeed it cannot be longer, for Jaqueline and Philippa will be back, and I promised Bessie . . ."

"Then sit down by me," and of itself his arm went about her.

But where it was now drawing her she would not have, for a ledge of rock among the bracken is one thing, and a seat in a summerhouse and an old bench at Dame Kate's are two more, but bed-edges are bed-edges and different again. And she had played with the children on the floor, so she placed herself at his feet with her head against his velvet knee and let his hands do as they list with her hair.

"Poor child!" she sighed. "If she could have riven Sir Mordaunt's banner in twenty pieces she would ha' done, just to keep him a bit longer, but it's been finished these three days. Any day they'll be setting up the pavilions in the quarry, for it's to be presented to him with ceremonies, by my lady herself. Bessie'll not believe but Hal's knocked on the head already, and when he tells her it's them that wears such gloves as hers that does the knocking she'll have none of it, but only creeps closer to him and weeps."

"Pish, tell her about all them that doesn't get knocked on the head."

"I do, and we all do, even the Lady Estelle, and she brightens up for a bit, but then it all comes over her again, and—nay, sweetheart, leave me a hair to my head!" For it was siesta-tumbled again, and all his doing.

"Then get up and sit by me."

"Not I, for I know you. . . ."

"Five minutes. . . ."

"And have Jacqueline and Philippa on us before we know, and Bessie with her bed to straighten again! That would be prettiness for a maiden's chamber!"

"Would it were your own!" and as she would not rise he slipped down, and there was a sighing silence for a space, but presently they began to talk again.

"Saints above, the thrumming you've made of me! The solar 'll see no more o' me to-night!"

"Let me see you with it right down, Jo."

"Hearken to him, first in my pearls, then in my green nets, and now like a cow's tail to switch the flies off! You'll be wanting me as I was born next! What speed are you making with that likeness of mine?"

"Likenesses are for when I haven't you," but suddenly she put her hand over his mouth.

"Sssh . . . listen . . ."

And it was nothing, yet not nothing, for it brought him back to where he was. He kissed the hand before setting it against his breast, but the outer door stood open, and what little light remained was beginning to glimmer on Bessie's white walls.

"I cannot say I like this new bower of yours overmuch," he said. "Think you it'll be long now before they're off?"

"I wasn't to say so, but it will be before another week, and oh, Willie, the ache I've been in to see you!"

Then out it popped. . . . "To tell me this about Ferdinand?" and he felt the sudden trembling of her hand against his breast as she began some pretence of not understanding.

"What about Ferdinand?"

"That he was to be dubbed a knight," and she drew back.

"Who told you that?"

"It's yourself I should have thought would have told me, but it had to be the treasurer," he answered, and suddenly the hand was snatched away. Straightening herself she was on her feet. Not even the children must see her disordered as she was, and she crossed to Bessie's white-clothed table, from which with her hands busily at her hair she spoke over her shoulder.

"I was under promise, Willie. I was under promise to my lord himself, and it had to be weighed with other matters first, that it wasn't for either you or me to ask questions about. But seeing Sir William's told you, and it's close at hand now, it may be I'm loosed. It will be the day they all go. The priest will bless the banner, and my lady will give it into Sir Mordaunt's keeping, and Ferdinand will have watched his vine-leaves overnight from his bed, but he'll have to be there whatever befalls, and now you know all there is," and she went on dressing her hair.

But Willie did not know all, and if things were as she had said it brought much of his planning to the ground again. There was little likelihood now that he would ride out with Hal to water the horses, and while the grooms waited by a lake-side would wander off with him as he had wandered with Bartholomew Rhys, and pick up no matter what so it but brought things to a head with the treasurer and opened a door it might be to nowhere, but it might be to Augsburgs and Nurembergs of gold. Within a week! The day was Tuesday. So soon, and still not a dozen people in Gwlad had been told of it! And now so slowly was she dressing her hair that she might have had all night to do it in. He was in a nook of the castle where it would be at his peril he was found, and suddenly the hair-dressing was finished. She turned, advanced, and stood before him, the two of them of a height, she with her hands again beseechingly at his breast.

"It shall not be here again, Willie, and do not blame me, but to-night is their last together, and oh, have a thought for me too! Lady or not, think you my life's anything but a hunger and a wasting away? With a sick boy in bed, that would have had a sort of prettiness had he not been pampered from his cradle and picked up and married when he should ha' been playing hoodman-blind, a babe in my arms where a man should have been, and me sometimes fit to curse my own father, that riches wasn't enough for him but he must sire a bought title too! Willie, love! They try to comfort me as I try to comfort Bessie, but I cannot shut my eyes to what I know in my heart. Come Christmas I shall be a widow, for me and his exercises will have finished him. Nay, I meant no harm, that was but a child in knowledge myself. Philippa and Jaqueline know as much as I knew then, but a widow I shall be, and this chamber wasn't my thought, but Bessie herself. Open your heart a bit, Willie, for I haven't yet seen it as wide open as mine is to you now. Shall I tell you something?" and now it was she who might have had but a single garment to her back, not velvet and pearls, but a shawl to wrap her head in, and an apron to rest the babe on her knee, and her hair to cover her at nights.

"What?"

"Let me bury him first and get my mourning over. Then, if you will, one quiet night we'll steal out o' this place, not to Dame Kate's, but a long way, wherever you say, sweetheart mine. And my father can do what he likes about his new-bought Lady Joslin, but I shall be just Jo again, a mercer's daughter, that walking along a gallery one day saw a face that no more belonged here than her own did, and what with this and that wasn't able to help herself, but did what she did, and if it was wrong you must try to forgive her, but if it was right —nay, I cannot go on, for 'tis too like imagining his death! But come in your old clothes, red splashes and all—just Willie, my own lad. . . ."

But suddenly she saw his face fixed on the doorway. There, hand-in-hand in the last of the daylight, the two children stood.

4

THE DRAWBRIDGE OF GWLAD NOW STOOD OPEN FROM SUNRISE TILL eve for the coming and going of those within and without. So greatly did these last exceed the first that the waste itself had become a camp, and the cattle had gone, and the fires of the soldiery lighted the outer walls at night, and hardly for an hour were the trumpets still. For now the tidings were that half the Marches were on the move. Dusty messengers flung themselves from their horses, for news not received with speed is no news at all, and from the waste the watchfires reached out to the huts and hovels of the township itself. The solar casement was closed for the clatter of the horses that crowded the back-court about the smithies. At the octagonal kitchen pickets had been set, for there were too many strange faces to be watched, each of them with a mouth and a belly beneath. And the stay-at-homes of the household thanked God it would only be for a few days, when as suddenly all would be peace again.

But in the lists by the quarry they were preparing for ceremonial. No tilting-barrier was being dressed, for it was not the time to be maiming men, but up they were going, the timber frames for the galleries, the pavilions, the presentation-dais with its tester, the fencing to keep the beholders back. All day the hammering sounded, and the marshal's men looked up at the skies, but they remained cloudless, and now the secret was out, and there was not a scullion who did not know that nine-tenths of the garrison was for the field at once, leaving only a few behind. Indeed, the Lady Estelle had already gone, accompanied a full post by my lord himself, back to Ludlow and His Grace, a bristle of spears glinting away down the sunny southern road.

Grave in his mulberry velvet, heavy with thought, Willie Middlemiss moved among the marshal's men. The poles and frames were ready for the panoplies, and a couple of tents were already fluttering their silken spreads like vessels in the breeze. One of them was Sir Mordaunt's, all gules and bars, sables and feathers argent, but Willie saw no Hal, nor had he seen him all that day or the day before. Instead he saw Sir Baltasar, my lord's chaplain, who was to bless the banner, as grave of demeanour as himself, but he turned away, wondering which of them had the better reason for his gravity. Sir Baltasar was only there to assure himself beforehand that no rope or roughness of the ground should trip him during the performance of his solemn office. But Willie? Now?

If only he could have seen Hal, just for a few moments! Or Bessie, or Jo! But now the ladies were keeping to their own apartments, and he supposed Jo was with her sick boy, and Bessie instructing her charges in modesty of demeanour as they carried the ewer and basin with their eyes prettily on the ground. But at the worst Hal could only be knocked on the head, and now again Willie was telling himself that there was nothing at all to fear. Two children, hand-in-hand at a door! Pish, there were twenty ways out! In a trice she had driven them away, in another he had been over the window-ledge and half-way down the turret again. On his way back to his chamber he had met nobody, and say Jaqueline or Philippa did babble, the way children did, and some jealous lady-in-waiting pricked up her ears and began to whisper and question further? Jo and Bessie would see to it. Jaqueline had been dreaming, Philippa had been overtired. Bessie would swear she had been at her post. Jo was in favour again and would bear her out. Piff! Willie had been in a hundred worse predicaments!

But still he could not shake it off, and now he had himself to blame for a hardly less dangerous thing. Had it needed all this about Welsh colliers just to bring a locket to Sir William's notice? How did he know in what words she had rallied the treasurer about having a goldsmith in the castle and then giving him no work to do? Oh, so lightly she had passed all *that* over! So ready had Willie been too, to drink it all in! But why had Sir William come into Willie's chamber that morning, and picked up three impressions in green wax, and then asked Willie whether he was a courtier too, to hear secrets by side winds and then flatter an infant knight-to-be with a picture of the lady of his heart? And the soft-footed Punshon, what of him? Now all coming together it troubled Willie. From the exercise-ground he had passed through the garrison arch into the grass-court. Even there strangers came and went, and he stood by the sundial again, looking at its motto. '*Labuntur et Imputantur.*' Time steals on, but it brings its reckoning with it. A pretty thought that for one who was trying to look on the bright side and tell himself all was well! Turning away to his own chamber again, he got out one of his pieces of green wax and stood looking at it for a very long time. Now she wanted him to wait only a little while, and together they would steal out one dark night and would not return, and he knew now where they would go. They would go to London, where he had never been. There the real nobility dwelt, not these castle-bound country cousins, sunk in debt and glad to pawn their scions to the first merchant's daughter who bid the price. London! Even proud York subjected itself to the London assay. It was there the Goldsmith's Guild was, and in Cheap where her father had his shop the goldsmiths too were gathered. Not a doubt her father knew them, and they met in one another's houses, and the fewer titles they had among them the more it was Maister This and Maister That, and to marry money and rub shoulders with it was better than to be a Bartholomew, dreaming of it in the bowels of the earth. . . .

Suddenly he heard a 'Hem' behind him. It was the black-liveried Punshon again, and he turned, for though he had friends there was no coming at them, and as things were he must account even Punshon his friend. But Punshon's face had little on it to cheer him.

"What's amiss, Punshon?" he asked, and the clerk shook his melancholy head.

"I misdoubted it was too good to last. Heigho! We have to take it as it comes."

"What now?"

"It's the weather. He always says he knows when it's going to change. He's on his couch again."

"Sir William?"

"Ay, and if I were you I should keep out of his way. He was asking for you this morning, but I said you weren't to be found."

"What does he want of me?"

"Somebody to wreak his rheumatism on, so let him wreak it on me that's used to him and his ways."

And this Willie would gladly have done, but to be sent for and not be there was not the way to favour, yet it was above all to comfort himself that he answered Punshon as servants should be answered.

"Nay, you could have found me, for I was only watching them set up the tents. I'm under the treasurer's orders, and it's my duty to be at his call. I ought to need no bidding either. Is he to be seen now or is he sleeping?"

"Best for all of us if he was," Punshon muttered, and that settled it for Willie. Let Punshon cringe. He did not know the Latin for it, but if all had to be accounted for so let the duty and obedience be too, and it seemed to set matters right with the sundial again.

"You'll find his door open, and don't say you weren't warned," said the clerk at the foot of the stairs, and without further words Willie walked along the passage.

Change for the better or break for the worse, no outside weather ever altered the light of that apartment with the painted window, outside which there now paced not one sentry but two. The treasurer lay on the couch in his cloth-of-gold, his low table by his side, and it seemed that his door should not have been left open, for he raised his voice in choler, but seeing it was not Punshon checked himself somewhat.

"Cannot yon proud-stomach of a clerk shut a door now?" he complained. "A man's but to fall sick and every back's turned on him!" and when Willie had closed the door he demanded to be told whether the rain had come yet.

"No sir, and yet it has come over sultry," said Willie, standing before him. "I'm told you sent for me, sir, and I was not to be found, but I was there or thereby, and now I've made all haste," and now he had his portion of it too.

"I want none of you, for I'm weary of your faces all of you, now I'm on my back again and cannot see an order carried out. I could die alone for all any of you'd come nigh me—aaoh!" for a cramp had taken him and he was twisted with it. "It has to creep but a bit closer my heart. . . ."

"Command me, sir. Shall I run for the physician?" but the spasm passed and the sufferer answered wearily.

"Nay, they can know no more than what you tell 'em about yourself. But there's drops in that phial. Count me out six, on sugar," and his eyes blinked towards the table. "Ay," he said when Willie had done the measuring, "I thank you, young man. It seems I have one near me after all—ay, I thank you," and as Willie passed him a napkin to wipe the drops from his fingers he added, "That rogue Punshon . . ." and closed his eyes.

And now Willie was set up with himself at having done the right thing. If, just once, he had seen cruelty peeping out from below Sir William's fluttering lids, why, Sir William had much to suffer, so let him keep his cruelty for others. He had taken Willie up, and praised his art, and only lately, picking up one of Willie's bits of green wax, had smiled and asked him if he was a courtier too. At the treasurer's bidding he sat down. The drops brought some ease, and Punshon did not know the trick of respecting others and oneself too, for now Sir William was looking at him with thanks in his eyes.

"I see you've changed your suit," he said, and Willie withdrew his eyes from the phial, for he was thinking that if those drops brought such relief he must be ready at need to go to the physician for more of them.

"Yes, sir, for I was watching the setting up of the pavilions, and all who were not working seemed to be in their best, and you haven't told me why you sent for me."

"Nay, it has gone from my mind. May you never suffer in your limbs as I do wi' this overcast weather!"

"It's to be hoped it holds up till after the presentation, sir," said Willie cheerfully, for he had always heard that cheerful company is a physic, but Sir William's lids were blinking again.

"The presentation?"

"The banner my lady's to bestow on Sir Mordaunt, sir," and the treasurer passed his hand over his brow.

"Ah, the presentation! Sick men forget the world goes on just the same. I'm getting too old for changes, and indeed many changes are coming, young man."

"So I hear on all hands, sir."

"Another week and we shall be but few in Gwlad . . . women and children, servants and old men and such a cripple as you see in me . . . and all the treasure gone with 'em. . . ."

"I'd had it in my mind at one time to go myself, sir," said Willie, but at that the treasurer shook his head.

"There's plenty in brigandines without putting artists into strait jackets, and that brings it back why I sent for you, but 'tis naught. We'll let them get out o' the castle first."

"Would it be too bold to ask where they're going, sir?" Willie ventured, and Sir William placed two finger tips on his eyelids as he paused.

"It's all who does the asking, but let me see. Isn't it from the North you came?"

"From York, sir."

"To be sure, from York. There was something about two Henricus H's back-to-back. Were you ever in Middleham?"

"Never, sir, but I've heard my Lord of Salisbury has a castle there."

"His castle's there still, but not him. Yet he has but a weak force, and these from Gwlad are setting out to join him."

Willie suddenly felt himself a heavily responsible person. There was he, in his mulberry velvet, being told high matters by Sir William in his cloth-of-gold, when Punshon himself, who knew the treasurer best of all, had bidden him beware. But of such matters he was well aware that he knew nothing, and silence is always golden, and it would show a proper discretion to return to the matter in hand.

"Yet . . . you sent for me, sir."

"I did. Measure me three more of those drops, for it keeps it off," and when this was done, "but as I say, 'tis naught, naught that half the world hereabouts doesn't know. Which way did you come to Gwlad from York?"

"Over the mountains, sir."

"What? Alone?" and Willie hesitated, yet having started on the truth, judged it best to go along.

"I set out alone, sir, but I picked up with some on the way."

"Who were these you picked up with?" and Willie became warier still.

"A pack of Welsh miners, sir, that called themselves a *cenedl*. They were travelling the mountain way so as not to be pressed."

"On which side were they?"

"On neither side, sir," and Sir William sighed.

"There's little of that you can tell me if they're Welsh! But you say they were miners. Were they then mining on the mountains?" and this time Sir William rested his eyes by closing them.

And now Willie was all a-quiver. Here, after his best thought and contrivance and care, was the opening he had sought, offered him by the treasurer of Gwlad himself. No watering the horses with Hal, not a finger to lift, only to answer Sir William's questions, slowly, bearing in mind all he knew, with his eyes open and placing himself in the best light. From heaven itself the occasion came, and would to the God of it he had had something to moisten his lips with, for never had they been so dry.

"Not mining, sir. 'Twas ironstone they mined, and had there been any there was no fuel to be had. They were from Carlisle, and the last I saw of them they were bound for the Forest of Dean. But there was one among them, a man curious in such things. . . ."

"Yes?" said Sir William softly.

"He knew more than the others. He was forever picking up stones as they went, and crushing them in a mortar, and sifting and sampling them. . . ."

"Yes?"

"And he marked 'em all down, pyrites or shale or whatever it might be," and Sir William opened his eyes again, blinking with interest.

"On what?"

"He had a sort of map, that he'd made himself. . . ."

"That he marked down what he found on? Have you seen this map?"

"Yes, sir."

"Yourself? You have not just heard of it?"

"With these eyes I saw it, sir."

"Did you by any chance ever take a copy of this curiosity of a map?"

"No, sir, but . . . it may be it's not for me to say so, sir, but what my eyes see they remember. . . ."

And the look Sir William shot at Willie at this was the most gracious and flattering of all, for it was a tribute to those same eyes in Willie's head. He did not speak, but Willie glowed with pleasure, and now the way stood broadly open, but Sir William still had questions to ask.

"These of this—whatever the word was you used—did they too know of this you're speaking of?"

"That would be hard to say, sir. Not more than two or three of them spoke English. But I doubt if they'd make much of that map, for certain signs were neither in English nor Welsh."

"Yet travelling together, they could see all there was to see for themselves without a map?"

"It may be, sir. Indeed, they must have known there was silver round Carlisle."

"You said ironstone. Was silver too marked?"

"With an '*Ag*,' which is neither Welsh nor English, but Latin."

"So you are a Latinist too!"

"Indeed no, sir. I heard all the Latin I wanted at Valle Crucis. But every goldsmith knows '*Ag*' is silver, and '*Aur*' gold," and suddenly the treasurer astonished Willie by addressing him by his name for the first time.

"So, young Master Middlemiss; but let me tell you all this is something and nothing. Draw the matter that way round and you'll hear these tales of silver and gold on every tongue. Tell me what, in your proper judgment, is the best way to keep a secret?"

"Tell it to none, sir," said Willie promptly.

"Ay, that would keep it fast enough, but after that?"

"None but them you could trust," but again the treasurer shook his head.

"Not so. Tell all the world. Show 'em your piece of gold. Let them take it in their hands. Then ask them if they can guess where it came from, and whatever they say, then say, Ay, so it was. Do you take me?"

"Only in part, sir."

"Then hear, young goldsmith. Take a walk one day on the waste yonder. Speak to the first you meet, and if you lead the talk rightly soon he'll be whispering in your ear there's gold in these very mountains. Nay, and he's right too, as I can give you evidence. Bet let another come, and ask them both where it is, and see the loggerheads they'll be at about it! How many did they number, these miners of yours?"

"Twenty—thirty . . ." said Willie, picturing the *cenedl* again, strung out over the misty mountain-top, Pugh a dot away on the left, Iorwerth on the right, and the jangling of their implements and the thin notes of the horns that kept them together.

"And how many are there in this castle? Five hundred? A thousand? What becomes of a thousand men once they're out on these hills? Think you they're not swallowed up? What's more, these hills are my lord's, and do you tell me that pushed as my lord's been pushed, and as I'm pushed now (for my lord has many matters to weigh him down and it's on the treasurer it all falls) . . . think you it hasn't all been tried, and tried again, eating up yet more money, till none but a fool would put his hand into his pocket any deeper?"

Crestfallen and abashed, Willie found not a word to say, but the soft voice went on.

"But you have seen a map and you have eyes to remember with. Tell me now what sort of a map you could make out o' your memory, so as maybe to open things again, though God wot I thought I'd finished with the folly! A hundred men couldn't be spared, but with good hap a dozen might."

But now that Willie tried to do so even in his own ears it sounded the lamest of tales. A lake of which he did not know the name: an estuary, but Gwlad was nowhere near the sea: Bartholomew's '*Aur*,' the unskilled letters themselves sprawling over it might be twenty miles of ground: the more he lost himself the more closely the treasurer questioned. But he hinted and helped too, letting fall little things, and one would have said he commiserated with Willie, forgetting even his own aches that the further it went the more he must extinguish Willie's hopes. The band of miners he swept wholly aside. They were but twenty or thirty ignorant labouring men. But one among them had knowledge, and knowledge, ah, knowledge, was all! Let Willie but say he could produce a map. . . .

"If there was a map in this castle to start me, sir. . . ."

"One might be found. It wouldn't be my lord's map, that has closer secrets on it than all this hoodman-blind of gold. But the marshal will have maps, but yet there's another matter. Say you found what you seek. What next?"

"That would be for him that's lord of the land, sir."

"But not of the gold in it. Even my lord would have to pray for a licence to work it, and some o' that would go to the crown, and some to the Church, but it would be my lord who had the wages to pay, and God's eyes, he's paid enough."

"My lord has but to pray for his licence to get it, and for the rest he'd have his hands on it, and them that has their hands on a thing first, sir . . ." and again the treasurer asked Willie to measure out the drops. They must have been some tincture of mint, for now a faint odour of mint seemed to emanate from the couch, suffusing the air as the reds and blues of the window stained the light, and had not Willie now all he had ever dreamed of and in the fullest measure? Secret or no secret, here he was at the very heart and centre of it. Not only had Sir William listened attentively; the pressure of his questions was

gentle, and if he must disappoint Willie he was doing so with the least
hurt, patiently showing him reasons. And suddenly he raised himself
on one elbow and told him to call Punshon, bidding him bring his
keys. Willie did so, and under the treasurer's direction the clerk carried
forward the heavy iron-bound chest from the other side of the apartment, and turned a key in it, and was then told to be gone again.
"Open it," said the treasurer, and Willie lifted the lid. In its upper part
was a tray, and Sir William had said no more than the truth, for search
in the mountains had indeed been made. Lying there in compartments
were ores and stones, some cracked and crushed, others in the lump,
each with its legend or note.

"That was some of Pietro's work," murmured the treasurer, his
eyes now on the ores and quartz, now on Willie. "Pietro is a Venetian
and a skilled and learned man. Indeed his skill and learning would have
landed him i' trouble had he fallen into any other hands than mine,
for I found him at Gravesend, and not knowing our English ways he
had lighted on evil company, of which he had to be cured. But I was
loth to be too heavy on one who had worked in Venice, under Montigliani himself, ay and in his own cabinet, so I chid him and made them
suffer that deserved it. I cannot get up into mountains myself, nor have
this twenty years, so I cannot tell you which parts these are from.
Can you read Pietro's lips?"

"No, sir."

"Nor can I when he tries to speak English with 'em, but these are
his findings and glosses, that worked under Montigliani's own eyes.
You've heard of Montigliani?"

"Never, sir."

"No matter, seeing he's more a searcher into things than a profiter
by them. It was something for Pietro to do in his cellar. It's your
Bartholomew I'd liefer see than any o' them," and Willie started
violently, for never at any time had Sir William heard the *pen cenedl's*
name from Willie's lips. "And bear it ever in mind, if Pietro shows
mutiny you've but to do this," and with his crooked finger the
sick man again shaped the diagram of a square in the coloured
air. "But it is time we drew to some point. How think you matters
stand now, you that's done everything but hold this gold in your
hand?"

How indeed? Was that coloured window never opened, the air in
that apartment never changed, or was it that some lingering heat from
the cellars below never altered? Heard but unmarked, the two sentries
outside had not ceased to pass and repass, but now Willie was conscious
of their footfall for the first time. "It's your Bartholomew I'd liefer
see than any of them" but how had this man come by Bartholomew's

name? To whom in that castle had Willie ever breathed it, ever had occasion to breathe it? Only to one, and now the skies themselves seemed to darken outside the coloured window, some unwholesome heat to distil from that flaccid body. The last time his fingers had drawn that sinister square in the air had been that morning when he had supported Willie up from the cellar, and given him wine to restore him, and said he had but been probing him and putting him to the test, for how should he take a man into his privy service without knowing the make of man he was?

And that same morning, when the wine had brought Willie round again, he had shown Willie the gold knob of his stick, and the deadly thing had come apart in his hand, showing its thin envenomed point. Oh, a cruel man, with a fastidious stomach for cruelty, taking it as he took his drops, one sugared drop at a time and then a delectable closing of the eyes as he savoured it! How did matters stand now? Only one other pair of lips in Gwlad could have spoken Bartholomew's name. She had told a long story, but what story he had not even asked her. Now the invalid's lids were fluttering again as he watched Willie from the couch.

"Those artist's eyes of yours! If they have but carried a map as they carry daintier things! Say, unless I pry (for indeed it has a bearing): the Lady Joslin so soon to be, did she sit to you for the medallion you're so prettily at in your green wax?"

"They sit best when they least know it, sir," Willie managed to get faintly out, for it came over him like a sickness, the perilous new scent the man's nostrils might be at now.

"True, but what I would know is, just how comes it you catch the image so that the very eyes cry 'Ha?' By what process, for even the heavenliest of gifts cannot work but by a process."

"It's not a thing I can explain, sir. . . ."

"But you see my drift. A face or a map, it is the same faculty, and I cannot advise my lord to sink yet more money lacking some sort of trust or warrant."

"Then think no more of it, sir, for with any wit I might have known," said Willie humbly, his head on his breast, but Sir William caught his glance which was on the open chest of stones, and he spoke as one might hush a babe.

"Come, come, a better heart than that! With such luck as has been yours already! As Tull tells me, you began with vine-leaves. That guided you to the one lady in all this castle that could help you at a leap higher. With such a lady taking you up, and coming to me on your behalf with a jewel in her hand I should have grieved to miss . . . this spate of arms and marching is only for a few days longer and then we can all take to our peaceable occupations again . . . nay, so protected and favoured, you cannot lose heart now!"

"I have naught to say, sir."

"Ah! You would remind me she is a wedded lady, wedded and out of reach! But fear nothing for that, for provided it is chaste all courtesy and chivalry allow it and extol it! The air is never still of their rondels and vilanelles! For a touch o' the fingertips they die happy slaying Turks and paynims i' battle! They vow to make themselves monks for the kiss of a petticoat hem, and visit them at night only as angels visit 'em, i' their dreams! Think you we've forgotten the sweets of life, us that lies sick, forsaken by all but their physician and such as they can hold in fear?"

And now the eyes were blinking so rapidly that each eye might have had a reptilian double lid, baleful and veiled, and it rushed over Willie that those same eyes were reputed to know where every piece on his charge was at any moment of the day or night. Even Punshon lowered his voice, saying that the very stones of the walls were ears, and Punshon crept into chambers when their occupant was not there, and reported what he saw, so that presently there was Sir William himself, advised of his moment, and picking up impressions in green wax and comparing them with the mould that made them. Now the soft voice was smothered in its own sweetness.

"But to return to that map. Soon they will be off, but my lord remains behind to set things on a footing before he goes too, and how his eyes will sparkle and dance! For always 'twas I who held him back. Ever he believed in it, as I believe myself, ay me, could we but find the spot! The Great Salt itself could go but he'd find that gold, and there are the workings, for Punshon has seen them, but alas they're worked out! Now the map's the miracle that changes all. This is no wish of mine, but my lord's himself, and I can see the leap he'll give when he but hears the word! But you see what will be necessary?"

Willie, his head still sunk on his breast, made no reply.

"You cannot be set to work in your present chamber, for there's naught in this castle half so precious as this is now. Your map will have to be made in secret, under my lord's own eyes and mine. It's what I sent for you this morning for, when you were looking on with Sir Baltasar. The chaplain has a cabinet next to my lord's. There's one chamber between his and this, and it's there I shall place you. Punshon will wait on you as he waits on me, whatever you command. I fear you'll miss your liberty for a few days, but if we cannot lay hands on this Bartholomew it cannot be otherwise. Did you hear that sentry that passed? Beyond my lord's apartment he turns again. He passes the chaplain's room, then yours, then this, and turns again. Would I could see you lodged myself! But Punshon will see to it, as he will see to all. Nay, call him now, that I may give him his orders myself—and remember 'tis but till your map is ready and the place is found."

And Punshon came, and carried the chest of ores back to its place again, and showed Willie out of the coloured room by an inner door and into another only a stride or two beyond. There his belongings were carried down that very afternoon. But though Punshon locked no door, Willie needed no telling that he was hardly less a prisoner than the tongueless Pietro in the cellar below.

5

THE CEREMONIES WERE OVER, SIR MORDAUNT'S BANNER CONSECRATED,
little Ferdinand Covil had knelt and risen again Sir Ferdinand,
chaplain Baltasar absolved and blessed the men-at-arms. The banner
was hung for the time being behind Sir Mordaunt's place in the great
hall, and Sir Ferdinand was put back into his bed again. Now what
had been solemnity was all noise and merriment. The pavilions and
fluttering stages were placed under guard, the exercise-ground was as
crowded as a fair, and out on the waste was the fair itself. No more
marching and counter-marching, no discipline of captains or orders
save the general calls of the trumpets; the soldiery were making holiday
and to-morrow would be on the march. The hall was appointed for a
night of revelry. Hal, as departing, was given a place at table and
waited on by a page. He and his glove were going, but not for long or
far, not to France or anywhere across the seas. Still on English soil,
assuredly he would be back before the winter, with a new-healed and
handsome scar it might be, but a pair of spurs on his heels too. Thus
Sir Gaston, the languishing French prisoner, still waiting for his
ransom, but a few moments later he was debonair again, receiving the
angelic custody of Bessie with a pledge to Hal, and my lady herself for
his witness. It was late that night when they sat down to dinner.

But in a closed room next to the treasurer's, Willie Middlemiss sat,
gazing gloomily at his untasted food.

From the waste to the hovels of the town was also a press of preparation. The rain had held off, but the month was September, the Year
of Our Lord 1459, a mid-solstice. The sun sank early, a yellower light
glowed on the outer walls, for they were burning up the encampment
rubbish, and the air was smoky with the moving torches. Here on the
waste too were tents, not silken pavilions or galleries gaudy with
blazonings of arms, but the workaday booths of common people,
pudding sellers and vendors of trotters and porringers of pulse and pease.
Besides the great loaded military waggons were wains and barrows
and tilts and handcarts, and in and out moved Mother Jule with her
crutches and her beard, telling fortunes.

By the whipping-posts two tumblers performed their antics, and
with the sun now sunk beyond the western mountains the crowd but
increased in numbers, for they were ejecting all strangers from the

castle and closing the bridge. With their pickings in their pockets they poured out by the wooden approach, some singing tipsily as they came.

But in the room next to the treasurer's Willie Middlemiss still sat, eating nothing, and Punshon took his supper away again, but still he sat. The room, like the treasurer's, had a couch under the window, but though the window was of clear glass it was placed too high for him to look out of without getting on the couch. He heard the passing of the sentries without seeing them, and he had no second room. Carefully taking off and folding his doublet of murrey he lay down on the couch.

He was awakened the next morning, a couple of hours before Punshon appeared with his breakfast. It was still only half light, the trumpets were blowing without ceasing, but that was my lord's side of the castle and so the quietest and when the trumpets paused no lesser sounds reached him in between. And the devil take him if he was going to lie there, straining his ears but hearing only the trumpets, and he got up, and put on his doublet again, and opened the door and was walking out. But at the turn of the passage he met Punshon, who fixed sorrowful eyes on him.

"Have you not slept well, sir?" he asked.

"Well enough," said Willie, and Punshon stood aside as Willie made to pass on, but he saw the shake of the clerk's head.

"As you will, sir, but 'twill but end in a chiding," he said, and at the way in which Punshon spoke the last word Willie stopped abruptly. He remembered that Pietro too had been "chidden." He had been apprehended at Gravesend, in the wrong company, and his luckless companions had not escaped with a chiding. He stared at Punshon for some moments, who made no attempt to restrain him. A chiding, but Sir William was not the man to chide twice. The next was a square drawn with a crooked forefinger in the air, and Willie knew now that Montfaucon's gibbet was a square one, set on a little hill, and that there they could be counted as they dangled, thirty at a time. Dropping his head he returned slowly by the way he had come.

So past the entrance of Gwlad's quarry the men-at-arms marched out by companies. By the southern valley way they had come in, but to join those advancing from Middleham in the north they now issued again by the postern. The castle trumpets played a Loath-to-depart, the ladies waved handkerchiefs from that portion of the walls overlooking the backcourt where Willie's own turret had once been, and it was as if the castle itself sighed when the last man had gone. Now again my lord would appear at the board or not, as might befall. Only a semblance of garnish would be set out on the sideboards, the hanap and the Great Salt would be seen but fitfully. Willie was alone,

with only Sir Baltasar's closet to separate him from the apartments
to which my lord would withdraw himself. If the treasurer on his other
side visited the castle's master Willie would know his passing by the
tapping of his ebony stick, but so neighboured he must keep a decorous
silence, move about with the least noise possible. The weather would
get no better, nor with it Sir William's health. It was the report he had
first heard of him, how ill a man he was to cross when his rheumatism
shook him. Punshon went in fear of him, and now if Willie was to
have speech with Sir William again apparently it must be by way of
Punshon.

His prison needed but a little furnishing to make it, though small,
the handsomest apartment Willie had ever seen. It seemed indeed to
have been a guest-chamber, for the lodging of great personages, for a
cusped and ornamented canopy overarched its window and its walls
had been diapered with a pattern of gold lilies. But now furniture had
been taken out to make room for a large working-table. As before he
had been given goldsmith's tools, so now he was supplied with rules
and compasses and squares, and on the table was spread the marshal's
map. And by comparison with Bartholomew's ragged rivering and
sprawls of lakes the marshal's map was a map indeed, but any help
it was to Willie was as nothing to the distractions it raised in his head.
As a map he could have pored over it from sunrise to nightfall. Every
castle in the Marches it showed—nay, in the whole Western Kingdom,
from Haverford and Pembroke to Harddllech and Caernarvon in the
north, the roads, the overwhelming woods, the harbourages of the
coasts. But it said nothing of '*Ag*' for silver or '*Aur*' for gold, and
Willie knew already that he had done ill to ask for it. Instead of pegging
him to the ground it scattered his thoughts like a flock of birds.
Ludlow: that was where His Grace lay, and the castle there was
Wigmore. Wirral and Hope and Caer: that was the country he had
crossed with Matthias. There was Valle Crucis by its stream, and here
Gwlad itself, with Willie Middlemiss lodged in it. But he had best set
it aside. He was not there to lose himself over maps, but to make a
map—nay, one point on a map, which if he could but hit on his troubles
were over. For half a day he dreamed and fretted. Then slowly he
dropped his head. When he lifted it again it was to push the marshal's
map away. This was not the way to do it.

Then what way? Perhaps a short sleep, for he had slept little, and
on his couch he stretched himself. To the sound of the sentry's feet
he slept, nor did he wake till again Punshon brought in his food,
which this time he did not refuse. Sleep too had shown him how plainly
this was *not* the way. Bartholomew's notions too must be set aside.
They became ever the vaguer with thinking on, and Willie's first plan

had been the best. If not with Hal, then with another, it was to get up into the mountains themselves. Was he a magician, to lie there on a couch and direct others to gold? Try; and if nothing then try again.

And now he despised Punshon only less than he was beginning to fear his master. That too came back with his daytime sleep, his padded footsteps, his treachery, his spying. It was Punshon who had spread the net that had brought him into those crippled hands. It was Punshon who had nosed about Willie's upper room, and reported what he had found there, so that up at the chosen moment Sir William had come too, to see for himself. It was Punshon who had led Willie on with his talk of gold, and had shown him his ledgers, and talked about listening walls, yet had not scrupled to seem to betray the treasurer even while he served him. Now Punshon was his gaoler, who did not close doors but warned Willie that if he used them he would be chidden. The door opened and there he stood, again asking Willie whether he would not take a cup of wine, Punshon, who had feigned a drunken sickness when he had been no more drunk than Willie himself. But now Willie had the measure of his man and a show of civility was the best.

"I thank you, Punshon, but no, for my head must be clear for what I have to do. Is our master easier of his pains to-day?"

"Up one minute, down the next, sir. I dread the winter with him."

"Think you this Welsh air·may not suit him?"

"He's tried many airs, sir. It goes deeper than that, and you don't live all those years with a man without knowing when he's due for it again."

"What, have you then served him a long time?"

"Before we ever saw Gwlad, sir. I was in London with him, and Harwich, and Bristowe, to say nothing of Calais and Flanders and the Poitou ports and the Isles."

"And what is this he's due for again?"

"A shaking passion, sir, a very palsy of fury, that always follows on the mint. First the wine I thank you for that warning of, then the mint, and I've never seen him that far yet but the other followed."

"Nay, the poor gentleman! And can naught be done?"

"That's all according, sir. Let the rage work itself out and he's a lamb again. But sometimes you'd shiver at what comes in between. Yet he'd seem to be different when he's with you, sir. *I'd* never ha' ventured in on him the other morning the way you did, and my lord himself doesn't always handle him the right way, for just when he's needing a rest my lord's all on the jump about that gold again. You're the one that seems to have the trick of it. Lodged like this i' one of the chosen chambers, that Dauphins and Infantas have slept in before now! Nay, nay. In my judgment, *you're* the medicine for him, sir!"

("And if I can but get *you* outside this castle, and my hands on that false throat o' yours, you lickspittle rogue, I'll be your medicine too!" Willie muttered, as Punshon brushed a speck from his black livery and glanced to see that Willie had all he wanted and took himself noiselessly off again.)

It was sometime during the dead of that night that Willie woke to it in all its sudden blackness. Yet there was a lurking, glimmering light in the blackness too, that seemed to persist out of some dark dream. Never, never, would he make that map. It had never been there to make save as a memory of another's memory, that he had not been able to question. He did not even know whether that ragged *cenedl* had been there, or whether it rested on hearsay and surmise, as Bartholomew surmised so many other things, the metals that married, the oil-well that burned yet could not be brought to melt the iron out of the stone. All that he knew the treasurer too had known, as every rascal on the waste had heard of it, and the treasurer too had tried and failed and tried again, with Pietro below to crush and sift for him, till he had deemed the money still in hand to be the best and had sponged it from his mind. But now my lord himself had been roused to it all again. Fain would Sir William have had his hands on this Bartholomew Rhys, but now they had Willie instead. Dauphins and Infantas had slept under that same canopy, but what a fool he had been not to know that first thoughts were always right! His impulse had been to steal the map. There then the map would have been, to speak for itself, and after that Willie could have washed his hands of it all.

But say now Willie had had the map, what the better would he have been for it? Say too that by some twist of luck the very spot was found? Then my lord would pray for his licence, and would get it, but still where would Willie be? He shivered. That inner midnight light shone on himself too, lighting up his path to its fatal end. Such secrets were not for journeyman-goldsmiths who came unasked to castles and slept first among the horses and their fodder but now in a royal lodging. The moment the gold was found he would be questioned. He would be kept away from the place, told that it was all a flash and nothing, bidden produce this Bartholomew, charged with misleading, chidden. Of a certainty no more liberty would be his in this castle that was now forcing its very stones apart with things that did not meet the eye. The way to keep a secret? Tell none? Tell all? Ah, but there was a still better way, and that was not to have one!

Chidden. As Pietro had been chidden. The gibbet for the others, but for Pietro they had had a use and they had but chidden him. So Willie would be chidden, left without a tongue to tell that he had

ever known anything; so now, while this light-in-darkness lasted, was
the time to be taking the necessary steps. No door was yet locked on
him, not yet. For a light offence they could still only rebuke him
lightly, and he had been free to go to the ceremonies at a very little
risk. Therefore his map must still see him through. He must affect a
diligence at it, remember other things Bartholomew had told him,
dream them, make them up, tell them all was on the way, ask for yet
other maps. Then, but how he could not think yet, word must be got
to Jo. What she had let slip or not let slip must wait, and who was her
pimple of a spouse to stand in the way now? Sir Ferdinand! Dub a
cheese-maggot and see it skip on the platter! She had been forced into
marriage with her breeches-button of a boy. He had known it was but
a peanut of a marriage ever since that first headshake that had said
No but all the time her eyes had said Yes. But let there be no more of
this talk about waiting till after Christmas. It must be on the first
quiet night, just before they closed the bridge. Punshon should smart,
but Sizar the smith was a good fellow and it was not far to the smithy.
He would have an accident with his pair of compasses so that they had
to be straightened. Sizar had friends among the servants—he should
be given a note, to be conveyed to her. . . .

He was busily composing his note when the light-in-darkness began
to blend itself with another light, and the window over his head became
grey and the golden lilies began to glimmer palely again on his inner
wall.

And now let tale-bearer Punshon be given the right kind of tale
to bear, for the part he must play in his map-making was an immediate
one. Punshon had his chest of stones, but Punshon had never been
under the tuition of an eminent geologist like Bartholomew Rhys, not
a profitless prober into things like this Montigliani, but a toiler and
labourer at it, yet with the blood of kings in his veins too, so that he
sought kingly things in a kingly way. The prodigious natural philosopher that Bartholomew Rhys had been must be conveyed to Punshon too, by hints and signs and profundities of nothing. And on this
airy meat Willie began to feed Punshon that very morning, as he bade
him run to the seneschal's office for balsamed paper he could see
through, and such other maps as were to be had, that Willie might
seem to be tracing it all back, step by step and inference by inference.
Then let Punshon go and tell it all to Sir William, and let Sir William
pass it on to my lord. Nay, even this buffoonery must be given an air
and semblance too, and Willie saw that he had been wrong in turning
back at Punshon's gloomy hint that if he moved twenty paces from
his room he would be chidden. He ought to have taken no notice,
stared at Punshon, pushed past him and gone to those ceremonies. A

prisoner, he? He was far less a prisoner even than the French knight was, for Sir Gaston had given his parole, and Willie had given none. Out of his own grace and reasonableness he had accepted it, that such a secret was a matter only for my lord, the treasurer and himself. If Sir William meant "Punshon shall bring you your food, and see to your close-stool, and you may bid Punshon do whatever you are in need of, but do not set foot out of your chamber," then let Sir William say so. He turned to Punshon again.

"But see you say nothing of what I'm imparting to you, for indeed I ought not to be saying it at all; yet ah, if I could but tell you a quarter of the things that prince of philosophers told me!" he said with a sage headshake. "When I used to stand back in awe of him, and tell him surely he had the gift of divination, see the way he'd shake that noble head of his! It was but the ripe fruits of experience, he'd tell me, running his fingers over that map and then pointing to the ground and bidding me dig, for he always had a spade with him and made me carry one too. Would you could have seen him, you that has a chest of stones of your own! . . . 'Gwilym,' he'd say, for he never called me aught but Gwilym, as if I'd been his own son, 'Gwilym, I see a stone there with a sort of sheen on it; put it in your pocket and remind me when we get back where you picked it up; then I'll likely tell you what it is just by the look o' the land,' . . . and never yet have I known him wrong. But I don't doubt I shall manage without him, so get me that balsam paper to lay on the map, for I've this minute bethought me of something else."

It was while Punshon had gone that the accident happened to his compasses. Setting them on the floor he placed his heel on them in such a way that when he picked them up again the points were bent in different directions and would by no means meet. Then with his compasses in his hand and his note in his breast he put on his mulberry doublet again and strode out. Straight to the smithy he went, where he spent ten minutes in talk with Sizar, and then, sniffing the air, saw no reason why he should return immediately, very good reason why he should now find out Sir William's mind. He therefore crossed the back-court, but found it a melancholy sight. Menials were idling in the sun, at the kitchen doors cooks and panters stood in gossip. The pavilions had gone from the lists, the barrack-room into which he looked was empty. Determined to prove Punshon wrong, he strolled across the grass-court, past his own door to the herb-garden, and then back to the court again and through the outer arch to the moat. But he approached neither the gatehouse nor the bridge, for he could see across to the waste without. Thrice the ordinary numbers seemed to have assembled there, and they were squatting about a couple of fires they had lighted, and the hollow drubbing of a drum reached his ears, and a thin piping, for even the draggletails that ever follow moving troops were draggled by those who sought to entertain them. Strollers and thieves no doubt, and now he had done enough to put this about the chiding to the test, and he returned to his own quarters, where he found Punshon again, either in fear for him or simulating a fear.

"Oh sir, have a care!" was all he said, but Willie only gave him an indifferent laugh.

"What ails you now, Punshon?"

"Sir—never say I didn't warn you. . . ."

"No, I'll never say that, good Punshon, but I bent my compasses and took 'em to Sizar to heat and straighten and they'll be ready in an hour, so be you ready to fetch 'em back. What's all this to-do on the waste?" and Punshon trembled again.

"Don't tell me you've been out on the waste, sir!"

"Not I. I but saw 'em across the moat. There seemed to be music."

"There'll be less when my lord holds his court, sir."

"A court? My lord? What court?"

"Halve the guards of this castle, sir, and see what starts among the baser sort. Gatehouse or postern, through they'll slip, or some o' them inside will slip out, and it's nothing but wenching and pilfering, and four o' the rogues has been taken already. All such is to deal with before my lord's free to go, and them you saw are just a pack of idlers and witnesses and hard-swearers, and I wish you could keep yourself a bit more within rule, sir, for it's as I say when he starts on that mint," but now Willie became lofty.

"Punshon, you put me out of all patience. 'Tis you doesn't set about such things the right way. What Sir William requires of me needs no orders, and when will he be ready for me to see him again?"

"Can I tell him you have aught for him?" and at that Willie broke imprudently out.

"No, but hearken to what you can do, and stir yourself about it too! You can go to the kitchen, and see what's for dinner, and bring me the choice of two or three dishes. Then when I've had it you can go get those compasses from Sizar. Did you get the balsam paper?"

"It's on the table, waiting for you, sir."

"Then do as I command you, and let's have no more of this talk about orders that haven't been given nor likely to be," and shocked at the outburst Punshon went dejectedly out.

But the devil take it that he had lost his temper and raised his voice in that way, forgetting what chamber he was in. No invalid wishes to hear voices raised only a yard or two beyond his door, and Punshon bringing in his dinner, conveyed Sir William's request with it. On,

Willie's other side was Sir Baltasar's room, my lord's beyond again, and Sir William's concern was not for himself. It was lest my lord should have been disturbed, which was hardly to be believed, but Willie had been reminded of his situation. If, a prisoner, he wished to brawl, there was down below for that. He had not seen those prisons down below. Pietro's hot cellar had been prison enough for him, but Pietro had the air of the moat-end and a grating through which the sunlight slanted at certain hours down the wall. It was not to be supposed that the castle had no worse dungeons than Pietro's, and now he was told that my lord was to hold a court. Now too he remembered, which he had entirely forgotten, that he had been railed at by an old hag of a silkwork-woman who for a year and a half had not seen her own two sons. One had sold bread of his own baking, the other had shot a falcon with a bolt, but if anything went amiss, to sell a loaf of bread, to shoot a bird, to raise a voice to a servant—which of these crimes was likely in my lord's eye to outweigh the shattering of a cherished dream, and now this dangerous hoodwinking about a map? This dust-in-the-eyes to gain a little time, time for another to contrive things, and send him secret word, and be waiting one evening in the shadow of the guardhouse before they closed the gate, and off together to London, where her father was, and the most famous goldsmiths were, and when Sir Ferdinand died her white arms and bosom to receive him? Oh, if Sir William were indeed a cruel man what daintier cruelty could he have contrived than this, so soft, so gentle, never a finger lifted, and the victim himself telling himself that all was well?

And how much better was this creeper back-and-forth between them, able to give messages what twist he pleased, ready at any moment to run to Sir William to tell him that Willie was taking it thus and thus? Sir William had only to remain invisible and Willie himself twisted the cords and chose among the irons, even as he sat with his head between his hands over his balsam paper, trying to remember word-by-word what he had written in the note he had committed to Sizar. Now even that note had gone the way of Bartholomew's map. He had written it in perturbation and haste. By some means she must contrive to see him for a few minutes, as always she had done the contriving, and what had she not contrived? Always she thought of something. Assuredly she would think of something now, and all that afternoon he sat there, telling himself that there was no need for him to be sitting there at all, for he was still free to come and go provided he did not raise his voice and disturb Sir Baltasar at his prayers in the next room.

Then the more glowing things began to steal over him again. The Yes of the eyes had belied the No of the headshake from the very beginning. He was sinking to his knee before her again in the drapery-closet, showing her that trouble of a locket among the bracken of the quarry, telling her he had no pretty mistress, watching the alarm on her face when the thwacking of the staves had ceased and she had realized that the exercises were over. She was in the herb-garden again in her crimson and pearls, in the close gown of green with the ripple of daisy-buttons he had kissed her, the two of them sinking into the kiss together till the light had died about above them as if they drowned. Oh her boy-nibbled, hungering mouth, given its sustenance at last! No flimflam fare there, to be helped on its way to the sighing of a vilanelle, but solid mutton and pudding for a tradesman's daughter, as he was no more than an artificer himself. That hair of hers, thick as a truss and long as a cow's tail and walnut-black and scented like the wall-flower in the quarry . . . but suddenly Willie's heart gave a check. Through the masonry of the wall itself he seemed to hear the treasurer's voice again, pressing home its gentle questions. That impression in green wax: if it was not to pry, how did he make such likenesses that the very eye cried 'Ha?' Was it the same faculty and gift by which he was able to remember maps? Now what in the devil's name had the treasurer meant by that? Sir William did not ask questions at large. They were to the point, like his stiletto, that did not prick deep but God help him it pricked at all! What had his nose picked up now?

He started out into a sweat. Not that broken old turret on which the new solar-building abutted! Not that upper embrasure only five feet from the ground, or Bessie's white cell with the bed, and the room where the two elder children lodged beyond! Yet even at that he had hinted. So it remained but chaste all courtesy and chivalry allowed it! For a smile they took themselves overseas, and died happy fighting Turks, made themselves monks for the kiss of a garment's hem, visited them only as angels visited them, in their dreams! Willie wiped away the sweat. There was no sweat. Pietro was doing something on his hearth below.

For the making of his map he had put aside his mulberry jacket. Now he put it on again. There at the door the two children had stood, and he had not seen her since. The ceremonies had raised her to the degree of a lady, and Willie too sat in a chamber with golden lilies and a canopy over his bed. But Willie sat as suppliants sit in some high and gilded but public antechamber of a palace, with twenty others pondering their suits, while expressionless servitors appeared at door-ways, beckoning forward this one or that. And as he sat there suddenly there reached his ears the distant call of the barbican trumpet. The trumpet always sounded for the arrival of messengers, except that this time the flourish seemed a little prolonged. It ceased, but Willie's mapping ceased too, and he sat down on the edge of his bed, listening to the two sentries passing, first my lord's apartments, then the chaplain's and Willie's, then the turn beyond the treasurer's coloured window and back again. He was thinking of Bessie's white room again, of the two children hand-in-hand, but leaving nothing unexamined now, no minutest question unasked.

It was perhaps an hour later that Punshon entered. A servant to his bones, he had forgotten Willie's roundness with him, and again his voice was as deferential as his footfall. "Sir William grieves to put you to trouble, sir, but they are my lord's own orders. For maybe a day or two you will have to be disturbed."

"What's afoot now?" Willie demanded.

"News from the south, sir, and brought by two of the first importance. They are to be lodged here, close to my lord."

"In this room?"

"In this room, sir."

"When?"

"After supper, sir, or whenever my lord has finished conferring with them. 'Twill but be for a day or two—and two such—if I might venture a word, sir, it would be best to submit in grace. . . ."

"Bien. Then make my room upstairs ready," but Punshon did not move.

"I said two of them, sir, and they are my lord's express orders. Your chambers in the turret are also required," and Willie rose.

"Why then, since it must be so, very well. Where then is Sir William placing me.

Two hours later he knew. The bearers of the news from His Grace were lodged, the one in the apartment with the golden lilies, the other in the turret that overlooked the castle's central court. But my lord would still have Willie near him, and his balsam paper and map and board were being carried to Pietro's cellar down below.

6

WHAT HAPPENS WHEN TAPESTRIES FRAY, AND THE BRIGHT BLOOM FADES, and only the slackened warps remain, no more now than a few naked events, knotted together with dates? Of the eggs of the moth the antiquary is born. It is his lore that here, on such-and-such a night, my lord slept, or woke to read his letters again, while down below another also sleeplessly tossed. A learned man, he knows that Blore Heath, in the hundred of Totmonslow and the county of Stafford, also came within the honour of Tutbury, three hundred and fifty-three souls were born and lived and died there somewhere about that time. There every third Tuesday a court of pleas was held for the recovery of debts under forty shillings—all these things he knows.

But where my lord held his court in his castle of Gwlad the tapestry shows only a hole. Scarce a thread is left to tell that close by was a herb-garden, with an espaliered apple that bore no fruit. Blore Heath was over before Willie Middlemiss heard of its narrow glen and of the bloody nicking that befell. When he did learn of it it was only that an Egerton or an Audley or a Tatton fell, for tapestries are for the nuptials and obsequies of the great, and none has needle and thread for such as are born under a bush.

But it was stirring news for my lord, and if Willie Middlemiss had got himself into a hauberk in time he would have been in at the stir too. But six paces under a grating were now all the marching there was for him, six paces and back, whereas the sentries had sixty; but let him count his advantages too. The sentries must pace whether they wanted or not, but Willie could please himself. If he was a prisoner he might account himself almost a prisoner of state, for Punshon showed him more deference than ever, bringing him food of the choicest. He shared it with Pietro, who fell on it like a famished animal. Even flowers were carried down, to remind him it was not for long, but the flowers missed somewhat of their aim, for at the sight of them Pietro made such a strange noise far at the back of his throat and for a moment staggered so that Willie hurriedly ordered Punshon to take the flowers away and bring no more. But it was Punshon who brought the news of Blore, and even Punshon was stirred out of himself, but Willie's first question was for Hal.

"Hal?" asked the clerk, as if wondering who Hal was. "They say

Sir Mordaunt rendered a worthy account of himself, but it's my lord who's the joyful man now! Such as we cannot conceive the load that's off his mind! Ah, if any wanted a favour of him now would be the time to approach him!"

"This is a good cut of beef," said Willie, for the fare that day was more than commonly excellent. "And these messengers I've had to turn out of my bed for, when do they depart?"

"When the court's been held and my lord leaves to join His Grace."

"And Sir William? I pray he's taken a better turn," said Willie, on the point of forgetting to set some of the beef aside for Pietro.

"He'll maybe tide it over. Like all in Gwlad, he's more himself again with this grand news. He took no drops yesterday."

"Think you it could be conveyed to him how I wish to see him?"

"I'll be the bearer of anything you have to say to him, sir," and Willie remembered Pietro's share in time.

"You're a good fellow, Punshon, and I thank you, and you can tell him this: that I'm ready to give my parole or aught else, but this isn't the most suitable of places for what he's asking of me. I've certain things in my mind, and with two horses, me on one and you on the other and a day in the mountains themselves . . . but don't give it in any sense the appearance of a complaint. Say I'm well content with whatever he's pleased to think best, but even to stretch my legs in the herb-garden for an hour—you take me . . .?"

"It shall be told him," said Punshon, and departed, and Willie was left to the company of Pietro again.

And now what sort of company was that? Worse than none? Strangely, no, had Pietro but had a tongue to speak with. For two days now Willie had been watching Pietro. His furnace-flame had desiccated him to the dryness of an old root, the acids he breathed must have eaten half his lungs away, he crooked his knees as he moved, had been rendered perfect to suffer, and could have told Willie a fearsome story. But he had only his eyes to tell it with, for he had worked in Montigliani's own cabinet and his eyes had been spared. Look at those eyes with sternness and down dropped the lids, but show them commiseration and they became profound black pits of unextinguished and inextinguishable life. To this Willie's food added life again, and any third person would have thought it a strange sight, the two of them squatting after dinner under their grating, eyes fixed on eyes as they fumbled with crude signs. Paper was too long, too much trouble. Looking into Pietro's eyes Willie could no more have drawn that square with his finger in the air than he could have spirited himself through the grating overhead, and suddenly he bethought himself of the ores in Sir William's chest. They had been Pietro's work, now they had become his own, and he had Punshon bring them down. With a single lamp on the table, and the marshal's map, and the irons and retorts and crucibles and the phials that crowded the walls and their eyes and fingers to talk with, the ores and quartzes became their counters of exchange.

But with the ores Punshon also brought gladder news. Sir William had his message. He sent his high consideration to Willie, and his request was granted, for Willie might walk in the herb-garden for an hour in the afternoon. The treasurer also commended Willie for his patience in their little domestic difficulty, for indeed it was no more. So for one hour, in the afternoon, between three and four . . .

And when Punshon had gone Pietro, who was dumb but not deaf, looked at Willie again. Then he picked up one of his pencils. With it he wrote on Willie's balsam paper an English word. The word was *"Lies."*

But now the morrow and the augury of it seemed a life's length away. The summer-house again, and my lord with the sunshine of victory in his heart! Surely his joy would irradiate the whole castle! The court he was about to hold would be a court of mercy and for-getting, and if she had had audience of him in the grey days, what could she not ask of him now? Willie was willing to seek his gold like another. If he did not find it, why, what the worse off were they? The minutes, the hours crawled on. When the sun shone on his blank of wall Pietro knew them as if it had been the sundial itself. Willie washed himself, put on his grave suit of murrey. He had totally forgotten he had no appointment, only leave to walk in the herb-garden alone by himself for an hour, but such assignations were not made through Punshon. They made themselves, and to doubt would be not to deserve. At three o'clock on the morrow he was passing the closed door of Sir William's room, standing in the arched passage, pushing at the green door.

He saw the change in her the moment she appeared. He had had no reply to that note he had committed to Sizar, but now he looked anxiously at her again as she stood before him. She might not have slept for a week. She wore neither pearls nor nets, but had tied her triangle of muslin hastily about her chin, as they do who are too burdened to care any longer how they look. Her eyes were red and heavy, the bloom had gone from her cheeks, and standing there by the briar, her mouth drawn down at the corners, all she could get out was a hapless, "Oh, Willie!"

"Did you get my note?" was his first question.

"Yes, two days ago . . . oh, Willie!"

"Stop. Wait. Who told you you would find me here?"

"Bessie."

"And who told Bessie?"

"Oh, Willie . . . Hal . . ."

Hal! And Bessie here and Hal away! But she couldn't mean that, and he spoke sharply. "What of Hal? What's this about a battle? I hear there's been a battle, and my lord's men routed 'em. . . ."

"They did, Willie, but they went after them too hotly, with Sir Mordaunt and Hal at the head of 'em, and at some place in Cheshire they rallied again, and surrounded them and took them prisoners. . . ."

"What! Where did you get that from?" and she looked at him as if she would have asked him where he got anything else from.

"And then?"

"Sir Mordaunt and Hal were taken with 'em, and there's no word of 'em since, but what's that to Bessie? And that poor wean of a husband of mine. . . ."

"Sit down. Hal's not killed?"

"We've heard no more."

"Well then. What o' this victory?"

"Victory?" she asked blankly.

"I was told my lord had won a resounding victory at a place in Staffordshire called Blore."

"He did, if they'd but broken off in time."

"They told me . . . from whom have you all this?"

"From my lady herself, that'll now have none but me by her, and it had to be given out to the garrison there's been a great victory, but not that all was undone again, and that's not the worst, and oh, Willie . . . my little Ferdinand. . . ."

They had sat down in the summerhouse, and he had taken her hand, but not to play pat-a-cake with now. He was holding the hand almost as if it had been an inanimate thing, and he was suddenly frowning, yet composed, for he spoke in a steady voice.

"Let's have the worst, Jo, and then we can look at it."

"At Ludlow things are little better. They're slinging stones at one another across a river, but the one side's as loath to start as the other, and the King's at Lemster with an army, and His Grace is outnumbered and badly placed, and he's waiting for a force from Calais that hasn't reached him yet, and now all's in doubt again. . . ."

"Are these the tidings these two messengers brought?"

"Which two messengers, Willie? It's all messengers now, coming and going."

"The messengers I had to turn out of my lodging for, two of such degree that my lord had to have them near him."

"It may be so, but I've heard of none such. What are their names?"

But now that Willie came to think of it he had not been told these messenger's names, or indeed anything else except by one mouth. Even soldiers are told of victories, never of the other, and that was my lord's tale too. But the Lady Margaret had lands and domains in her own right, and such ladies sometimes let fall what their lords keep close. Far from rejoicing in a victory, my lord must now be making ready for the next mishap. If what she said was true he was preparing for it now, busy half the night in that chamber next but one to Willie's, going through papers it might be, destroying these, keeping those, with carryings in and out of which Willie must know nothing. If those messengers had been of such condition as Punshon had described she would surely have heard of them, and hearing Punshon's talk Pietro had suddenly reached for Willie's pencil and on his balsam paper had written the English word, "*Lies*." He drew closer to her.

"Jo. It is Willie speaking. You got that note of mine?"

For answer she only inclined her head.

"The wording's gone from me, but you got the sense of it."

"You said you must see me and here I am."

"But how? How came Bessie to know I should be here, and at this time?"

"I'm too overwrought to think of it or she to speak of it. It was something to do with Jaqueline," and he jumped as if a cannon had been let off.

"*Jaqueline!*"

"Or it might have been Philippa, or it might have been them both. She does naught but rock herself and moan, 'Hal, Hal!'"

"*Philippa!*" He had turned as haggard as Pietro himself. "But—you see what that can only mean?"

"Tell me what it is you would have me do, Willie," she said wearily.

"It seems those infants have been talking. By God, it cannot be but they've blabbed, and some accursed she-tailor or tiring-woman's come to hear of it, and in some way it's got round to a pair of ears in this castle that's been wide open and waiting for just some such thing! Know you whose I mean?"

Slowly she closed her eyes, but his own were on the hellebore and the borage and the rue. He muttered to himself.

"By every devil in Gwlad, what you haven't told me now!" Then raising his voice: "Hark. Since I wrote you that note I've been shifted from my chamber and lodged in a cellar with the rats! Yon toad in that painted room sits there spinning things and contriving 'em, sending me fair messages, but him that brings them is the same spawn and marrow. . . ."

She opened her eyes for a moment. . . . "Have a care, Willie. . . . Remember too, I've done no more, ever, than you begged me to do," and Willie dropped his voice again.

"Nor have you, Jo, but see what's come of it. Word by word, I cannot remember how, he got it all out of me. Nay, sweetheart, you were in nothing to blame. If you spoke a name, as you must have done, why the man had a name, so what odds? Jaqueline! Philippa! For fifty Jaquelines and Philippas would I have missed those few stolen minutes, when like a sweet friend you'd taken them off Bessie's hands for an hour, and played with them on the solar floor, and came in all tumbled and your hair falling down i' lumps. . . ."

"Willie . . . don't seek to make love to me just now. . . ."

"Nor will I, for when you sorrow I sorrow too, but you see how it is. From all you tell me it's little of gold my lord's thinking now. Gladly would I serve him elsewhere, but I willn't serve the other, nor can I rightly see what he wants of me, and yet I can. He's a drunkard, Jo, but not wi' wine. He sniffs at you as if you were a fragrant thing, and settles himself down into the honey of you, and sucks it into himself and closes his eyes with the deliciousness of it, but always he leaves a little to suck again, and the choicest of all to him is when you wait for it, and then he doesn't do it. It's on my mind now that he's but allowed me these few minutes with you to sweeten his dish for to-morrow."

"I cannot believe there are such in the world, Willie."

"There can be and are. Listen, yet I wasn't going to tell you. When he would have melted my own work, just as I'm telling you, he never took his eyes off my face. He gave me wine while I was still shaking, and when I woke after it I was in a strange chamber, set high beyond my dreaming, for the higher he lifts you the longer his eyes can blink while you fall. He talked to me of you, and it's but a few days since he was speaking of knights dying in strange lands for ladies' sakes, and making themselves monks for angelicness, and all approved by the noblest and highest, so it was but chaste. And now he gets wind of you being with me in a chamber where there was a bed, seen in the ladies' own apartments, where it's death for one of my station to be found. A minute! What's behind this summer-house?"

"Nay, it's set back against the wall."

"Yet you knew I should be here, and now these uneasy tidings blacken all. My lord flushed with victory? It's now I begin to fear! Oh Jo—Jo of my heart! When is it to be?"

Her hand was plucking now at a coarse stuff gown such as nurses wear, but her toes were not rising and falling beneath its hem. He hardly heard her "What?"

"This quiet night before they raise the bridge. That that you told me in Bessie's chamber, with your hands on my breast and your hair set straight again, speaking sweeter than I ever heard a woman speak," and the head in its muslin cage slowly sank.

"I cannot, Willie. I said Christmas if it's then, or sooner if it comes."

"But that was before any of these troubles!"

"I know—but I cannot . . ."

"How, you cannot? The Lady Joslin cannot, or Jo?" and she lifted the red eyes.

"Willie, if you but saw him. He lies there in our bed as if his christening had been his shriving too, and he knows as well as I do, for he clings to me in fear and asks me what it will be like and turns away his eyes from his headpiece when I put it on the bed. Then he'll pick up for a bit, and say he's a Christian knight, but at the touch of my lord's sword on his shoulder he almost fell on his face, and my lady bade me bring him in, and there—there he lies now," and again Willie patted the hand as if it had been an inanimate thing.

"Ah me, the poor bairn! It isn't in nature not to sigh for him, and happy for him he's in your own gentle hands! But who knows what's to befall long before Christmas, for we're scarce at October yet? In whose charge will Gwlad be when my lord joins His Grace?"

"I hear it's to be put into a sort of commission, under the marshal and the seneschal, with the treasurer to preside."

"*What!*"

"Thirty will leave with my lord, leaving fewer than fifty here, but the Earl of Warwick's on his way from France with those from Calais, and it may be they'll turn the balance and the skies will clear again."

"And how we shall laugh when all's over and be as happy as a midsummer day again!" he said bitterly. "But we cannot wait for that. It's to-morrow or next week, not Christmas. Christmas! Yon bloodsucker in the cloth-of-gold will have died of his own ecstasy before then! Cannot you see where it all points?"

"It isn't that my eyes haven't been washed clean enough."

"It points to my lord himself, or maybe to my lady. I'm staying under no commission, not with that hangman of the ports! Dearest of Joes, graciousest of girls, you must set something going! If you cannot come at my lord you must speak a word in my lady's ear. I cannot think yet what you'll say—naught about gold, for indeed I see now I spoke above my knowledge, and gold would savour too much of what's gone. I can ride a horse . . . I could bear my lord's messages for him . . . or he could give me a steel shirt and buckler, for I always thought a man-at-arms had a carefree life of it," and she raised mournful eyes. Never, never another? Always, always himself?

"Willie, is it all you can find to say?"

"I grant you I'm at a loss . . . it's what I'm trying to think of, what's best to be done. . . ."

"Not a word about leaving it all just a little while, if only for honest appearance's sake and very shame?" and he looked at her as if he would have asked her what ailed her now.

"And haven't I thought of that too, and pictured it fifty times, little else these last days? You and me, making for London by quiet ways, missing their marchings and their battles? Getting to London and me joining up with those of my own craft, and you among these friends of yours again, meeting them in Cheap and these barges on the river you told me of? Then you'd be back in your pretty chamber, but not by yourself this time, sweetheart mine, but one with you to take you in his arms and . . . but it may be you're right and it isn't the moment. Can you still get the key of this garden?"

"Alas I cannot, Willie. The last I saw of it Hal had it."

"Hal!" and he started. "Then it's lost, and there'll be another to make. That's a job for Sizar, for a herb-garden with two doors is better than a herb-garden with only one. Or it may be he has one that would fit among a tray of old scrap I saw, or a blank I could wax over and take an impression . . "

"What's in your mind now?" she asked wearily, and he began to mutter.

"Ay, Hal would be the one to put a key into his pocket and never think of other people! But he oiled the lock when he was oiling Sir Mordaunt's coude-pieces. . . ."

"I must get back to my little sick man."

"Bide where you are just a minute," and so saying he rose. Lightly he stepped the few yards to the locked gate, stooped to examine it, measuring it with his eyes. But suddenly beyond the grille something seemed to be happening. Between the walls there was a confused moving of feet, not the marching feet of the sentries, for these feet shuffled as they advanced, and a voice was raised sharply in pain, as if under some blow of correction, and another voice urged and cursed the laggards on. They were from the guard-room, in the custody of four men with pikes in their hands, some six or seven of them, raggens and ragamuffins, the sheddings and leavings of the armies, men without home or trade. My lord, with a court on hand, was losing no time. From the waste they had been hunted out, to start the new calendar clean, and Willie saw their faces as they approached. Unshaven and unkempt they were, ragged and furtive-eyed, and they were on their way to the backcourt and the prison under the postern, and Willie in his mulberry was already turning away. What business of his were their tatters and their filth?

But suddenly a face looked through the grille, full at Willie. It was a face he had seen somewhere before, though of when or where he had no recollection, and from its turn as it passed the face had seen Willie before too. But there was no time for such things now. Already the shuffling was dying away, and Willie glanced down at the lock again and took a rough measurement with his thumb. Then he turned from the grille.

But the summer-house was empty, for she had gone.

SIZAR OF THE SMITHIES HAD BEEN PUT IN CHARGE OF THE ARMOURY too, but this added little to his duties. In the back-court two heavy waggons stood, stuffed with Humphrey Tull's gear and lacking only the horses to carry it off elsewhere, and such wearers of armour as remained kept it ready by them. Any morning my lord, rising from his couch, might call for his mail-shirt instead of for his robe, and the knights in personal attendance on him had now shrunk to four. The remaining two, lame Sir Etienne and another not much younger, came under the Lady Margaret's orders, and there was little enough for squires and pages to do at table now. The great hall was being made ready for the court. Its sideboards had been stripped bare except for cups and platters of common ware or wood, and Willie, on his way to the herb-garden on the following afternoon, stepped aside and tried the door of the chamber with the canopy over the couch and the golden lilies on the walls. It was locked, and as Punshon was not to be seen he stooped and looked through its keyhole. There in the middle of the floor stood the Great Salt, with the hanap by its side and ewers and other silver-gilt lying heaped on his couch. Small chests stood on larger ones, among them the chest in which Punshon kept his ledgers, chained to his waist when he lay down at night, and thoughtfully Willie turned away. So. His room had *not* been required for guests of consequence, but for a treasure-chamber.

Those of the household still had their dinner in the hammer-beamed hall, but half its table-length sufficed now. A rope from wall to wall divided the hall in two, and on the empty dais where the high table had been my lord's carved chair had been set back to the wall, with other chairs stretching to right and left of it. Sentries guarded the doors, the remnant of the garrison had been ordered to their own quarters, not a lady's face was seen, nor did Lady Joslin appear in the herb-garden that day. Willie waited his hour, and as he left again paused for a moment before the lavender-grey michaelmas daisies that flowered under the espaliered apple. A handful of them would not be missed. But he remembered Pietro and his stagger and that convulsive choke at the back of his throat, and withdrew his hand again. What should flowers be doing in a cellar?

Instead he left the garden that day with something in his pocket more to the purpose than flowers. It appeared that Sizar had no key that would fit the lock of the herb-garden grille, but he had a blank that would serve, and Willie had green wax. His dinner too was waiting for him, keeping hot on the hearth that Pietro had been using that day. Now to circumvent the soft-footed Punshon. When Punshon had cleared his supper away again he would have no further reason for returning that night, but lest he should do so Willie made ready for him. It was at the foot of the stairs that he set his trap, an old watercan for Punshon's foot. If he broke his neck that would not greatly disturb Willie, and he would have heard him coming. Then with vice and saw and file he set to work on his waxed blank. Pietro saw very well what he was doing, for he gave him the profound look, half-raised a brow, but turned his eyes away again. The key might not fit the first time, but a little trial and correction to-morrow ought to be enough, and all the evening he toiled, undisturbed by any sudden sound from the stairs. Then he carried in his water-can again and slept that night with his key in his pocket.

In two days it was perfect. Barring the gatehouse, where they knew him, he might now walk out of Gwlad whenever he pleased. There remained only Jo. Surely, having come once, she would come again?

Then round the castle the word went, and it struck Willie as odd that he should have it first from the tongueless Pietro. With the same pencil with which he had written the word "Lies," so now he wrote for Willie's reading that the court was for to-morrow. At what hour? Willie asked, and Pietro held up his ten fingers; it was for ten o'clock. For how many days? One, or were there more to be tried than could be disposed of in one day? But these things Pietro did not know, and for half that night Willie dreamed about his key.

And now he was going to that trial. He was going for several reasons, but chiefly because he had not been told he must not. Well or ill, Sir William would be there, and Sir William seemed to have forgotten Willie. To show his face might remind him that there was still a Willie in Gwlad. No word of Jo would reach him in that cellar though he waited there till doomsday, and Willie was going to that court just to see numbers of faces again, and to hear voices, and to breathe the air of the outer world.

And he was going to be seen, for what was the use of having a handsome velvet coat if half the time he took it off to waste his time over a meaningless piece of balsam paper? He made himself ready with such care that morning that Pietro trembled at the knees again, as he had trembled on that first morning when Willie and the treasurer had appeared together.

Up the stairs he strode as proudly as if the treasure in the lilied chamber had indeed been his own and he had just turned his new key on it for an hour. Sedately he marched across the grass-court, past the sundial, entering the hall by the inner way, the sentry stiffening as he passed. Into the great chamber he strode, his shoulders trim and his hawk's nose high, looking about him.

The space behind the rope was already a pack of the baser sort. In from the waste they had come, the cutpurses and the idlers, the bedlamers and the vagabonds, with the castle guards to keep them in order. Close up to the dais was a second rope, but the space in front of it was empty, as was the dais itself. It was in the space between the two ropes that the domestics of the castle were already assembled in numbers, liveried men, not in velvet like Willie, and Willie placed himself somewhat apart, under one of the wall-sconces, where he stood, looking at the row of chairs set back against the wall, with my lord's high-backed chair in the middle There where he was standing Sir Mordaunt had had his seat, with Hal to wait on him; just a pair of hot-heads, prisoners now, taken at Tarporley in Cheshire. At the corner of the empty dais the French knight had sat in his blue-black, a prisoner too for all the lightness of his chains. And instead of the court being late, as Willie had expected, it was punctual to the minute, as if time pressed. There was a general movement, a suppressed stir among those at the back, the voices of guards were raised. The bailiff of the court climbed to the dais and thumped with his staff. In they filed, the high officers, grouping themselves to right, to left. With slow pace my lord himself followed, and as he took his seat, with the treasurer on his right and the seneschal on his left and the others in their degrees, links of mail glinted for a moment beneath his furs, before he disposed the robe over them again. Sir Baltasar, the chaplain, pronounced a prayer. Another voice not unlike the chaplain's was raised. The court was in session.

After the first ten minutes Willie had little interest in its proceedings. All was much as he had been told it would be, he had seen such rascals before, they were getting no more than they deserved, and he had nothing but commendation for the summary way in which the court disposed of them. Huddled together by the pikemen, first this shuffling wretch was thrust forward, then the next. The voice that resembled the chaplain's read the charge, and almost before it had finished another voice demanded whether the accused had anything to say. Scarce one of them had, or if he had he stammered so that he could not get it out, there was an exchange of glances across my lord, who was reading a paper, a whisper, a nod, and the sentence: a whipping, the next. Had they been honest men they would not have been there. Only one roost-robbing fellow lifted his voice, requiring that some witness should speak for him. At the back of the hall the name was passed from voice to voice, but if the witness was there he took too long in coming forward and the time of the court was being wasted: a double whipping, and the next. And Willie was beginning to wonder how many more of them there were when he felt a touch on his shoulder. Turning he saw that the man who had touched him was directing his eyes to the corner of the dais where the French knight was wont to sit. Punshon stood there in his black livery, frowning and beckoning; it was evidently not seemly that Willie, so close to the treasurer's person, should be standing among the lesser servants below. Way was made for him, slipping under the rope he stepped up to the dais, and made himself a place against the wall.

Now, from above, he could not only see the prisoners better but my lord too, for a bare six paces separated him from the master of Gwlad itself. On his head was a round fur cap of estate, round his neck a heavy interlaced golden collar. Cares had seated themselves immovably on his brow, graving his lean face into unalterable lines, but his cares this morning had little to do with the court or its business. His thoughts were otherwhere, and even when the seneschal on his other side leaned across him to confer with the treasurer he still read his letter, signifying his assent with a slight motion of his finger—yes, a whipping or what they would. But unless the treasurer happened to lean forward too Willie could not see him for Punshon, who stood immediately before him, whereas as an inferior he should certainly have been behind him. He caught a glimpse of the crooked hands crossed over the ebony stick, but with my lord present in person his deputy was leaving things to the seneschal and the marshal. And now Willie was hedged about in yet another way. He had been summoned to the dais, but once on the dais none might leave till my lord himself rose to depart. So he watched my lord with his brow gathered over his paper, his collar, his cap of estate, and the glint of chain under his robe that parted a few inches whenever the dipping finger approved the whipping.

Close to Willie on his left stood a little table, except for the row of chairs the only furniture on the dais. At it sat two clerks, noting down the sentences as they were pronounced and occasionally turning over some register or list. Suddenly, he saw their heads draw closer together. They were approaching some case that was not common pilfering, trespass, brawling or any of the lesser infractions. Another name was called, and there was forced forward along the roped pen a pallid spectre of a youth with chains on his wrists and eyes that closed themselves against the light. Again there was the consultation behind his lordship's letter. "Bring them on together," and there followed the first spectre a second, whose new-born beard reminded Willie vaguely of Matthias. This time the bailiff's staff thumped more peremptorily, the announcing voice was pitched higher.

"... for that to the injury of my lord's settled custom and prerogative he did on certain dates to wit ... privily bake and feloniously sell ... three quartern loaves of bread of fine wheaten flour ... and Tobias his brother, on sworn evidence to be produced ... with a certain crossbow and without licence or leave did shoot a goshawk the peculiar property of our most illustrious lord. ..."

There was a sudden outburst from the back, scuffling and calls for silence, but no silence. It was the old quarrel of the pigeons again, breaking out anew now that the garrison was depleted and they had numbers at their backs, and over by the great window that looked out on the grass court a crutch shot up and above the growlings a thin and screaming voice was raised.

"Mercy ... pity, pardon for 'em, my most gracious lord!"

"Peace there!"

"Grace, my lord ... they were but lads then ... nay, raise me some of you, that my eyes may see their faces again. ..."

"Away with her and proceed," and after some minutes the tumult abated somewhat and the voice of Robert Burnage the seneschal was heard again.

"Which of these is the elder?"

"Tobias, sir."

"From whence are they?"

"From the back cells, your highness."

"Since how long?"

"The one a year and a half, sir, the other two years come Christmas," and again there were conferrings along the row of chairs. Then my lord was seen to lower his letter for a moment.

"What's this?" he asked, looking about him.

"It is a matter perhaps best dealt with by yourself, my lord. It concerns that goshawk and that other about your lordship's bakery revenue."

"What about a goshawk? Who spoke of goshawks? Is my hall become a mews? It has gone from me, with a deal more that can wait till another day. Can they fight?" but this time it was the marshal who shook his head.

"It will be many a day before those two have enough on their bones to fight with," and the answer was an impatient exclamation.

"Many a day, and men wanted now! What sort of talk is this? All this of a loaf of bread, mouldy this two years! Dispatch. 'Tis naught to me. Use them as you think fit, and how many more of such cases are there?" and with that my lord turned to his letter again.

But Willie was interested now. That was his idea of a lord, one who

did not waste his time on little things! A stern man it might be, but
one inclined to mercy and willing to let himself be approached, whereas
those about him barred the way to him, lest some deserving suit should
find a way to his heart to their own detriment. If these two had but
been as knit in their frames as Willie instead of being blanched white
by whatever *siambr ddu* they had been haled from they would have been
clapped into leather and would have heard no more about it! But now,
with my lord washing his hands of the case, the court could not
agree. Punshon, tardily remembering that he stood in Willie's light,
had moved to one side, and now Willie could see the treasurer too.
His health seemed better. Willie was not close enough to him to know
whether he smelt of mint, but he was able to attend the court, and Robert
Burnage was tendering his advice again. It was that the prisoners
should be put back, and Sir William was purring gently as he nodded.

"It is no bad lodging as such lodgings go, well away from the moat-
end. Does the marshal agree?" but now it was the marshal who
demurred.

"Loaves of bread are no concern of mine, but a falcon—that comes
within the scope of my exercises. . . ."

"True, true—it must be looked at in all lights. . . ."

So, as it was not a sentence, my lord's finger did not even dip assent,
and back the two spectres were marched whence they came.

Now, as whipping began to follow whipping again, Willie was
wondering why his watching of faces had run so much on the faces
of women. He had scratched his likeness of Bartholomew on his crust
of bread, but never such a fine man's face as my lord's. When Willie
had watched it on the grass-court it had seemed to him a crafty and
scheming face; now he found it full of deep thinking and power. Such
faces smiled little, but women made themselves supple and dimpled
and toyish for them and their scars. This was a court of mercy too,
for my lord forbore to press home rancours he had forgotten; look
at him now in his cap of estate, yet with the chain-shirt peeping from
the furred edge of his robe! A just man in his court, a prompt one in
the field, and a dozen times Hal had told Willie the order of their
arming. The linked shirt slipped on they began from the ground, the
left leg first. The greaves, the cuisses, the genouillières for the knees,
the breastplate, the back-plate—how Willie wished he had seen them
ride away that morning, visors up, the pennons, the plumes, the
caparisoned horses, a gallanter and a more stirring jingling than the
cenedl with its fire-tongs and picks and rakes! And suddenly behind
him there was a sound of a commotion and a making way. Somebody
had arrived in haste, and into the presence of the court itself there
strode just such a figure as Willie had at that moment been picturing.

Except for his basnet, which he carried in the crook of his arm, he was cap-à-pie in steel. His lip-high mentonnière jutted forward like the jaw of a pike, his cropped and greying head looked over it as a chicken's head looks over the edge of its shell. One gauntlet he had flung into his basnet, and the hand from which he had taken it held yet another letter. My lord had stiffened in his carved chair. With a rubbing of armour-joints the envoy dipped one knee, stood rigid again, and handed my lord his letter. It was not even read through, for its beginning seemed to be enough for my lord. He was on his feet. He said a word in the treasurer's ear and with his hand indicated the empty chair. The court was to continue its business without him. All stood as my lord strode out, with the messenger following behind.

And what now matters the letter that brought my lord from his court that morning? Over by Ludlow to the south the ballistas were still flinging stones across a river, but if the Calais men were not there yet they were thereby. A veteran lot too, drilled by the book and newly equipped by the Staple, they were not the lads to turn a victory into a defeat as rash Sir Mordaunt had done at Blore. Yet why fight at all when a free pardon is offered you if you do not fight? My lord is in his closet, frowning over his letter. His empty chair on the dais is more than he now, and in it sat a different kind of man, not the man to overlook forgotten offences, but a soft-voiced, infinitely-patient man, who in the presence of his victim could not keep his reptilian lids still, but blinked them ever more rapidly and the more he sported the softer his voice became. Whippings? One whipping was too like another. One yawned one's head off at whippings, and Montfaucon's gibbet too was not the sentence but the coup-de-grâce. With the seneschal on his right and the marshal on his left it was Sir William Stone who presided over the court, and Punshon had stepped behind Willie and was conferring with the two clerks at the table in a low voice.

Now Willie began to wish uneasily that he was elsewhere. Make a drawing of that fat, flat implacable face? The man's mind was as hideous as his hands were crabbed and cramped, and he was making the sentence a pair of ears now, or a branding, or the thumb-cord or a hand struck off. His stumps were folded over his stick, but Willie could imagine them in motion, drawing a square in the air, about to drop a locket into a crucible, and the marshal and the seneschal had nothing to do but gaze at their knees, for he had taken all upon himself. At the back too there was a silence, not of protest, but a breathlessness, a dreadful thrill of waiting, a shuddering as each man rejoiced that the savagery was not for himself, and suddenly there stood within the rope a gallows-looking fellow already quaking with apprehension of the worst. Willie was unable to look at his dribbling mouth and the things that were going on in his eyes. By God, he was not staying for this! When all was said Sir William was not my lord. He turned away as Punshon came forward again, carrying a paper from the clerks. His foot made no noise, and Willie was going out quietly and quickly too, but now where Punshon had been standing a man-at-arms stood, immediately between him and the door. As Willie moved, this man moved the same way, and Punshon had given the paper to Sir William, and suddenly Sir William's voice was gently but clearly raised.

"Let none leave the court during the hearing of this case," and Punshon took up his station behind Willie again, and the man-at-arms too resumed his former place.

It was a case particularly close to Sir William's heart. The ill-favoured, dribbling fellow had been taken with certain clipped coins on him, which might well happen to any who possessed a coin at all, but these coins were still betrayingly bright from their recent clipping and unhappily the filings had been found on him too. It was an offence my lord himself could not have overlooked, yet fear-ridden as the fellow's countenance was it was pleasant as compared with the treasurer's. He was questioning, not the wretch himself, but a witness who had suddenly appeared on the dais.

"He was apprehended where?"

"On the waste, most gracious sir."

"At whose instance?"

"At mine, sir."

"Tell the court what you saw," and the witness did so. It was flagrant and utterly damning, and the marshal and the seneschal looked down at their knees again.

"Your name?" the witness was asked.

"Marples, may it please you, sir."

"Had you seen the accused before?"

"Not in my life, sir."

"Yet he approached you, as you say?"

"If I hadn't gold then silver would do, sir, he said," and the questioning continued.

But now Willie had brought himself to look at the unhappy man, and looking could not remove his eyes again. It was the same man he had seen through the grille, being marched off to the *siambr ddu*, the man who also had seen Willie before, yet less than ever could Willie have told when or where this could have been. He only knew that he never wanted to see that face again, and he drew back a pace, but wished he hadn't, for he had been the only one to make a movement and for a moment Sir William's eyes had flickered his way. Then for the first time the treasurer addressed the man below.

"You have heard what you are charged with?"

One of the guards stepped quickly forward, for the man was on the point of falling.

"Your name?" but to that too he was unable to reply for fear, and Sir William gave a tender little sigh.

"And yet some would say it is a case I should not be trying, for in a sense I am a party in such cases and so should not be a judge too. . . . Bailiff, is this man deaf?"

"He heard well enough when we went to call him, gracious sir."

"Then is he dumb, for he seems neither to hear nor speak?"

"Ay, he's ready enough with his tongue too, sir."

"Then if he will not plead, he must be treated as recalcitrant. That, alas, is the *forte et dure*," said the gentle voice, but at the name of a pain so dreadful the prisoner gave a shriek.

"They took it down wrong . . . they moidered me wi' their questions. . . ."

"Ah. The *forte et dure* . . ." and Sir William smiled musingly.

"A snickle wor set for me, and then they got agait on me. . . ."

"And now that at last he utters, in what tongue is it?"

And the bailiff leaned over, no doubt to explain to the president that a snickle was a snare, but there was one within arms length who knew what a snickle was better than the bailff did. His name was Willie Middlemiss. A snickle! . . . It was a summer evening, on a northern common, yet not one evening nor one common but a remembered haze of them, golden and serene with sunset and all the evenings and all the commons running into one. A lad among others, who had never seen wire drawn in his young life, he yet had that slender loop in his pocket and a peg to stake it down. He saw his companions again, himself as ever their ringleader, scanning the ground for the faint trace of the run, marking the spot, driving in the peg, setting concealing grasses artfully over their little instrument of death, but by some magic the evening was already morning again, and the small victim lay there, its fur wet with dew. He knew that hard northern speech too, like stones knocking together as compared with all speech he had heard since, and now two voices were speaking alternately, the one as hard as stones, the other dulcet soft. The man below was wriggling as desperately as the trapped rabbit. His words had been taken down wrong, he hadn't known what he was setting his mark to, he was not the man they sought. Others had set him on . . . give him but time to think and he would describe them . . . he could remember nothing but they must have slipped something into his pocket lest they should be found with it themselves. . . .

"Yes? A gold half-noble in such a state as you never saw? Four sweated florins, and the parings too?"

"I know naught of it, dread sir . . . they moidered me wi' their questions. . . ."

"Your name?"

"Royds, your worship . . ."

"Your trade?"

"A'm a weaver, sir. . . ."

"From where?"

Willie Middlemiss, stepping back for air, suddenly found his velvet shoulder in gentle contact with the hauberk of the guard behind him. There was an impersonal whisper in his ear: "You heard, sir; none is to leave the court," and he missed the next, yet he had no need of it, for he knew now who this man was who had looked at him through the grille. Willie Middlemiss was not creeping about rabbit-runs now, but seated in a northern inn, before a table cut in one piece from the thickness of an elm. It had its bark still on it, and along the line where wood and bark met a horny thumbnail was being run. "You start counting here, Maister Middlemiss; eighty's been counted, but you can add another score to that; my father felled that tree."

It was the tree they had fettled up with bottle-glass because it would not take the plane, and Willie had rapped out exactly the same questions the president was asking now. The man was a weaver, when there was anything to weave, but for one reason and another Willie had had no desire for his company that morning, and others had been listening, and roughly he had told the fellow to take himself off. Now the prisoner wanted nothing better, for his name was no more Royds than it was Middlemiss. His name was Sagar, and he kept an inn out o' demesne. He had wanted Willie to go to it, for there had been picked up on a northern hillside, only a few yards from the body of a dead man, the female half of a coiner's die. They had wanted another made for them while Willie was still in the neighbourhood, and so stunned was Willie now, yet so fascinated by his own thoughts and the plight in which he stood, that he heard not another word of the court's proceedings till again the man's high shivering cry reached him, followed this time by a scuffle to silence him. Then, smooth as oil, he heard the president's next words.

"Unhappily the court is unable to believe your story. It is a story courts are too familiar with, that I myself am sadly familiar with. There are none so innocent as those who find themselves before a court. Always it is *their* hands that are clean, never are the guilty where they should be. They cannot remember names, always they have seen a man for the first time, never in my experience have the officers of the court written a true account. Yet . . ." and it was then that the change came over the voice that henceforward did not leave it again, ". . . all is *too* perfect, and the world, alas, has not yet reached perfection. We have ways of refreshing faulty memories. Nay, in one short half-hour I have known miraculous cures come to pass! Bailiff, take him back. No, not to the oubliette; let him wait in the other. Meanwhile I will consider what forms the questioning might fittingly take. The realm cannot suffer treason as long as there is hope that a drowsy memory may be stirred. Away with him."

If Willie now saw that face of Sir William's it was not directly but reflected back from that of the unfortunate down by the rope. As if in a mirror he saw a shadow of what must have been on his own face, that first morning in Pietro's cellar, the terror and the loathing and the sickness unto death itself. As the man dropped to his knees the cry of the anguish to come broke from him for the third time.

"Nay, honoured lord, let them two gentlemen but read me their paper over again! Flayed and moidered beyond my wits I wor . . . I'm but a weyver wi'out learning. . . . I wor led into it by others . . . it's them should be ligging i' my bed. . . ."

"If he will not walk, pick him up and carry him. . . ."

"Nay, sir, not one wi' scarce a pair o' breeches to his buttocks! Seek a few o' these that looks like maisterpieces and above it all, that hasn't to lig o' wastes, but sleeps downy and soft, no matter who shivers. . . ."

"Stay. Bring him back. What do you mean by that last?"

"Them that stand nigher to your lordship than I do . . . poor men like us knows more than knows us. . . . I'll speak no names for fear it should be written down agen me, but you can follow my eyes. . . ."

The eyes turned. At a gesture the guard nearest to Willie stood aside. The eyes rested on Willie Middlemiss, and the treasurer, first saying something to the seneschal on his right and to the marshal on his left, felt the floor with his stick and in agitation rose. His voice shook with emotion.

"The court," he said, "is adjourned. Such cases as have not been heard will be put back. Let this man be bestowed as I said. Punshon, lend me your arm. It goes to my heart, but it is as I have long tried not to think. See the guards have their orders and help me back to my couch."

Leaning heavily on Punshon he moved waddlingly along the dais. Pot o' One Sagar was hustled out of the roped pen. But Willie's two armed attendants stood waiting till it was his pleasure to move, for in his mulberry velvet he was still to be treated with distinction.

8

SIR BALTASAR THE CHAPLAIN WAS LOOSE-FRAMED AND LACKED NOTHING of six feet in height, but at such times as he walked in the grass-court, sunk in meditation, he was approached by none. Within his castle my lord had powers of life and death, but even he might not despatch a soul on its journey without Sir Baltasar and the consolations of his office. He had blessed Sir Mordaunt's banner and shriven the troops for Blore, but his society was little sought, as too often preceding a tolling, or worse, a muffled party under cover of night, a hasty digging and a covering over again. Less even than my lord at his private business was Sir Baltasar to be disturbed at his prayers, which Willie should have remembered when he had raised his voice to Punshon.

That same night, as Willie lay in his niche behind the rag of arras, there entered to him this figure, and at the sight of the sombre face even Pietro sidled away into the adjoining chamber, where he moved about setting things in order. Seating himself on an upturned tub Sir Baltasar addressed Willie in a lowered and secret voice.

"Can you guess from whom I come?"

Willie did not answer. The chaplain might have come from Sir William. He might have come from my lord. His office derived from neither of these.

"Are you of the Christian faith?"

Still Willie said nothing, but thought of Matthias and his "*Christianus sum.*"

"I saw you in the court to-day."

"I was there," said Willie in a low voice.

"I am willing to pray with you, but first, lest you be confounded, I would talk as a simple man to you. If you have in any way erred why do you not confess it?" but at something indefinable in the voice Willie became attentive. He had never been closeted with Sir Baltasar before, but these priests seemed to have such various voices. When Sir Baltasar said Grace at table he came near to singing it. In opening the court he had prayed like a lawyer's charge. Now he was talking confidentially to Willie, and Willie was not to be caught like that.

"What should I have to confess?"

"Is there any man so blameless he has nothing to confess?"

"Nay, nay, that's too broad. It would help a man better to know what he was charged with."

"How long have you been in Gwlad?"

"I reached here the same day as my lord returned from His Grace at Ludlow."

"Where did you come from?" and again Willie hesitated.

"With all respect and reverence, sir, is this bedroom of mine a court?"

"Yet you might do better than you know to answer me, for to my mind you are in need of it. Did you see me in the court?"

"As who didn't, that began it with your prayer, sir?"

"Can you see me well now?"

Indeed Willie could not see him very well. His niche was a recess in the wall, with Pietro's opposite, no more than two strides separated them. The priest sat on his tub, the single candle was fixed to the wall behind him in a sconce of Pietro's contrivance. And suddenly the priest looked up and involuntarily Willie did the same. Incredibly, a bird seemed by some means to have found its way into that cachot below the moat-end. It could not be seen, but there it could be heard, twittering in the vaulting, trilling a few notes and stopping and beginning again, and now Willie looked at his visitor's face. By God, he was no more Sir Baltasar than Willie himself was a priest, and the twittering stopped but still Willie stared. Then his voice dropped shakily.

"Who are you?" he asked, and the man answered in yet another voice.

"Let's deal with things one at a time. There are two guards at your stairhead. Who think you could get past two guards but a priest going to confess a prisoner?"

"How did that bird get in here?"

"It came wi' me. Would you hear it again?" and again the vault was filled with the twittering.

"But who i' the name of all charming are you?"

"Leave idle questions. I was in the court, but not starting it off with prayer. It's dim in these wall-windings, and Baltasar and I are of a height, and it's a poor mime I should be if I couldn't mime a man I've known half my life. I was at the back, close to Mother Jule under the window, and now I'll stay or go, but mark you, if I stay you'll answer my questions."

"Ask 'em," said Willie, dazed.

"There's few in Gwlad would be in your shoes if my guessing tells me anywhere near right. So to start with, what do you know o' this man Sagar?"

"He's such a weaver as they wouldn't have in the cloth-towns, so he kept a ken that seemed to suit a few such as himself. For all I know the rest of his tale's true, that he followed on the backside of the armies."

"And what does he know about you?"

"No more than that he came smouting after me one day, wanting something I was in no mind to give him, and now the devil must send him here," and with that the stranger began to make extraordinary grimaces.

"See what happens in this castle when I turn my back for a month or two! I cannot take the air to nick a few swans but something goes amiss! In whose employment have you been since you came to Gwlad?"

"In the treasurer's," but now Willie was beginning to assemble his thoughts again. He would have said that by that time he had begun to know a little of that castle's daily life, but always there must be those who, sent abroad on my lord's business and returning again, would ask their familiars who such a new-comer as Willie was. He knew the treasurer too, and if the treasurer could employ one treacherous instrument he could employ another, and again he asked, "Who are you?"

"I've been sent."

"Who sent you?" but scarcely were the words out of his mouth but he was certain without further telling who had sent him. God be praised indeed for such a friend! A deal of trouble would be hers before she forgot Willie! The passages were dim, the man's habit was grave, not a guard in the place but seeing him would suppose him to be Sir Baltasar on some spiritual errand, and she had contrived that too, as the very next words confirmed.

"Have you heard of a place hereabouts they call Dame Kate's?"

"Yes."

"When were you last there?"

"Maybe a week before Blore, maybe ten days, and Hal was at Blore. Have you heard aught of him?"

"Nay, I came by another way, but it was at Kate's that rogue with the clippings was taken, and now cannot you see what's gathering over your head?"

"It looked like a glimpse of it to-day."

"And have you thought of what you're going to do about it?"

"Ay, but two guards at the head of those stairs means thinking again."

"What's Pietro doing in yonder?"

"I take it he thought as I did, that you were Sir Baltasar, and who are you to know the names of them in Gwlad like this?"

"I know your name too, Master Wilson Middlemiss from York, and what's against you now isn't going to be heard in open court.

It'll be tried in that chamber of the treasurer's, and my lord will know nothing of it, for this is between you and Sir William, and he'll be your judge. Have you ever heard a case tried by Sir William Stone?"

Willie was suddenly silent.

"I heard him in London when Pietro was tried, and I've heard him in Harwich too. It brings your dinner up again to hear him. Robert Burnage can be hard, and the marshal harder, but trust them to see they have duties elsewhere when Sir William Stone takes charge. Looked at strictly it's above my lord's head too."

"For the love of God, who are you?" and now the rebuke came with sudden sternness.

"What, will you still be knowing things you're better not knowing? If you're asked to-morrow who visited you last night isn't it enough for you that you were with Baltasar the priest? You, that's in the hands of as bitter a hunter of them as there is in all England and the Isles and Poitou together! Out o' that stone bed o' yours!" he whispered with fierce urgency. "Has Pietro no eyes or ears? On your knees, as if you were confessing yourself, as God knows you've every call to be! Here, close to me, that always was church-given if I hadn't been set to do other things, and can sing plainchant wi' the best of 'em and play a regal too! Now shake as if this was your last night alive, and if you don't know the Latin mumble what you will . . . now . . ." and with Willie tumbled out of his niche and himself off his tub and the two of them kneeling side by side he began. "*Credo in unum Deum* . . . what's this way out that you say you have in your mind?"

"I've a key that opens the gate of the herb-garden."

"*Patrem omnipotentem* . . . what of the barbican and the watch?"

"I made friends of them when I was in my leathers and they get up on their feet for me now I'm in my velvet."

"*Visibilium omnia et invisibilium* . . . and what of him that pulls the sneck for him?"

"I don't take you. . . ."

"The hangman's sneck, without they swing you awhile before letting you down again—him that'll be wearing that jacket of yours when a row of crows is perching above your head—Punshon, his clerk. . . ."

"I've got it in pickle for him, too—if I can but get out o' this. . . ."

"*Genitum non factum* . . . and keep your tongue from idle threats, you with less in your head than Titus my marotte! Think you he won't be down here to-night, ay, and me scarce past them guards again? . . . *Crucifixus etiam pro nobis*. . . ."

"So . . . I'll keep my hands off him awhile longer. But will you tell her . . .?"

"She shall be told. Drop your head, for I see Pietro. Now the prayer. ... *Pater noster* ... stay on your knees a bit after I've left you. ...."

So Pietro too saw the confession, and Willie remained obediently on his knees until this strange priest had left him, for he who called himself Gandelyn, and passed a guard with two uplifted fingers when the passage-light glimmered dim but clowned with his marotte as he capered into camps in his red and yellow, knew better than to expose himself till he was safely out of harm's way again.

Nor was he wrong about Punshon and his visit. Willie did not hear his step, but the clerk had Pietro to pass, and as a poker fell to the floor with a clatter Willie looked heavily up to see him entering, but seeing how Willie was occupied he seemed about to withdraw again.

"Nay, sir, I did not think to intrude—I will come another time," but Willie was rising from his knees. Soon, Punshon—let Willie but get out of this. ...

"And the Lord forgive you and us all, Punshon," he said with a deep sigh. "I did not look to see you to-night."

"Indeed, sir, I had to come, for I know little of what's afoot, but as full of grief as I am I could not keep away. Is there anything you would like for your supper?"

"I thank you, Punshon, no. I'll fast till I know what their pleasure is," and with his hands behind him he began to move along his six paces of floor. "If only you would tell the treasurer that my duty has never failed him nor never shall," and at that Punshon too placed himself by his side and began to pace in sympathy with him. Then he spoke in an encouraging whisper.

"And yet, sir, I bring you good news. Would you hear it, or continue in your meditation awhile?"

"Nay, good news would be better worth meditating on than any I have."

"Then if you will receive it I am to tell you, sir. Sir William bids you be of good heart, for I never saw a man so nigh to weeping as he was when I left him. But it was no time for tears, he said, and he dashed 'em away. This that he must do to-morrow is his plain duty to my lord, but he has given it his best thought and you are not to let it weigh too heavy upon you. As if it was a charge against himself he feels it, and that rogue's word wouldn't hang a dog, and he's keeping all privy that it may be over and forgotten the sooner. He'll plead his rheumatism, that he's trying hard to struggle over without his drops. The seneschal and the marshal will see the court to the end, but he'll hear this himself in his chamber. All will be but show, to furnish a report for my lord, and if his brow seems heavy and his questions come near to you you're to take it in kindness. He bids you sleep well, and have you eaten since the court rose, sir? You have not? Nay, but let me get you something."

"Thanks, good Punshon, no. Convey my duty and affection to Sir William. At what hour shall I be sent for?"

"At ten o'clock, sir."

"And sleep you well too, friend, as I now shall," and Punshon retired again, and Pietro came in, not to shape with his lips the word "Liar," but to place himself in his niche opposite to Willie. He did not glance at Willie, but extinguished the candle in its sconce, and Willie lay awake, thinking now of Jo, now of this stranger she had sent to help him in his need, yet ever returning to Punshon and the rod he had in pickle for him.

He woke still haunted by broken dreams, but above all hungry. He had not been hungrier even on that morning when he had woke at a coppice-edge, with a smoke-blackened Matthias lying by his side, who had cried out overnight for water when Willie had had none to give him. On that morning Willie's breakfast had been his leather cap full of hazelnuts, and most of the water had gone to wash Matthias's face, but now his breakfast put new life into him, and when a questioning was going to be severe they did not give their victims such a breakfast as that. It was of rabbit, baked in a pie with other things too, small birds of some kind and seasoned blood to make it richer, perhaps the blood of a deer. Nor was it whisked away from him, for he was still eating when his two guards entered, and the clearing away of breakfast was no duty of theirs, and nearly half the pie was left for Pietro. Willie rose promptly at the summons. He put on the jacket that had once been Hal's. A form of trial for appearance's sake, none but my lord to report it to, Willie's own master to direct it, the real offender a rascal caught with the evidence in his pocket . . . briskly Willie told the guards he was ready. As they filed up the stone stairs to Sir William's room, what if he did not even see the daylight? Along such passages men who resembled priests might pass with two fingers raised and news of good cheer. Punshon, who had jointed them, opened Sir William's door, and they stood in the light of the multi-coloured window again, rich and subdued enough for a church.

Except that a small table had been carried in, at which two clerks sat, the chamber in no way resembled a court. Sir William's couch was where it always was, Sir William lay on it in his undress of cloth-of-gold, his low table to his hand. Only, as the door closed again the two guards remained standing inside it, and Sir William had assumed his part already, for he did not look up as Willie was marched in, and like my lord he was reading a paper. The clerks sat motionless with their quills in their hands, beyond the window the sentries paced,

Punshon had placed himself by the table to be ready with any paper the treasurer might wish to see, and Willie stood motionless, in the middle of the room, alone and waiting.

At last the treasurer looked up. He seemed out of pain, at quietude and ease. Though his words were formal his voice was low and conversational.

"I do not think this inquiry, which I myself am holding in privity for special reasons, need engage us for very long. As I am informed there is only one witness. So far as at present appears we are here to clear a character rather than to look for small blemishes in the innocent. For this reason I propose to take such matters as identification and what not as established, unless, which I consider unlikely, they are in any way challenged. The clerks are already instructed in that sense, so I content myself by asking, formally, whether your name is Middlemiss?" and he looked benignly at Willie.

"That is my name, sir."

"William Middlemiss?"

"No, sir. My first name is Wilson," and the treasurer showed mild interest and surprise.

"Indeed? That will be to emend. The error doubtless is mine, but the clerks have it down as William. Punshon, see a note is made of it. You were in my lord's court yesterday?"

"Yes, sir."

"In what capacity? Purely as an onlooker, as you were fully entitled to be?"

"As you say, sir."

"Were you present when one was brought forward who called himself Royds, though there is information that he also goes by other names?"

"Yes, sir."

"You saw that this man, when I ordered him away, lingered as if he had something to say?"

"Yes, sir."

"Yet—to my gratification—he did not say it? (Be at your ease, Master Middlemiss. These are not questions of any import.)"

"I saw what happened, sir."

"So, and I hope I am not pressing on too quickly for the clerks. Now Master Middlemiss," and he consulted his paper. "You will be anxious to be about your ordinary duties, and fortunately I know what these are. Under some pressure this man Royds has since made a further statement, of such a nature that he will have to be called. As between ourselves, I have seen his kind before, and to save their own skins and pass all on to others there is nothing they will not say.

Therefore—is it agreeable to you that we should finish with this fellow now?"

"I am in your hands, sir," said Willie in a low voice, and a sign was made to Punshon. Again the door opened. The guards stood aside as a chair was carried in, with a man seated in it. He was bare-necked, in his shirt and breeches, his head lolled on his breast and cloths covered his feet. The treasurer raised himself on his cushions and fastened his eyes on one of the men who had carried the chair in.

"Is this the same man?"

"The same, sir."

"Can he speak?"

"He has been revived, sir."

"Punshon, have wine ready in case it is needed," and with his ebony stick Sir William gave a sharp rap on the edge of the table on which he had laid down his paper. The man gave a sudden great sob and raised his quailing eyes without moving his chin from his breast.

"Your name?"

"S-s-sagar."

"If your later statement is read out to you can you understand it? Read it, Punshon," and Punshon, taking up a paper, read its contents aloud. It affirmed that on a bygone date, which he could no longer remember, a young journeyman goldsmith whose face he had recognized on the dais the day before had, at the request of certain men in whose company he had happened by accident to find himself, taken a wax impression of a Henricus head, and of the same had presently made a die, from which, when the superscription had been added, the witness himself had struck certain coins, being compelled by the threats of those who stood over him so to do. As it was to be doubted whether he now heard what was being read out to him he was given a sip of wine, which enabled him to raise his head for a moment. Then he dropped it again, and Sir William, his elbow on his cushions, addressed the air.

"And say he is now charged with a charge hardly less grave, that of false swearing, and taken away again and questioned further, will he still persist in this slander of my most tried and trusted principal assistant, and so in a sense of myself and my fitness for my office?"

At that the man gave the great sob again, but was past doing more, and the spectacle he presented in that tinted chamber was itself an affront, and again Sir William made the sign. "Take him back, but do nothing further for the present," and again the guards stood aside as the chair with the man in it was carried out. When the door had closed again Sir William looked at Willie as if he would have asked his pardon for something.

"Pay no heed. I would bid you be seated, but it is a rule that I may not do so, unless indeed it is as that man is seated. Will you, for the court's satisfaction, formally deny the statement you have just heard?"

"I deny it, sir," and Sir William sank back into his cushions again.

"Ah, the weight that is lifted from my breast! There is no shift these villains will not sink to! As I suffered with you, so now I rejoice with you! . . . But I see you hesitate. Is there something you would add?"

For Willie now was unable to keep his lips from trembling. Oh gross, that bodily torment should wring from a human frame first a Yes, then a No, as a fiend's whim might move him! Had that man's feet been covered with the cloths only for the sparing of Willie's apprehensive eyes? Granted that mankind could show nothing lower: should justice be therefore less than just? Willie's lips parted.

"Nay, sir, it cannot be taken both ways at once like that! I cannot be wrongfully charged and then wrongfully cleared in that fashion! Mangled as he is, spare him now, sir!" and Sir William, who had closed his eyes, opened them again. He seemed suddenly surprised.

"What's this, Master Middlemiss? You at the table there, is all this being taken down?"

"Faithfully, sir."

"That Master Middlemiss denies the charge? Is false witness then to go free?"

"Nay, I but spoke out o' such pity as you'd have for a dog, sir!" and the sick man eased himself among his cushions.

"So you did, so you did. Would my experience had left my heart more of it! But this rascal says you made a die."

"Never of a coin, sir," and again Sir William spoke with fervour and thankfulness.

"All heaven forbid! Then my heart would have been broken indeed! 'Never of a coin.' Is that down?"

"It is down, sir."

"Then leave out that Master Middlemiss pleaded for him. His heart shall not be his undoing, for all his gift that kings might covet and the licence his eyes must be granted to practise it! But such delicate arts have naught to do with common rogues. Had that shivering rascal much of it?"

"Sufficient, sir."

"Then at Master Middlemiss's intercession he shall be spared more. He shall hang before night. But let him be hanged for coining, not for false witness . . . so now . . . but stay . . . where does that leave us, Punshon?"

"Maister Middlemiss has been accused, sir, and has denied it."

"And yet he intercedes for him that accuses him . . . but it may be my memory is at fault. Read it out, Punshon," and Punshon read:

" '*Master M. denies that he ever made a die for a coin but not that he made a Henricus head,*' " and that too Sir William condoned and excused.

"The fashioning of heads in general being part of his trade and exercised under my own eye and supervision. Is there no more brought against him than that?"

"Not sworn on oath, sir."

"How, not sworn on oath?"

"Where Maister Middlemiss came from it is shockingly rife, sir. Trade is at a standstill because of it, all the way to Hull it has come down to concealment of goods and refusal to trade i' the markets, and all that ought to be in the open trafficked in at night by rascals with neither leave nor licence."

"Hull? What, is foreign money coming in?"

"Aught they can get their fingers and scissors on, and give 'em the head and there's fifty prentices can put the superscription round it, and if Sagar is to be believed, at a place called Ellbeck, where he was a weaver, an inquest was held on this very die, a Henricus half-noble it was, though none o' this was stated on oath."

Sir William's flat face had become a mask. His eyes were beginning to blink, and he murmured to himself, "Two Henricus H's placed back-to-back." Then his eyes were turned on Willie.

"Is this true, Master Middlemiss? Not that it can be used against you, seeing none's sworn to it, but can it be as Punshon says, trade stopped, and courts held, and a gallows in Hull with nothing to do?" and Willie gulped.

"I know naught of it, sir, save that I was asked to make a die and refused, and if Sagar says different I'll bear a hand with his hanging myself . . ." but again the treasurer's face had changed. He was not Sir William the invalid now, but an older yet a younger and a more vigorous Sir William, a Master of his London Guild again, appointed by his sovereign to cleanse the land of the corruption of its currency, zealous to do so and inuring himself to them eans. He made a private sign to Punshon, and not a sound was to be heard in the chamber as he turned to Willie again.

"Ah, the happiness of it that you refused to make that die! With a single pair of dies what mischief have I not seen done! Ecus, sols, moutons, Henrys, I have wept to see it, the trade of nations undermined, the king's licences set at naught, the laws flouted, every jack his own master to the confusion of the realm, and our hearts wrung dry even of pity, for when one villain is taken he must be used as a lesson to the others! Did I hear you offer to lend a hand with this hanging for the truth's sake? Nay, 'tis a thought! Not that it can be said his hands aren't clean, but for some employments not too clean is sometimes the better instrument. It is in such ways we learn their devotion. I am getting old, Master Middlemiss, and where is my lord to look for his new treasurer when I am gone? . . . Ah, I thank you, Punshon," and into his mouth he popped the piece of sugar over which the clerk had distilled a dozen drops of mint. He drew in his breath, inhaling the coolness of it, and slowly a dreadful look of benignity overspread his face.

"So. My lord's new treasurer. Not a Sir William, but a Sir Wilson, for I myself was not always a knight. Is there a piece in this castle you do not know, and alas much that is here no longer? Now I feel myself ready to pass my task on. I have but to commend you to my lord and he too will rejoice. But, coining or false witness, what matters it? Punishment is still punishment, and you cannot act the hangman in those fine clothes. Have I not seen you in others?"

Willie, standing there in the wavy, particoloured light that resembled that of a church, made no answer, and Sir William turned to his watchdog again.

"Had he not others, Punshon, stained with acid as I remember, and more suitable for neck-work than these?"

"I have kept them by, sir."

"But do not take his velvet from him. He may have eyes to please we do not know of. Nor on better thoughts shall the other be this afternoon. Give weaver Sagar another night. So Master Middlemiss quits himself and we start afresh. Now I am drowsy and will sleep a little before I see my lord. The appointment will be to sign and seal before he leaves. Warn Sir Baltasar. Until to-morrow, young treasurer-to-be . . ."

In his cloth-of-gold he sank luxuriously back. Punshon bowed low to Willie. The guards drew aside, Willie gave the man on the couch a long look, and then, inclining his head only, turned away.

9

BETTER NOW, A THOUSAND TIMES BETTER THE SIAMBR DDU. WILLIE DID
not know where that cachot lay, yet it could hardly be so deep under
the postern but that sometimes the faint clinking of the smithies reached
it, or the stamping of the horses or the rumble of wheels as the heavy
carts were driven away. There the young spectre who had sold the
bread languished, and his brother Tobias who had shot the falcon,
but Willie was thinking of that other cell, where lay a man who was
to hang to-morrow. It might be that he did not yet know that his
despatch was to come so mercifully quickly, and Willie wondered
whether he was sleeping and whether Sir Baltasar had been warned
yet. As for himself, God be thanked he had ways enough and to spare.
His burins were sharp, he had his knife. His wrists, the veins of his
straight young neck, the heart itself, and no Sir Baltasar either, for
what were Sir Baltasar's mockeries of holy words if the world contained in it even one man with such unholiness in his heart as this?
Trade and the currency of the realm and the sanctified mummery of
the laws! Nay, it was a world well out of if nothing in life came before
these! Now he had forgotten even Jo. He could do it now, or wait till
to-morrow, yet what to-morrow if he did it now? All to end thus?
Was it this he had sought with so much toil, and what matter when
he did it since in a time that seemed to him suddenly short it must
come to all?

Pietro was in the other chamber, doing something at his hearth.
No more than Willie's own were Pietro's hands unspotted; spotted
hands for foul work, yet even Pietro had been spared this. Nor did
Willie now even wish to see that other, Jo's messenger who had passed
the guards with two uplifted fingers. There was something he must go
through alone, spend that night with alone, his only company a man
who could not have spoken if he would. He was back in his leathers
again, but he had not taken off his velvet doublet without thinking of
Hal. Hal, seeking knocks, had got what he sought, but Willie, seeking
he had never known what, had got nothing. He had been warned too,
for now had come the thought of Matthias. "And how if your place
in the hall is empty one night, and some ask what has become of Sir
Willie, but those who know only bid the musicians play louder?"
Except the trumpets and the drums on the waste Willie had not heard

K

a note of music all the months he had been in Gwlad. Once he himself had played a whistle, but thievish Welshmen had stolen it, yet even they had not lacked their music, and Willie, stretched in his niche, remembered the voices he had heard as he had lain in Bartholomew's tent, the desolate and homeless hymn, uplifted to an ironstone God. But as they had drawn nearer to the Wales that was their home their hymn had become a hymn of battle. Whet thy axe, Cadwgan! Whet it against the Saes, and after the battle the carouse and the sweeter sweets . . . he remembered the very tune in which they had bawled for women too, not ironstone women, for women of flesh and blood, to solace the harshness of their lives—

But suddenly the tune running through his head was interrupted. Again Pietro had dropped something with a warning sound. In his leathers Willie got out of his niche and peered past the rag of arras. Gods' thunder! Had the soft-spoken deformity not finished with Willie yet? Within the arch, still dressed in his cloth-of-gold, Sir William leaned on his stick, with Punshon behind him. And for Willie's last night he had been heavily at the mint, for Willie smelt it faintly through the fumes that never left that working cellar. He wondered that he should have come again so soon, and with his hands crumpled over the stick he was leaning forward, saying something to Pietro in Italian, and Pietro was bending at the knees again.

Now the treasurer was looking round the cellar. At the end of the hearth, between it and the grating, Willie's disordered working table had been pushed back, with his rules and compasses and the marshal's maps, swept aside by Willie days ago. The treasurer's eyes rested on them, then were lifted to the implements on the wall, the phials and crucibles and the forgotten samples of old ores. They met Willie's as he drew aside the arras.

"Good e'en to you, Master Middlemiss," he said as Willie took a step forward. "I grant it's somewhat late for another visit, but new matters are best dealt with as they appear lest they grow into something out of nothing. Do I bring you from your rest?"

Willie found his voice. . . . "I was lying down, sir. For resting I will say nothing."

"Well said," and the treasurer picked up Willie's piece of balsam-paper. "And to what state of advancement has this got?"

"It is somewhat backward, sir. Lately my mind has been taken too much off it."

"To be sure. There is too much going on these disturbed days. We will get to-morrow over first. Have you never seen it? The prod to the stolen animal that drags on the rope? 'Tis naught. Youth soon shakes these things off."

Willie, watching the hand that idly fitted the tracing to the marshal's map, moving it this way and that, made no answer. Then the treasurer picked up the compasses that had been bent and straightened, but put those too down again.

"Yet all this can wait. 'Twas another matter I wanted a word with you about. I see you're back in your working-clothes."

Still Willie made no reply, and now the treasurer's hand was fumbling for something inside his robe. In silence he brought it out and stood looking at it as it lay in his twisted hand. It was the key of the herb-garden gate.

"Punshon found it in your velvets," he said, dandling it in his palm as if he was judging the weight of it. "And the light here is not good, neither is it in my own chamber, but I cannot have sentries looking in at my panes as they pass. So I carried it out into the air where I could see it. This is a new key. It still has traces of wax on it."

And now Willie remembered that there was nothing about such processes that this man was not familiar with. He had questioned him about the marks of the master-workers of York, in what their practice differed from Lincoln or Durham, had picked up Willie's impressions and the mould from which they had been made, comparing one with another. He, who had not always been a knight, knew all about key-blanks and green wax, and now he had put the key back inside his robe again, and with his back to the table-edge was looking at Willie fixedly, patiently, waiting for him to say something.

"I cannot deny it has started things in my mind that I was willing to let rest, Master Middlemiss," he said slowly. "It was in the garden I looked at it, and something put it into my head to try it in the grille. It seemed the lock had been oiled too. A turn and the grille opened without a sound. What have you to say to this, Master Middlemiss?" and Willie moistened his lips.

"I cannot betray what's not mine to tell, sir."

"Ay, I'd missed that key," Sir William murmured to himself. "Now I come to look back I'd missed it since Blore. Is it possible somebody had it in his pocket, and took it away with him, and now cannot send it back?"

Even Pietro was not more dumb than Willie. What did this man not know? Blore meant Hal. He knew of his meetings with Bessie, of the secret assignations at Dame Kate's, doubtless of Willie's own private comings and goings too. And having let Willie see the key he showed it no more, but had picked up the balsam-paper again, which again however he put down, for he was a methodical man, who dealt with things one at a time.

"So, a key having gone, another had to be contrived. With a blank, easy enough to shape at the smithies, and a touch o' green wax, a little sawing and filing, and there is as neat a key as you could wish. Had you then some thought of leaving us, Master Middlemiss?"

Thought! For how many days now had Willie thought of little else? And what imp of forgetfulness had brought it about that in doffing his fine mulberry and getting back into his worn old leathers again he had not remembered that in his pocket was a key? But Sir William went unrelentingly on.

"Us that have cherished you, and naught too good for that precious gift of yours, so that from the smithies you were taken under my own wing, and how it wrung my heart when I had to set you to this sad business of melting, and then to crown it all it appeared you had this wondrous knowledge that would have ended our troubles for good and all . . . have you forgotten these things, that without a word you would leave us now?"

"Indeed, sir, you abase me that you can think I meant any disloyalty by it. . . ."

"And these others you cannot betray because of secrecy and breaking faith—(oh that I were young again!)—have you never heard that there are two things in this world that cannot be hid?"

"Sir?"

"A light—and love? Nay, young man, as if every elder in Gwlad hadn't smiled to think of blunt, simple, honest Hal! Why, it was my lord's own fondest mirth that he was supposed to turn a blind eye to it, as he did! Ah the pretty days, the pretty days when you are young, that you have to make the most of while they last, and alas never do! But mark you, Master Middlemiss. Hal is a squire. Sir Mordaunt himself answers for Hal so he but keeps up a show of discretion. And do not believe all you hear o' my lady either, for in truth she is of a good disposition to the very least of her ladies!"

Sickeningly Willie saw it all coming. He spoke of Hal and Bessie, but was only keeping the other back a little longer, and where was the escape now? Punshon was standing back immovable in the arch, at the head of the stairs were the two guards. Pietro, softly blowing at his hearth, was heating some portion of a trinket, sent by one of the ladies to mend, as blind and deaf to what went on as he was dumb. "Finish, you Satan in your cloth-of-gold!" Willie wanted to cry but could not, and again he smelt the thin odour of the mint that never failed of telling its hideous tale. And now Sir William was beginning to lose control. The lids were beginning to quiver, the long-damped fires to awaken in his eyes. He himself was resisting it, husbanding it, delaying the nameless paroxysm that, once spent, would leave him a normal man again; but the ecstasy would no longer be held off, and when next he spoke an angel might have pitied him in the grip of that last fierce approaching self-torture that was also his bliss.

"Yet see how it all adds together!" he cried in a tremulous voice. "What of that man this morning and the report he brings? Is that why you begged mercy for him, as always they will beg for another's mercy that stand most in need of it themselves? What of all this?" and the balsam-paper on the board shifted and slid under the shaking hand that was laid upon it, and Willie broke out.

"Give me a few days there among it . . . give me a few men to dig. . . . I saw it on that man's map . . . it is close to the lake. . . ."

"Or under a lake, or to dig half-way to hell for, but is *that* the tale you came to me with? . . . Nay, I must keep myself still . . . let none look at me for a moment. . . ."

"I never set up for a magician, sir. . . ."

"Not when to forge a key will easier serve your turn—nay, that key!" and his voice cracked. "I'll pardon that man! Let Sagar be pardoned! I'll pardon him for having opened my eyes to the truth! Why should I hurt such a wretch more? Punshon, are you there? See his pardon's written out!"

"Then the Grace of God on you too, sir, for he's no worse than others," said Willie under his breath, but the man in the cloth-of-gold turned on him.

"Aha! The Grace of God! But I said nothing about *you*, without whom such cannot lift a finger! Stop, Punshon. If I pardon him this other will not have him to hang—but let it stand. Let him be pardoned. Oh, I am sick with struggle! I would have ease, ease! He planned to slip away with that key!"

"Indeed it has that look, sir."

"He comes from this place in Yorkshire . . . this Yorkshire must be getting due for a visit! . . . Men cannot trade there, nor the taxes of the lordship be collected, and soon along there comes a Cade to band the mutinous rascals together, and York and Lancaster together cannot find a better way than mine. . . ."

"'Tis a sorry picture you paint, but a true one, sir."

"So what; Punshon, not to commit ourselves but to be considering it, what—it begins to swim together in my head—is this Wales we are in?"

"The Middle Marches, Sir William."

"Ay, ay, ay. Gwlad in the Middle Marches. Now I call it to mind I have seen scores of 'em. They put their eyes out and then turn 'em loose on the mountains to look for gold. In Bristowe, but that was only the lesser ones, we struck their right hands off and let 'em go. That's dainty, an artist's eyes and his right hand! But there's them among 'em so headstrong and stubborn they'd but start again with the hand that was left 'em, by some sort of feel or itch they seem to have! Are the guards posted above?"

"Doubled, sir."

"Then let me think. Ah, I have it." Then suddenly to Willie, "What did you say of that young bull and his tit of a governess?"

"I said nothing, sir, nor shall."

"Firmly spoke, but show us the decoy and we will guess the springe! Do you call to mind a headpiece you silvered the vine-leaves of?"

"It was a task set me by Maister Tull, sir."

"The casque if I remember of a young gentleman of birth that's now a knight?"

"All the castle knew of it, sir."

"But the silver had to be got from his lady, and with what's left of it you're now making an image of her for his comfort where he lies?"

Willie neither moved nor spoke.

"A kind and well-favoured lady, a thought simple-hearted, the sort to give you a lift in Gwlad, but—be wary, young artist with a hand and eyes to lose!—a wedded lady, under powerful protection, and her virtue to be answered for and her good name to guard?"

Still Punshon stood immovable in his arch, Pietro indifferently occupied at his hearth, Willie without speech. '*Labuntur et Imputantur;*' it was upon him, from the least of his offences to the direst, all heaped together at once. But not so was it to be meted out to him. It was to be delicately measured, till he himself could bear no more, but besought the end as a boon, and now the man himself could contain no longer, for it was bubbling and boiling to a head.

"A master-coiner and an accomplice of coiners, he makes his way over the hills to Gwlad with some old-wives' tale of mountains and their gold! Cunningly, a step at a time, he perfects his plans, weighing what acquaintance he shall make, setting lark-traps for their eyes that glitter! Who shall be the next to help him to his horse? Ah, a comfit-box needs his skill or a broken chain to mend, or what you will, so all is up, up, up! As fair and fortunate a marriage as you would wish, solicited and brought about by my lord himself, that too! He corrupts my own servant, with his 'Sir William the treasurer, what is his mood to-day, are his pains heavy or light, slept he well or ill?' All this subtlety to *me*, in my own private chamber! Punshon, did you say the guards were doubled?"

Willie was standing as he had stood at ten o'clock that morning, looking down now at his weather-worn and acid-splashed leathers.

His tormentor had advanced, his weight on his stick, but the stick itself was unsteady with the shaking of the tumult within him. Then it broke. He swayed this way and that with his passion.

"Nor did he spare even the eyes of the young innocents! The little ladies soon-to-be, dutiful over their pretty lessons, ah, there was a vile thing! In a forbidden chamber—(Lord of Heaven, send it now and quick!)—in a maid's chamber, contriving with a happy wife till *he* came creeping into Gwlad—where it is death for such as he to be found he forced his way, by a sly window and into a chamber with a virgin's bed! Now by the Hart's Nine Lives he shall suffer for it! Set all free, but not *him!* Is this Wales? Then he shall be tried by the ancient laws of Wales! His trial hushed up in my closet, him? In the open air he shall be tried, and from the least to the highest all, all shall be his judges! Know you the laws of Wales, you that came to Wales to coin its gold?"

"Soon I shall," Willie muttered.

"From the meanest to the highest I say! Hear the Institutes of Hywel Dda, framed for such and imprecated with the malediction of God on whoso should violate them! In Gwlad he has been under the protection of Gwlad! Not one i' this castle but was his surety! He had the protection of the steward from the serving of the first dish till the lowest had been fed! He had the protection of my lord's court from the calling of the first case to the last, which shall be his own! He had the protection of the chief huntsman for as far as the barking of the dogs could be heard, and of every doorkeeper for the length of his arm and his rod, and of him that held the horses for as long as it took the smiths to make their four shoes and their nails! The chaplain protected him as far as his chapel, and the falconers while the goshawks flew, never was stranger protected as he was protected! Now all have been flouted, and all shall be his judges! He shall receive the punishment of each, and as my lord's deputy he shall answer me the last! Before the eyes of all men he shall be tried, out on the waste or some public place—not in a dungeon, but where the sun shall shine on him for all to see—but that for which *I* shall try him will be the peculiar honour of my lady, who must be jealous to guard the purity and virtue with which she is surrounded! For as long as Gwlad's stones stand it shall be remembered that one came to this castle and found it a fair and pleasant place, but was minded to leave it a stews with his greed for gold and his lust for its women. . . ."

The stale mint was being breathed on Willie's face. The traitor Punshon in the doorway was doubtless meditating his tale for to-morrow, how he had pleaded with Sir William, and would still plead. But Pietro had made an unexpected movement. His occupation with his trinket had brought him close to Willie's table, where a candle burned, but the candle was not enough light for him, and suddenly he did an unimaginable thing. There too on the table lay Willie's balsam-paper and the marshal's maps. Indeed the mute must have gone suddenly mad, hearth-mad, melting-mad, fire-mad, burning-mad. There was the brushing sound of papers being swept together. Dropping his trinket he was gathering them together in his hands, making such ruin of them as he had made of the scrap and the dross. Into the fire on the hearth he was thrusting them, where the brittle balsam-paper caught, flared, filled the cellar with a pale yellow light. But the stout maps burned less readily, and Sir William had fallen back, his mouth open, the pelican-folds about his fleshy jaw a-quiver. The marshal's maps being destroyed before his eyes by a suddenly demented mute! A rack of emotions mingled and played over his face. Dropping his stick he shot out his deformed hands to save the precious things. A poker lay on the hearth, and in his delirium he seized it, but Pietro's movement was that of a cat. The ebony stick was no longer on the floor but in Pietro's hand. No more Montfaucon squares drawn with a finger in the air, no more admiration of the exquisite work of that orientally-patterned knob! He had touched the spring. The stiletto was naked in his hand. And as well as Punshon, Pietro knew the treasurer's habits. His robe was of cloth-of-gold, but the shirt beneath it was cloth-of-steel, invulnerable to that dainty point. Suddenly the wrist above the crippled hand was gripped, forced down to the hearth. Slowly, choosingly, wholly rapt in what he was doing, the mute pressed the point into the back of it. Then he cast the weapon also into the fire.

Punshon had fled. From the stairs came his muffled cry, but Sir William Stone did not hear it. His face had become ovine, blank, as he tried to believe the unbelievable. Nor did the four guards come tumbling down the stairs. Instead there descended from somewhere above a long-drawn, hollow sound, a sound to curdle the blood at such a moment. Vacant and echoing, it came again, the lonely cry of an owl, followed immediately by a woman's shriek.

"My lady! All who hear me, to my lady! The Lady Margaret—stop her. . . ."

There was a heavy crash, as of some vessel being shattered, and then a man's voice.

"To his post, every man! Fire! *Tan!* Fire!" and then the high female cry again.

"Nay, hold my lady . . . she has flung herself from the solar window . . . she is in the moat. . . ."

"To my lord . . . they have broken in from the waste . . . *tan!* Fire! *Tan!* They are seeking to breach the postern!"

"Hark the prisoners are rising . . . sound the trumpets!" and a clang and a crash of iron. Again the hoot of the owl, as the bird had twittered in the vault, other cries, runnings. . . .

But Sir William Stone, ovine and glassy-eyed, was watching the blood gently welling from the back of his hand, with less than half an hour to live.

10

STRANGE THAT SUCH A COMMOTION SHOULD BREAK OUT IN THE NIGHT, yet in the morning each man should look at his fellow, and say, "Didn't you hear it?" and all should suddenly doubt whether they had not been dreaming! The gaoler, questioned, could give an account of every prisoner in his charge. The guards of the back-court knew nothing of any inrush from the waste, and no burning of pitch or resin scorched the postern doors. My lady had indeed fancied she had heard sounds, but the nights were getting chilly and the solar window had been closed, and the hooks of the men who for assurance's sake were set to dredge the moat encountered nothing but mud and rubbish and the snaky stalks of the lilies. True, flinders of a broken ewer were found on the turret stairs that rose outside the seneschal's room, and on the landing above it a breast-plate had fallen from its hook in the wall. As for owls, they were to be heard everywhere. In short, those who had been the first to join in the tumult were now the first to feel themselves foolish.

One discreet rumour however there was. Sir William Stone, Gwlad's treasurer, had had another of his seizures in the night and his room was not to be approached. They were my lord's express orders, conveyed through Punshon, for when suddenly an important pair of shoes is to be stepped into it is best to say nothing till the matter has been deliberated upon.

But Sir William Stone, still in his cloth-of-gold, lay on his couch with his hands turned in and a napkin to cover his face, which was probably heavily discoloured, and for the moment my lord had more pressing matters to attend to.

This time it was Humphrey Tull who had brought the news, and Humphrey was none of your hard-riding young gallants who could gallop a horse to a standstill and then without taking breath throw himself on another. At his age he liked to take things more gently, for the prime of his days was over and he had seen too many changes in the world. He had hardened himself to it that massive engines should throw stones over rivers, for so the titans of old had hurled their rocks in battle. He had become broken to it that armour, which he had dreamed to make so supple and easy that its bearer would hardly know he wore it, had now become as heavy as a pavess and so cumbrous that the very saddles had taken on the look of Sir William's curule chair. But speak of gunpowder and Humphrey sunk his grizzled head between his hands. Sappers with their kegs of gunpowder and their petards could reduce the castles themselves, so that soon men would no longer build them, and farewell to his plumed burgonets and his damascening in silver and gold and all the famous artistry of his craft. And now, though it was no longer the news it had been, Humphrey brought my lord heavier tidings still.

It was in my lord's own apartment that he bore the heavy particulars, seated like a privileged familiar, with only one other present. The door was locked, wine stood on the table, and between sips he answered my lord's slow but weighty questions.

"Overnight, you say?"

"Overnight they crossed over and ranged themselves on the other side, with Mundford and Trollope."

"What! And those two with their pockets lined with my cousin Warwick's money?"

"My lord of Warwick should have left them in France instead of wasting good Calais money on red jackets for such crow-pickings," Humphrey growled.

"And Warwick?"

"What could he do with a free pardon offered? When desertion sets in there's no stopping it, and the Welsh broke away too. They're for their mountains again."

"And His Grace's orders to me?"

"A ship awaits him. He's in Ireland, to continue from there. In the meantime your lordship's to do as you think best, but they have their Bill of Attainer all drawn up and beyond a doubt your lordship will come in for some attention."

"What of Ludlow and his castle?"

"They marched in and found nobody, and now they're plundering castle and town alike," and thereupon my lord turned to the third.

"And what's your counsel in all this?" and the third voice spoke.

"Get the women away first, next the treasure," and Humphrey Tull filled himself another cup of wine.

An hour later he was in the smithies, silencing a man who clanged with a hammer and calling for Sizar. With Sizar he conferred in the back-court.

"What's in them two closed carts standing there?"

"Most of what's left of the armoury, sir."

"Have them opened and let me see," and Sizar called a couple of smiths. No loveliness from Milan had been packed into the carts, no florid inventions from Germany, nothing knightly and precious from

Spain. Only Wrexham bucklers and undressed pike-heads from Sheffield faced them, a few boxes of spurs and oddments from Ripon, cases of rivets and hooks and buckles and piles of hides, nothing for Humphrey to break his heart over, and out of the carts he ordered them.

"Get four men, two to pass 'em and two to stack 'em. Fit fresh bars and locks, to fasten from the inside, and have them two made into strong-rooms on wheels by this afternoon. Then—say this is from my lord and me—see what other carts there are in Gwlad and find out from the grooms how many horses, for they'll all be wanted and them with feet can walk. See they're assembled by nightfall. Have all washed out, and if they don't dry put braziers into 'em. Bid your men stir themselves," and he stood looking at what had been unloaded and piled against the armoury wall. Leather, leave it; bolts and nuts, arrowheads, bowstaves, there wouldn't be room for them; an odd casque here and there, a body-suit, back and front, ay to be sure, pretty enough, but nothing for Humphrey Tull to break his heart over, and he turned his broad but aching back and took himself off to give fresh orders, but first looking into the smithy again.

"Young Middlemiss, where is he?"

"With the treasurer 'tis likely, Maister Tull. Sir William had it again i' the night and it's little we've seen o' the young gentleman while you've been away. Might we ask what's to do, Maister Tull?"

"Ay. When your men's done what's set 'em, but not before, you can tell 'em they can be looking after themselves too, for Gwlad's packing up. Then, if Sir William's ta'en ill, will young Middlemiss be acting in his stead?"

"Either him or Punshon, sir," and the master-armourer turned away.

But it was Punshon who, that same afternoon, had empty boxes carried into the room with the overhead canopy and the gilded lilies, and the Great Salt and the hanap were wrapped in straw and packed into them, together with the mazers and the ewers and the plate and all else from the great hall's sideboards. Out into the yard they were carried, where the two carts had been fitted with stronger fastenings, and Humphrey and Punshon saw to the loading. But room was left inside each waggon for four armed men, over and above the strong guard that also had been warned, and Humphrey turned to the other carts that crowded the back-court from the postern to the wicket that led out to the quarry and the exercise-ground.

Tell one tell all; now it spread through the castle as if tinder had been ignited. There had been a victory; there had been a defeat; they were making haste to place themselves under His Grace's protection, they were summoned to share in his rejoicing; but in any event they were moving, and at once. In the solar, in the wardrobes, in the drapery-closet, the women ran here and there, assembling inconceivable bales and packages. Told by the seneschal's officers that nine-tenths of them must be left behind they strewed them about again, in search of this or that that on no account could be dispensed with. The children were scolded for getting in the way, packed off and bidden to be good and amuse themselves. In the octagonal kitchen the cooks sweated as they had never sweated, preparing provisions. It was not possible to be out of earshot of the stamping of horses, the rumbling of wheels, the hammering as cases were nailed up and the swearing of men as tilts and hooded wains were hurriedly converted into litters. But one of the smaller ones stood apart. Mattresses and pillows had been carried into it, and on the pillows, until the head itself should rest there, reposed a silvered headpiece, laced over with a delicate pattern of vine-leaves. Humphrey Tull himself had given it a polish before placing it there, in the hospital of Sir Ferdinand Covil and of the lady who was to tend him on his way.

But now the width of the moat cut off the castle from the waste beyond. The drawbridge was raised, for you cannot seize folk's chickens to feed your falcons and entomb their sons alive and make the whipping-post a daily spectacle but tempers will rise. More than ever of them were assembled now, barring the way to Ludlow and the south unless it was forced, and my lord, closeted with the marshal and with that third again, was for forcing it, but the marshal was of a different mind.

"Cumbered with waggons we are at the mercy of the slowest," he said. "A wheel's but to come off or a stone or two to be flung and all might take an ugly shape," and my lord continued to pace his apartment, greaved and shirted in steel as to his body but his unarmed head now no more than that of an elderly, spent man, more fitted to take its rest than to struggle longer.

"Would you tell me I am besieged by these rascals in my own castle?" he demanded.

"That court of your lordship's would have been better held at another time," the marshal told him.

"But save this check at Tarporley none of this had happened then," but again the marshal shook his head.

"It's been happening for years back, and one of 'em, an old witch that swings between crutches, is rousing 'em over her two sons, back in the cachot again," and my lord, willing to shift the blame to no matter whom, flashed out.

"What, two I was willing to let go? How comes this?"

"Nay, if your lordship had but said so plainly, but you left it, and

as for the seneschal and myself it was ta'en out of our hands, and . . ."
but the marshal did not finish. The sentence finished itself, with a
picture of a man in cloth-of-gold, lying only three rooms away, whose
end must be concealed till fresh plans had been devised, and again he
broke out, that weary man the most illustrious John, lord of the
baronies of Wickware and Wharram and Tollington and Wyke in
England and of Quellyn and Coed Isaf and Coed Uchaf and Gwlad in
Wales.

"Then keep it hidden as best you can from the women, but you,
marshal, get together such men as we have and you and I will lead
them! This afternoon we'll make a sortie, and fall on the rascals, and
burn those hovels of theirs and see what a shower of bolts and a few
pikeheads will do! What! My own castle! Have I fed and protected
the mongrels for this? Now they shall have something they'll remember!" but at that the third stood like a tall confessor behind him, he
who ventured unarmed into armed camps and whose bag of tricks
rightly used was more than an armoury of leather and steel.

And who are they, these wandering and nameless shadows of the
great, half their time away on secret errands and on their return so
privileged and indulged that they may tender their advice unasked?
No part of the tapestry's pattern in their own day, how shall they be
known when both they and tapestry are gone? They are the changelings
and the bastards and the rousers of men, who in their youth sell their
swords but when they are older their wits. History disowns them, but
rejected by history they peer with protean faces out of ballads, that
no man writes yet they are sung when the ordinances and the laws
are forgotten. If they are false they are the claimants and the pre-
tenders: if they are faithful they follow their masters through the world,
and the confined king hears their voice outside his prison-wall, and the
unravelled stocking draws up the cord and the cord the rope and
presently the king is free. What is it but their own lives? Unbidden
this man spoke.

"Give me leave, my lord. Pikes and bolts are for when all else has
been tried. What have you to do with Ludlow and the south? With
women to get away the postern by night is more to the purpose than
a sortie in the afternoon. I haven't nicked your Swans for nothing
and there's a price on all your heads. His Grace is making for Ireland,
Salisbury and Warwick are helter-skelter for Calais again. Half a
year I've been away from Gwlad and it may be I'm back just in time.
Get me across the moat in the ditching-barge. Give me a couple to
help me with a foolish contrivance I have. And while I'm fooling 'em
at the front gate get you gone by the back, and to Ireland and His
Grace all of you. Have I your lordship's leave?"

And my lord hesitated, yet pondered. . . . "What's your trick now, Gandelyn?"

"A sortie, and but fifty men left to guard the women and the treasure! Nay, leave it to me!"

"Fifty, that were five hundred," my lord sighed. "It goes against my pride, but let 'em have their prisoners back. That was Sir William's doing, and what use have I for a treasurer now? But you? Shall I see you in Ireland?"

"That is as it may be, my lord," and after some further talk, Gandelyn had leave to go.

All over the waste men were assembled in shifting groups, but groups without any purpose. They formed and melted away again as if of themselves, for there was nothing to say that had not been said a hundred times before. Yet ever to the whipping-post they drifted back, though the last whipping had been two days ago, and there the post stood, just an upright baulk of wood like another, the ground about it perhaps a little more trodden than elsewhere and the timber perhaps a little stained, but the groaning and the shuddering over. One man returned to it from time to time, as if by some sort of fascination. He wore neither doublet nor shirt, only a woman's cloak thrown over his shoulders, but he too could find nobody fresh to tell his tale to.

Sometimes the groups would make a set towards the moat, as if moved by some common purpose. Many carried cudgels and iron bars, and their pockets bulged and their faces had a dangerous look. But across the moat nothing was to be seen. The drawbridge was clamped up to its wall, the portcullis beyond it was dropped, if imprecations broke out there were only the grey walls to address. Occasionally a stone or two was flung, but they cracked only a little way above the massive base, and in those wall-slits were arrows and bolts ready to be loosed. So they turned away again, this time to the battered and broken row of cowsheds and stables.

Here, however, was one not to be wearied or worn down. In and out of her door Mother Jule would hobble whenever there were any to exhort or harangue or revile. Nay, let a dozen gather and she would forget to close her door, chilling the air even for her silkworms, spent with shrillness yet summoning fresh strength the more stood by to listen. In her shawl and steeple hat, her crutches sunk into her armpits and her clubbed foot swinging as if she would have kicked them to it, she scolded and told their fortunes and cursed them all at once, and sometimes they guffawed, for it was an entertainment when Mother Jule began to curse.

"Nay, shut your mouth and your door, Mother Jule, or your silkworms will take their death in this air," and the hag's voice cracked.

"Were they twenty times dead my Comfit and my Dewdrop are more alive than some of you that's shaped like men! I was lifted up in the court and I saw 'em, my own two babes that I suckled, and white as they were they had more blood in 'em than you, you pack o' pissweeds! And they ordered 'em back again—ay, them coffin-faces i' their high chairs, they ordered 'em back where they were brought from, to ironmould and mildew to their deaths. . . ."

" 'Ware the post yonder, Mother Jule. . . ."

"Ay, 'ware your own cowardly skins all of you, and there was one came to me one day from that accursed place, and I told him as sweet a fortune as heart could wish so he'd put in a word for my Edward and my Clem, but he was like you, he had better bums than mine to wipe, so I cursed him, as I curse you all, and your generations for nine generations to come!" and slamming her ricketty door behind her she tottered back to her silkworms in their nests.

But Dame Kate's, the five-square dower-house with the broken and ivy-draggled wall, was now avoided by all. This was not because it stood a little further back, but because a felon whose impending fate they shuddered to think of had been taken red-handed there, and thanks to God he was a stranger. Formerly they had stripped it of its woodwork for their fires and carried away its stones to patch their own falling dwellings; now, as if to advertise the dreadful spectacle to come, for two nights strange sounds had been heard to issue from it, moans but not the moaning of any known creature, the whimperings of a dog but not at the moon, and sometimes a ghastly laugh. They knew nothing of the man who lay in his cloth-of-gold with the napkin over his face, but alive they had heard his cruelties in the court. This would be a cruelty to remember, and already, as very soon the legend was born, it was as if some foreign soul, cast out from heaven and rejected by hell, plagued the air about Dame Kate's.

Its doorless entry looked towards the whipping-post, and here, among the bits of old capitals and fragments of broken glazing, the kennelman had had his home; but it had an inner door, that led up shaky stairs to the only remaining upper chamber with a roof left to cover it. Because it had a roof it had been turned into a general lumber-room for such furniture as had been moved in from the remaining portions. A carved and testered bed occupied half its floor-space. On this articles had been heaped but removed again, and the bed was now evidently in use, for a woman's garments lay upon it. And set out of the way, on the piled benches and boxes that hid the whole of another wall, a broad double board had been lifted, cumbrous with hidden mechanism.

The room's single window looked out towards the barbican, and by it stood a girl. She had seen the half-hearted stone-throwing and the men who had drifted away again, and could still see the castle walls, forbidding and isolated and all entry denied. In little more than another hour the sun would be down, nay, as she moved to the other side of the window it had left the lower levels already, for to the west the wooded mountains rose, evergreen hardly to be distinguished from oak against their solemn scarp. It was late October, in another month the world would have wrapped itself up for the winter again. She was weary of wandering, but at least here was a roof, and for the rest she was ready to see what came.

But suddenly she moved further aslant the window. Away by the angle of the barbican a glimpse of the turning moat could be seen, and something was moving across it. It looked like a coracle of hides or a small wooden boat, and there were three figures in it, one of them manipulating a paddle. But as they made their boat fast to a willow she could see little more, for first more willows hid them, then the frame of the window itself. They had however landed, for a light wind caught the boat and swung it out over the water again, still tethered but empty. Turning away from the window she unbarred the door, which had been bolted.

It was nearly a quarter of an hour before she heard voices below, for with communication cut off any approaching from that side must skirt the waste if they wished to approach Dame Kate's unseen. Then down the stairs she softly called a name.

"Is that you, Gandelyn?"

But there was no reply. She called again, but only a cat answered, and cats or birds twittering in roofs or these new noises and bumpings of furniture that he said might keep the over-curious away, there never was any sense or reason in the man. Nor had it happened yet, that creeping round the bush or across the barn floor, and placing herself by his side and just lying there waiting. Perhaps in a castle it would not happen, for castles would have eyes that spied and tongues that whispered, and of that or the winter out of doors she would almost have preferred the winter, but knew that when it came she would soon be thinking twice about that too. Now that she had made up her mind to it it no longer troubled her. Where other girls settled down, she only rested awhile and was off again, and should it happen, and a baby be born, she would be like Meg, a few hour's sleep, a munch of cold bacon, and once more away with the babe at her breast.

The stairs creaked lightly and she stood listening, but as likely as not it was only another of his tricks. Owls, mewings, creaking stairs, knockings, if he wanted Old Kate out of her grave again, why let him.

Except for these things he was easy to get on with, for all his mutterings about Yorkshire, east Yorkshire, a long time ago. If there was anything to tell he would tell her in his own good time. But she would have liked a roof over her head for the winter.

But the creaking came again, and turning she found herself suddenly face to face with a woman.

Save for heaviness it would have been a young and pretty face that looked back at her from the opening of its half-drawn hood. But the large inky eyes were tired and underscored, and after their first long stare at her they had moved round the room itself, as if she had been there before and in some way it had changed since she had seen it last. But Hannah, looking back, saw that her mantle was of fine dark blue cloth and that the rest of her clothes were no less costly, and that she wore them as if for a journey. She was wondering whether such as she had not best be addressed as Madam when she heard a low shaky voice.

"I wanted . . . I came . . . do not think it too strange . . . would you stand by the window for me?"

And Gandelyn might whiten Hannah's face for her, making it ghastly with whatever he put on it and then wiped off again, but it had its own curded pallor and was now proof against all the looking that could be brought to bear on it. Who thinks of these things with eyes and knives to watch, and breath to hold lest any moment should bring a slip, and unless she schooled her tongue something that was not a slip? It was the woman who was looking at her so hard who would suffer, and wipe it from her mind, and then suffer again, but to the end of her days would never know what Hannah knew now.

"Please turn your head," and Hannah standing by the window turned it and her visitor gave a tremulous sigh. "But your hair . . . it is not the same. . . ."

"Madam?" said Hannah.

"Will you tell me why you came to Gwlad?"

"I was told I should find employment in the castle as a seampstress, Madam."

"Do not call me Madam. Only to find employment? For nothing more?"

"Ha' you finished looking at me?"

"No, it is not the same. Before it was in a lump, but now it's all great wormcasts o' red gold. . . ."

"I heard your step, Madam, but it was Gandelyn I thought to see," and her visitor, still only a yard within the door, leaned her hooded head against a box that stood on another box, resting it as if its burden was too great for her.

"Gandelyn? Is he back? He's been away half my time in Gwlad, and as for my lady wanting seampstresses, to-night we're being bundled out and where we shall all be to-morrow night only the good God knows. But for all your hair I should ha' known you," and Hannah stiffened.

"I am at a loss for your meaning, Madam. It's for that cage of wire he makes me set at the back of it. He wanted to gum it, but I was having none of his gumming, and I cannot make out either why you want to look at me or why you cannot keep your eyes from ranging round this room as if they were counting every stick in it."

For indeed the heavy eyes were doing so, much as Hannah had moved everything about to her own use. Now the tired eyes were looking at the bed with Hannah's cloak on it and a couple of bundles at its foot, now at a saddle thrown down on the floor. She covered her face for a moment; then, putting aside the blue hood again, gazed at Hannah in a way that put Madams out of her head once for all.

"Would you—" she faltered, "—would you suffer it if I embraced you?" and Hannah took a step back.

"Nay, woman, you're in trouble! What is it?"

"What isn't it! My husband, myself, and now this . . . but I had to come . . . I had to see you with my own eyes. . . ."

"Nay, come over and sit down down on the bed. Who are you?"

"Jo Covil. They call me lady now, but I do not know myself by the sound of it, and it would be like an act of Jesu if any called me Jo at this moment. . . ."

"I'll call you what you will, but what's your grief? Do you say you have a husband stricken down through these dreadful wars?"

"Ay, when they fight in the nursery and marry in their swaddling-clothes. He's fourteen, the mammet, and married a year, and to-night he'll be put into a litter with his new helmet to play with, and after that it's only which mile o' the road he dies on."

"Nay, poor lady, the shame!"

"You're called Hannah, aren't you?"

"Ay. Did Gandelyn tell you?"

"I think I should ha' known you. Are you not wondering why I came?"

" 'Tis easy to see you came for comfort."

"Did you not see who came with me?"

"I was at the window and saw there were three of you."

"And are you not going to ask me who the other is?" and from the bench-end to which she had sunk Joslin Covil lifted her brimming eyes.

Hannah was still standing, rustic in her homespun, only waiting to be told in what she could help, but at something in the tone her face changed. The remorseful dark eyes, the questions about her hair, the looking and looking again, her being there at all . . . could what the woman had come to say be as difficult as all this? And now when she did say it it was not her lips that spoke it. She put out a tremulous hand to Hannah. In it something glittered like a coin, that broken, ill-fated locket. The next moment it was in Hannah's hand, silently telling her all.

But not in any way that she could at first comprehend. Again they danced through her head, her visitor's glances round the room, that timid desire to embrace her, her longing to be called by her familiar name. So *that* was where she had seen her hair before, and been perplexed that it was not the same; and it was not the Hannah of a moment ago who spoke now, but some former Hannah, long a stranger to herself.

"How came you by this?"

"Gandelyn pressed it into my hand—he said he'd picked it off a rainbow. . . ."

"Not so!" That would not do, not for a moment would it do! "Gandelyn gave it to you?" and the eyes closed and the head rocked itself against the wall again.

"Ay, why should you believe me? It makes it easier. Now I can go, yet I cannot, but I could not rest till I came."

And now it was Hannah herself who was looking round the room that was her own room no longer. Its bed, its chests and boxes, everything in it had been there before she came, and others than she had used it before ever she had seen it. To be ordered to place herself by the window, to be told her hair was not the same, to be offered a treacherous embrace, up they flashed, knife after knife, and now having finished with him she was returning him to her and wanting all as if it had never been! Now it was Hannah who would not let her face be seen. Oh, suffer all to come a little near, for in this world we have to live with 'em, but none too near, nor ever the same one twice! And let her get it over now and those knives were like Gandelyn's, they didn't hurt, but that didn't mean this weeping woman! No, not the weeping woman! Let her keep her tears for the next man to kiss away, and the more the head against the wall rocked the more Hannah stood watching her like a red cat.

"So! And if Gandelyn wanted me to have this why didn't Gandelyn give it to me?"

"Oh that I had never seen it!"

"And Gandelyn's only this day or two back, and it hasn't been in Gandelyn's pockets all this while! It would seem if this locket had a tongue it might have a tale to tell!"

"It's told me all the tales I wish to hear of it," the unhappy woman sighed. "He showed it to me in the quarry, and told me it was no more than all journeymen carry with 'em to show their masters. Then I offered to show it to Sir William for him, as would now I hadn't, and how Gandelyn came by it I cannot tell you," and Hannah flashed.

"Yet *you* can come to *me* with it in your hand! But your pardon, Madam. I know naught of your Sir Williams, that am but a poor seampstress looking for work," and the other moaned monotonously, piteously.

"And I'm but a mercer's daughter, that a thousand times has wished I'd never left my home! And now my lady that began by scolding me will hardly let me out of her sight for clinging and loneliness, and me with my way to London to make and a burial on the way!" and she gulped again, but still Hannah did not move, but only looked her up and down.

"That's a fine mantle you're wearing, Madam, and I don't doubt your grief's eased by those shoes on your feet, but let's finish with this that's in my hand. Weeping, when every sob you give and every stick in this room is mocking me with it all! Fie on you, Madam! At least shed no tears over it! But there's one thing you don't weep over, and that's why you come to me now, bringing him and this with you! Was it so you could say to yourself, 'Ay, I'd a fancy to see what she was like, her that knew him before I did, and now I see she's such-and-such, nothing by the side o' me, but it's another hook to hold him by and seeing her's been like meat to my eyes?' Was *that* it?"

"O that I were in my grave!"

"And now you tell me he's downstairs, what should bring *him* at this time o' day? Did he come willingly? Did he run? Couldn't you hold him back for his headstrongness and haste?"

"Oh, how little of the truth you know!"

"Then pray help me, Madam. Would he ha' wed you?"

"There was a time not long ago when I'd have wedded him."

"*Us* break *their* hearts!" Hannah muttered to herself, then swiftly turning, "And would you not wed him now?" but the head against the wall was rocking again.

"It wasn't that he couldn't even wait till my little milk-tooth was put to his rest. It wasn't his pomping in his new clothes when I'd ha' taken him in his old ones. And you can't even bring yourself to embrace me, but it began by my asking him who his pretty mistress was, and he answered as I said, but now the rest needs no more telling than I know in my own heart. Through mirk and mire you've followed him for love of him, in a way I never could, and I know there's no talking to him for thinking there's nobody in the world like himself, but I thought between two women . . . yet even for comfort and gentleness you cannot bring yourself to call me by a sister's name. . . ."

Hannah had moved slowly away to the window. What new thing was this? Followed him through mirk and mire for love, she? Oh, a little nearness for all, but nearer for none and never for the same one twice! For a time not to be counted as time she looked out at the castle walls; then slowly she turned the differently-dressed head.

"Listen, lady. It was unmannerly of me to speak of your clothes the way I did, but last spring I set out on a pilgrimage in the clothes you see me in now. With one of my own kith and kin I journeyed, but she died in my arms, and the galloway I rode on's down below now, and soon I shall be off on it again. But it wasn't for love of him, if it's any ease to you, lady, never, never was it for love of him! I set out not knowing who or what I was, and it was that, nothing else, I found on the way. And I know now why *you* came here, but less than ever can I see what brought *him*."

"I could see you didn't know."

"Then tell me plain."

"He's downstairs there, but if it's a while since you've seen him it's to be doubted if you'd know him. These last weeks he couldn't ha' got out o' Gwlad if he'd tried. He'd got himself a fine new suit of clothes, but he was as much a prisoner in 'em as he'd been wi' the others in the dungeons, where but for Gandelyn he'd be now. And now there's a dreadful whisper about, that for my life I durstn't tell you, except that him that comes next to my lord himself is dead, and he and another are held answerable for it, and at any other time he'd be for the torture now. But now every soul in Gwlad's on the move, and in their haste even the dead man's still lying when they put him, but if they drag the backwater again, as they did only a day or two back, they'll maybe find another among the lily-stalks, a servant and a spy—but you mustn't ask me more, for I cannot bear to think of it all. . . ."

Nor could Hannah have asked her even if she would, for there were sudden sounds from below, not up the stairs but from the back. The door of a shed was being unlocked and an animal was being got out. Two men's voices were heard, speaking in low tones, and the moving and knocking of wood. Then all at once there rose from below a chilling, long-drawn howl, like that of some solitary wandering animal, seeking its love or its prey. It died away again, but Joslin Covil had sprung up from her bench in fright. Flying to the window she had flung her arms about Hannah, who held her close but spoke composedly.

"Quiet now. 'Tis only him and his Dame Kating. Hush now as I bid you—ay, Jo or anything you will. . . ."

There was a foot on the stairs and Gandelyn appeared. From the pile of boxes where Jo had been sitting he began to get down his board. Then he turned to Hannah with a sort of basket-work wheel of light wire in his hand.

"We cannot lose any more time because of the light," he said. "It's past Mother Jule's, the end shed. He's taking the galloway and the stage over, and you know where the paint-pot is. I'm chancing no knives in the dark, so be getting yourself ready."

11

SAY THEN IT WAS BECAUSE OF THE LIGHT. THERE WAS A CASTLE TO march out of and leave empty, and the last hour of the day was best for keeping a rabble's eyes on one spectacle when for so many reasons it was desirable they should be diverted from another. The wind, from the south-west, wisped a quarter of the sky with mares-tails of thin cirrus, but high over these other gigantic vapours towered, pile on pile of celestial fortresses, lifted on their level bases from the earth and thunder-still. Their cragged and creviced contours were bathed in a false light, and the whole sunny system showered its illumination down on Gwlad's turreted walls and mirrored itself skyward again from the turning of the moat. It would be another hour before the first star.

But in the backcourt and about the postern all was assembly and haste, with lanterns unlighted yet and as little noise as might be. The guard stood about the treasure-carts, the tilts and litters were horsed up and awaited only their occupants. Only at the last moment would the gates of the cachots be unlocked, and in the quarry they were digging a hasty grave, that doubtless would be opened again in time to come. Over Punshon's body lying at the bottom of the backwater the dabchick bobbed and dived as before.

It was the humiliation of having to release the prisoners that came nearest to my lord's heart. To-morrow his castle would be ransacked, his private apartments befouled, his goods carried away piecemeal, but that could be dealt with later, for he was but going to Ireland for a breathing-space. He would return, bringing harrying and vengeance with him, and return he did, bringing harrying and vengeance in full measure. But now the marshal on one side of him and Robert Burnage on the other were trying to hearten him as he strode up and down his empty hall, weary of life and the worst of his troubles coming at its end.

"When I return . . . I can spare a wretch or two when I think of the toll I'll take of the rascals in six months or a year from now. . . ."

"Nay my lord, you as good as pardoned half of them in your own court. You'd all but set 'em free before any o' this!"

"Ay, I would have freed 'em, but that it should even seem I was driven to it . . . have they buried Sir William yet?"

"Sir Baltasar has all in hand now."

"And my lady, who is with her?"

"Your lady bears herself well, my lord, seeing Lady Joslin cannot both be with her and with Sir Ferdinand too."

"Is all victualled and the treasure well guarded?"

"Both, sir, and do you take a cup of wine now."

But there was none to bring it, and the three-decked sideboard was empty, and only the sconces on the walls were left against their smoky patches, and to-morrow any looking in from the grass-court would see the table-trestles blazing in the midst of my lord's hall, and a pandemonium of beggars and bedlamers swilling his wine, and hear their riot and ribaldries as they installed Mother Jule between the carved bedposts of the Lady Margaret's own bed.

But Mother Jule knew nothing yet of the dignity so soon to be hers, and a few broken sheds away from where she poked her beard into her silkworn-nests there moved a leather-clad figure who might have been one of themselves, so unnoticed did he move among them. Indeed he had found one of them to give him a hand with what he was doing, in return for a small service, for with a burin he had prodded a couple of holes through the woman's cloak the man wore, but the cloak was in his way as he worked, and when he shook it off it showed his back and shoulders, wealed and excoriated with the stripes of a recent whipping. The shed had a sort of half-door or parclos. Inside it stood a galloway, but it had been off-loaded again and Willie Middlemiss had been instructed in the setting up of the light structure. Now, raised from the ground a couple of feet, it ran outwards from the parclos, three boards wide and some five yards long, and Willie was inside the shed again, hanging out a rent old backcloth and trying not to look at the other man's back. But he moved like one without strength. In one short week . . . but that too he tried to put out of his mind. Not Punshon, for in that he had had another to help him. The clerk should not have been there on the moat-side with Willie's mulberry on his back just as Willie and the man who passed in the half-light as Sir Baltasar had been stealing out from the herb-garden grille. Do it and be free or do not do it and remain, and drowning a man was not the same as swinging him up and watching him awhile and then letting him down again . . . but let him not think of it. None of it had happened, but he was as haggard and spent as if it had, and he wanted to tell that man to cover his shoulders again, but could not bring himself to the effort, so continued to watch them.

And now that upper room of Dame Kate's was a drapery-closet indeed. One of the bundles on the bed had been unpacked, and Gandelyn had taken the other when he had fetched the board, and Joslin Covil's eyes were dry again as she stepped back and held her breath at Hannah's transformation. The ruddy wormcasts of her hair had been carefully let down again and the nimbus of light wire secured to her nape by a couple of tresses knotted behind it. Hannah held it in place with one hand, and like a tiring-woman Joslin Covil was separating the heavy clusters, drawing them outwards into rays. A paint-pot stood on the window ledge, and Hannah's face was plastered over a dead and terrifying white. Out of their darkening her eyes shone from it witch-like and tranced and glassy, and Jo Covil did not cease to catch her breath and to ask her questions.

"But what does he make you put on your body?"

"Marry, whatever comes into his head. If we're among Red Roses he'll ha' me all white in my smock, mopping and mowing and cursing me, clowning and anticking like a madman wi' his knives in his hand. If we're among White 'Uns he'll ha' me as red as a John in a niche, or as blue as a Mary for all I know or care, for I have his fierce face to watch. But him, the other. Did you say he'd changed?"

"When I saw him again in the boat my heart leapt into my throat. But do you do all this as you go from place to place?"

"Ay, or if it isn't this it's something else, for he's a bottomless bag of it all. What trouble did he get into this time?"

"I do not know for sure and if I did it's not to be spoken of. It seems he knew where there was gold. And what are you putting on yourself now?"

"Nay, he said nothing but that I was to make haste, so I shall e'en stand up to him as I am. Gold? Where?"

"He'd heard there was gold in these mountains, and you don't know them in Gwlad or you wouldn't ask what happened. From that moment on he lived from minute to minute if he'd but known it. They'll not have such knowledge going loose about in Gwlad. Mother o' God, I'm making you into a sunflower bigger than the sun himself!"

"Let me look in your glass. Ay, that's it, and you don't tear it out by the roots the way he does. But hearken, Jo. When all's said such things are his trade. I'm not starting you off on your poor young Sir again, but . . . you're young and beautiful and it's out o' nature you should be left alone . . . tell me, did he ever make a locket of you?"

"He started something, and nothing but mischief came out of it."

"In London, with folk over him to rule him . . . he'll get there in the end if he has to whistle his way there on that whistle of his . . . I've travelled alone too and God knows what would ha' come of it but for this mountebank I somehow cannot bring myself to part from . . ." but at that moment the mountebank's voice was heard below.

"You up there, are you ready?"

"Ay, in a minute. . . . Burdened as you are there's things he could do on the way for you, men's things, that they can do better than us. Who's putting you back over the moat?"

"I need none to put me back. There's a river in London broader than their moat, and I've been in boats before."

"Or Gandelyn could, for I sometimes think he could make himself

wings o' darkness and fly over battlements, but Willie Middlemiss . . .
with twenty nooses round his neck still something fresh would catch
his eye . . ." and again the impatient voice below.

"The light'll be gone . . . stir your shanks. . . ."

"Coming, coming!"

"And I with you. Holy Mother, the look of you! Here, let me put
my mantle over it—I'll take yours—so, and keep it up with your hands
and see you do not shake it on the stairs," and she held open the door.

Gwlad's gaoler was one of the few in that castle Willie Middlemiss
had never seen. All he himself knew of gaolers was that one of them
had unlocked the fetters from Matthias's wrists, but hearing the
explosion of a petard had fled without loosing the shackles from his
feet, and his face would have whitened like a willow-leaf in a wind at
the sight of the squinting monstrosity, with arms as long as an ape's
and thicker from back to front than he was sideways, to whom word
had just been brought. His cave was next to the *siambr ddu*. He neither
saw nor wished to see the day, wherefore it was fitting that the bearer
of the order should also be inured to twilight, and deliver it by signs
for lack of a tongue, for Pietro had been forgotten and the servant
who had passed the message on had had no liking for his errand. Nor
did the gaoler hold with all this releasing of men, and his face was as ugly
as his iron keys as he slouched along his stone tunnel, carrying them
like some bunch of hideous fruit. Several doors already stood open. A
whipping or a branding and their tenants had been free. But into the
smallest of the oubliettes the greatest number had been crowded, and he
could not bring his tongue to utter the word. Therefore he did no more than
set the door open, and hove himself sullenly away again, with the cowering captives still lifting their eyes to the open door yet afraid to move.

But now muffled sounds and movements high overhead reached
their dull ears. The postern gate stood open, the half-dozen outriders
had already gone forth. The baggage-carts were piled high, seated in
the litters several ladies waited. But the chief litter, which was the
Lady Margaret's, was still unoccupied. Her talbot-face was heavily
veiled, but again and again she put the veils aside to ask where the
Lady Joslin was. But for that, she vowed, she had never in her life
been so glad to leave a place; it had not been the same since that fracas
in the night, of owls and moans and crashing crockery, just before
Sir William had died. But Lady Joslin was not to be found, though in
his litter Sir Ferdinand moved his head weakly from side to side,
now toying with his headpiece and telling those who looked in that
he was a Christian knight, now whimpering that he would whip his
wife and confine her to her room for leaving him so long.

And now all were looking for Lady Covil, and my lord was fuming, for the treasure-carts were to travel in the midst of them and it was time they were on their way. But Lady Joslin was out on the waste, though none at the gatehouse had seen her pass, and now they themselves were but four. Behind a torn and knife-rent old sailcloth slung like a curtain across a broken cowshed she was waiting till Hannah Thirlow should have finished what she had to say to Wilson Middlemiss. They were in the shadows at the back, where Hannah's dim face was like a deathly white flower in the dusk, surrounded by a dull lustre of radiance, and this is what she was saying:

" 'Tis naught to me, Willie, nor has been these three years and more. Do you mind a spring nightfall before Thirlow stopped work, while my father was yet alive, and the hawthorn past the top o' the tenter-frames fit to make you drunk wi' its smell?"

"I've forgotten," he said, but his face was only less pallid than her own.

"If you'd but lifted a finger I was all spilling over for you under them hawthorns. You'd just to whisper 'Nan' and I couldn't have helped myself. But one came to seek you, and gave a whistle, and you shoved your face against mine and were off, as twenty times since then it's been the same. You cannot wait for ever for them that's always somewhere else, and that was the end, as I knew then."

"One midsummer morning, when you were cutting teasles . . ." he began, but she would hear no more, for Gandelyn was growling, "The light, the light!"

"Now a stranger comes, and he'll be to learn the ways of too, but he's not the sort to court all the love away, and if he never courts me, so, but it's all one to me if I never sleep under a roof again. But her there, she's not the one to sleep under stars. She's for London, and I know without your telling me it's London you're thinking of. But you'll find all's to begin from now."

"The light, Madonna, the light!"

"I'm ready . . . go to her now, and take this with you, for I truly think it's i' these things your heart is," and thrusting the broken locket into his hand she sprang to the board that darkened the parclos.

The sun was off the waste, but still the gigantic crests cast down their thunderous sheen. It lighted the faces of the disease-stricken denizens of the waste and the staves and rags and bundles of the sturdy beggars and wanderers who had not ceased to assemble about Gandelyn's stage ever since its erection had begun, for a show is a show, and if when it is over a tin dish is rattled it was no more than the palmers did and the hedge-priests. In their impatience they raised their voices and clapped their hands, and even Mother Jule had come out to see, and none paid any attention to two figures that slipped out by one side of the parclos, as there sprang out from the other a tall, lithe, zany of a fellow garbed in yellow and red, who was on the stage in a bound, menacing them with a basket of glittering knives, so that one after another of them flinched before his fierce gesture of hurling. He mopped and mowed, and raised one supple leg high above his head, where he held it stiff as if he leaned his cock-crested head against a yellow whipping-post. Then down it came, and up he sprang as if shot out of a jack-in-the-box, his legs a diamond in the air. "The Devil forget you all and God gi'e ye good-e'en!" he bawled, and spun round like a top and cried "Hark!" and seemed to listen, but only guffawed when every head turned and there was nothing to hearken to. "Oyez, worthy citizens of Gwlad! Grimble-gramble and knives to whet—where is she that I may see the colour of her blood? Up, you WhiteJezebel—up to your carving-block!"

But the two had slipped by unseen, and it was time to hasten, but the shoes on her feet might have been of lead. Now she hurried a few paces, now dragged again, and unless it was said now it would never be said, yet there was nothing to say. They had passed Mother Jule's before his lips parted over his broad teeth.

"Go now," he said chokingly. "My lord and my lady will be in a rage," but he who had held her in his arms did not now approach within a yard of her.

"Take me to the moat and unfasten the boat for me and push me off."

"Ay, I can do that," but they had left Dame Kate's behind them before she realized that she was still wearing Hannah's frieze cloak and had left her own mantle of dark blue cloth in the cowshed. They reached the willows where the coracle was tied, and he stood with the loosened rope in his hand, but still there was nothing to say except to tell her to get into the boat.

"There's a stone for your foot. If we stayed here for a year it wouldn't alter things. Get you in," but she did not put forth her foot.

"Is that all you can find to say, Willie, 'Get you in'?"

"I'm thinking to say nothing becomes me best."

But it was she who that day on the Bridge of Sighs had first lifted the eyes that said Yes while her headshake said No. It was she who had had perfume-boxes to mend, and a broken girdle-chain to hunt for and a locket to show to the treasurer. It was she who had remembered the morning exercises in the quarry, and had first thought of the drapery-closet, and later of the herb-garden and Dame Kate's behind them, and that unalterable thing that is in each of us remains with us to the end. For lack of a comfit-box a cloak would do, and now over the walls and across the moat there reached them the mingled noises of the forecourt. He hardly heard her words.

"Nothing can be changed of a sudden, Willie. All must go forward as it is. After that I'm for London and my father."

"Ay, and you're losing time. Make an end."

"But my lord's ship is waiting for him at Portmadoc, and my lady's bestowing me as near as may be to Stafford, and . . . and . . . which way will you be making?"

"I cannot tell. I know 'em at Valle Crucis. For all I can see it's there again."

"But you can take this cloak back to Hannah. Not that she isn't welcome to mine, but . . . should you find yourself near Stafford before long . . . I mustn't linger now, but at Stafford there'd maybe a minute to say good-bye. . . ."

Only now did he lift his humbled head. . . . "Stafford? What would I be doing in Stafford?"

"Oh, I must begone! And I could send Hannah something else another time, and you'd be bringing me my mantle back, and nay . . . if you won't ask it, a God-speed now if you like. . . ."

They stepped back into the willows. On a windless evening the willows alone moved for a few moments. Then she was in the coracle and he was thrusting her out over the moat.

But fascination and rapture kept the air still where the platform ran out of the cowshed. There, in the shadowless cloud-shine, a motionless white face over which a spell seemed to have been cast held every eye. In such a pallor of panic did it seem to be that a thistledown of whiteness should have emanated from it, but instead a flaming monstrance surrounded it, an exploding crater, that scattered itself in a flaring wheel. Knives hemmed the outspread arms about, brushed the chalk-white cheeks, lodged themselves between the fingers, and with each knife the torturer in yellow and red launched a new imprecation. So were his eyes everywhere that if a prying rogue at the parclos chanced to see a knife flash out of sight to bury itself in the rent cloth behind some fresh devilry had followed before he could speak, and now he had no more than two knives left in his basket, and what would he do with those? He displayed them; he juggled with them; he cut his own throat with them; all were motionless as he prepared for the final butchery.

"Her eyes . . . they're for her eyes. . . ."

But Gandelyn never threw the two knives. A head had turned, and another and another. A shout was raised, so sudden that the conjuror himself stood still. In the last of the cloudshine a straggling company of a dozen was approaching. They stumbled and halted. Some helped others to walk, one man was being carried by those who hardly had the strength to carry themselves, and suddenly there was a scream. It was from Mother Jule.

"My Teddy! My Clem!" she cried, and the next moment was

swinging like a pendulum between her crutches, toppling forward at every step to take them into her thin arms again. They were the prisoners from the dungeons, who had at last summoned courage to walk out of the open door, and about the platform and the knifeboard not a mother's son remained.

It was they too who brought the news, that my lord and his following had gone, but there was a castle to sack, and now history puts forth her monitory hand. What has all this been while her back was turned? No more truancy: in what county is Blore Glen? What was the date of the battle of Wakefield, of Barnet, of Tewkesbury, of Bosworth Field? When does modern history begin? Who were the Lollards? What do you know of the *forgæ errantes?*"

But now the cloudshine tips only the craggy crests, and over Gwlad's walls and waste the shadows creep, and the tapestry itself has become too fragile to handle. Held together only by history's protecting glass its threads sag thin and hueless, and the antiquary has yet to find, in some fragmentary household-book or inventory, the name of Wilson Middlemiss, sometime goldsmith of York, or any piece of his stamped with a London mark. There is no trace in the Stafford records of whether he met Joslin Covil there, and one is as likely to find in some grey old village church the wall-tablet that sets forth the virtues of Sir William Stone's private life as the place on the way where little Sir Ferdinand was laid to rest. Only in a ballad does Gandelyn live, and it says nothing of his red-headed mort or whether she crept to his side one night, or whether she bore a child or not. Now the waste is empty, from the crests the last light has gone, no more sounds come from Dame Kate's. Only in Gwlad's hall is a muffled uproar of rioting, and as the wooden tables blaze on the floor fantastic shadows leap across the great window and are cast out over the grass-court as far as the sundial itself.

Yet through it all, there steals a note that cares nothing whether it is heard or no. It is faint and sweet and far-off, dewy and fresh as February hedge-buds that have buffeted the winter through, a morning-song, sung to a lost tune by an unknown voice now five centuries still, the song of a younger Gandelyn, who sold not his wits but his sword:

> "*I heard the carpynge of a clerke*
> *Al at yone woodes end . . .*"

—it seems to die but the memory is not left empty, and for a little longer than we hear it we are willing to believe that all was so.

A Few Words No Longer in Daily Use

★

WAR, ARMS, COSTUME, ETC.

Ballista a war-catapult.

Basnet a visored headpiece.

Brigandine a footman's corslet.

Camlet a fabric of silk and long wool.

Cotte a woman's under-smock.

Coude-piece an elbow-piece.

Crinet a horse's neck-armour.

Cuisses thigh-pieces.

Destrier a war-horse.

Greaves shin-pieces.

Haqueton a stuffed jerkin.

Hauberk a tunic of ring or chainmail.

Hennin a steeple headdress.

Mangonel an engine for casting stones.

Mentonnière a chin-piece (as coudière, genouil-lière, etc., pieces for elbow and knee).

Murrey a mulberry-colour and fabric.

Pavess a standing shield for a footman.

Sallet a 'tin hat.'

Saye a fine serge.

Wimple a nun's cover for chin and cheeks.

MISCELLANEOUS

Aumbry almoner's office.

Bateleur a producer of rabbits from hats.

Cariad (Welsh) sweetheart.

Close-stool a night-cabinet.

Cupel a small crucible of bone-ash.

Ddu (Welsh) black.

Dortoir dormitory.

Dwu (Welsh) God.

Enula elecampane, horse-heal.

Hanap a large service-vessel.

Leman (here) a light lady.

Lymer a bloodhound.

Marotte a jester's toy with a clown's head.

Mawr (Welsh) large, great.

Membrane a skin for writing.

Parclos a half-door.

Pistyll (Welsh) a runnel or spout.

Planish to level or smooth.

Saes (Welsh) Saxon.

Siambr (Welsh) chamber.

Slub wet cloth 'in the grey.'

Solar a sun-parlour.

Taid (Welsh) grandfather.

Thole to endure, put up with.

Threap to jockey out of.